TABITHA, GET UP

LEE UPTON

Sagging Meniscus

Set in Sabon with LaTeX.

ISBN: 978-1-952386-89-3 (paperback)
ISBN: 978-1-952386-90-9 (ebook)
Library of Congress Control Number: 2023952260

Sagging Meniscus Press
Montclair, New Jersey
saggingmeniscus.com

In memory of Alice Faye, beloved sister

Peter made them all go outside. After kneeling down, he prayed, turned to the body, and said, "Tabitha, get up!"

—Acts 9.40, The Bible, International Standard Version

I have been to lots of parties
and acted perfectly disgraceful
but I never actually collapsed
oh Lana Turner we love you get up

"Poem ["Lana Turner Has Collapsed!"]—Frank O'Hara

Tabitha, Get Up

MESSAGE TO PUBLISHER

Dear Rosamund,

I know every woman looks better after a divorce, but you looked PHENOMENAL in that photograph above that article about some awful charity event in *The Post*. I recognized you instantly, what with the light emanating from your face in a way that lets everyone know your wealth isn't only inherited!

Rosamund, I must say: the orchids you keep in your apartment are so drop dead gorgeous anyone would want to abduct them. It's like they're skinned from some rare being from a planet where cow's milk sits up and talks. I mean, those orchids—they bellow that you have refined taste.

Well, enough flattery. You know me well enough to know that money is an issue.

And so this is a direct request. I won't mention an amount because I don't want to sound mercenary, and I'm sorry that the best work I've ever done, *Annie: Her Life Story*, never quite hit the best-seller ranks, even (especially) among my relatives. Yes, please forget that. Because opportunity has just now reared its head. Its two heads.

So here is what's happening. The actor Brent Vintner is in Midlothian! Brent Vintner: so good looking they should bottle that man and spray him on belligerent people as a form of crowd control. And Piper Fields—the children's book author who on the side writes filthy novels—she too is in Midlothian! (I've already read part of the opening of one of her smutty novels. Ritualized ceremonies, melted candle wax, incense. If I didn't know better I'd think it was written by a priest.)

What I've learned from Alyse at the bake shop (where she studies credit card receipts for big fun and eavesdrops better than I do) is that both Brent Vintner and Piper Fields may be here for months. Which is convenient for my purposes. By my writing their biographies—two tell-all or tell-it-to-me biographies, unputdownable, bursting with juicy bits—we're poised to do some business. And I am herewith making a commitment to take scrupulous and cleverly labeled notes to keep myself, so to speak, on the ball.

At any rate, please let me know how the advance can be made more attractive to me.

Sending love and not using those little x's and o's.

NOTE TO SELF

Good going! Established tone of authority. Emailing with tone of authority should guarantee advance. Besides, those short celebrity profiles I wrote caused problems, which means some people actually read them. Unfortunately, I'm no longer allowed to conduct interviews with any entertainer at the Empireum. Still, it's undeniable that I have a gift for ferreting out embarrassing information. In those celebrity profiles I got some good material about the two most shame-producing aspects of those minor celebrities' lives: finances and parenting.

I'm sure that becoming a publisher was only supposed to be a half-way entertaining hobby for Rosamund to complain about. Yet I do believe she might give me an advance because 1) she is not at all risk-averse, 2) there's something complicated going on with her taxes, 3) she owes my mother an emotional debt, and 4) she has a bet with her ex-husband concerning me.

Note to Remind Self: Do Not Do the Following Again

So how do I gain access to Brent Vintner? His agent. Normally I wouldn't go through an agent, but in this case maybe I'll win her favor and be allowed on set. Additional access. An introduction to Brent Vintner would be nice, of course.

I do my research. Brent Vintner's agent likes large dogs—obvious from Facebook. I change my profile picture to a Labrador and friend-request her. No luck. Still, her privacy settings are really not smart. She's practically begging for identity theft, and therefore when I call her office I know a few things: she knits, grows vegetables, and hand cranks an apple contraption to make unpasteurized cider.

My first mistake: identifying myself. Conversation moves in the following direction:

Me: I write celebrity profiles and I would like to write a full-scale biography of Brent Vintner.

Agent X: Don't ever call this office again.

Me: Do you want me to use your home number? I can tap it in right now.

Agent X: No, I mean, don't ever contact Brent or me. The work you've done—irresponsible. You're irresponsible. You have a really gaudy imagination, I'll say that.

Me: Gaudy imagination? I like that. Can I quote that? A gaudy imagination. That's interesting. Really. You read my profiles? I didn't know you had a clipping service.

Agent X: The last time I checked there's such a thing as the internet.

Me: Yeah, but those were really tiny local outlets I wrote for. I don't even know if they have websites. Or no, I think they pulled the stories.

Agent X: I'm going to make sure you never talk to Brent or anyone who works with him or anyone else who has anything to do with anyone who means anything to anyone . . .

Me: That's so ambitious of you! You're incredibly ambitious. I identify with that. Where did you learn to be so tenacious?

[Note to self: I am lowering myself too much. Because, note to self, I am being lazy.]

Agent X: [deliberate silence . . . five seconds and counting]

Me: I'm going to have to tell Brent Vinter you denied me access right at the point when I could help his career—and your career.

[Note to self: Hang up. Hang up. Hang up.]

Agent X: I know women like you. Trolls, loud mouthed, pushy women who think that they can just write anything, indulge in any fantasy.

Me: I want to give an honest account. I'm a biographer, not a writer.

Agent X: How can you *not* be a writer if you're a biographer?

Me: It isn't the same thing.

Agent X: [Deliberate silence]

Me: As a biographer I'm ferreting out truth, outlining a life until the contours are visible. It never feels like writing to me. I'm not inventing anything. I'm releasing a life, clarifying a life. I'm more like a painter or a photographer than a writer. I hardly even work in—in—words.

Agent X: I'm hanging up now.

Me: Do you have to? Do you have any more questions for me? I'd love to answer them. It's really a pleasure to talk with you. I hope you'll reconsider. Hello? Hello?

Message to Publisher

Dear Rosamund,

I'm already making excellent progress! These progress reports you're requiring me to write should hardly seem necessary, especially now that you've agreed to the advance. After all, I'm a person of my word.

I've spoken with Brent Vintner's agent, and she was full of questions for me. I felt like the tables were turned and she wanted to write my biography before I even met Brent. Not that I'm on a first name basis with him—not that we've met. Obviously I have to do more research first. My methods, I've never revealed them, but I will give you a taste—you've heard of the photographer Clarice Bearbuereton? Truly exceptional portraits. Before she met her subjects she walked the streets they walked, learned from waiters what their favorite liqueurs were, stalked around the gymnasium they frequented in high school . . . I don't mean to suggest that I need elaborate preparations. But I do want to say that the preparations I'll make eventually will save much time at the other end of the project and will cause the biography of Brent Vintner to give off a luster, like a masterpiece glimmering with hints of autumnal burnt gold hues.

EMAIL MESSAGE FROM PUBLISHER

Tabitha,

You are shitting me.

I don't know why I let you convince me to bankroll you. What about Piper Fields? Start with her. Forget Vintner. His agent isn't going to let you get within ten feet of him. Piper Fields is only a children's book author and a novelist—she could use some positive publicity. Those trashy novels of hers bit into her kiddie book sales. Try her.

Dear Rosamund,

I understand entirely. I'll try Piper Fields soon. The biography should write itself.

My Life Is Not a Journey

An ad just came up on my laptop for a book with the awful title: *Chart Your Life's Journey Now.* Why am I selected for such an ad? Hate when people refer to their "life's journey." Like journey has destination. Other than death, where does journey lead? Also, like journey is planned. Like we booked the flight and now are innocent travelers. Not true. Some of us are going nowhere or endlessly traveling back to where we started!

Job listings. What's needed locally: warehouse associate, forklift driver, more warehouse pickers. I have survived in Midlothian on advances for the biographies and profiles I wrote or attempted to write, but mostly, to be honest, I have survived on part-time jobs. Waitressing. Stocking or clerking at two grocery stores. I can't go back to those places. I have a reputation, unfortunately. Must, however, finance my own life while trying to write biographies.

Must not be frantic. Must slow down.

No need to remember all my mistakes, those worthless memory spikes. Best not to look backward, into the past. Why shouldn't I try to avoid my own pain by writing about the pain in strangers' lives?

And yet: there's so much I don't need to forget—although sometimes at night I writhe around from memories. Oh how could I have done what I did—the instances are legion! Like the time I wore a fringed vest and was so proud—feeling beautiful!—and then found out later . . . must stop. The embarrassment still burns. Could use some additional forgetfulness.

Must focus on the future: I will find a way to write both biographies pitched to Rosamund. Will regain sense of meaning once I've begun. After all, writing about other lives gives life meaning. I don't know why everyone in the world isn't writing a biography about somebody else. So many people are interesting, and how else are you going to get them to talk to you unless you give them an excuse?

An Unexpected Voice Mail

"Tabitha! I have a question. What sort of outfit should I wear to Corinne's wedding? I know it's months away, but she already sent one of those hectoring Save the Date cards. Now I feel like I should make plans. At least I've already settled on a wedding gift—a six-pack of my homemade candles, vanilla scented. I plan to sprinkle dried petals in the wax, so save all your dead flowers for me, okay? The wedding's not until October which means I've got time to figure this out. I don't want to wear something that shouts 'Autumn!' Nothing too pumpkin-y. Or dark gray and red—nothing that shouts Thanksgiving turkey gobbler. Oh my god, what am I doing? I don't know why I'm asking you, of all people, what I should wear. I hope I'll never again see you in that atrocious yellow dress—the one you wore to the Pick a Wick Charity Ball when you had eye trouble and had to wear a patch. You looked like Big Bird's diabolical sister. And that navy blue outfit from the last time I saw you at Avery's—everyone thought you were a crooked river boat captain.

"Anyway, start saving your dead flowers. The way you are with flowers—you're worse than a funeral parlor. By the way, isn't this great? I found out how to send messages directly to voice mail. Your phone won't even ring. This way we can save time—no unnecessary blabbing! That's what your brother always used to say! No unnecessary blabbing!"

My brother is my mother's favorite person in the world—even though he never visits or calls and decamped down to Florida three decades ago. It's his wife, Gaia (her preferred name—she used to be Ginger), who keeps in sporadic contact, sending self-help books to me. Last month I got a package with a note: "Thinking you'll love these, Tabby." Inside: two second-hand paperbacks: *You Ain't Done Yet* and *You Need a Dog*. She has had much to bear: placating my silent, brooding brother who avoids our mother when, really, our mother, in her late eighties, is navigating a life he can't comprehend. As she likes to say, it's a miracle women of her generation, given the crap they had to put up with, didn't all scoot around like lemmings and jump off cliffs.

NOTES TOWARD A BIOGRAPHY OF PIPER FIELDS

Settling down now after getting that voice mail from my mother.

Reconsidering Rosamund's email—of course Rosamund thinks I'll have better luck with Piper Fields. Because Rosamund thinks another woman might have mercy on me. She assumes that because Piper Fields writes for both children and frustrated adults I'll understand her more readily than I will an actor whose face has emblazoned the sides of buses. No, Rosamund thinks Piper Fields is a safer bet, on multiple fronts. And yet—I wonder.

Oh no, the man in the apartment on the first floor is doing this weird thing where he makes music by pushing air with his mouth through a garden hose.

Back to work.

Hard to verify anything on the internet. Photographs of Piper Fields aren't all that helpful. She never looks the same in any photograph. Fierce makeup. Changes of hair color and hair length. Still, even though she never looks the same, she gives the impression that she must be pretty all the time. Even "drop the suitcases beautiful." Decades ago when my mother was in Boston on a historical tour a man caught sight of her and dropped two suitcases. I want to find my mother's story charming, except it's been used against me too often. As a child I was always confused by her references to beauty. She once called me "drop the toothpick beautiful" when I was thirteen. My mother let me know that her metaphor had to do with how much the object weighs. As if I didn't already know what I looked like. And I didn't.

Piper Fields's books for children put children to sleep: that's their function. Beleaguered, exhausted parents read her books to their children and in minutes each child's head is nodding, unconscious—you couldn't do a better job with a brick.

Three years ago her former agent (a duplicitous man who wrote his own memoir) divulged that, although Piper Fields was the author of children's books, she was also (under the name Bunny Swift) the author of erotic novels. Once the cat (Bunny Swift) was out of the bag, Piper Fields published all her books under her own name. A stir was created. Comparisons to Beatrix Potter, but like Beatrix Potter bit heads off bunnies. *New York Magazine* called her "Mary Poppins Porno." Okay by me. I've always found Mary Poppins unsettling, perhaps because my mother complained about the movie itself as Very Disturbing. Especially the Dick Van Dyke character. My mother said, when I was a small child, "Don't watch that man. If you cut off all six of a Daddy Long Leg spider's legs, and left two of them, that would be that man."

What I need: to discover more controversy regarding Piper Fields. Fresh controversy. Or something at least minimally interesting. After I make contact, I'm hoping Piper Fields will let her guard down and tell me about her inspiration for the dirty books she writes for so-called adults and why she writes them. The ones with the subtly depicted orgies. I can't help but think of that headline from three years ago. They called her "The Cock Whisperer." Right in the *New York Times* too. Anyway, they got away with it because she'd just published that kiddie book about the shy rooster.

The End of the World

Let us go then you and I when the evening is not exactly spread against the sky but more like smudged, let us go then—and maybe by myself—let us go then to that little bar where I can sit in a booth and not be noticed and drink a Peppered Snog, which is lovely and has an orange peel that's on fire, so much so that I'd never dare to light one like that at home! And the bartender, Leon, is my nephew and so I'm safe there! And welcome like a blousy old aunt who tips very well despite the fact that her advance is just about whittled away already!

I feel proprietary pride. I helped Leon name his bar. We spent much of an entire night considering names. Eggs & Pudding (No, Leon said, people will expect eggs, and pudding), Pearls & Swine (No, Leon cried, people will expect pearls), Doin' It To Ya (suggestion by Leon's old blister pack of a buddy from high school, obviously no), Pops on Top (too Seussy), I Give Up (one of our top choices), DrinksALot (too clever, Leon said—but there could be a Camelot tie in, with round tables?), Leon's (too solipsistic).

When it got to be 3 a.m. Leon looked out at the night sky from my balcony and said, "Let's go with the next words we hear." Fifteen minutes later, a man yelled, "Fuck you to the end of the world, you bitch." Once we made sure the guy he was yelling at was okay, we went with it: The End of the World—after we argued about naming the bar The World Bitch, which would be preferable, but Leon . . .

What would I do without Leon? As my mother likes to remind everyone, she had me twenty years after she had my brother. My brother and Gaia got married when they were both still teenagers and had Leon a year before I was born. I suppose my nephew and I both benefited from being inseparable when we were growing up, and from the fact that we lived like feral dogs, wandering the neighborhood unless Mattie, my father's mother, caught us and brought us over to her place and fed us and turned the garden hose on us and brushed the burrs out of our hair. I like to think that Leon and I knew how to thrive on neglect, like certain shrubs.

Of course I love my brother, but I think of my nephew Leon as more like a brother than my own brother. There's not a human being I'm closer to than Leon which, I'm sure he'd say, is pretty sad, but there you have it.

All the sparks in Leon flare regularly, and as a result he may be tending bar for a very long time, and that was another reason for naming his bar The End of the World—in hopes he'd live as long as the world—at least those were my hopes, unvoiced. Last August as soon as Leon turned fifty-one he said he felt so much younger than when he turned fifty. After you hit thirty, it's the years that sit on the decade marker that make you feel dried up no matter how old you are. The thing is, Leon looks younger than me although he's a year older. You'd think Leon would have more wear and tear on his body and soul because of his first divorce after seven years with a woman who didn't appreciate his sense of humor. Rochelle complained that he was too footloose, too silly. She thought of herself as a serious, sensible person. A confirmed atheist, which in her case meant unwavering allegiance to articles of faith and ritualistic confrontations in which she could strong arm those of less traditional faiths.

Rochelle claimed that Leon willfully misunderstood her, that it was a family trait. (She said this in my stunned presence—I really couldn't figure out what she meant.) The entire marriage was misbegotten, in part because she kept using confusing atheistic logic on Leon. She might as well have argued with a leprechaun. Why he remarried her after their first divorce I'll never know.

Divorce isn't cheap either. Rochelle's long shadow casts itself over his life too often, especially after the first time he divorced her. I can't imagine it's any easier now that he's divorcing her again.

Poor Leon. But it's not the end of the world, he likes to say. Speaking of The End of the World, while we were still debating what to name the bar we spent time thinking about what people would do during the end time. We settled on the most likely three choices: praying, holding loved ones close, and drinking to numb the pain. You can do all three simultaneously at a bar. And the name stuck.

So much to admire about The End of the World: the barn doors for tables, the dim lighting, the booths that allow for privacy, the small scattering of tables, the restrooms modeled after farmyard milk stalls, the long shining mahogany bar, and the lit up mirror casting bright liquidy horror film light over tiers of bottles. That was another name Leon was considering for the bar: Liquid Tears or Liqueur tears or Lick Your Tears.

I was taking notes—little things that struck me, notes to self, you know, all of which require immense concentration, and that might have been why I startled when the woman's voice broke my focus. In the bar there's a juke box and an old mini grand piano that my nephew got for free by taking it off someone's hands, and that woman was wriggling atop the piano and growling.

Why don't you ever see men doing that? From a corner, from a rounded booth near a partition, chortles emanated. That's not a word—chortles—I've ever before used. But these were nothing less than chortles. Enraging sounds—those deep in the throat sounds, huffing. Choking laughs, aggressive.

The people laughing—it sounded like a group of maybe three men—were enjoying the woman's humiliation, for there she was, winding herself around like a python in a parody of frustrated sexual desire. Which is something I actually know something about. Honestly, that woman reminded me of what it's like to wipe off a sticky table with a dishrag when you're ready to fall asleep. That was the way her bottom half was making the rounds on that old piano while the song playing was like Frank Sinatra light. Like someone was trying to be Frank Sinatra but never had a bad day in his young unblemished life. And to the sound of this lightweight ballad the woman in her low-slung black dress was rear-end mopping the piano, which I knew for a fact hadn't been tuned in years.

It is a terrible thing to see anyone humiliating themselves, especially another woman. As a gender, haven't we been embarrassed enough, made to see ourselves as others see us too often? We've been shamed forever—seeing humiliation close up, it seems like overkill.

The woman gyrating was one of those people who inflates her own sense of attractiveness. I love people like that and sometimes I've been one of those people, and why not? She was singing-moaning words that I couldn't make out, and the chortles from the back booth grew louder and more guttural and I couldn't help myself. I sprang up and marched to the chortlers.

"That woman," I said, pointing to the woman on the piano who was ignoring me, her eyes closed, so involved was she in the activity of sponging around on the piano—I said, "That woman is doing something none of you have the guts to do. She's enjoying the music. She's moving herself around to enjoy the music." I turned to make sure she wasn't paying attention. "I know it looks like she's crying for attention—and she is—but she's a human being with a human soul and she doesn't deserve to be laughed at. Look at you! Just look at you." I wanted to insult them—because it felt good to be enraged and virtuous—and then I looked at them.

The one nearest me, shading his eyes as if staring into the sun, was beautiful. More than beautiful. An oasis to anyone dying of thirst. I could only see his chin and the really sweet tips of his ears, but I knew beauty. And then he pulled his hand away from his face.

I heard the rush of wings behind me. It was the piano woman, her dress swishing, wedging herself right up next to me. She leaned over toward a bald, dark-eyed man and kissed him and said, "Darling, how'd you like it?"

And the man she kissed said, "You're adorable." He looked at me, glowering.

The woman turned. "And you are?" she said.

MESSAGE TO PUBLISHER

Dear Rosamund,

You know how you wanted me to work only on Piper Fields? To gain her trust and convince her to allow me to be her biographer? Or should I say, I myself wanted her to realize how lucky she'd be if I were her biographer? Well, shove that possibility aside because, by lucky accident, I met Brent Vintner in the most casual and friendly way. In, of all places, my nephew's bar.

Brent Vintner was there with some of his friends (movie types here in Midlothian "shooting"—movie lingo) and he invited me to join him. Just like that. He saw, he conquered. I don't pretend of course that it was a matter of hearts beating—I'm at least fifteen years older than the dear child—but it was a case of Brent Vintner recognizing that I'm a person of interest. At any rate, he insisted that I join him at the table with his friends and then proceeded to feed me like I was a wee bird. French fries.

A funny thing . . . The woman who was at Brent Vintner's booth had been doing a bit of improv on top of my nephew's piano, wriggling upon the broken down instrument like she was destroying enemies. I didn't even realize who she was. I've seen her in at least three movies. My god, in real life she looks completely different. Smaller. Insect-like. Scorched. You know how the features of famous people are often a little off, too large or too small for their heads? Maybe allowing them to fluidly express emotion by moving parts of their face around? Not that my features aren't more than a little "off," but good god it just shows you what kind of fantasy world we all live in—she does not look like herself, is all I'm saying. But Brent Vintner—this is the miracle, the stupefying fact: he looks better than he looks onscreen.

Nothing can capture it. Maybe it's his smell. You can't capture that in a movie, try as any director might. He smells wonderful. Not like cologne. No, like an alpine breeze in a meadow where streams straggle down rocky cliffs and the wind blows the fragrance of never discovered snow blossoms.

Rosamund, aren't you glad you're going to send me another advance? An advance on the advance, because in this tiny town coincidentally two people I'm going to immortalize are here for possibly months and already will become deeply invested in my well-being.

It may not seem like work—what I'm doing, but believe me it's like my nervous system is being power washed.

No need to send the advance immediately but soon. Soon is best.

NOTE TO SELF

Am I going too far with this made-up scenario? As if Brent Vintner would ever feed a middle-aged woman French fries. Unless it was his terminally ill mother and even then I'm doubtful.

But he did put his hand to his mouth in the universal sign that means "Stop Talking" when A. F. whipped over to the table, her hair in her eyes, her tiny cat body already drooping as she slid into the booth with the men, laughing, delighted by herself, gulping herself down.

Humiliation. I had been embarrassed for A. F. before I knew she was A. F. and when I thought she needed me and that I was her warrior.

I slunk away after she came to the table. It is humiliating to act righteous when no one is doing anything wrong. It smacks of the Inquisition.

ATTEMPTING TO CALM DOWN BY WATCHING *LES DIABOLIQUES*

Alone in my apartment, I watch *Les Diaboliques*, even though it takes me half an hour to get the English subtitles to work. The movie is about a wife with a heart condition, her husband, and the husband's mistress (hateful word) played by Simone Signoret. The two women form a bond and agree to drown the husband in a bathtub. Friendship! Next they drive back to the hideous boys' school where they work and dump the body in the swimming pool.

That gruesome swimming pool is covered with algae. It reminds me of what people always say about marriage—you can't know what's going on below the surface. Like there should be a dead body underneath the floating rot in every marriage.

Back to the movie. Those women went to so much trouble! Soon, the odious husband's body disappears from the swimming pool. At any rate (spoiler alert) the mistress (hateful word—can't say that enough) turns out to be in league with the husband, and they're attempting in a very convoluted and ham-handed manner to make the wife die of a heart attack. Eventually, when the husband rises from a bathtub wearing white rubber discs over his eyes so that he can delude his terrified wife into thinking he's a corpse, she actually does die.

Depressing. Nevertheless, after the movie ends, I find myself gathering strength, readying myself for the battle that is my life. After all, I would not have been fooled like the poor wife in *Les Diaboliques*. If my late ex-husband rose up from the bathtub after being apparently dead I would not have been shocked. I would only have been surprised that he rose out of a bathtub and not a shower.

STRATEGIES

Could not sleep after watching *Les Diaboliques* and so just gave up and read a dystopian novel (absorbing survivalist ideas) until dawn. Feeling restless, not frantic after sleepless night.

Must take a walk. Walking is soothing?

Seven a.m. and shops are closed. The lonely hour. The Health Food Emporium—it looks like it's probably still in business despite those tainted muscle milks. And up ahead: the produce market. That market has always seemed like a front for local organized crime, which is basically disorganized crime or no one would tolerate it. And there's the Cliftdale Foundation where Leon got fired because he wouldn't peach on that idiot who meddled with the toilet tank. Leon: too loyal for his own good.

If Bosomy Bouquets were open I'd make my way down the steps to ogle the blossoms. I pass two tattoo parlors and Walker's, a restaurant where I used to work until I quit in protest when the cook insisted he didn't need—ever—to wash his left hand, and also because he always came to work with a giant scab on his forehead and wouldn't listen when I made first-aid suggestions.

Soon I'm outside the State Farm insurance office. I used to meet in the back room with an environmental group. It wasn't much of a group: just Leon and me and Furshenker. Heady days. We called ourselves, for clarity's sake, Clean Water! We were exceptionally serious and did improve local water quality even though going to town council meetings left us dredged with the breadcrumbs of boredom.

Furshenker—that name sounds like a primitive tool for skinning an animal. The funny thing: he was an amateur taxidermist. For a while he was in trouble because the police thought he murdered someone. And then it turned out that he did, but it was later and in another state. I wonder if Furshenker's out of prison. Maybe I could write about him?

Up ahead, Tappity Doo Dah, closed so early in the day. The parking lot is empty except for one car—the one car that always seems to be in every otherwise empty parking lot. Tappity Doo Dah—the name of that bar promises too much. As if a good time could ever be had by all. No wonder the awning droops. It takes so much energy to please people. I've only been inside the place once—I never returned, out of loyalty to The End of the World. At Tappity Doo Dah I encountered what you might call a "body wall" in every direction—that's how popular the place is. Brightly colored neon tubing overhead, poundingly unrecognizable music, and the general spore-like diffusion of wiggly sex chemicals.

That place is designed for a sensation-seeking clientele, for fleeting, superficial experiences. Maybe Tappity Doo Dah's customers, after a night of intense pheromone dispersal, ought to walk to The End of the World, calm themselves down and steep.

The End of the World has depth. Depth! I want to shout as I turn away from Tappity Doo Dah. And intimacy! Being inside The End of the World—it's like floating inside a glass of whiskey: golden brown, warming, where everything you see is distorted. If you spend time at The End of the World you feel righteously stained.

Must focus. Must remind self: this is my own life, no one else's. Yet—to be a biographer may mean I'm subsuming my own life, as Leon's friend Clover says?

Such a shaky business.

Must remember dignity of profession. Search for truth online, and in person, and in printed materials. Fulfill my life-long aspiration: to be someone others will tell their stories to, to be a biographer, which means to understand how others make their lives their own.

To do so I must be alert to the following:

People lie about themselves.

People may not even be aware that they lie about themselves.

Denial creates all-encompassing fog.

It is difficult for anyone to see themselves. I must see for them.

A feeling-full, well-practiced imagination may come closer to the truth than facts.

Memories of "facts" are dubious, subject to distortion.

Why clip coupons and then forget them when paying at grocery store—death wish?

Am I emotionally ready to check bank balance?

Why is it that, after you're no longer related by marriage, you are contacted by former in-law?

Cannot eat meat—ethical issues—yet remember how fortifying bacon can be.

Why "rescue" two cats unless unconsciously aiming to pressure self to remain viable as living organism out of sense of obligation?

Remember: observe your surroundings.

Look for an angle when engaging in research. Or at least a corner.

An Expected Voice Mail From my Mother

"Tabitha, have you made a living will and a regular will? It's very important, I'm told. What I'm thinking: you know that golden pony on your shelf? I always liked that pony, and I hope when you make your will you think about who it's going to. I would take very good care of it! I know that little pony came from your dear departed father's departed mother. You don't want it just ending up anywhere. Please think seriously about this!"

More Strategies

Tell Leon he gets $25 every time he calls and/or texts to let me know that Brent Vintner is at The End of the World. Assuming Brent Vintner will return. $25 every single time. No exceptions. Will bill each $25 as "expense." Which it is. Plus, Leon really needs the money. Plus, must not spend all my resources on Piper Fields.

Research—Worthwhile "Facts" Regarding Brent Vintner

Internet reveals:

He likes the color green! (Must wear green when interviewing him—gain advantage.)

He used to make ice cones as a child and sold them!

Worked summer stock—*Seven Brides for Seven Brothers*, repeatedly. Very unfortunate. Production amounts to advertisement in favor of serial kidnappings and evident rape. Really crazy patriarchal stuff that reveals basic fabric of society. He played one of the brothers—none can be told apart from the others. Sociopaths.

Best known as male companion of central star (G. G.) in *What About Ducks?* In recent years works in low budget indie productions. Apparently to gain respect. Possibly sympathy too. Played Hamlet in college—entire production in large water bed onstage. Production panned in merciless college newspaper as "Hamlet: Bed Wetter."

All reports refer to solid, well-intentioned parents. Myth?

Message From Publisher

Tabitha—

Are you working on the biography about Piper Fields? Didn't I ask you to try Piper Fields FIRST?

Message to Publisher

Rosamund—

I have been stalking her. Have not forgotten. In fact, I now know where she goes for breakfast.

Have faith, Rosamund. I am killing two birds with one stone.

Piper Fields: Making Contact: Stone Canoe Cafe

No one looks like their author photos. I don't know what they use on those things—some sort of filter that turns human flesh into misty cloud spume and star sprinkles.

I only know what Piper Fields looks like because of Alyse at the bakery. Alyse, who has small children and relies on Piper Fields's books to get them to sleep—she recognized the name on the credit card. She had to describe Piper Fields to me because the woman never looks the same way twice in online photographs. Alyse said I'll recognize Piper Fields because she's pretty and has a "blurry face."

I didn't think Alyse was being helpful until on Wichita Street I saw a woman who exactly matched Alyse's description. Pretty with a blurry face. Someone who looked like she was in disguise by not being in one of her usual disguises. I stared long and hard. She didn't appear to notice, like she was used to being stared at. Which was further evidence she was Piper Fields.

I've become a regular now, waiting for Piper Fields each day. Delighted to discover that she's here at ten nearly every morning. One waffle for her, on the side one scrambled egg. A cup of tea. She eats like she's at a four-year-old's imaginary tea party. Yet there's something animal-like about her. Animal-like in the manner of an extinct animal. How she writes those orgiastic novels, I don't know. She can hardly manipulate a waffle.

What is the key to this woman? A hybrid person, pleasing both children and the most terrifying category of adults. Is she a house divided against herself although she can, evidently, stand? Is her personality the result of an overly reclusive upbringing or a too indulgent one? Cult or commune? Does she inhabit an imaginary world because she's uncomfortable in her own body and thinks of herself as stuck in a plaster flesh cast?

My plan: make humorous remarks to her from my table. Eventually she'll reveal that she writes children's books and I'll ask her to tell me about them. No, rethink. Do not want to snooze.

She is examining her waffle like it's a chessboard and she's remembering losing a match. Has anyone ever eaten a waffle square by square? And the little silver pitcher of maple syrup. She's now pouring the tiniest stream, like a fairy wets its lips on top of the waffle and she has to direct the stream into its pinprick mouth.

She lifts her right eyebrow. A perfect eyebrow, like it was painted by an old Dutch master. I think of the sculptures of Dutch heads in my apartment. Stupid impulse purchase.

The waiter whips over to me because there are only two customers in the place and I always tip beyond my means. I've waited tables enough to know how treacherous the job is, how poorly remunerated, how everything can fly up in your face—like blood. That happened once when I cut my hand on a steak knife and had to give the customer his meal free even though he devoured the steak, soaked up the blood with the entire contents of the bread basket, and as an insult tipped me a nickel with gum on it.

I order a Mid-Loaf-Ian: fried banana bread. Also eggs over hard. I make the gesture of flatness with my palm to emphasize "over hard." And then, as insurance, I say "please don't let the yolks be runny." Because a runny yolk destroys all serenity. And coffee of course. Like the kind cowboys make on the range, the kind that burns through the kettle.

Today: a bit of a shock. She looks up, smiles, nods. Recognizes me as a regular? Knows me by reputation?

The cafe door slaps open. In the entrance: a bearded man, immense, in a red flannel shirt—plaid. Paul Bunyan. I wonder: Did Piper Fields conjure him? Is he a character from one of her children's books? A giant logger who defends those winsome rabbits she writes about? Flannel in early April suggests the wearer is reluctant to accept the tender warmth of spring. Clutching a bag patterned with tiny donuts and the word Alyse's in gold scroll, he struts to a table, angles his chair to face Piper Fields.

With a hand flap, the man in flannel dismisses the waiter and inches his chair closer to Piper Fields's table. Ears lowered, he's hunched, sucking in his breath like someone who will, at any moment, lunge. He leans forward, his hands holding up his chin, elbows on thighs. No intention of hiding his interest, assuming it's his right to observe this tiny woman. I mean, I've been observing her, but subtly. His attention amounts to a threat, to shoving her with his eyes.

Time is slowing, as if what is happening is occurring in the past.

Piper Fields's fork hovers in midair.

I do what anyone with half a brain would do. I stand, launch myself at the man in flannel and shout, "Out! Out! Out! Out!"

He rises, stumbles backward, rushes to the door. I follow, shaking my fist. The man is fast—zigzagging down the sidewalk.

When I come back inside, Piper Fields is standing beside my table, her eyes watery.

"Thank you," she says.

"Who was he?" I ask, desperate to know. "Tell me everything." I can't believe my luck. Here she is: the subject of my biography, although she has no idea she is the subject of my biography. She owes me so much. It takes effort not to reach out and clasp her hand.

"You've had a shock," I say.

She laughs—small white teeth. Like teeth in a children's book. I have never met anyone so ruined by their profession. "Oh, every day's a shock," she says. "You shoved that man right out of here. He's a thousand times bigger than you are and you did that."

Hot-faced, I want to hear more. "Really? I mean, he was big. That's true. He smelled like vomit. I have no fear of vomit. I'm a cat owner. Tell me, who was he?"

She looks behind herself. We are almost alone. Just a waiter with a mop by the door. "Do you need help?" I call over to the waiter. Startled, he looks away.

Piper introduces herself, assuming that I don't know who she is. I point to the chair at my table. She sits down on the chair's edge, obviously not intending to stay.

I try again. "Do you know that man who—?"

"I have no idea who he is." Her eyes look incredibly moist.

And then I confess. "I actually know who you are. You're a children's book writer. You put children to sleep."

"You're right. The books bore children to sleep. This is the story I usually tell about it: I started babysitting when I was fifteen. It was a way to survive, learning how to get children to sleep so I could rummage through their parent's refrigerators."

"Did you find many sex toys?"

She tilts her head.

"I don't mean in the refrigerator," I say. "I just mean, you know, nosing around in the parents' houses."

"It's funny that you said that because once I did find something that resembled a sex toy in a refrigerator. It whirred."

I want to change the subject to something more relevant to the biography I plan to write. I ask, "What is your creative process like?"

"Seriously. You actually want to know?"

"I'm deliriously interested."

"I really can't tell you what my creative process is like."

"Is it—a secret sauce?"

"Very secret sauce. So secret I don't even know how any of those books get written."

I think I understand. "You feel like after you write something it's erased from your memory? You've exorcised the demon that possessed you?"

"We're talking about the children's books or—"

"Any of your books," I say, encouragingly, hoping I don't sound like I'm interviewing her, although I obviously am.

"I can guarantee that my demons haven't been exorcised," she says.

Sensing that I might be annoying her already, I ask a simpler question. "What attracted you to Midlothian?"

"There's someone I need to meet with occasionally who doesn't live very far from here. Besides, Midlothian's a nice, quiet town where no one—I thought until this morning—would bother me."

"Good for writing, I imagine."

"I wouldn't know."

"What do you mean?"

She looked away. "I'm having a bit of a—block."

I find myself really liking this woman—so ready to reveal her vulnerabilities. I feel less alone, I can admit that!

She looks over at the table she abandoned. "Well, I guess we're both safe. I can go back and rescue my waffle."

She smiles sweetly. I'm almost rendered helpless before I say, "Oh bring that monster over here. I'd love it if you stayed. We can ask for hotter coffee. We can make a united stand and request a fresh pot."

She delivers her plate and silverware. My sudden boldness makes me shy, and for the next few minutes I can hear myself chew. I fear I've gone too far too fast, ruining everything. "We should exchange numbers," I say. "Call me if that guy ever bothers you again. I can scare him off."

We actually exchange numbers, clumsily. Then we talk a bit about the rabbits in her books. Before she leaves, I ask, "Do you want me to check outside? Make sure you're not followed?"

I pop up before she can refuse my help and charge out the front entrance. A mother and daughter bouncing along, a young guy in a wool coat too heavy for the weather. No plaid flannel. Just strangers straggling. When I return, Piper Fields is gone—out the back exit.

The waiter is picking up her dishes. I help him and he says, "You have to stop."

I say, "I can't help it." What I mean is, I'm happy and need to do something with my hands. It is a lucky, rare thing—to get a phone number quickly, easily.

MESSAGE TO PUBLISHER

Dear Rosamund,

Contact established! Piper Fields is eating out of my hand like one of her infernal bunnies in that series of bunny books she wrote. Those tragic bunnies. More on those later—I'm learning a lot! On the other hand: why wait? Those bunnies. You know the ones in her illustrations that are pink and gray and look like they have a contagious skin disease? She used to own two bunnies like that, although she kept saying she wasn't comfortable with the word "owned," and was only using the term for convenience. No, it was more like she lived with the bunnies, she said, and when she said that, Rosamund, I kept picturing her all bundled up in a burrow snuggling with those rodents. The bunnies liked to hide in high grass and her father mowed . . . I'll say no more. At any rate, that series of bunny books is actually an elegy. The subtext is brutal death. "But at least they were together," she said.

Anyway, Rosamund, my ethics dictate that I reveal to her my plans. First, though, I want her to like me a little bit more than she does, you know? Besides, I'll say that the idea came upon me gradually—the idea to write the biography. One that's authorized and that will make you some money, Rosamund, because Rosamund, you may never know what poverty feels like, but that doesn't mean you aren't interested in seeing what can happen to your many bank accounts when the biography of Piper Fields sells and sells. And then, too, there's what you really want: the prestige. Because that's what I can bring. For you. People will forget all about that horrific bust up from your husband, the court case, etcetera. A new year. A new you. Because you and I share the ability to ask questions and to seek answers.

I'll keep you informed. I'm very excited, Rosamund—in case you didn't pick up on that because of my (enviable) subtlety?

RESEARCH

Note to self: must pry from Piper Fields more about the identity of the man in flannel with the threatening demeanor. Is he, indeed, a stranger? Or was Piper Fields lying? She seemed so—I don't know?—accustomed to what happened. I mean, she sat there frozen and also like "Oh god, here we go again." If that had happened to me I'd be swinging for the doors. I'd be picking up and hurling a chair. I'd be myself, and I myself would be very good in a fox hole, thank you. But I must say that, upon reflection, something seemed "off" about her. Once or twice I caught a look on her face that suggested a quality I have admired in others but never found a way to emulate: cunning.

Have avoided reading Piper Fields's writing at any length. Must begin at last but face internal resistance.

I start with *Bunnies! Bunnies! Bunnies!* Brave of her to draw the illustrations herself and not leave it to a professional. No dimensionality. Bunnies look like road kill.

On to the adult novels—maybe just try one. Or complete first as well as second chapter of one. Murder and orgies. Or not. Try again tomorrow?

Perhaps link between kiddie books and erotic novels? Bunnies? Rabbits lead exceptionally smutty lives?

Resist calling Piper Fields. Do not want to seem like insane fan. Practice being patient.

REFOCUSING

Plowing on, as if I have enough in my bank account to eat. Must open another credit card. So. Strategies: Piper Fields appeared to like me, yet she has not texted or phoned although we exchanged numbers and I saved her from the rude intentions of logger. Remedy: soon I'll text and ask if she'd like to meet me at nice little lunch place. I can serve as body guard and get to the bottom of mystery of her personality.

Discovery: there's a new restaurant outside of town, and they don't know my reputation! I can apply for a hostess job—or any job. The website refers to the restaurant as "fashionable." That's a negative. But website photo of carousel horse in the entranceway looks promising as does laminated menu of breakfast platters. I apply in person and am turned down instantly, denied even an opportunity to fill out an application. Will not describe more of encounter. I can't help but feel my age and my looks and my attitude are held against me.

Afterwards, Leon sees me slumping my way across the parking lot by The End of the World, pulls up in his car, climbs out, and calls over, "Good God, Tabitha, you look like Leonid Brezhnev in that coat."

I immediately feel better. Heartening to be able to blame the coat.

MESSAGE TO PUBLISHER

Dear Rosamund,

I'm sorry that my ex-brother-in-law contacted you. I can assure you that I never gave him your number, nor would I have ever encouraged him to ask you to invest in his macabre business. I hardly know the man, frankly. He has been trying to get me to buy one of his products for the past three years and has been keeping a spoonful of my former husband's ashes in reserve just in case I'll be in the market. Perhaps you'll believe I'm being heartless because I do not find the need to haul around my long ago divorced spouse's ashes in a locket. Or maybe you understand completely. At any rate, I'll threaten my ex-brother-in-law to the best of my ability. It occurs to me now that possibly he has hacked my email and my phone.

How Many Times Must I Say No?

Take positive action to get ex-brother-in-law off back. NO, Thomas, I do not want to buy one of those memorial necklaces which hold my former husband's ashes. I realize that my ex-brother-in-law makes his living selling those necklaces online. Nevertheless, the offer to send a necklace with a spoonful of my ex-husband's ashes does not entice me to spend the astronomical amounts he's charging. Conrad was more than two decades older than me at the time of our marriage and went on to marry and divorce three other women. I'm sorry that he died three years ago, but I do not want to wear his ashes around my neck. Bless his heart. It was hard enough dealing with him while he was living. So, no, Thomas, no. If Thomas doesn't stop calling I'll have to change my number and then how will Piper Fields reach me? I've already communicated with my ex-brother-in-law too often about this issue. The last time he called I asked him: Thomas, why don't you just sell jawbones on a string? He laughed. Apparently his grief hasn't lingered.

Strategy

At possible future lunch with Piper Fields, hazard the idea about writing her biography. Mention other biographies I've written. Pretend to be humble, casual, let drop fact that, other than a few brief celebrity profiles, I've only ever before worked on the dead. Make joke about how easy dead people are to write about? They can't dispute one damn thing! Not from a perch in Hell!

No, rethink. Make joke about how I'd like to work with the living to make sure to get all facts straight. Continue on, trying out that argument I once used with Rosamund: about how easy it would be simply to vacuum up facts from the internet, put in some general contextual speculations, and call it a day. But NO—I am an artist, not composing a biography like an anteater snuffling up squirming digital trifles. Make comparison to Piper Fields's own occupation. How we're craft-persons. Establish trust. Let her know I understand her outsized wishes, that she's a woman of many dimensions, and we have so much in common! I write too and can't keep a job for the life of me. I'm meant for solitary and unproductive labor. Genetically we must have a ribbon of DNA in common? Suggest that a biography would combat the hostile perceptions she endures after it became known she writes not only bedtime books for children but bedtime smut for adults.

Order more of her adult novels. Fill in the gaps. Sure, they're close to pornographic, luckily enough, and that creates tension and traction: how can the same author who writes the most benign and innocent woolly-lamb style of children's literature also compose cult novels about harrowing . . . ? More important, how did she keep secret for many years her second identity as a writer of novels for adults with obvious personality disorders?

What are her passions? Her influences (boring but must be referred to, glancingly at least)? Her great regrets (if lucky will be many—must press her on these, gain trust, appear sympathetic)? Plans for the future (hope these involve transgressive desires not just some boring holiday in Maine Airbnb picking blueberries)? Relationships with famous people (cross fingers and hope)? Cooking recipes? Other failures?

Dread making timeline of her life but must be done. Cannot make timeline of past month in my own life. But must UNDERSTAND time in relation to Piper Fields. Also is Piper Fields her real name? Name is too conveniently writerly for children's book author. Like the name of the Pied Piper who leads clamoring children away from their cheap parents, and thus Piper Fields's sweet lullaby bunny books suggest treachery? Or is Piper Fields more befitting a name for purveyor of adult novels even more than her early pseudonym, Bunny Swift? Piper Fields sounds like an itinerant schoolteacher who invites lumberjack for pancakes in Pornhub feature . . . Must approach name issue cautiously.

Strategy: Try to write in full sentences.

Also: Observe surroundings. Notice things. Like how many windows are in a room, color of carpet, extraordinary smells, background noise.

Be present in the world. You have senses. Use them. This will allow you to understand what you otherwise miss because you live in your head like it's a mall.

From The End of the World:

Text from Leon:

Your pretty boy is back

Text from me to Leon:

I'll be there

Quick Action at the End of the World

No time to slip out of what I'm wearing. Unfortunately, I'm dressed in the same clothes from the last time I saw Brent Vintner. Not green, his favorite color. He might remember me as the woman who accosted his table in defense of the person rubbing herself into the bar's piano, rubbing like she was my nephew applying turtle wax to his used Impala if he did so with his rear end. Seriously though, Brent Vintner might remember me enough to think, Oh I know that woman from somewhere, but where? Maybe he'll mistake me for a member of the film crew. Like I applied light reflecting dust to his cheekbones. Tabitha, the makeup artist.

It's barely endurable, walking in. My mind is showing itself right through the bones of my skull. Even with my head down I can tell that a male presence is alone at the booth up against the old Burt Lancaster poster, and thus I settle only narrowly within the sightline of the male presence. My face is so hot I'm afraid I've caught a shame fever. I lift my chin, try to look through my eyelashes.

"Jesus, Aunt Tabitha, you're late." It's Leon. I didn't see him hop over the bar. He lowers himself, whispers in my ear. "He's still here. I'm pretending that you have a reason to be here that doesn't involve him, you know?"

I love it when Leon calls me Aunt Tabitha. The word "aunt" sweats respect.

"Thank you," I whisper as he bolts off.

Without asking, Leon flies back in an instant and hands me a frosted mug of beer.

I slowly angle myself in the direction of the male presence. Wrong man. I swivel. Brent Vintner is behind me, sitting alone. His head snaps forward.

"Join me," he says.

Of course I'm dreaming.

"I remember you," he actually says.

"Oh," I say. I apologize again. "I didn't realize that the woman on the piano was who she is and I thought your table was being—cruel. I shouldn't have—"

"No, you were fine," he says. He's drinking something that looks like glue we used in grade school, the glue that comes with a thick red rubber tip. All cocktails should be dispensed like that, with a thick red rubber tip.

He says something, and I can't make it out. He turns away. I have the horrible thought that he's invited me to sit with him and my silence has been interpreted as rudeness, or at least lack of interest.

I pick up my mug and my purse and stand in front of his table and gradually lower myself into the chair opposite him and realize I shouldn't be doing what I'm doing because the look he is giving me—frozen horror. Like he's endured this before and thought that in this small town he wouldn't have to face a crazed fan. His face—it's like Piper Fields's face just before the strange man had to be pushed out the door.

"I'm sorry," I say. "I thought I didn't hear you and that you invited me to join you. I'm so sorry. I keep misinterpreting situations. I do that so often. Something happens, and I do exactly what I shouldn't do. Like here you are, an actor, probably after a hard day of shooting and you want to have a moment to yourself in this out of the way place. Or maybe you're waiting for friends and now I'm sitting with you and you're not going to know how to explain why I'm here. Or there's someone you're pursuing—man or woman I don't know—and it looks bad, like you're sitting here with an old hooker or with, like, a cranky relative and there's nothing you can do. You're trapped by your own good manners. When really you ought to have body guards at this point in your life. And you're wondering what you have to do to get rid of me or if you should just walk out the door but you haven't paid for your beer yet and you have an order of fries coming. And you're wondering: Is this woman going to cry? Because you hate seeing that. Men crying. Women crying. Children crying—that's normal. But you hate to cause pain because in movies that's all you do, simulate pain. And that's what movies do: entertain with pain. They ought to make that a slogan: entertain with pain."

I feel breath coming down onto my scalp. It's Leon standing over me.

"Another beer?" he asks Brent Vintner.

"Sure," Brent Vintner says. He nods to me, "And you? You want another? Or maybe you've already had another?"

Never before had I noticed that The End of the World has only two windows and they're relatively high on the wall. No carpeting, only dingy boards fermented in old whiskey and tears. The bar's smell is quite wonderful—vaguely peach, cinnamon, mint aftershave (Leon). There are whispery noises as if old ghosts rustle under floorboards.

Message to Publisher

Dear Rosamund,

I had beers with Brent Vintner last night. Three beers. He bought. My confession: I was with him, and my nephew Leon attests to that fact, but I have almost no memory of the night. I could have spent hours in a ditch or attending a baseball game—I would not have known. It's as if my mind went blank for hours, which attests to Brent Vintner's—I don't know what to call it—virility? I don't mean anything sexual was occurring. Of course not. I'm fifteen years older than he is and my charms have not been appreciated since my deceased former husband first met me. Nevertheless, I must have found my way home (I'd walked to the bar) and in my own bed, fully dressed. And what information, what new insight do I have to offer that would help me write a biography of Brent Vintner? Plenty, once my mind heals from the obvious seismic cracking it endured. Somewhere in the course of the night I did inform Brent Vintner that I was writing his biography and there was nothing he could do about it. I do remember that.

Don't lose faith in me, Rosamund. I'm enjoying myself too much.

The Return of Memory

It's coming back now. In splinters. I wasn't drunk. Three beers is nothing to me. Nobody gets under-the-table drunk on three beers. I really think my mind went empty for hours because I was—for lack of a better word—happy. Brent Vintner, he listens. He listens like he's memorizing lines from a script. "You're talking my ears off," he said—and he smiled. Like it was a marvelous thing to have ears lopped off.

Really, how am I going to write about this man?

"Are you desperately lonely?" I asked him at one point. I was lubricated by the third beer, I admit. "Are you so lonely that sometimes at night you talk to the plates in your kitchen? You hold up a plate before your face and try to see your reflection in it and then give up and have better luck with a stainless steel pan and you say to the pan, 'Will anyone ever love me in any way?' Do you go to bed and gnaw on your bedsheets and sit up in the middle of the night and catch a glimpse of your reflection in the mirror and for one wild instant imagine your reflection is your very own demon lover? And then when you see it's just yourself you think: tomorrow I will change. Tomorrow I will send out so much love into the world that love will come right back to me? And then the next day you go out to the animal rescue farm and you rescue two—two, mind you—two cats who are already named: Pert and Pretty, and pretty soon you realize that they despise you, that those two cats are like everyone you knew in middle school who turned away from you when you tried to join their dance circle at the Snow Ball. Pert and Pretty. What kind of company are they? They nip, they swagger, they swat at one another and only become compatible when they join forces to hiss. No wonder they were abandoned! That rescue place. I should have known it wasn't the right place for me to find companionship. I only saw rich people there. My cats expected a higher standard of living and now they won't forgive me."

He smiled. A gentle smile. I realized it was my opportunity to learn something about him. I tried again. "Do you ever yourself, not that you would ever have any need to feel that way, do you on any occasion ever feel lonely?"

"Right now. At this instant." He smiled again. A little up-teasing of the mouth.

He swallowed. I waited. I could tell he wanted to say more.

At last words came from him. "On set everyone knits."

"They knit?"

"I know. I don't knit. So many of them knit because you wait a lot. You wait more than anything. And so people knit. I don't—it makes me feel—alone."

"Well, to hell with that," I said. "Knitting. I've never trusted people who knit. Well, some people. I've known some saints who knit. There's probably a saint for knitting like there's a saint for everything else. It has to be some martyr tortured with yarn. But, you know, I think that a lot of people who knit are just working out tension, right? It's like they don't want to pay for a therapist, and so they keep their fingers busy making socks or scarves no one in their right mind would ever want to itch through winter in, you know? You start moving your hands regularly in a certain way and you can't stop. It becomes a way of life. Nothing else matters."

He ordered another beer, kept looking toward the door.

"Are you expecting someone?" I asked.

"I was, but I think they're a no-show."

"Does that happen to you often?" I couldn't imagine it did.

He didn't answer. I tried another tactic. Sometimes people really need to relax and require another person to needle them into it. "You know," I said, "they have drinks here that they can light on fire. Leon, that's my nephew, he can take an orange peel and make it spurt flames. Have you ever had a flaming drink?"

"Years ago."

"Was that at, like, the Charles Manson ranch or something?" I asked.

I don't know why I said that.

"Why did you say that?" he asked, blinking, leaning closer, like he wanted to see if the pupils of my eyes were doing anything.

"I just—I think in California if you're an actor you must know everyone. Sometimes you wonder," I said, "given corporate greed, how come that ranch isn't like a theme park by now."

He sat back, picked up his mug, drank, set the mug down harder than it had to be set down. "When can I see you again?" he asked.

"You're saying that," I said, "so you can get rid of me. You'll put a fake number in my cell phone and then toddle out the door, thinking you've soothed me and that I won't follow you and destroy your life. You're thinking that by acting as if you want to see me again I can be got rid of now. You're thinking that I'm one of those people who actually likes delayed gratification. No, I'm not one of those," I said, laughing and laughing.

Leon and Gregory came running up to the table. "Aunt Tabitha, are you all right?" Leon asked.

Gregory said, "Don't choke like that. You make us worried."

I said, "Is my laugh that awful?"

Leon nodded his apologies to Brent Vintner. "She's always been like this. She can't help herself."

And that was when the miracle happened. Brent Vintner leaned across the table, picked up my hand, and before he let it go, he said, "I have all sorts of ideas about how that laugh could be put to use. Let's have your phone number."

Leon cleared his throat. "She's not just anybody," he said.

Gregory chimed in. "She's been drinking here for years and has never before this date caused too many problems. She's just—Aunt Tabitha to all of us."

I turned my head slowly and looked up. "Gregory," I said, "you're seventy seven years old. I couldn't easily be your aunt at my age. Do the math, honey."

And that's when my memory went blank again. Because nothing much else happened. I did watch Brent Vintner punch his phone number into my phone and my number into his, and gather up his squeaky leather jacket. Next he was moving toward the door, his buttocks making an inspired sliding motion in his jeans. Anyone from a mile away could tell he was an actor.

PHONE CALL TO LEON

Me: Are you busy?

Leon: Are you kidding? I'm tending bar. I'm never busy at work.

Me: Great, because this might take time. Can you describe for me Brent Vintner's appearance?

Leon: You saw him. You were here with him.

Me: I know. But I don't quite—anyway, can you just tell me what you think he looks like?

Leon: There are photographs of him all over the internet.

Me: I know. I want to hear what you think he looks like.

Leon: Watch one of his films. You can catch them on Netflix and YouTube. I saw him on Netflix the other night. The movie where he's a firefighter? No, that was another movie. He was a detective. He kept going into dark rooms and finding bodies. I wanted to shout, "Can't you turn on a light switch?"

Me: I know I can watch his movies. I want to hear how you think he looks.

Leon: Weird. Okay. He's about six feet, big shoulders, slim waist, his pants slip down a little. Probably got a nice package.

Me: Speak English.

Leon: Okay. What else do you need? Tabitha-Tamitty-Ramma-Dulah. I like that name for you—like you're a guru and a midwife.

Me: His face?

Leon: Eyes. Mouth. Nose. Dark hair. Sort of a narrow face. Good hairline. Is that enough?

Me: Thanks. That helps.

Leon: Anytime, Aunt Tabs. Wait. Your book about him—it's not going to be long right, like your book about Annie?

Me: God no. Short and sweet. Simple language.

Leon: Good. Because a long book is like a short church service. It could always be shorter. Keep it short and you'll be A-okay, Tabbity Dabbity Ding Dong.

Me: Leon, please don't.

Leon: Sorry. I won't make a long apology. A long apology is like a cashmere sweater on a moth farm. It's always full of holes.

Me: I have to go. I can't keep talking.

Leon: A short goodbye is like a kangaroo without a pouch. Just: Anybody see my baby? So long, gotta hop.

Celibacy

All these years when I am not having sex I could be more ritualistically inclined. Once you give something a name you're consecrating it. Basically, I think of myself as unendingly lonely. Instead of admitting as much, I can say: I'm practicing celibacy. It's a practice, isn't it? You renew the vows daily? It would sound so much better—celibacy—instead of what it actually is. Realize I could have been a member of the Shakers, a remnant of the last truly happy people.

Apologizing to the washing machine at the laundromat after accidentally kicking it isn't wrong.

Must fulfill promise to Rosamund and make extended contact with Piper Fields. Must also be prepared for such contact.

Trying Again to Read One of Piper Fields's Novels

Question: Why does everyone in chapter two wear a shower cap? Not erotic.

Question: Why do people look shorter when naked?

Don't just plan to call Piper Fields and invite her to lunch. Actually call her. Why not? I am not crazed cult member—not her typical adult reader.

Research in Cafe With Piper Fields on Site

The surprise: Piper Fields agrees to meet me at The Gradual Eatery & Cafe.

I arrive a half hour early, take a shady booth as far back from the door as possible.

Five large windows let in streams of syrupy gold light at one end of the cafe. No carpeting but flooring is much scuffed, old brown boards with artificial knot holes. Smell of linguini and parmesan and disinfectant. From the kitchen the hiss of rising steam, a low whimper, the rubbery sound of something hitting the floor.

Except for a couple of businessmen I'm the only customer. One of the businessmen glances at me, turns his back, twists close to the other businessman and whispers. The other businessman peers over at me. I don't know why. What is this? *The Nosy Businessmen*? Which sounds like a light-hearted opera by Mozart, one of those confections that makes you think he predicted capitalism. It occurs to me that the men may imagine, because I'm alone, that I'm some sort of superannuated sex worker. Which would be fine, except that sort of work must be incredibly difficult, similar to cutting heads off chickens at a processing plant.

And then—there she is—possibly! Yes, it's her. The blurry face. It's Piper Fields, in a short skirt and high collared blouse elaborated by a red cardigan. Much alertness at the table of two businessmen. She slides into the booth, and her smile is so wide her eyes disappear.

"Let's look at the menu first," she says, "and then let's talk."

There is a moment when you know that another person is someone you want to be absurdly loyal toward, when you figure that maybe if a grenade got tossed near them you'd prostrate yourself upon it. That's because she said the magic words: "Let's look at the menu first." How polite is that? Let's look at the menu first so we're not making the waiter wait, so we're not distracted, so when we talk we can concentrate fully. Already she seems like a very different woman from the one I saw frozen over a waffle. Less delicate, more human-like.

The light from the hanging lantern above our booth shines down on the straight part in her hair as she studies the menu, and it occurs to me that I won't be able to write a word about her that is honest. I'll have to be careful not to turn the biography into one of the lives of the saints.

She looks up at me, the dimple in her right cheek deepening. Something crosses her eyes—the light shifting. She puts down her menu.

I can't help but stare. She's wearing an extraordinary amount of makeup and the outline of her lips shades too far toward her nose. If I didn't recognize her voice and her way of holding herself and tilting her head and her general blurriness, I might think she was another woman.

She blinks rapidly and ages before me, her forehead furrowing, the skin under her eyes webbing. "You're one of them, aren't you?" she says. "I should have trusted my instincts." She pulls her enormous carry-all satchel closer, draws it up on her shoulder like a holster.

"What?" I say.

"You're like the others. I wasn't sure—but the way you're looking at me. I know that look. I've lived with that stare for years. Because of the novels. I know for sure now. I googled your name and couldn't believe it and didn't want to come and came anyway, thinking that maybe you're not going to exploit me, but you are, aren't you?"

With horror, I realize that I have to try not to cry. "I confess," I say. "But don't worry. I'm not a fan. I can't stand your books. I'm a biographer and I want to write about you—that's all. Really. I think your children's books are exactly what I would have hated as a child. I think they're propaganda for neglectful parents. I think they're secretly dusted with narcotics. And your novels—they're not even vivid enough to be pornography. They're more like pretentious erotica, which has never done anyone any good."

Her face begins to relax, unknotting.

To keep her from thinking about what I've just said I ask, "You own a cat?"

"How can you tell?"

I nod. She looks down at the hair on her sweater and says, "You like cats but you don't like anything I've written. If so, I think we can get along."

She brightens before my eyes.

The waiter, very young and contemptuous, slumps over to us. Piper Fields snaps shut her menu and orders shrimp in a basket.

"They don't even come in a basket," I inform her.

"Should I change my order?"

"No, I just meant—I hope you won't be disappointed."

"Does it bother you—disappointment?"

I don't have to think about it. "If it bothered me I'd be dead by now."

Above us to my left is a long shelf arrayed with teapots—the most perfect little teapots, one shaped like a cabbage, another like a bunny, another like a pumpkin, another like a tiny cottage, and the others are simply round and teapot-shaped and in lovely colors: blue and aqua and mint green. I'm hoping she appreciates them. It's like we've landed inside one of her children's books where her bunnies would serve tea, their ears trembling while they tipped the teapot with their fluffy paws. Even though I abhor those sorts of books, the decor on the wall next to our booth is pleasant, and the pumpkin-shaped teapot reminds me of my mother, in the best possible way.

I go on. "I write biographies that aren't entirely conventional. I've written two so far—and some short profiles of celebrities. I really think my publisher is using me for something to do with a tax write-off—I can't understand the math—but my biographies rely a good deal on imagination. My own. They're almost—spiritual."

"You channel spirits?"

"God no. I avoid even writing about anyone's ancestors. Everyone skips that part in biographies anyway. Who cares about the Duchy of Puddlelump or whatever."

"I'm trying to understand," Piper Fields says. "You read—auras?"

"Not if I have any self-respect. You mean, like the colors surrounding you? Because you're surrounded by blue flames or something? I once heard of a woman whose aura was mustard yellow. She said it made her feel like a hot dog. No, I can't even comprehend the idea of auras. I intuit life stories. Think of what a fabulous story I could make of your life! But I promise—in your case I won't write a word about you unless you approve. Anything I write—you can see. If you agree that I can write anything at all. I'm respectful. I listen. Probably no one really listens to you—you're alone in town, aren't you?—and I can listen. You'll need that—a listener?"

Our lunch ends soon after our desserts arrive, for although at first she eats delicately, when Piper Fields decides to make an impact on rice pudding she can't be held back.

Message to Publisher

Dear Rosamund,

You'll be surprised to learn that Piper Fields is a kleptomaniac—is there really such a thing, or is she just a common ordinary thief? I'm not sure if my question can ever be answered. I guess it's like asking if there are nymphomaniacs anymore when you're really just asking if there are common ordinary women.

At any rate, we had a quiet, perhaps too quiet lunch today. As we were leaving the restaurant I noticed that in her satchel I could see the clear imprint of a teapot. Yes—through her open carryall an actual cabbage-shaped teapot was visible, the teapot that had been on the shelf directly over our heads at that secluded restaurant, a place I'll never be able to return to because I'll be assumed to be the thief, not the sweet, blurry-faced woman, the true criminal. Although the fact that she was wearing a high collared blouse like a shorter Mary Poppins should have made her the suspect instantly.

But isn't that interesting that she stole a teapot?

Thanks, by the way, for the advance. As Mary Poppins would say in that snuffy accent, it's a bit trifling, but I appreciate the thought. Rosamund, that advance can't even be considered a mental calculation.

The Meaning of a Teapot

I'm bothered that Piper Fields stole that teapot. She had to do it while I was up by the cashier examining the carousel of cakes. What could her thievery mean? Teapot associations: warmth, steam, roundedness, brewing, tea, pot. Stealing? Maybe she's trying to communicate that she's in hot water?

Does every action mean something? Maybe she just thought: What a cute teapot. I'm going to take it home! Must have it now!

Unlike me, she can afford a teapot. Many many teapots. She could fill a swimming pool with teapots. She could live inside a mammoth teapot-shaped house built to her specifications.

Oh, but when is anybody satisfied?

Maybe I am obviously overlooking some slutty teapot angle.

Additional Message to Publisher

Dear Rosamund, (email not to be sent),

Tell the truth.

You love to gamble and you love power and you love to know that I am reliant on you, in no position to do anything but beg (discretely) and therefore I do not exactly beg, Rosamund. You can keep me on a string with the most paltry advance with the requirement that I send you regular follow-ups, while I pursue a weird author of children's books and of erotica, a teapot pilferer, in order eventually that you yourself possibly might meet her when her lawyers arrive at your office, intent on suing unless you agree to withdraw the manuscript. And you will withdraw it, all the while vibrating with excitement because your little hobby has once again given you the thrilling experience of engaging with an alien world.

You'll have had the benefit of the tax advantage and of a little publicity and an opportunity to surprise the subject of my biography with your politeness, your ready compliance, your sympathy. Is that what this is all about? You really don't care that much if what I write sells because your money stocking is the size of Montana plus Texas.

Of course, Rosamund, I won't send this to you—this daft letter written at 3 a.m. when I cannot sleep and have imbibed a snifter of low-grade brandy that ought to be used only medicinally . . .

Message From Publisher

Tabitha, you should not drink. You're hallucinating. Deadline: at least three chapters two months from now on one or the other of these people or you're finished. Why do I put up with you? I'm not laughing.

Tell your mother I'll be shipping her another armchair for repair earlier than I said. Maybe by Monday. No one upholsters like your mother, and there's no one I admire more or feel a greater debt toward. She was such a support to me during the worst period of my life.

"To Speak of Woe That Is in Marriage"

I know a little bit about how Rosamund was supported: my mother put her phone on speaker and cleaned out her refrigerator while Rosamund recited the miseries that characterized her marriage. My mother told me everything. It sounded like that Robert Lowell poem where the wife complains that the husband "stalls above me like an elephant." My mother has never been a good listener, but she can give the impression of being one to anyone who doesn't know her well.

Establishing Rules: the Necessities

Don't over-rely on anyone—ever.

Try to save money or at least don't go broke weekly.

Pay attention to your surroundings to stay safe. Notice threats. Do not push large men out through doors. Not again or at least not regularly. Use imagination. Consider possible negative scenarios attending brash actions.

Don't neglect physical exercise. When walking in park pick up pace. Do not dawdle. Take actual strides.

Be bold. Assume you might eventually know what you're doing.

Establish routine for creating progress reports for Rosamund.

Take notes feverishly.

Strategize.

Record thoughts that get in your way so thoughts can be kicked curbside.

Be bold. That can't be said enough: Be bold.

Keep temper around your mother. She's your mother. Hardly replaceable.

Breathe.

Observe surroundings. Be alert.

Keep equilibrium. Do not entertain absurd levels of expectation.

An Expected Voice Mail

"Tabitha, are you drinking too much lately? A little bird tells me you've sent an intemperate email. Whiskey is fine, just don't touch champagne. It looks so innocent but, believe you me, those bubbles are the devil's air pockets. I don't often talk about my regrets. You know what preceded both of my pregnancies? Champagne. It's like it was more involved in the process than your father. Well, who ever knew what your poor dear departed father ever wanted? What do men want? I wished someone knew the answer to that."

After listening to my mother's voice mail I attempt to take her question seriously.

What Do Men Want?

Everything. Everything that women want except they believe they deserve it. Not my father, probably, and not all men but enough of them. And that is one of the reasons why I can't help but defend (occasionally) my mother: despite everything she was told to expect from life as a woman, she still wants everything and believes she deserves it.

So few understand my mother, and I admit that sometimes I'm among them. Years ago I had a friend from my community college days who met her and said "With a mother like that I'd be on suicide watch"—which really made my mother laugh when she overheard it. A sense of humor—that's a blessing, although I admit that if you always find things funny you're not paying attention.

The Surprise

I was scrolling through my phone trying to figure out why I had so few contacts when I came upon Brent Vintner's name and number. My memory was right: he actually had put his number in my phone. And his email! I have only seven contacts and two of those are for my mother and one is for Piper Fields, so this new unexpected name and number and email address (he actually typed in his email address!) leapt out.

What an immense surprise.

And that's when a beautiful idea was born: Brent Vintner was obviously lonely—why else would he leave what looks like a legitimate phone number?—and Piper Fields was obviously lonely, otherwise why would she steal a teapot? I could get them together on the basis of loneliness alone. Get them both talking about themselves, record their conversation on my phone, and in no time at all I would have enough material for two biographies about two personalities who were sure in the future to be regarded as compelling far beyond what, at this point, I could reasonably expect.

I screwed my courage to the sticking place and called Brent Vintner. He didn't answer.

I left a text:

There's someone I want you to meet Not a rabid fan An entirely sensible woman (beautiful) Writes books for children also filthy stuff Can't wait for you to meet her

[Realization: he won't think I'm suggesting a threesome? Of course not. I'm fifteen years older than he is. I could have been his babysitter. I could have been his teenage mother.]

Decided to text again: This is not for a threesome Little j

Decided to text again. By little j I meant joke Ok?

NOT A SURPRISE

No returned text.
No returned text.
No returned text.

My phone says "sent" but maybe his number is wrong. His fingers might have slipped. Or he put in a fake number.

So glad I haven't yet told Piper Fields she was going to meet Brent Vintner. Maybe Piper Fields won't want to meet him, although that's doubtful. A celibate nun would climb every mountain to meet him. *The Sound of Music*—what kind of plot was that? That woman yodeled her way out of her virginity.

No response to my text.

SURPRISE

Text from Brent Vintner:

Sure! Sorry to be slow Too busy fending off knitting lessons

Is 8 ok? At your nephew's bar?

My response to Brent Vintner:

OK

What online photo should I text to Piper Fields to get her to agree to meet Brent Vintner? The one of him as a Trojan in that movie about Achilles? Too much leg hair. Too sweaty. Really, you look at that photo and you smell him. Which would be great.

I send it.

Waiting at the End of the World

We've been at the bar for a half hour, and Brent Vintner hasn't shown up, and already I have to excuse myself and pull Leon away from Piper Fields.

"What? What am I doing wrong?"

"Don't pretend, Leon. You shouldn't hang on to her like that. Brent Vintner will be here any minute, and he won't like the way it looks."

"I can take him."

"Hell, Leon, *I* can take him. He's shorter than he looks. But that's not why Piper and I are here."

"Why are you here?"

"I'm writing about both of them, and I want them to talk with one another. I want them to draw one another out in a way that will give me information I wouldn't get otherwise."

"Why don't you just ask them questions?"

"That's unnatural, Leon."

We look at one another. I say, "Leon, have you ever read Jane Austen?"

"Do I look like I read Jane Austen? I'm a Brontë man myself. Tabitha, of course I've read Jane Austen."

"Okay. You can talk to Piper about Jane Austen. But don't hang off her."

"Why do you want me to talk to her about Jane Austen?"

"Because I know you. You'll say things that will offend her and she'll be all the more ready to welcome Brent Vintner. When he comes."

"He's not coming."

"Of course he's coming. He's been held up by knitters lately."

Piper Fields is uncommonly quiet as she nurses her beer, and so I observe my surroundings. The dim barroom recesses of The End of the World. An optical illusion, making the bar appear extended. Corners where people can go unseen. High sided booths should you wish to execute a crime boss. The piano that, although a mini-grand, takes up an ungodly amount of room. In the near darkness it looks like it's breathing, like an enormous bull got stuck and couldn't squeeze its way out of the bar.

"He'll come," I keep repeating.

Piper Fields sighs and says, "I think he'll be able to resist us."

A group of teenagers swagger in. Immediately Leon is on the phone to Blowman who lives two doors down. It's like rousing the Kraken. Within two minutes Blowman hurtles through the door and up to the teenagers. He uses his hammered-by-nails face to his advantage. The teenagers don't even dare show their fake ID's. They jostle one another as they trot out.

"That was beautiful," I tell Blowman.

What a gem! Blowman works with such quiet dignity for Leon, bouncing out any potential troublemakers and helping Gilbert in the kitchen.

It's hard to believe Blowman used to be a monk. What is the attraction of being a monk? Must not be flip or irreverent but feel a certain affinity nevertheless. I myself have never had to take a vow of Poverty. Most often it's been a lifestyle. Also, I took no vows but I am experiencing Chastity, as I keep noting, and generally exhibit Obedience to a superior (my mother—out of love). In addition, I wear the same outfit often and tend toward repetitive thoughts in a form close to prayer because of general attitude of supplication.

There's a strong possibility that Blowman knows all the Gregorian chants. Personally, I cannot understand the appeal of Gregorian chants. Musically gifted people call them beautiful, but those chants sound like the souls in hell breathing into a harmonica.

Blowman doesn't stay long enough for me to introduce him to Piper Fields. It's evident he's heading back to his bed, apparently to nap like a hibernating animal. Interesting fact: skunks do not hibernate. They engage in something called torpor. First they eat a great deal for months so that they can live off their own fat. Feel much admiration.

And then—there he is.

Brent Vintner slides up to me. Something on the bottom of his shoes makes him actually slide. "Special effects," he says. "I want to keep these shoes when filming's over. I tried to get away sooner. No luck. I'm really sorry."

Short introduction to Piper. She's staring, dog-like. I want to tell Brent Vintner to turn down his wattage. I get into the booth next to him. Leon comes over and runs his hand down my arm. "Isn't she something?" he says to Brent Vintner, and it's obvious he means me ill by batting his eyes in a fawning way.

"You're not selling me," I tell Leon and turn away from him.

Leon hobbles back to the bar, obviously pleased with himself, God knows why.

Heroic Realization

Nero fiddled while Rome burned and he's considered a monster. The musicians on the Titanic fiddled while the lifeboats were lowered and they're considered heroes. What I mean to suggest: context is everything.

TRANSCRIPT

Transcript of conversation between Piper Fields and Brent Vintner at The End of the World from my phone's recording app:

So you're Tabitha's friend.

Not exactly. She thinks she's writing a biography about me.

She isn't?

Not if I can help it.

Why are you here?

The chance to meet you . . . you seem interesting.

I'm not.

Well, you could pretend to be interesting. Tabitha, it's obvious you're recording this.

Come on, Brent. Let's make things interesting.

I've never made things interesting in my life.

I forgot—you're an actor. You need a script.

No, I mean things are either interesting or they're not. If they're not it's almost impossible to force them to be interesting.

I've never seen any of your movies.

Aren't you the lucky one.

What's not on my phone's audio, because it's not hearable, only a visual: it looked like a spider was on my arm and I jumped. It was only the shadow of Brent Vintner's departing finger.

More audio of conversation:

Piper Fields: Where are you shooting?

Me (turning to Brent Vintner): I bet you're shooting all over town! Doctors' row and the old defunct airport and the cement factory and downtown by the caramel candy corn and licorice shop. We're big on our caramel candy corn around here, more than our licorice. But I bet you're not staying in town. I bet you and the crew are out in those hotels by the highway. Or in those suburban rentals.

Brent Vintner: You're right. Exactly. I'm really getting to know Midlothian and the outlets by the highway. Do you live here year-round, Piper?

Piper Fields: No. Just staying until the end of summer. For peace and quiet.

Brent Vintner (turning to me): How do you and Piper know each other?

NOTE TO SELF:

I'm dying of boredom.

SMALL TALK

Can it get more miniscule? Any smaller and it would be something you sweep off a picnic blanket. Failure of courage: Why can't I ask an interesting question, if I could think of one?

Additional audio:

Piper Fields (to Brent Vintner): Are all the sex acts you've performed in movies simulated?

Me to Brent Vintner: You don't have to answer that. Anyway, I think most sex acts are simulated. That's why they're called sex *acts*, right?

Brent Vintner: Exactly.

GOING DOWNHILL FROM HERE

Reminder to self: don't try to bring people together who have nothing in common. It never works. Even if they have everything in common it never works. Remember how you tried to bring Leon and that woman from that ceramics class together? Such a mistake. I liked her immensely. In fact, I wish she hadn't moved away. She was always giving me statues from her ceramics class. They didn't really make many ceramics in that class. They mostly painted ceramics. I have five panda-shaped cookie jars.

That woman started leaving mugs shaped like birds and cats on the counter at The End of the World. Leon kept trying to give them back but she'd always say, "No strings attached," like her gifts were actually free. Well, Leon and I have such a history of candor that he confessed to me that the ceramics woman was making him want to die. He actually said, "I want to die every time I see one of her mugs." She was an aggressive gift giver. Each of those mugs meant something obscene, it seems to me. Like Leon was the mug and what she wanted to fill him with was exceptionally hot.

Looking at Piper Fields and Brent Vintner as they talk quietly in my nephew's bar—the obvious antipathy. What does it remind me of?

Years ago I had a dream in which I was a bumblebee spun between the knees of two strangers sitting across from one another at a table. Their knees would have touched except for me. I was the bumblebee between their knees and my bumblebee body kept turning around and around. Somewhat like a ball of yarn.

Piper Fields and Brent Vintner aren't turning me around, certainly, but I believe that both of them are using me to keep their knees from touching.

The piano over by the wall appears to be expanding. A. F. sure was daring to get right up on that instrument and gyrate. What absolute guts. The splinters on the top of that piano are nothing less than crunchy. Never would I have the courage to mount that piano, and if I did it would buck me right off. A. F.—those breathy expulsions by the men watching her were tributes to her charisma, to the fact that she was still getting up and performing just like when she wasn't a millionaire but a little kid indistinguishable from every other member of the Irish step-dancing troupe at the county fair. She manhandled that piano. She might as well have hog-tied and branded it.

That piano—ever since that woman sat atop it, that piano has so much more presence at The End of the World.

Leon dances over, winking at me. Kind of him. That's a signal to let me know that all is okay, nothing's burning in the kitchen, and his friend Blowman probably is asleep by now but is on call if anything goes awry.

Piper Fields gathers up her enormous satchel, says she has to be off.

"Does your writing call to you?" I ask.

"God no," she says. "It never calls."

That strikes me as very sad—making me think of someone alone at night waiting for the phone to ring. What a sad life she must lead. New thought: writing about human intimacy all the time like she does in her erotic novels—that's basically simulating the most intimate of all acts?

Before I can make the above point, Brent Vintner says, "It was great to meet you, Piper," and she mutters something in return and edges out of the booth. Leon, being the thoughtful person he wants people to imagine he is, walks her to the exit and tells her he hopes to see her again at The End of the World.

She's forgotten the name of the bar, I think, because she turns and frowns. Then she must remember the name of the bar and tells him, "When hell freezes over."

An Attempt at Meaning

If I'm really honest, which sometimes I hate to be, I have to admit that I'm almost enjoying this period of my life—this period when things don't quite happen. True, I met both Piper Fields and Brent Vintner, but it's all going so poorly my life is held in suspension. Perhaps life is meaningful because much is held in suspension rather than immediately sinking.

Piper Fields: A Woman Who Cannot Be Understood

"Don't do that again," Piper Fields says when she calls the next morning. Her voice sounds suspiciously low.

"Are you a smoker?" I ask.

"No, why would you think I'm a smoker?"

"Your voice sounds so—sultry. Like Lauren Bacall. That's a compliment. She was gorgeous, with eyes like an enraged cat's, and she had this sort of frog effect in her voice. Some people have a more mucous-y effect. Her voice was lovely. People fall on their heads for that sort of thing."

"You mean fall head over heels."

"Either way."

"What I want you to know is that you really shouldn't try to make me find someone like Brent Vintner attractive. Or try to get in my good graces by putting a man in front of me. He's so—packaged. Those good looks. I've always found really handsome men a turn off. Do you understand?'

"Not at all."

"The real point is: I found the whole experience off putting. You shouldn't have had me go to that bar to meet him. I know why it's called The End of the World. It's like you could get diphtheria there. It's like a place designed for transmitting infectious diseases."

I agree. "Like infectious diseases go there on their dates!"

"If you know that, then why did you have me go there to meet Brent Vintner?"

"It's a family place. My brother's son, Leon, owns the bar—he led you out. If more people go there and buy liquor he'll eventually earn enough money to clean the place up."

"Well, good for Leon. We're good, right? You're obviously a very sensitive person. I don't want to hurt your feelings."

"You're having a good time saying awful things and my feelings aren't even hurt!"

Afterwards I felt bad—for Leon. The place isn't filthy. Not for a bar. I wonder how many bars Piper Fields has been in? What does she really know about diphtheria?

Will not try to get her and Brent Vintner together again. Worse than oil and water—oil will float on water. She will not float on Brent Vintner. Nor he on her. Sad for them both. Or perhaps it's like a movie where the people who hate each other fall in love by the end of the movie? That happens exclusively in movies. People who hate each other in life may at best pretend to tolerate each other and inevitably shorten each other's lives.

Must not get carried away with possibilities for joint interviews/audios. Must not skimp on required digging for truth. Biography: like ditch digging but dirtier. Like ditch digging in a trench filled with melted marshmallows.

Starters

It occurs to me that I've been writing these notes as a way to avoid composing even a sentence or two that would constitute a start on one of my proposed biographies. Must screw my courage and try to make forays that will entice potential readers.

Trial Openings

Piper Fields is a woman wearing many masks. Who is this woman who draws a cult readership of the bizarre and depraved to her orbit through her novels and yet manages to tell stories to children that sweeten their dreams? How can a woman who sketches the most amateurish little bunnies—bunnies that a seven-year-old would be ashamed to draw—manage also to titillate adults with fantasies so bizarre they might have been hatched in science fiction?

[Question: Why? I mean, it seems preposterous that this woman has a career in children's literature. Don't those parents putting their children to bed with books by Piper Fields endure a sensation of queasiness? I would.]

Or: Piper Fields is a woman stripping away many masks, allowing adult readers to see that the author herself is not the same as any single character in her putrid novels.

[Question: "Putrid"? Too harsh?]

Or: Piper Fields is a woman who no longer wears masks. Once writing under the name Bunny Swift, she hid her second identity as a transgressive novelist. After her identity was revealed, she continued her reign as a publishing phenomenon, proving that books don't make the woman and that her readers accept that the 21st century Beatrix Potter is also the 21st century Marquis de Sade.

[Question: Am I flattering the audience too much by stoking their buried dreams of sophistication?]

Or: Piper Fields: the patriarchy's nightmare, for here's an author who does it all and feels no shame, who proves a woman can be both an inventor of delights for . . .

[Question: Perhaps sideline references to her children's books? I'm beginning to wish her identity as a writer of erotica was never revealed. Much easier just to focus on how she transgresses stereotypes rather than how she both transgresses some stereotypes and affirms, possibly, others? Would like to avoid all mention of children.]

Or: Piper Fields changes direction, committing herself fully to writing novels for adults, novels that now mean her previous career in hard bound picture books is but a distant memory.

[Question: How will I convince her to give up writing for children? That's where the money is. Could this be an unsympathetic biography? I've never done one of those!]

Or: Piper Fields, ploughing in the dough by writing about squishy rabbits, hypocritically composes novels for adults in which rabbits . . .

[Question: Would this opening require reading all her novels to detect presence of rabbits? Or would using search function on digital copies suffice? Would my biography seem like it's mirroring one of those hideous movies of the 70s in which a woman is a prim schoolteacher/librarian/watchmaker by day and an uninhibited libertine by night, steeped in angst and steaming like a teapot left too long on the stove? Reconsider, although there could be possible (wink wink) teapot tie-in.]

HAPPINESS

Pot of Gold discounted box of chocolates arrives from FedEx. Plus spa gift basket of lavender bath oils, bath salts, bath lotion, and fluffy net thing for scrubbing! Double discounted. Little luxuries help when mood is down.

Sudden sadness. Remember in far misty past being a child of nine and dropped off at annual 4-H Fair for six hours to wander among livestock stalls. Touched bunnies in crate until boy shrieked, "Get your dirty paws off them!" Felt especially filthy afterwards although had no paws. Wandered farther. Began to itch.

Was that the date when my bath fixation began? Deep appreciation for scented soap, hot water, and soaking as antidote to being perennially unclean?

Hour of bliss—must not eat chocolates in tub decorated by little fluffy net thing in corner. Wait until out of tub. Towel off briskly. Pert and Pretty fascinated as usual. Fear that cats are reincarnated dirty old creeps. Cats—who knows what goes on in their minds?

Suddenly cannot help but wonder about those cats in nursing homes who trot down the hall to show off that they know someone's dying, heading toward said person's bed, jumping in, and snuggling. If that happened to me I'd yell, "Get the hell out of here!"

Great luck! One clementine not totally sunken-faced discovered in kitchen. Gnash chocolates with clementine for citrus plus sweetness effect.

Regift small fluffy net thing as toy to Pert and Pretty until realize nylon from net could stick in throats. Attractive choking hazard. Throw fluffy thing in trash. As I told Brent Vintner, I didn't choose their names. The original owners did. Pert and Pretty. Their names sound like the manufacturer's label on an old brassiere.

Read *Northanger Abbey* and endure general sense of unease because in certain moods feel like Jane Austen is scolding me. Listen to old jazz disc Leon left at apartment. Wake to drum solo. Fall asleep on couch again, abandoned by Pert and Pretty who lounge on bed pillows, like head warmers when head is not there.

Message to Publisher

Dear Rosamund,

I'm making staggeringly good progress! Don't want to give away too much. Suffice it to say I've been recording some interesting conversations. Don't worry about legal ramifications. No one will know.

Message From Rosamund

GET PERMISSION. GET SIGNED LETTER OF PERMISSION. You CANNOT record conversations without permission. I am not about to pay your legal bills. Either stop recording or do what is required BY LAW.

An Unexpected Visit in the Morning

Even before I drink my coffee my mother turns up at my apartment. I haven't cleaned my glasses yet. She appears so smeared. Mostly, I listen:

"Tabitha, sometimes I forget you're my daughter. I look so young. I wouldn't be your mother if I didn't get pregnant too young and have your brother first, decades before you came along. I waited for ages to have you accidentally, almost long enough to forget the experience of labor. It was hell. You were a breech birth. Like Nero."

I clean my glasses and stare at her astonishingly wide face. Someone extraordinarily beautiful, maybe Catherine Deneuve, said that after a certain age you can keep either your face or your figure. I don't think she was talking about men, but she should have been.

It feels nice to look at my mother. So often she only phones and doesn't visit, but here she is—her remarkable face, powdered so that her skin looks softly folded and refolded. I like to think of her studying her own face in the mirror each morning with conviction and applying makeup as a defensive art. In my family it is nearly impossible not to look like a bulldog when you pass forty-one, true, but the look suits my mother and reflects how much power she summons. The tunic she's wearing is gorgeous and shimmers with silver detailing. She will not be drab, she will not be defeated.

I say, "What—that's new, isn't it?"

"I'm glad you like it. The chain doesn't hang too low, does it? I don't want it to be a beacon drawing all eyes to my chest."

"That's not—"

"Oh yes. I've always liked Thomas. Too bad you didn't marry him instead of his brother."

"Is that pendant—meant for carrying someone's ashes? Dad's ashes?"

"No. I was thinking more of—yours. Or maybe Leon's. Whoever dies first. Tabitha, you know how to make spice jars, don't you? You layer spices in jars? I hope you're up for it. For charity. For selling to help out the firefighters? I promised you'd help out. The firefighters are counting on you. Just toss together any old spices you have in the cupboard and pop them in a jar. You must have spices in there old enough to have mummified the pharaohs. I hope you're up for it! Well, that's it. I have to rush. No unnecessary blabbing!"

Meeting With Piper Fields at Squallie's

The restaurant: a diminutive from of Squalid, I presume. The atmosphere brings back memories of when I waited tables. The kitchen in that restaurant housed giant vats—like footage of early nuclear power facilities. The specialty of the house: chicken dinners with mashed potatoes. The mashed potatoes were made of dried flakes and the chicken was breaded to the bone. I don't eat meat or poultry, and so I should have been thankful that very little chicken went into the chicken.

Piper Fields is seated at a table suitably distant from a window. Good choice. Unfortunate carpeting. Comet cleanser smell and sticky table top. Occasional shouts from kitchen, nothing overtly violent. Nothing here for Piper to steal unless she likes old license plates and they're nailed to the wall. I don't presume to understand decor: aside from those license plates on all walls, artificial dwarf palms droop in enormous pots next to each table. Like fake greenery creates serenity, unlike living plants with their inexhaustible demands. No booths, unfortunately, even though the restaurant booth is one of the marvels of past centuries. Who invented the booth? Thank you, adulterers.

Resolved: will not ask about teapot. Congratulate myself for realizing it's best not to pretend to be court of law. At the next table a couple are making a waiter play loaves and fishes to keep refilling their bread basket.

After our orders are delivered (we're both having the spinach quiche—regrets later) Piper Fields lowers her voice and leans halfway across the table.

She begins on an apologetic note, which I enjoy. "I want you to know, even though I said what I did, that I do appreciate your wanting me to meet Brent Vintner. I didn't mean to sound so harsh the last time we talked. It's just that I'm not much for movies or movie actors. I know—makes me a freak, doesn't it?"

"It does. Who doesn't like movies? They're our guides to life."

"I'm just not intrigued by actors the way you are."

"Am I intrigued? Did you get a good look at Brent Vintner? I know that the bar is poorly lit. Nevertheless—"

"I hope I'm not overstepping." She puts her fork down and slides her plate to the side of the table. "I keep replaying that night, and I just can't help but think you were trying to get me to become interested in that man—the way you pushed us together. He had to be uncomfortable too."

"How could you tell? He's an actor. There's no way to tell if his body language follows his actual thoughts. He has to be skilled at deception."

"Really, Tabitha. Anyway, it doesn't matter. The thing I want you to know is that I'm not going to cooperate with the biography. I don't mind having you as a friend. That sounds wrong—I mean, I might begin to like having you as a friend."

"You're making me blush. No one has ever said that to me before! Are you sure?"

"No, I'm not sure. But I am sure that if we're to be anything like friends you need to stop writing about me in any way."

"But I—accepted an advance to write about you."

In a tight voice she says, "You shouldn't have made such a promise."

"It can't hurt you, my writing about your life. I won't say anything that isn't—authorized—by you. I like you already. I'll be careful. Your double life, the way for years you kept hidden your second career as a novelist—I would use your own words about your choices. An empathetic portrayal, that's what it would be. And it would be short too. Maybe not much longer than a pamphlet in the end. You don't want to be known? To have your life presented three-dimensionally? I've read some articles—that "Cock Whisperer" one. Hard to forget. A biography could help people forget."

She stirs in her seat. "No, Tabitha. I don't think I should have to say another word about this. I wouldn't have had lunch with you if I thought I was going to be harangued. Really, I thought you'd accept a clear refusal. I made the mistake of thinking that you would be sensitive about my feelings."

The air around my head thickens, becomes gluey, and stretches. Everything in my peripheral vision warps. My right leg gallops under the table. I cry out, "You really are a children's book author—the sort that makes children never want to wake up! You've put me in an awful position! I was ready to sanctify you! Now I don't know how I'm going to earn a living. My publisher gave me an advance! An advance! I hope you pay for this lunch!"

She claps her hands over her mouth then pulls her hands away as if her own mouth bit her. The waiter approaching our table pivots and hustles off.

Piper Fields hisses. "What does it matter what you know about my life? Really. I don't even have a life of my own. So does it matter what you think?" She slaps the table top and her voice rises. "Sometimes I'm so fed up with my life being appropriated, with my body being used and used and used. You can't know what I'm talking about. You wouldn't understand."

Her voice rises even more. "Imagine being an actress and no one knows you're playing a part. They think—that's just YOU, that's all you are, you have no other life. It's your body and voice—that's what you're selling."

I wave my hands in front of her face. "Oh please, can you be a little quieter? And please don't sell your body. You're making me so jumpy."

She lowers her shoulders and her voice softens. "Oh, who cares? Who cares about the whole ugly charade. Who cares anymore?"

"I care," I say.

Her eyes enlarge. "You want the truth? Are you ready for the truth?"

"I'm always ready for the truth. I live for the truth."

"You're not ready for my truth."

"Well if it's your truth—but your truth—"

She makes a funny noise to shush me. I'm so confused that I do stop talking. Her eyes have the look of cunning that I recognized when I first saw her at that breakfast place. She lowers her head and says, calmly now, "I don't even write the godawful books!"

"You don't write the books? You've been fooling me. You're not Piper Fields?"

"Of course I'm Piper Fields."

The skin on my face is shrinking.

She sits back. "Is it that hard to understand? It's my name on the books, but I don't write the books. The real author doesn't want to be known, she has her reasons, and so she says I write the books. I sign her contracts, make appearances, do whatever she would normally do. I sign her idiotic books at book signings. I make up stories about being inspired to write the books. I deal with all the after effects once the books are published. There, are you happy that I've betrayed my friend?"

"Yes! Yes, I am!"

"Well, she uses me. What can I say. It's been building—my rage. I get lambasted by cult readers of her stupid porno novels, and then I get letters from little children and sometimes they send me videos of themselves reading the stories. Think of that—it's horrible. The real person—never mind her actual name—publishes her crap under my name and I get to walk around in the world pretending to be her and I have to survive the blowback. I don't know how much longer I can take it."

The waiter appears, asking if there's anything more we'd like. When he leaves, almost trotting to get away from us, I ask, "Why do you do it—if that's what you do?"

"I wanted the money and she wanted the privacy and the control over her reputation. And she didn't want the fuss. So, you know what? I'm trapped. How can I get out?"

"I can tell the world!" I whisper.

"No, you can't. I'll deny it. No one will believe you because, frankly, look at you. You told me yourself that you have a gruesome reputation for those celebrity profiles."

"I didn't make up anything. Those people—they told me too much and then denied it and brought out their bad-tempered publicists! People always tell me too much! That's why I'm remarkable! Something about me—"

"I really don't care to hear about you, Tabitha. I've heard enough. Anyway, at least it's good to vent. I have to find my own way out of this. Perhaps I'll die—that way she'll have to stop publishing under my name."

"Oh, your friend is a woman. You let that slip—multiple times. But you know what? She won't have to stop publishing even if both of you die. Posthumous publication. People publish a lot more after they're dead. It's physics . . . Emily Dickinson. Charles Bukowski . . ." It occurs to me once again that I have the most experience writing about dead people and that perhaps in the future I will have better luck writing about whatever was never alive.

She sighs, crumbles up her napkin. "Did that quiche taste funny to you?"

"Yes. I think it was frozen back in the 60's or something. I also think it wasn't really spinach but dandelion greens with bologna and bacon bits. This place—let's not return."

"Agreed. Tabitha, you know what? You know what? I really don't care if you keep my secret. It doesn't matter and no one will believe you, like I said. It's too odd."

"The real author must be so much more interesting than you are, Piper! Did she choose you for your name?"

"Probably."

I try another possibility. "All I have to do is look in your grade school yearbook to find the real author? Maybe?"

"What makes you think we went to school together?"

"A neighbor girl then?"

"You'll never find out her identity."

"Okay, maybe you really want to keep on impersonating her. I mean, there are the creeps who come after you, but you also get adulation and respect. If you retire, I'll take over. I'd love the life you're living."

"Aren't you happy now—happy and free?"

"Have you met my mother?"

"Well, you'd still have a mother."

"She'd disown me if she thought I wrote the dirty novels you—or whoever the writer is—writes. All those orgies. Subtly depicted. My mother can't stand evasiveness. You realize I'm writing a biography about Brent Vintner too? I have my hands full. I wanted to crush two birds with one stone."

"Isn't it kill two birds with one stone?"

"You know, maybe Brent Vintner isn't really Brent Vintner either—actors never are themselves anyway. Maybe all his acting is done by a stunt double and he does all his own stunts. Did you notice his skin?"

"Why? He has normal human skin."

"No, it's like he came air brushed."

"He was probably still wearing makeup from the set or something."

"Oh. You're dashing my dreams."

"It's all an illusion, Tabitha. Wake up. Now."

Message to Publisher

Dear Rosamund,

You won't believe what I've discovered—although possibly it's all a lie. Piper Fields says another woman uses her to "present" herself as the author of the children's books and those sweaty novels. The actual author remains incognito. Piper Fields is getting fed up with the charade. She vows she won't let me know who the actual author is. I don't know if she's telling the truth, but I'm sure I can break her. What do you think? Worth pursuing?

Text from Rosamund:

You need help

Text from me to Rosamund:

Very cruel of you to say that

Text from Rosamund:

No I mean I'm sending my niece As your intern She can help

Text from me:

I don't need your godawful niece

Text from Rosamund:

Her name is Tinker Flatts she's not a pushover you need her help

Self Study and Philosophical Interlude

Rosamund often gives the impression that she wonders why she puts up with me. The answers are, I believe, legion. Because of loyalty? Self-dramatization? Self-sabotage? Also, taxes, bet with her ex-husband, simple authoritarian impulses on her part, allegiance to my mother, etcetera? Better question: why do I put up with Rosamund? Because she forwards advances? Loyalty? Self-dramatization? Self-sabotage? Because it is wonderful that someone pretends to believe in me—somewhat? But now: a sign of disbelief: she's sending her own niece. The nepotism, frankly, trots. It's enough to make me question everything. And my life is already all about questions.

Question for anyone I interview:

What is the meaning of life? I was once in an auditorium and a famous scientist was asked that question. "This," she said, pointing around to everyone in the audience, "This is the meaning." I have never seen a crowd of people look more disappointed.

Meandering Meaningfully

I am meandering on the empty sidewalk down Shiawassee Street, meandering because I am hoping to discover what course of action I should pursue. Soon I'll have to put up with someone named Tinker Flatts. She sounds like a plateau. And all my hard work reconnoitering with both of the subjects of my next two projects will be compromised. With my luck, Tinker Flatts will probably make a deal and each biography will be marketed with the heading "as told to Tinker Flatts."

Eventually, I find myself across from Jesmun Park—full flush of spring, the air softening, many shades of green. The color green won't let you forget how various it is, how many ways it lights the world. Along the southern embankment the leaves of the hosta lilies loom so large they appear prehistoric.

And then I'm peering over toward what used to be Mattie's cottage tucked away across from the park entrance on Peach Street, more of an alley than a street. Oh Mattie, how she would hate that the new owners repainted her blue cottage. It's now orange. Everything and every color in every room of Mattie's cottage was chosen with care. A smell of sandalwood and lemon furniture polish. The lovely dark fabrics, the shawl on the back of the main armchair. All gone seventeen years ago.

How lovely that cottage was, how the book shelves were magical portals into other lives. Book shelves around each corner. She must have owned every book about Eleanor Roosevelt and written by Eleanor Roosevelt. She had a lot of books about Emily Dickinson too. For a middle school report I had to write about that Dickinson poem "Hope is the thing with Feathers" (I forget where the dashes go) and Mattie was so patient with me. I kept saying "Why doesn't she say Hope is a bird if she means a bird. Why does she say 'Hope is a thing with feathers.' A bird is not a 'thing.' "

"I don't know, Tabitha."

I loved her answer—so different from anything I'd ever heard my mother say. They didn't have much in common, my mother and

Mattie. They had that tense mother-in-law/daughter-in-law thing going. Mattie never said anything against my mother, though she worked her mouth a lot, silently talking back in her own head.

Mattie once offered me some advice about my mother. "You should always respect her. You may not know exactly how to appreciate her now, but someday you'll learn something very important from her. Tabby, sweetie, with some people it's like you're one of the 49ers panning for gold. You may think you're just getting a bunch of decayed, crumbly old rocks but eventually—honey, are you listening?—there will be a beautiful nugget just for you."

So strange, some of her opinions. "She understands me," she used to say about the poet Sylvia Plath. "I know," she said. "Don't you laugh. That's not right to laugh. She understands me. I mean that. She needed hope. I wish I could have given her that."

Understanding people's lives—that's what interested Mattie. Books, she used to say, are one of the best ways to begin to figure out other people. You can find the little pockets in a life, and in those pockets are the silly happy things and the little sad things and the terrible tragic things that make people who they are.

I cross the street and head into the park. In a grassy swale, right in the middle of the park, that's where the Midlothian Library stood until it was razed five years ago. When I stop walking I imagine I must be in my favorite section of the library, right where the comfy reading room was located. Here was the mammoth armchair with its ornate red and white lily design, and here was the old fireplace, never lit because old books are kindling, and here's the round braided rug, and around every wall shelves of books fretted by mealworms rise to the ceiling. And somewhere in the foyer/entrance area Mrs. Mulwaye takes off her glasses and rubs her eyes. We adored one another—or I adored her, at any rate. I spent every hour I could in that library and sometimes brought Mrs. Mulwaye apples from the wormy tree down the lane from my house. Never once did I take a book out of that library, preferring to keep them there, for books are friends to one another and must never leave one another for long.

Ahead, the pathway is dappled with light and shadows. "Dappled": I first saw that word in a poem in grade school. Even now I feel a tremor. Dappled—that perfect word. I remember the page from a scrapbook and how I pasted the poem (what poem? I can't remember) next to an image from a magazine. The picture was of a forest where pink light dappled the forest floor. Dappled. A smattering of light sprinkled flat. Little round ovals of light passing through leaves in spatters on the ground. Light splashes.

A tap on my shoulder. I jump.

"Sorry," Brent Vintner says. "So sorry. Tabitha, you should disable the location setting on your phone—for Facebook. You should also check your privacy settings."

"You scared me."

He apologizes again and we move forward. The light from my glasses, I see now, is dappling the walkway. I tell him and he says, "Really?"

"Do you like that word—dapple?" I ask him.

"Dapple. Dapple. Dapple. Great word," he says. "I never thought about that word before. You like the word because you like apples? It's like shorthand: Hand me dat apple? Dapple?"

A bicyclist speeds by. The bicyclist's breath is a tiny warm wet huff that makes me swat my neck.

We stop by a lilac bush so over flowering with blossoms that my head wants to get entangled in the branches. "Whoa," Brent Vintner says. "It's a good thing you don't have antlers."

"Thank you," I say, as he pulls me out. And then I'm thanking him for not pulling me out right away and thereby letting me linger among the lilacs long enough for my whole head to be suffused with the fragrance and for my eyes to be empurpled and my skin to be stipple-touched with blossoms.

We walk on, and I can't contain my curiosity any longer. I ask "What do you want? Why are you here?"

"They don't need me on set today. I'm escaping the knitters. I had a talk with my agent. She said something about being called up by a woman with your name? Said you wanted to interview me? Here I am."

"Your agent allowed this?"

"Actually—" he brushes petals from his shoulders.

"Shake your head," I say, "you're lilacked."

"Actually," he continues, "she said I'd regret having anything to do with you. She said you have a reputation."

My chest swells with pride. "Tell her I say thanks!"

Another bicyclist veers close. More breath on my neck. Brent Vintner takes my arm as if there's something wrong with it.

"Why don't you come to my hotel," he says. "There's a decent bar there. I have a pretty well stocked mini bar in my room too. I could call down to room service and get you a dapple."

Incredulous, I look at Brent Vintner's beautiful ears and say, "Are you kidding? You joker! How long do you think these lilacs are going to last? One stiff wind and they're gone. This isn't a day that anyone should be spending indoors! How long do you think the weather's going to hold? Don't you know how few days like this there are in any spring? You've been around those knitters way too long!"

MESSAGE TO PUBLISHER

Dear Rosamund,

Please reconsider sending Tinker Flatts. She may be your relative but her name gives away her basic non-serious nature. Whoever in your family named her Tinker must have known she was destined to while away her life with nonessentials and frivolities. And however the name Flatts came about I really don't want to know. Perhaps there is a geographical expert back in the genealogical records?

This Tinker Flatts person will only delay my work. Seriously. Return to sender before she gets here. Where is she, by the way? When is she expected to arrive?

Email from Rosamund:

Tuesday 4:45. I've arranged a car for her. She'll be staying at your mother's place. She's unusually mature and committed. I think she could learn from your mother, my dear friend, about what counts.

The Intern's Arrival

I suppose I must blame fate. My mother has a reputation for upholstery, and after Rosamund shipped a family relic to be reupholstered, that simple business proposition began their friendship on a level that inspired trust. I do believe Rosamund wishes she were like my mother, which would mean Rosamund would be in her later eighties instead of in her later sixties and possess incredible self-assurance, vitality, charisma, and the key to immortality.

Tinker Flatts, upon arriving at my apartment rather than my mother's place, asks for popcorn and homemade fudge. Doesn't like brand of Rose tea in my cupboard. Tells me she thinks I must have got hooked on that tea when the package included miniature plastic turkeys. She's smarter than she looks and she looks extremely unprepared for interning.

At same time, I must admit she might help with Brent Vintner. She's twenty seven but looks about fifteen. Perhaps she will throw herself at him and announce herself as age appropriate although not quite, given that he is thirty-five. He should be older for her. That's how it works in Hollywood. Subtract twenty years from men's ages and add thirty-five to every woman's. Shirley Temple was out of work by the time she was nine?

Notice that Tinker Flatts continually looks me up and down, disapprovingly.

Late Night Thoughts

Insults uttered by Tinker Flatts—only now recollected because insults may be slow to arrive, like words are being shyly courteous and unwilling to harm, unlike the person launching said insults. Tinker Flatts said, "You look like a little schoolmarm in those glasses. Like you jumped off a rerun of *Little House on the Prairie*." She did not stop there. She said, "and those funny sweatpants. They're red and have that long aqua stripe. Like something from decades ago. My cousin used to wear pants like those until I chanted 'You've got a stain in your pants' and then she buried those things."

Yes, those were insults, but possibly Tinker Flatts is trying to help me? Get me to go out and buy more attractive fashions? Yet she insults my glasses. But must wear glasses. Must SEE. Tried to wear contact lenses once and only succeeded in breaking foot.

So Much to Teach My Intern

If she insists on being my intern, why not teach Tinker Flatts the craft of biography? Expend knowledge. Cultivate her gratitude and respect. Perhaps I can be helpful in launching her career. Being an intern must be painful—can relieve her pain!

Can discuss how I construct timelines, ways to interview everyone connected with subject. Online searches. Review reasonably sound, efficient practices. Reasonably sound, efficient practices might work for her though never did me any good. Intention: save her years of effort, unnecessary fumbles, collisions with lawyers. Inform her of importance of noting eating patterns of subject. Even if subject is dead, family members will remember. No one forgets how people eat.

Self-respect: soaring!

Reminder: Tell Tinker Flatts writing about dead is preferable.

Addendum: Realization: Tinker Flatts truly does plan to take over my projects? My present life could be plot of *All About Eve* except Eve Harrington at least pretended to be nice.

I head over to The End of the World. Familiarity does not breed contempt. When I pop into the kitchen to get some extra limes for Leon I find Blowman tossing stuff into the kitchen trash bin. It's amazing to see him, always. A little like coming upon a woodland bear who has wandered into a garbage dump. He's muscled up in a way that reminds me again that we're all animals. I am an animal and have always liked animals. Before I leave, he gives me what might be a frown-wince-smile. Some people have a gift—without saying a word they make you feel better.

Phone Call From Piper Fields—A Reversal

As she speaks, I walk to the balcony, the phone clasped against my ear. Piper Fields is taking her time to get to the point. I don't know how long we can talk about the weather. At this height I'm near the treetops and the leaves are thrashing, and I want to think that the leaves are happy, applauding me. Those trees have already seen plenty of people in bad shape. They deserve to see more of us in better shape.

At last, Piper Fields says, "Listen, Tabitha, what I told you over lunch—that was the drinks talking."

"You had lemonade. Maybe it was that quiche from the 1960s talking."

"You're right. It was talking and I wasn't. I don't know why I was teasing you like that, pretending that I'm not who I am."

"I know. It was really confusing. I kept thinking: who are you? And then I was thinking: do we know who anyone is? And I got caught up in my own mind, wondering about identity."

"Thanks, Tabitha. Thanks for understanding."

"Of course!"

Making Sense of Conversation With Piper Fields

Obviously, Piper Fields enjoys lying. And thievery. Surprised she isn't banned from libraries.

Why Writing About the Dead is Preferable

Easier to construct a narrative arc: beginning, middle, END.

Can pray to the dead in own mind: "Help me find out what you did in 1957 and I'll make you live forever!"

Dead do not steal teapots. Do not steal. Period.

I cannot disappoint them, only their relatives. One less person to offend.

Dead do not lie. Only leave, possibly, record of lies.

Addendum: The difficult thing: it's hard because the person dies. When I wrote about Annie's death I could hardly bear it. I covered her death within one sentence. No more words.

But my Killdeer biography—that was made possible because he was dead, after all, and donated all his journals, without restrictions, to the Midlothian Historical Society. I found out more than I expected. While he told *The Midlothian Express-Times* that the entirety of his paper doll art was destroyed in an electrical fire at his home, his journals told an entirely different story. He burned the dolls himself.

At least some of his photos survived. Interesting: he made paper clothes for extant statues of Lenin—not that they ever made it to the statues. He also made replicas of what he called "paper people" resembling human bodies freeze dried and stacked. Disturbing. Next: ant art. Ant-sized art for ant galleries. Again, conceptual art. Art that ants would enjoy seeing—magnified crumbs, for instance. He followed up with stacked scale models of human body parts in cheese. He thought there was commercial potential, imagining something on the order of Edible Arrangements. Then he went back to ant art and began drawing pictures of buff ant body builders because ants lift more than twenty times their weight.

Next, he started believing, like ants, that he didn't have ears or lungs and that puncture points in his body did all his breathing for him. He swore that crockery and tea kettles were inhabited by spirits, and that the whistle of a steaming kettle was a cry for help. With a micro-pen he drew inside bowls and ceramic kettles and frying pans, drawing delicately, with each swirl of the pen attempting to lure spirits out of the interior.

I had to piece together so much of Killdeer's life. I have no doubt whatsoever that Rosamund actually enjoyed dickering with his descendant's lawyers.

Piper Fields certainly isn't predictable. I still think she may eventually consent to my writing her authorized biography. Then again, I can always write an unauthorized biography, though having actual facts from the horse's mouth would be nice. The question remains: will the life of either Brent Vintner and/or Piper Fields offer enough drama to satisfy readers? Unlikely. They continue to seem helplessly normal. Perhaps normality is exotic. It is for me.

Milieu Is a Disgusting Word

Phone call:

"Tabitha—it's me."

"Who is this?"

"Brent Vintner."

"Really? How do I know?"

"You know, Tabitha. Anyway, I want to invite you to a party. I know you want to know more—for the biography. Maybe you should get a sense of my milieu."

"Your what?"

"My milieu. You know, people I work with."

"That's a disgusting word. Oh—wait. I misheard. Your milieu. Okay."

"I'll pick you up at 8. Your address?"

"Oh, just stop by The End of the World. You can pick me up from there."

ANTICIPATION

Why did I accept Brent Vintner's bizarre invitation? I won't be comfortable at any party, especially one with strangers, especially one with his co-workers, although I admire actors. I admire their ability to remember their lines, their ability to take risks, their incredible dedication, their resilience in the face of rejection.

I accepted, of course, because of the thought of Brent Vintner's face. And duty to my vocation.

What must it have been like for his parents to live while watching Brent Vintner's face grow? Maybe people always think their babies are beautiful. I remember a friend's brand new baby. When my friend peeled away the baby's blanket, I jerked backward and hit my head on her China cabinet. Her baby looked exactly like a rat. A rat in a blanket. I think it's in *Alice in Wonderland*—that part where Alice sees what she thinks is a baby until she realizes she's gaping at a pig. It's like I have something in common with Lewis Carroll. There's no way he wasn't writing from experience.

Brent Vintner—how strange for his parents that he kept getting more and more beautiful. The photos online of his childhood years—you wonder how his parents managed to endure all that light beaming from his face. They must have been regularly startled.

A party with actors. They'll be good-looking, distinguished people. Nevertheless, I'm beginning to feel excited as well as nervous. Nervous-excited. I pray it won't be like one of those *Vanity Fair* parties you see photos of in *The Post*—parties where people are taking selfies and holding strangely shaped drinking straws and everyone seems to be stuck together in weird combinations. Like, people you'd never think should be on each other's laps are caught laughing on each other's laps.

No, I want it to be like one of those parties in old movies where people sing beside the piano player and other people dance and the atmosphere used to be what's called "festive." I want the party like the one in *White Christmas* where Rosemary Clooney snubs Bing Crosby and where the piano is a gorgeous black shining boat-like object and people cluster around it. Though that movie—*White Christmas*—kind of ruined Bing Crosby for me. I know it's considered his best movie, but when he suggests that Clooney should drink butter milk all the romance drains off the screen.

Will everyone be dressed up, or will they be dressed down in that calculated way that proves they can throw on even goat skin and it will be perfect, expensively patched and distressed? I settle for my simple black dress that's relatively tight because I don't want to look like I'm intolerant. My simple black dress—the one I save for funerals. I wear my hair up too. I'll be decades older than anyone there but I have power over younger people.

So excited. Too excited. Can hardly stay inside skin. Feel like skin should be unwrappable so soul can run free.

We arrive at a property on the south side of Midlothian rented by a producer.

The rooms are crowded, and you have to pass between people by scooting low. To keep your balance you momentarily put your hand on some stranger's back which is uncomfortable for anyone involved and may seem like groping. A wall lined with windows. Floorboards shining golden, islanded with throw rugs aggressively placed to trip the elderly. A crisp smell like dry-cleaning, a fug of smoke, weedy, the humming of voices, and to my left is the woman who sat atop the piano at Leon's bar. At present she is sitting atop the man who is presumably her husband and apparently has never gotten tired of this sort of display. As if he too, like a piano or a dying whale, cannot object.

This is Brent Vintner's "milieu."

Breasts. Obviously this is a place where women's breasts are prominently featured. I've never understood that. I look down at my dress and feel pride in the fact that my breasts are not prominently featured. No, they are basically burrowing. Nostalgia: remembering when I grew breasts. My first reaction: these are going to be inconvenient.

I almost recognize a few actors, vaguely, and not by their names. It is, after all, a small, independent film that Brent Vintner is in—something smart and uncompromising and maybe a bit boring because it's so intense, who knows, and so pretty much none of the actors have familiar faces. Delicately, Brent Vintner has me by the arm. It occurs to me that people think I'm his elderly aunt, and I'm being smiled at, nodded at. A little tremor of curiosity flows around the room like no doubt people would enjoy the spectacle of my having a stroke.

"Want a little drinky poo?" a very drunk man asks me. He's stringy with a long neck that periscopes.

"We're all set," Brent Vintner answers for me.

I bristle. "I can handle a drink," I say. "Is anything flaming? I'd love something flaming."

Brent Vintner whispers in my ear. "I don't think it's safe to have matches in here."

"Because of the knitting?"

He smiles in his awkward way—too awkward for someone with his astonishingly good looks. "Yes, the yarn."

I eavesdrop as I wander through rooms with Brent Vintner until I begin to understand what the movie he's making is about: a singer gifted since childhood who lands in prison and then breaks out and under another identity becomes a renowned composer of a South Korean symphony. Can this be correct? It sounds like the movie is called *The Hair on Her Arm*?

It's unfortunate if the movie documents the singer from childhood. Is there anything worse than children's singing voices? It's not like they're going to keep those voices for long. There's something temporary, decaying, about children's voices.

I whisper to Brent Vintner, "Is the child here—the one who plays the part of a child?"

He whispers into my ear. "No. No children are on the premises."

"Thank god," I whisper back.

She's upon us then—a celebrity whose face I recognize, except because her face is right in front of me I have to assemble it. It's like a Picasso painting of one of his innumerable female victims. The woman breathes into Brent Vintner's face. Her lips are uniquely alive, I realize with admiration.

"Your lips are so alive," I say.

She turns to Brent Vintner. "Who is this?" she asks.

My elbow is being scooped up again by Brent Vintner, and then we're outside, on a balcony, a drink mysteriously in my hand.

"What do you think of these people?" he asks.

"They're so—alive."

"I know, but what do you think of them?"

"I don't know. They seem—happy."

He looks into the distance, toward the illuminated water tower. The sky has a just erased chalkboard quality, the starlight a smear. I breathe in the fresh, unperfumed air and the wonderful smell of Brent Vintner.

"You know," Brent Vintner says, "the second time I saw you, you talked about being lonely. Are you?"

"Of course. I've always been lonely."

"Don't you have a family?"

"I do, but it's not enough."

"I know," he says. "It's not quite enough."

I realize that the biography will have to account for his pensiveness. His childhood—that will have to be investigated. The biography—suddenly it seems like too much work.

"Do you ever feel that you can't make yourself understood?" he asks.

"Always," I say.

From the roomful of people behind us laughter and shouts erupt. I will never fit in with any of the beautiful people in that room. I'm not bothered by that. I don't have to fit in. I chronicle those who do. It's important to be an observer, outside the tide of human affairs.

More people in the room are dancing. Loose limbed. Casual seeming. Like dancing is natural instead of a symptom of strained social relations. Dancing actors. How easy it is for them. I do dance—at night—with the blinds closed. I'll dance to anything. I can't help but throw myself into my dancing when I'm alone. Sometimes I imagine dancing with various nice people. Then I feel that I'm being watched and have to stop dancing by myself because I'm throwing myself into the dance in a way that would embarrass the watchers. I try to imagine other scenarios. For instance, it's a wedding and people of all ages attend and a lonely seven-year-old boy asks me to dance. He's an incredibly polished dancer and I follow his exact moves—pretty wild, arm flailing moves—and my dancing isn't considered embarrassing because I'm being kind to a child.

"Thank you for a really nice evening," I say to Brent Vintner, "but I have an early day tomorrow."

"What's up tomorrow?"

"My cats. I made an appointment with them."

Keeping My Promises

I had told the cats I'd be there for them.

Post-Party Remorse

What did I do wrong? I don't think it's especially neurotic to wonder, is it? I can't control the feeling that I did something embarrassing at the party. The sensations I experience may spring from deja vu, that is, from an incident when I was at a party years ago. I sat on a bunch of blankets on a couch and didn't realize anything was wrong until a half hour later when a woman's hand reached out from under me and a man came running over and shouted "You suffocated her." I didn't, but still.

Usually I would be reading a novel at night but my mind won't settle. Netflix. Always avoid the documentaries. Although they're fascinating, afterwards I want to disappear into the bitter bowels of the earth. Even though I know they're not "real," the effort to appear real is there.

In mood for movie thriller with mammoth plot holes where a man jumps over roofs then slides down roofs and drives a car off a cliff and survives, bubbling up from underwater like a rubber duck.

Have hidden two chocolates from Pot 'o' Gold collection so that when they're found will spark exhilaration.

After twenty minutes realize I've seen this thriller before. It's because of the nondescript title that I was fooled. Something like: *It's What It Is*, or *Anything But Interesting*, or *Death to a Kill*, or *Kiss Me With Tongue*.

Pert and Pretty are becoming less dismissive, although I know they prefer my nephew Leon. I must try harder.

Resolved: use credit card to buy cat toys. Be wary of possible choking hazards. Also pick up a carton of that pretend cat milk that doesn't mess with their stomachs but initiates memories (for them) of early breast feeding experience. Breast feeding. It's not like breast milk comes in chunks. Breast-drinking sounds wrong, however. Can't win.

STARTERS

Concentrate. Turn off phone.

I've lingered too long on these notes and must at least attempt to write directly about Brent Vintner for biography, given that I've been introduced to his milieu. But what to write?

Possibilities for opening of Brent Vintner biography:

How does Brent Vintner look at his own face in the mirror every morning to shave without being temporarily blinded?

Remember when people used to talk about "the male gaze" like it was a thing? Now it's like we're being gazed at by artificial intelligences, and desire seems all wonky and hard to express—even though expressions of desire have often, throughout millennia, been artificial.

[Question: For the opening of the biography, do the above sentences appear too distant from the ostensible subject: Brent Vintner?]

[Question: How did Brent Vintner's former girlfriends/partners survive losing him? Any murder plots or just slow deaths of despair?

Or did those love interests try to restrain themselves, possibly at the start of each affair by getting a tattoo that says "EXPECT NOTHING" in funky calligraphy?]

Help me God, I must do some laundry. Have used up all laundry baskets for laundry. Can't avoid doing laundry and simply go to Wal-Mart and pick up yet another laundry basket again.

Might as well turn on phone. What if someone desperately wants to reach me?

An Unexpected Voice Mail

"Tabitha, I must say that Tinker is like the daughter I've always wished I had. She has a girlfriend from Nigeria and another one from New Zealand, has interned at major art studios, and plans to specialize in marketing at Rosamund's company. What ambition! Tabitha, you should consider taking a leaf from her book. Bye bye now."

Beautiful Discoveries Part I

My loneliness—why does it exist? I have Leon at the bar. I have my mother, for what that's worth and it's worth a lot. She's the sort of mother you never have to feel guilty about neglecting—she won't let me and, anyway, she's the most fulfilled person I've ever met. And now there's Tinker Flatts—she's clearly rooted in my mother's life. Solitude is not loneliness and can never be overrated.

My intern wears combat boots—I'm serious. I do admire her tattoos, not the boots. Her boots make rubber marks on the floor—big swirling black snake-emulating designs. But her tattoos. Every day she wears something that exposes a new tattoo. A very slow strip tease.

Her tattoos are always of items you can find in your refrigerator. I do not understand this and ask her to explain.

She stomps her boots, no doubt leaving a mark (I'll check when she steps away). "That's so when the apocalypse comes, people will remember what food products looked like."

"Is everything organic—all the tattoos?"

"Man, no," she says, sounding like such a throwback. "Man, no oh no. I want a little humor in there. I've got ketchup." She lifts up her shirt.

"Is that relish?" I ask.

"Yeah, it's a little too wobbly looking—like the relish is going to erupt."

What can I say? My intern. I'm stuck with her.

"Your mom really is a treat," Tinker Flatts says, pulling down her shirt. "I've never known someone to have that many Halloween decorations. She says she keeps them up all year round. It's like she's way ahead of her time. Like you'd think someone that ancient wouldn't still be into skulls. Maybe everybody used to be into skulls but she's like—whoa."

Drafting Portion of Brent Vintner Biography—Various Starts

Must recreate "milieu":

Brent Vintner mixes drolly among party goers while two dogs are having sex in a far room, and a woman whose lips seem weirdly alive bends toward Brent Vintner's perfect ear. The milieu is apparently not unusual for Brent Vintner to inhabit—this mix of low level jazz and high level cleavage, the combined smells of exotic perfumes and cheap pharmaceuticals. Brent Vintner, however, isn't entirely at home in such an atmosphere. He twists on the sofa, looks from side to side, hardly speaks. A new drug is being cut on the glass coffee table. Brent Vintner ignores those sniffing at the suspicious gray power (called snuffer-doodle or snuffydoo or snuff). He is a creature not made for unknown nasal substances but rather for the rural plains of Michigan.

Note to self: must look up facts about Michigan.

His childhood in a rural hamlet hardly prepared him for this sort of sophistication. As a child he picked radishes in the family garden until his arms blistered.

Note to self: check on this with Brent Vintner.

His first romantic date amounted to a backyard barbecue tryst with a young lady who snuck into his home and deposited an open beer in his sock drawer.

Note to self: check on this with Brent Vintner.

Research

I'm attempting and failing to watch movies in which Brent Vintner has a role. I keep experimenting with trailers and having to pause—that face! The way he moves his face around. He wags his face, basically. You can't help but smile—it's like when a dog wags its tail.

Prefer when he blinks. Simply cannot look at his face without flinching. Like looking directly into sun.

Is Brent Vintner more effective in comedies or dramas or dramadies?

What does the word "effective" mean? You can be effective at anything. Effectively stupid. Effectively foolish. Effectively gullible.

Is it superficial to spend much of a biography chapter on a subject's clothing if subject isn't Coco Chanel? For instance, turquoise shirt worn by Brent Vintner—could spend considerable time on 3-D effects it creates?

Researching more internet "facts" about Brent Vintner.

Oh my god. He's dated everyone. Disastrously. At least he didn't tattoo all their names on himself. There's that to be thankful for. Not that I should care. Not that I'm going to see every inch of his body. And why should we all be so intent on thinking about other bodies? Aren't there other issues in the world? Admittedly, all of them affect bodies, but still . . .

It's amazing, isn't it, that people tattoo the names of their loved ones on their bodies—while those persons are still alive. After the person's dead, that's okay—unless maybe you discover a trove of incriminating letters or their internet history. But tattooing a living person's name on your body—what an act of faith that is. It's like you're just tempting a divorce lawyer to pop out of the bushes . . .

Transcript: A Phone Call From Piper Fields

"I was going to go for a walk in the park and it occurred to me that maybe we could talk."

"You mean a real interview? I'd love that! Let's do it. I'll be there. Jesmun Park?"

What does Piper Fields want? Will she confess the truth? Does she need a friend more than a biographer? Could there be something desperately wrong with her—that I could write about?

Meeting Up With Piper Fields

She's standing alone beside the giant oak that a van crashed into last month—everyone lived—and she's looking smaller. I am beginning to recognize her easily, no matter what she does with her hair and her eyes and her mouth.

"Did you shrink since I last saw you?" I ask.

"What do you mean?"

"You're not the same. You're smaller."

"I feel smaller."

There's a cool breeze but strong sunlight—the way sunlight is when the wind is up, like the sun is in competition with the wind. I can tell that Piper wants to tell me something, that her conscience is bothering her. We begin walking.

"Piper, did you ever kill a man?"

"What?

"You're guilty," I say. "What did you do?"

She stops, turns to me, her mouth open.

"What is it?" I ask. "You're going to lie again. It's so obvious. You're not going to let me interview you—not really."

She blinks her reddening eyes and closes her mouth.

"What is it?" I ask again.

"I can take you to her," she says.

"Who?"

"The real Piper Fields. That's not her name. She's not me."

I am speechless for seconds and then of course I jump at the chance to meet "the real Piper Fields," although I can't believe anything Piper Fields tells me.

I ask when I can meet "the real Piper Fields." This woman thrives on trickery and chaos and is too cunning. How can I ever trust her to tell me the truth?

Oh, how far I've come in my perceptions of Piper Fields since she was being uncommonly gentle with a waffle.

Note to Self

Sudden lack of faith in profession: why commit life to telling stories about personalities of various sorts? Would do better if picked names at random. All lives = interesting? But not all interesting to me?

Piper Fields: more interesting now that she once again declares she's not who everyone believes she is. Why would best-selling children's book author and indecent novelist deny her identity? Mystery. To create mystery? Plus, if she's not the actual author, why did she make up a story about bunnies massacred by a lawn mower, and about learning to soothe children while babysitting? Also, what about her claim of finding sex toys in refrigerator? Are these stories invented to bolster a false identity when she was still committed to admitting she's the author of her own books?

Although I am, as usual, tempted to destroy all my notes, I will not do so. There's no telling what they might reveal in time.

I have never denied my identity—not that I can recall. Have written anonymous notes, but that's not the same thing.

Secret Suspicions/Questions

What if Piper Fields and Brent Vintner are working together to slyly make sure both biographies are never completed? Again, that's another problem about working with the living.

Sudden realization: What if person being written about uses biographer's questions only as a way to frame their own memoir? Danger about working with the living: they can tell their own story, thereby throwing you out of the running entirely. Who do they think they are?

Back to Piper Fields in particular: I assume she is lying about her identity and is actually the author of her own kiddie books and novels. Regardless, I need to gather more information about her. For instance, what are her work habits like? Pen or pencil? Laptop or ancient hieroglyphs (little joke). Does she write the children's books in the morning, the smut at night? Or does she divide up the year? Children in the spring? The novels, for the rest of the year? Or does she write the children's books in the course of one morning? And the adult novels in the course of one hangover . . . ? These things matter to the most regressive readers.

Preparing to Meet "Real" Author of Novels by "Piper Fields"

What offering on Netflix could prepare me for meeting with both Piper Fields and woman claiming to be actual author? Spy thriller? Ravishingly beautiful East German agent strikingly similar to a young Angela Merkel must lure CIA agent to turn over nuclear scientist whose small daughter is stuck in Tennessee cave. Fall asleep and wake up at part where woman disrupts Soviet sable industry by mating sables in Stockholm? Sables—jumping mink-like creatures—are freed from rusty cages. Realize it's a double header with *Gorky Park* and must consult Wikipedia to understand plot. Seems perfect mental exercise for next day's adventure with Piper Fields.

Meeting the Real Piper Fields Who Isn't Piper Fields

Piper's car: clean with an almost new car smell. She drives the way she eats: cautiously at first, then with a heightened recognition of danger.

She slows as we pass a farmhouse with a horse-shoe drive but doesn't turn in.

"Do you want to blindfold me?" I ask.

"Why?"

"So, you know, I can't tell anyone the location."

"I trust you. You're not going to tell anyone the location."

"What's her name—this person who, you say, really wrote all the books?"

"I'll let her tell you that—if she wants to. If she decides to trust you. You know that all this is deniable, right, if we don't like how you handle the information? Your reputation—it's not great. As I keep reminding you: people won't believe you."

What is Piper Fields's motive for this charade, pretending she's not herself? Is she trying to make her life sound more compelling than it could possibly be? Isn't that my job?

"Do you have some sort of secret sorrow I should know about?" I ask.

She continues to stare forward, one of those drivers who misses seeing anything on either side of her. A cow could be juggling orange balls in the next lane and she wouldn't notice. A small child could be competing on a balance beam with a duck and she wouldn't notice. Flames could be shooting out of a garbage truck driven by a squealing groundhog and she wouldn't notice.

I ask again, "Do you have a secret sorrow?"

Finally she says, "What kind of question is that?" She jerks the wheel although there's nothing on the road to avoid.

"It's the kind of question I ask everybody—eventually." When she remains silent I say, "Why don't you want to be known as the author of your own books? Don't you like being a writer?"

She thumps the steering wheel. "I don't understand how anybody would ever want to write books. Sitting there. Locking yourself in place. Dreaming up paranoid fantasies. Do you believe me now? I wouldn't want to write a single one of those books."

"No. I think you enjoy deception."

We were about twenty five miles east of Midlothian when she pulled into a driveway. A tiny yellow house. A fairytale house, I tell myself, already narrating the story in my mind. Possibly inside this house resides the true author of narcoleptic children's books as well as filthy adult novels. She'll greet me at the door with a warm smile and force me into her cat-strewn dwelling.

Or it's actually a man. A small frowning man who dislikes children, not just their singing, but their existence. If he could have once avoided being a child he would have, jumping from afterbirth into, at least, early middle age.

The door opens. A woman, older than Piper by several years. A fluttering of her hands. She's wearing a blue and white checked shirt, a navy blue skirt, fuzzy knee highs.

She leads us inside. Seven windows, fluffy beige carpeting, a rose perfume smell and also something urine-like. Scratching sounds.

Cats, of course. Three. The buttery yellow bruiser sort, broad shouldered bodyguard cats. With a piercing sensation of homesickness I think of my cats, those brave foot soldiers reluctantly tending my own loneliness.

No sooner am I seated then the fluttery-fingered woman begins to explain herself.

"You must think I've been incredibly selfish. And I have been. It's just that while my husband was alive he disapproved of my writing." She's wearing a long pendant that rises and dips as she talks. I wonder if it's one of those pendants my ex-brother-in-law sells and if her husband's ashes are swinging in it.

I catch up with her when she says "I couldn't help myself—it was a joy to be indiscreet privately. I suppose that's not being truly indiscreet if no one knows, is it? For years I thought no one would discover that the children's books and the novels for grownups were from the same author. Well, poor Piper—" she nodded toward Piper who was staring out the window at a sycamore waving its branches—"poor Piper has had to deal with the downside. The overly solicitous fans. I never meant for her to be so implicated. It's true—instead of a pen name I have a pen person—dear, kind Piper—who has pretended to author everything I've written. At first I didn't think it would be a burden. Who would care about the author of those children's books? But then when they served a need . . . Piper has freed me up to write as I wish and not feel the pressure to conform that another author might feel."

The woman still hasn't given me her name, and I haven't found any handy addressed envelopes on the table next to me, nor did I notice a mailbox when we pulled into her driveway. I could always interview her neighbors to find out what she calls herself.

She gazes over my head and continues. "Well, you see, Tabitha—such a great name—Tabitha, it's all gone a bit tits up. That's a British expression, isn't it? So helpful. Anyway, I think Piper is getting a little tired of the charade."

Piper shifts and murmurs, "Certainly. Really, the readers are making it impossible."

"So true," the woman says. "Not that I've had to endure it. I understand, from Piper's account, that you, dear Tabitha, witnessed one of my readers accosting Piper."

"That's right. A very threatening fellow. The red flannel shirt said it all."

The woman levels her gaze at me. "It's past time, I know, for us to be thinking of ways to get Piper out of this mess that I put her in, and we've been wondering if you might help us."

What does this woman want me to do? Possibilities flash through my mind. How am I supposed to kill Piper Fields?

I ask, "Do you want me to unearth the truth in the biography, or do you want to publicize the truth yourself so that it doesn't seem pried out of you?"

"I think we need to consider multiple alternatives. I hoped you might have some ideas."

When I'm silent for nearly a minute she says, "Options, options, options. Various plans: Piper—you could unmask me. You could say you did it for all these years as a favor because my husband threatened me."

"Isn't that the truth?" I ask.

"At first, but he's been dead for twelve years and there's a time stamp on that excuse." She paused dramatically before going on.

"I guess Piper could say that's how it started and then we didn't want to upset readers. We carried on the masquerade—successfully. More successfully than we hoped to."

The room descends into silence. One of the cats is batting at what's either a moth or a fly.

The insight comes upon me with such force that I'm ready to bolt upright from my chair. Instead I stay seated and speak in the calmest voice I can muster: "You're lying. I can tell you're lying. Everything you say sounds—rehearsed. Piper, you wrote all the damn books. You're trying to get me to agree to an enormous lie—for publicity. And you're going to use all my earlier mistakes against me. Those celebrity profiles in which I got things a little too provocative for some people—not due to any fault of my own—you're going to make sure I ruin my own career to advance your own, and then you'll sell even more of your sex-addled novels, Piper, and parents will pick up your dimwitted kiddie books out of sympathy. This is a bad, bad plan."

The woman winks at Piper. "How did she guess?" she asks. "How did she figure it out?"

She winks again at Piper, who bears a look of agony on her face as she mumbles, "I tried, Maryann, I tried."

"Oh, how did I know?" I ask. "How did I know?" I can hardly breathe—because I don't know how. I just know. The way I know that Brent Vintner's arms had been blistered during childhood while he picked radishes, the way I know that Brent Vintner's face would never be loved enough by the camera, because the camera doesn't convey touch. Indescribable, unsupportable truth. I know.

"I think you're stuck being me," the woman—who I now know is named Maryann—tells Piper Fields. "You're stuck with the fans, with the notoriety, with the strange, sad, atrocious letters and emails and tweets, darling."

Both of these women look so deflated that I can't help but reconsider—temporarily. "Okay," I say. "Okay. If you're telling the truth you can just announce it yourself, can't you? There's nothing holding you back."

"I signed all her contracts," Piper says. "I guess I'm owed something." I realize that these two women hate each other. Oddly, the image of Tinker Flatts floats before me, her large feet in her large boots, and I think about how lucky I am not to hate anybody, not even Tinker Flatts.

"I guess we would rather have a go-between, someone to tell our story sympathetically," the woman named Maryann says. "We were hoping it would be you."

On the drive back, Piper is silent. Before I step out of her car, I'm expecting her to either stare straight ahead or to glare. Instead, she turns to me and her eyes are wet.

"I'm sorry," I tell her. "I just can't do it. And I know you're lying."

"But you look like you're broke and really so—naive," she said. "We thought you'd do anything."

MESSAGE TO PUBLISHER

Dear Rosamund,

Piper Fields is what my mother, your devoted friend, used to call "a pill." I do not take pills. Not even aspirin. I'm sorry I ever suggested she'd make a good subject for my next biography. She's far too complicated, and I have pride. I will not be used by a liar. I've already been married and divorced, and although that happened long ago I lived a lie long enough to know better than to entertain additional lies.

Just to be clear (I'm trying to be clear to everyone today) I am formally announcing, to eliminate any possible misunderstanding, that I will not be writing the biography of Piper Fields. I will only be writing Brent Vintner's biography. He's remarkably forthcoming. Piper Fields, however, plays too many games. It's best that I concentrate exclusively on Brent Vintner, maintaining singular focus. I have already established an atmosphere of trust and inserted myself into Brent Vintner's milieu. Plus, he should be a target of general interest. He's in the process of making a remarkable movie, very top secret, one of those indie films, a vanity project, and it's called something absolutely fetching in an absurd way. It's either *The Hair on Her Arm, The Skin on Your Arm*, or *The Harem of Yarn*—quite possibly the latter, given that many of his co-stars are knitting addicts. Attached please find receipts for a few (minor) expenses.

Email to Piper Fields

I won't be writing your biography. Just to be clear. No need to respond.

Notes from Actual Conversation with Tinker Flatts

Aunt Rosamund wants to know the real story about why you're giving up on Piper Fields.

Because she's a lying psychopath.

But that's all the more reason—

Tinker, you can write her biography.

Really?

Really. I give you my permission.

Can I have your notes?

No, but you can ask Piper Fields where she got her latest teapot. That's a good start.

Gosh, thanks. I guess I'm settling down for a while then. Your mom wants me to sign a six-month lease.

Really?

She says I'm like the daughter she never had.

You are like the daughter she never had.

A Beautiful Day

There is, I admit, something luxurious about giving up a project. What's not done emits a glimmer, a special luster. I say this because it's a beautiful day and because the lilacs that Brent Vintner has had delivered to my apartment are so gorgeous that I sit beside them as if I'm consulting them, asking them, Why won't you stay, why won't you stay forever? Their time with us is so short. Lilac time.

I should never have told Brent Vintner about my loneliness that night, three beer mugs down, at The End of the World. And yet if I hadn't told him, would these lilacs have appeared by themselves? When I was a child we lived near scratch woods, a patch of weedy tangles, and amid those tangles grew the most unforgettable elderberry bush. When elderberries pop in your mouth the actual taste is purple. A tart purple. Likewise, the violet color of these lilacs which Brent Vintner has had delivered to me, these heavy drown-drooping lilacs—you can almost taste their purple and violet petals.

I text Brent Vintner: "You have answered my prayers. Thank you!" I send a photo of Pert and Pretty sitting beside the lilacs just before they swat the vase. No matter. It wasn't the vase I loved.

I find another vase in the cupboard and settle the lilacs next to the golden pony given to me by Mattie. What a wonderful woman my grandmother was. She loved Diana Ross fiercely and was always playing "You Can't Hurry Love," by The Supremes. She liked to sing the lyrics and tell me, "Tabitha, you can't hurry love. You can't hurry luck either. You can only try to give it a head start." She liked to say, "Tabitha, there's an old saying by an old Greek or whoever: 'Hurry slowly.' I know you, honey. When you get nervous you say what you don't mean. You got that from me, honey. You have to learn to slow down. I hurried love and it all worked out, only because I was lucky."

I once had a dream about Mattie after she died. In the dream I'm swimming underwater wildly fast. Afterwards, I sit in the sand for a long time until Mattie comes out of the water dripping with amethysts and diamonds and rubies and emeralds. Because she took her time she saw treasures under the water. She saw and gathered all that I couldn't. When I woke up I felt stung by that dream.

The golden pony. Under the gold paint it's plaster. It's lightweight, easy to break, which is why I keep it up high on my bookshelf, away from Pert and Pretty. Whenever I look at it I tell myself: Don't hurry. And then I wonder if I haven't hurried enough.

The Language of Flowers, or: Is Brent Vintner Trying to Tell Me Something?

The Victorians, in particular, attached a great deal of meaning to flowers. Which really does suggest that they were hopelessly repressed. After all, how much can flowers say? Lilacs, for instance, according to Wikipedia and the Farmer's Almanac, are connected to the memory of love—the freshness of early love or the loss of that love. That's not telling you much. Then too, plenty of what's called the language of flowers is contradictory and hard to translate. Why do begonias mean "Watch out?" Why do daisies mean both "Your secret is safe with me" and "You are pure." If you're that pure why is your secret problematic? Petunias (who gives petunias, they're so floppy and the color of flags at an auto dealership?) mean "I resent you" and also "Soothe me." And peonies can stand for wealth and happiness but also "bashfulness." Although peonies don't look bashful. They look like they just put on every dress they own and are headed to a very demanding party.

The sad thing about lilacs, as I keep mentioning: their blooming time is so short. But then they make such an impression on all fronts. What they say: I may not stay long—and you will never get enough of me.

NETFLIX—WITH LEON: AN ATTEMPT TO ENGAGE IN CINEMATIC RESEARCH

Leon is stretched out on his couch and eating a bowl of popcorn off his stomach. Very perilous, eating like that on a white couch and expecting not to drop greased kernels. He's put on one of Brent Vintner's movies.

"I always like it when you talk about Brent Vintner and use his full name," he says.

I don't ask why. I know he'll tell me after two more handfuls of popcorn.

"His full name creates distance, you know?" Leon says. "Aesthetic distance. That's a giveaway. I've been thinking he isn't really Brent Vintner but a stand-in, you know, and he's pulling our legs. Yours especially. When you first said his name to me you said it with a touch of irony, you know? Like, 'Hi, Leon, here's 'Brent Vintner, the act-or,' and you chuckled. Like you meant, 'Jesus Christ, this dude thinks we really believe he's Brent Vintner.' "

"But he is Brent Vintner."

"Is he really? Do you really know?" Leon shoves his popcorn around in the bowl and says, "Okay, time to watch the act-or, Brent the Vintner."

WATCHING

Brent Vintner is very young in this movie, and smiles softly from his poreless and pleasant face, which makes me feel older than I am—although in a distinguished but eerie way: the sort of person who says "Dah-ling," like Katherine Hepburn in *Suddenly Last Summer* when she tries to get Elizabeth Taylor lobotomized. Or Katherine Hepburn in *On Golden Pond*, that movie about two elderly people torturing their daughter, poor Jane Fonda who can only earn her father's love by executing a backflip off a dock.

"Stop studying me, Leon."

"You can't look at him for more than a second or two? Ouch, here he is again."

At the end of the movie: a wedding. Thank god Brent Vintner is the best man, not the groom. Still, as I'm watching the movie a bad memory crops up from when I was eighteen and made the mistake of getting married. Back then, as a wedding gift, my mother gave me the same oak hope chest her own mother gave her—the size and shape of a coffin. On my wedding day, right when I learned I was getting that hope chest, something horrible happened. After the ceremony I was standing on a balcony and someone bumped me from behind and I shot off into the shrubbery.

I don't think that hope chest can possibly be lucky. I still own it and have never opened it—and it's been thirty two years since the wedding. I really should give it away except I don't want to put a curse on anybody else. That chest makes me think of all those sad folktales about the bride who ran away after the wedding. Or so everyone thought! Decades later the bride's body is discovered in the wooden chest where she went to play hide and seek, planning to pop out and surprise her husband. In all those stories there are always scratch marks inside the lid of the chest.

I'm shivering now just thinking about it.

Piper Fields Is Becoming Such A Nuisance

Piper Fields asks to meet me—surprisingly. We agree on the place: Tiffany's Rhubarb Hospice. It's a restaurant "to die for," according to the website.

"Why," she asks after the server takes our order, "why did you push that Tinkerbell character on me?"

"Tinker Flatts? She's capable. Her aunt is my publisher. Her aunt worships the ground her boots walk on—"

"Those boots—they're loud and they leave marks."

"I know, it's impressive. It's like she leaves a map of wherever she's been for every day of her life. Her aunt will make sure your life story is written up—and nicely packaged too. They'll hire a book doctor, etcetera, and it will all work out. Snip snap."

"It's not my life story. I'm not the author of those books. I don't know why you don't believe me."

"Because you're such a hustler. I can't trust you. Listen, I finally read more than a few pages from one of your novels."

"What? You never even read one of those novels I supposedly wrote?" She digs into her linguini. It is far too cheesed. In fact, avalanched.

"I read part of one, and I almost made it through one of the children's books but then I fell asleep."

"Well—that's perfect. I can't believe you didn't—"

"Listen, I really did read more than a few pages of one of the novels—"

"Which one?"

"I can't remember the title, but a goat was prominently featured."

"*Satan's Goat.*"

"I don't know who it belonged to, but it was a goat. There was a portion about a wedding? I can't help it, I have such a hard time reading about weddings. Especially fancy weddings. You know the old saying: the costlier the wedding, the sooner the divorce. Or maybe it's something like: the longer the wedding, the shorter the marriage. I really don't know."

I don't tell Piper Fields about the hope chest and how I got bumped off the balcony, but I do describe the catering at my wedding: a plated dinner with sea bass drizzled with truffle oil. The oil made the fish taste unwashed. A cake beribboned and enormous, almost like one of those cakes in old movies, the kind where a woman leaps out and tap dances. Maybe a woman should have popped out with a machete.

I go on. "But the wedding in your novel. That was quite a wedding. I'm surprised anyone lived through it. Well, not everyone did, but still. You know it's lilac season? I hope someday I'll go to a wedding and there will be lilacs everywhere. Big bunches, bigger than bunches of grapes, and the air will be fragrant, and no one will die. Sorry, it's spring and I get carried away. About your novel, though—that was something. I never expected the ending. Well, I read part of the beginning and skipped to the ending. I might have missed something . . ."

Piper Fields sighs and says, "*Satan's Goat* is actually a political allegory with insight into contemporary reality."

"Fuck me with a spoon. I had no idea!"

"The thing is," she says, rescuing a strand of linguini, "call off that girl. Tinker Flatty or whatever her name is. She's stalking me and I can't stand it."

"You're right. She's right over there, watching. Taking notes."

Piper Fields jackknifes around. "Where?"

"I'm kidding. God knows where she is. She's probably with my mother. I meant to ask: where did you dig up Maryann?"

"I told you. I've known her since childhood."

"She looks just like you, but she's easily at least five years older than you. So she wrote the novels? Ha ha. No, she did not. I know you wrote everything under your name. Your sensibility—it speckles everything."

"You are wrong, Tabitha. It's like a genetic characteristic: your wrongness."

"You know what they say about being wrong? Taken to an extreme, it's a form of genius."

I was very proud of myself during that lunch. So proud I forgot to take home my linguini leftovers, which was just as well. The cats greeted me at the door, communicating how frustrated they were while I was away, communicating by nipping at my ankles, demanding wet food from my own little wet market in the kitchen.

An Expected Voice Mail

"Remember when you were a little girl and read that Beauty and the Beast book all the time? I've been thinking about that. Tinker mentioned you have a new friend? She said someone saw you with an actor from that low-budget movie they've resorted to making in town? But anyway, about Beauty and the Beast. Funny that you loved that story. Tabitha, remember: the beast transforms in the end. It was a gamble for the girl, but I bet she was tipped off. They never reverse the genders, do they? You don't happen to have that old green spatula I loaned you, do you? I was thinking of borrowing it back and hanging it on a nail—for a cute effect. I know you don't use it. You've never thoroughly scraped out a jar of mayonnaise in your life."

Work Habits

I may not be especially particular about cleaning out mayonnaise from the jar but I have exemplary strategies I intend to employ:

Concentrate. That biography of Brent Vintner won't write itself.

Nap when necessary. Before nap, assign self a question, such as: What interests you most about . . .?

Relax when not napping. Good ideas come when least expected.

Peanut butter is inexpensive and a fine protein source for maintaining stamina.

Continue being diligent about notes.

Take notes about notes.

And then take notes about those notes.

A biography is not only about the biographee but about the conditions that make writing the biography possible. That is, biography is the essential art: otherwise, how can we discover how other people manage to stay alive for years?

Remember not to disappear down the rabbit hole of another person's life.

Practice humility even though you'll know so much about the subject of the biography and can correct others repeatedly and with ease.

Do not take notes in pencil. Smudge. Use laptop for greater storage potential. Smudge-less.

If people do not want to tell you the truth, be silent. People can't stand silence and will TALK.

Expect to be misunderstood.

Beautiful Discoveries, Part II

Concentration isn't easily achieved. It's best not to beat yourself up about it.

Watermelon—it's too early in the season, and yet I go to Giant and there they are—an entire bin of seedless watermelons. I lift a few. Heavier than pumpkins. I wonder if the insides are like pumpkins—a bunch of strings and seeds.

The funny thing: Pert and Pretty and I are eating a very nice dinner together and the watermelon, which I'd set on the floor next to the radiator, rolls right over to us. Like it's alive. Like it wants to eat something too. The cats sprint out of the kitchen, and I sit there looking down at the watermelon. This is the discovery: a watermelon is beautiful because it looks like a bad paint job. Like something hand painted in a ceramics class. Which makes me think of that woman who used to be in love with Leon. Sad. Leon never drank from a single one of her many mugs.

Surprising Text

Oh—text from Brent Vintner:

R u Bzy?

[Me wondering but not texting the words: Who texts like that?]

I text back:

How old are you? 10? You're talking to a middle-aged lady
[Note to self: Middle age is beautiful.]

He texts back: Are you busy?

I text back: Why?

He texts: Interview me now? Too much knitting here

I text back: Can you come to my apt? 44 Bitumen Apt 3?

He texts back: In a jif

I should not have spent so much time with a hairbrush. Before I can change out of pajamas he's knocking.

He looks around. "What the hell?"

"What? What's wrong?"

"It's just—not what I expected. It's so—bare. Did you only recently move in?"

"No, I just have no time for fluff. I grew up in a household where one holiday was celebrated year round. I just prefer a more—"

"Hermit-like home?"

"Is there anything wrong with that? I suppose your home is entirely outfitted with troll dolls."

Hands on hips, he swivels. "You don't even have pillows on your couch."

"Arrest me. I have cats, although I don't know where they are at this minute. They would do harrowing things to pillows. Be alert. They might jump out at any minute. They've become very protective. Recently they put it together that I feed them and now they don't want me to die."

I point him past the corner to the alcove where my bookshelf stands—which is not at all denuded of items that express personality. He looks over at the Dutch heads and the golden pony and the vase of lilacs and the many books on each shelf, and then he steps toward the towers of books on the floor, the ones that can't fit on the shelves. I'm so glad I put all my self-help books behind the other stacks and they're not visible. Not that anything's wrong with self-help books. I've needed help, and where was I going to get it genuinely, if not from myself? He runs his hand over the top of the stack of poetry books—Berryman and Plath and Lucille Clifton and Gertrude Stein. Texts from my old college classes.

It's clear that Brent Vintner is a genuine reader by the manner in which, as if magnetized, he touches the spine of my second-hand Brontë and lingers over a novel by Thackeray on the shelf. A minute later he turns back to the stacks of my books, piled high and ready to topple across the floor, and picks up *The Merry Adventures of Robin Hood* by Howard Pyle. An illustrated children's book.

He sets the book back on top of the stack. "I turned down a part—I was going to be one of the merry men but something better came up."

"What could be better than being a merry man?"

He laughs. "You're right. I regret that."

"You should. Think of the time you could have spent up in a tree. And you could have eaten without cutlery at a banquet and downed tankards of ale. You could have worn the color green for weeks. Do you want to sit down? The couch squeaks a little. I hope that's okay."

He sits next to me and the couch shrieks. He holds his head in his hands, his shoulders moving up and down.

"Don't cry," I say, thinking he's upset that I live in my admittedly pitiful apartment. "I love my life."

He looks up and laughs. "No, I'm not crying. It's just—restful here in a refreshing way."

"You keep laughing."

"I know—it's just my way to relax."

"You're laughing about my couch. That's okay. My couch appreciates it. No one ever sits on it. Well, Tinker does. Tinker Flatts, my intern."

"You have an intern! How great! That's so—I didn't expect that."

"Neither did I. She's worthless. My mother likes her, and that's a plus. It keeps my mother busy, complimenting Tinker during phone calls to me. But never mind my life, let's hear about your life. This is an interview, right?"

He leans back on the couch, extends his right arm over the back.

"You have a very wide arm span," I inform him. "I read something about how the length of your arms combined is the length of your legs. You have long legs and maybe that's not true in your case, because I think your arms are shorter. Okay. The interview. My first question: were you born looking like this, and where can I get some baby pictures of you that aren't already online?"

He withdraws his arm. "I can see what my folks have. They can send you some photos."

"Oh, great. And I can talk to them too?"

"They would love that. They'd love you. You're very much like—something about you is really familiar. I feel—almost at home."

"That's odd. I never feel at home. Even when I was a child at home I felt: dear God, who dropped me on this godforsaken doorstep? But back to you. Did you always want to act, or did it come upon you like a compulsion? Or were you discovered? Or did you have to submit to the cuddling couch?"

"You mean the casting couch?"

"Dear God, I'm sorry you had to go through that."

"I don't mean that I—no. I acted in high school, and afterwards joined a local community theater, then a small professional company. I auditioned. Lots of auditions. Lots of luck."

"Your face—you really won the genetic jackpot."

"I've never felt that way. I'm kind of alienated from the way I apparently look."

"Do you watch your movies?"

"Never."

"You know, that's funny. I'm the same way. I can't get through a single one of your movies. I try, but I keep pausing to stare at your face. It's like your face on the screen, even on my laptop, it's like your face is this hallucinogen. I get dizzy. I almost fainted once just looking at you. Even now I could lose consciousness. It's humiliating. I know age is just a number but you're fifteen years younger than I am and I feel—what?—like you're older. Like even though you must be about six feet tall you're this tiny little man who's come to visit. This wee little feller. It's the strangest experience. Like I aged backward and you aged forward. Back to the interview. What's your most humiliating experience?"

"You mean—excepting the present moment?"

"Obviously."

"I kept falling off a horse. For a movie. They put a brace on me and I still fell off the horse. The horse almost broke its leg. Thank god the horse was okay. In another movie—it went straight to video—I was supposed to dive into a lake and I couldn't do it. My legs wouldn't let me. I was terrified—and it made no sense. I was a competitive swimmer in high school. Maybe my instincts told me the film wasn't right for me."

"Or maybe under the water there was a giant steel spike and you would have been gored."

"True," he says. "Absolutely true. Why are you such fun to talk to?"

"I'm not, I'm really not. Have you been drinking?"

"Speaking of which—" He goes over to where he had draped his jacket over a chair and pulls a sack from the pocket. "Just some rum I had in my hotel room. A lubricant. To relax us both."

"That sounds so seedy, Brent Vintner. How long have you relied on the devil's juice?" I laugh to let him know I'm saying something outrageous.

"Do you have glasses?" he asks.

"I'm wearing them."

"No, I mean for pouring the drinks, Tabitha."

"Oh, certainly. Come into my kitchen. I bet that's where the cats are hanging out, by their watering hole. I mean water bowl. They're such animals. Oh, I meant to ask you, are your costars making you knit yet, or do you have to hold their balls of yarn for them like a kitten on a postcard?"

I open the cupboard and pull down an unchipped glass. Then open the dishwasher to find another unchipped glass. No luck. I give him the unchipped glass.

Once we settle back on the couch I tell him, "If we drink too much and too steadily I won't be able to ask the best questions during this interview." He shifts and the couch executes an enormous yawn.

"We'll pace ourselves," he says, patting my cheek. His fingers are uncommonly warm.

"Your fingers are uncommonly warm," I tell him. "They really are. Feel them. It's like you toasted them."

"Your cheeks are uncommonly cold," he says, running his finger down my left cheek.

"What about my right cheek?" I ask. "Are they both cold?"

"Oh they're freezing," he says.

I pop up. "Damn my landlord. He's always adjusting the furnace."

"Come back," Brent Vintner says. "We don't have all night. You're supposed to ask me questions."

"I should call my landlord—tomorrow. It would be rude to call him tonight. You're my guest. Also a meal ticket because I'm really relying on the biography to pay my rent. My publisher—her name is Rosamund—gives me such paltry advances. No one gets paid for anything anymore. So, okay, let's continue. What else humiliates you?"

He looks away. "Trying to be understood and failing every time to make my intentions clear. It's a problem I have. A big problem. If I want—something—I usually can't say it directly or make much of a move, unless I'm acting and then it's not real, it's acting."

"You know what I always say to myself when I have that problem?"

"I don't know, Tabitha, what do you say?"

"I say what Shakespeare wrote. I tell myself: Screw your courage to the sticking place. The only bad thing about that is that I think Lady Macbeth said it, and she's not exactly someone whose advice you necessarily want to take, you know? Plus, it's hard to remember the exact words. I keep forgetting the part about the sticking place and then it has another meaning. It's just like: screw your courage. Which is funny."

Brent Vintner takes my hand. "We're getting nowhere, aren't we? You don't like rum?"

"Oh I do. Rum makes me feel like a pirate. Like I could run a sword through someone and bounce around deck, you know? Then I think: why? A pirate's life is not for me. What did you want to be when you were growing up?"

"It's funny that you mentioned pirates. I thought I'd be one."

"Didn't you play one—in one of your first films?" I like the rum. I'm glad it's Captain Morgan's Rum, like someone is getting credit for it.

"You saw that! Really, you saw that one!"

"I kept having to pause it, but I did see part of it on YouTube. I saw part of the ending because your back was to the camera." My glass is already empty.

"That's the best thing I've ever done."

"You die in that film."

"I know. That's one of the best roles you can get—if you don't have to die too soon in the movie. To die at the end. That's a—gift."

"We all die in the end, don't we. Not to be philosophical. I'm speaking more—biologically. I think—I'm very tired now. Rum tired. It was gorgeous, that rum. Like drinking perfume and apricots all pressed in a giant drum. Like I'm being gently clubbed by lazy pirates. Can you forgive me, Brent Vintner, I'm very tired."

"Oh, Tabitha," he says. "I'd forgive you anything."

"Please don't," I say. "I would take such advantage of you if you did."

The Next Morning: A Proposition Sent Via Email

From, of all people, Piper Fields:

Can you come with me (I'll pay for your assistance) to a book signing/launch? At Bookits. Tomorrow. Ten a.m. for the children's book; 9 p.m. for the novel. As you know, it's really Maryann's work (even though you refuse to believe me or her) and now I have to sign the damn books. I really wish Maryann weren't prolific. She always finishes the books simultaneously. I don't know how she doesn't go insane. But would love company (i.e., bodyguard).

I Respond by Phone

My first question: "None of the children at the book signing are going to sing? Right?"

"What are you talking about? No. Why would they? Sometimes children hum. Otherwise, there's no entertainment. It's a small bookstore. A miracle if anyone shows up."

"Oh they'll show up. Parents are always pulling their kids out of the house. They don't want to be in a confined space with them for too long. And your cult readership—anything to meet other cultists."

"They'll try to steal the book."

"The children?"

"No, the cultists. I hope they don't try to steal the children—that's why the launches are set far apart."

I ask, "What do we do between the launches?"

"I think I'm going home to nap. Feel free to do whatever you'd like. There's a cot in the backroom of the bookstore, if you'd prefer to stay there."

"I don't know . . . I've never been in a bookstore that isn't haunted."

"I like that. I'll tell that to Maryann. Maybe she can write about a haunted bookstore where an orgy takes place—or where bunnies run the register."

"I wish I really knew why you want this sucker, Maryann, to say she wrote your books. Maybe you should say you both wrote the books and subdivide the unwanted attention that way."

MESSAGE FROM PUBLISHER

Tabitha, try not to have such a snotty tone in your emails and texts. That's not YOU. As you like to say, Screw your courage to the sticky place. Reconsider whether or not you want to write about Piper Fields. Think about it, Tabitha. She's a good bet—a better bet than Brent Vintner. She may be complicated. At least she'll give you the time of day.

Email to Rosamund and carefully NOT SENT because it's beneath me and an old bad joke that no one has ever laughed at:

Dear Rosamund,

I don't need anyone to give me the time of day. I have a watch.

BOOKSTORE HAUNTING

Who is talking? I look down and see a tiny girl in a purple satin tutu.

"What did you say, honey?"

"Are you the bunny?"

Earlier, I had tried on a blue and white dress with puffed sleeves then quickly peeled it off. The outfit looked like something an unhappy prairie wife would wear to run away from her husband. I chose this pink dress with a puffy bodice, hoping it suggested optimism—to myself. I did not realize I look like a mascot.

Another child peers up at me sulkily: "What are you?"

"I'm Piper Fields's friend. I'm here to help keep things organized."

Clots of parents. Some look like cross-over readers familiar with Piper's adult novels. Much non-discreet rubbernecking from that contingent. Other adults have that excited-to-see-another-adult look. Piper in a modest beige cardigan is lodged behind a table and signing books with a long thick purple pen adorned with an enormous ball of fluff.

"What are you?" This time the words emerge from a small boy wearing denim overalls with a sunflower embroidered on the bib. His mother has edged him forward to ask this ridiculously insulting question. She's the sort of parent who probably embroidered that sunflower. The sort of competent person who eggs her son to be assertive even in the presence of strange adults. It's unnerving.

"I'm Tabitha," I tell the little boy, as gently as I can, through my clenched jaw. "What's your name?"

His mother frowns and rubs his back. Next she'll give him mouth-to-mouth respiration because I'm not smiling as much as she'd like.

When it's her turn up front, the mother bends close to Piper Fields and looks back at me. She thrusts a book at Piper Fields who signs it—a very small signature, I can tell by craning. Not like the big scrawls with sweet little drawings she usually makes. The woman hustles away, nearly shouldering me as she heads out. Her little boy lags behind. I give him a high five and we're both happy.

A child throws down a stuffed animal on the signing table. Oh—a bunny. It looks positively maimed. Very floppy, apparently its insides sucked out. I manage to move closer to get a better look. A few of the other children are holding similar bunnies. I realize: of course there's a product tie-in with Piper's books. I should have known.

You can speculate about what these children are going to be like as adults by the way they treat those bunnies. One little boy is cuddle-kissing his while another bangs the bunny's head against a rack of Legos.

I'm supposed to be protecting Piper Fields but in this crowd I'm spending a lot of time looking down. Such short children. A sensation of wetness. A toddler is sucking on the hem of my dress.

Inches from me in line stands a woman in a dress as pink as my own. I tap the woman's shoulder.

"Your little girl is—here," I say, pointing down at the toddler.

"That's not my child," the woman says, glaring like I'm trying to pawn off this sweet little girl barnacled to my dress. I begin to sweat and look around, guilty already.

Once in Walmart I witnessed a child wandering and crying. I hurried up to her and said, "Sweetie, are you lost?" As if summoned by horn, the child's father barreled from behind a carousel of coats and shouted "Get away from her!" I was only saved from arrest because I'd known one of the store clerks since grade school and she vouched that children don't even like me.

"Is this anyone's child?" I ask the air, attempting not to be too loud, too disruptive, imagining that the parent can't be far away.

A flutter of interest. Much pulling of children closer.

The little girl gumming my dress isn't looking up. She'll scream when she sees I'm not her mother.

From my vantage point the child's right foot is visible and part of her left—tiny white sneakers with butterflies. Surely someone loves her. I just have to wait.

At last a man in a faded Chapstick t-shirt turns away from the signing table where he's been leaning closer to Piper Fields than a dentist, and duck-walks toward me. He strips the little girl's hands from my dress, hoists her, and says, "What you been up to, monkey?"

The woman I thought was the child's mother pivots to say "You shouldn't talk to her like that."

"He's not talking to me," I say. "I don't even know him." I look up at the man, "Do I know you?"

He ignores me, masterfully, before he says to his little girl, "Do we know her, chubby monkey? Do we? Who wants a cupcake? Chubby monkey wants a cupcake!"

He's holding not only the child, I see now, but his other hand, dangling, clutches a copy of Piper Fields's newest children's book *Bunny Carnival*. And—there it is—peeking from under the bunny book, a thicker book. Piper's name is on the spine. He's a cross-over Dad, getting double-duty out of the occasion.

Sudden suspicion: did that Dad force the toddler to grip my dress? Like I'm an old hitching post?

So much time to kill before the night-time book signing.

Napping in the storage room of a bookstore—how bold is that! For bookstores preserve within their confines compressed desire, and here they are, cartons of books upon books, all fudged with human misery. Napping is a little dangerous in case the spirits in those books enter the sleeping soul. I check to see if my biographies are here and they aren't. The smell of books, like time concentrated and stuffed into a leaf pile. As I drift into unconsciousness I say a little prayer for my publisher Rosamund, that she not abandon me, for I know not what I do.

I wake to the sound of voices. I'm not sure where I am, and then I see the boxes towering around me and realize I've probably slept for hours and should be out front, bodyguarding Piper Fields. It's comfy on the cot and the air is warm. I imagine that long lines of cultists are forming—those seriously disturbed people who aren't embarrassed by their fetishes being revealed by the fact that they're buying one of Piper Fields's supposedly transgressive novels. I think of my mother who claims the books are less transgressive than her old Betty Crocker cookbooks. "There aren't even directions!" my mother has complained.

And then, standing above me, looms a stranger. It takes me a moment to realize that under all the makeup it's Piper Fields. She's stuffed into a black corset and fishnet stockings. I expected more originality from her than a reprise of a Halloween costume from the mid-twentieth century. Her eyelashes are immense. She blinks and it's like her eyes are strained through baleen.

"Will you get out there with me!" she hisses. Her lipstick, a ghastly whale blue, almost matches her eye shadow, a ghastlier Edgar Allan Poe gray. She hisses again, "What am I paying you for?"

"The children thought I was a bunny," I mutter.

"Well, they're children. They're hallucinating, what do you expect? Come on, up and at 'em. I want you to look severe, like you won't let anyone mess with me."

It occurs to me that by having a signing/book launch for her new novel she's asking to be messed with. People want to see the face and body behind the near-pornography. As if she's read my mind, she says, "It's not pornography. Maybe it's erotica—but only for the imaginative. Basically, the books are realistic portrayals of the inner lives of average everyday people."

"There are no average everyday people," I say, defensively. "People deserve to be treated as if they're each—original."

The sound system has been playing classical music, and now there's a break in the music and applause.

"That's your cue," I say.

I wander out with Piper Fields, the florescent lights making me blink, and once again I regret my pink dress. How bright it looks, how sweet and comforting. How out of step with current reality. The pink is lily-livered, such a declaration that I can't hold my own in a fight. I try to relax and observe. One of the strategies I still need to perfect: observing my surroundings. Amazing how various the couples in the crowd are, some clearly just past driving age with elderly grandparents holding on to their arms. Some loners, fidgeting. Stick and poke tattoos, very well done on some. I'm smiling at these book lovers, even though a few are doused in patchouli oil, the last drip from Hell's furnace.

All gazes are on me, and the air bends.

One of the cultists—a short woman with so many spikes in her face she looks like a line drawing of a virus—thrusts Piper's new novel at me. Bodies are closing in, tightening in a circle around me. I realize with a start that these people think I'm Piper Fields. They are blinded by the disjunctive energy my dress is spewing, and this is infuriating.

"Go ahead," Piper Fields whispers, her corset creaking like wicker, "sign for me. I'll pay you double."

I whisper to Piper Fields, "I can't sign your name—that would be wrong."

"Just scribble," she says, "and then draw a house, like a little child would draw a house. They'll eat it up."

She pushes me into her chair behind the signing table and hands me a pen.

"What happened to the pen with the purple pompom?" I ask.

The new pen, fringed, looks like what a miniature Christ would have threatened the money changers with at the temple.

The first person at the signing table, a redhead with a daisy-bedecked bun, says "Book 5, Chapter 4." I turn to Piper Fields, who is standing behind me with her hands on her hips. She says, "I'll explain later."

This continues—the strange mathematical notations. Pretty soon I've figured it out. It's about which book and which chapter in that book meant the most to the person before me. I'm once more glad not to have read much of Piper Fields's oeuvre. I crane to scan the crowd and feel a wash of relief when I don't see the man in plaid flannel. Probably, though, unless he was wearing the same flannel shirt as when I first saw him I wouldn't recognize him. While protecting Piper Fields and her waffle I had never entirely "seen" the man. I saw plaid.

You would think, wouldn't you, that, as an author of biographies, I'd be accustomed to signing books. But Rosamund, for whatever reason, discouraged me from meeting the public. I've never signed a copy of one of my biographies, and after I tried to sign one for my mother she pulled the book away and complained about my ruining resale value. When my second cousin moved to Florida she actually gave me back my own books. Leon—world's best nephew—kindly had suggested we hold a signing in his bar for my biography of Killdeer. Why did I decline the offer? Rosamund had been antagonistic about the idea, almost as if she didn't want the book to sell. And then when I published *Annie: Her Life Story* I knew I'd think about my beloved Annie and burst out crying every time I signed a book. Then again, would The End of the World be the best place for a book signing? Drunks. Sticky tables. Old peanuts underfoot. Yes, yes it would be.

While I'm signing books with a flourish—sketching mountains, rockets, doughnuts, to everyone's weird delight—I experience surges of power. I should have brought spice jars, I realize. This crowd might find a new use for one of the rubs. Everyone at the signing looks radiant, like the whole bookstore experience qualifies as rapturous mischief. You can't help but wonder if the person handing you a book for signing has a fetish for deviled eggs and totalitarianism, especially if that person is carrying a tub of deviled eggs and sports on his wrist a tattoo that looks like Stalin with a hangover, but you do feel a sense of wonder. All these people in love with the written word, and no matter what's in the books it's unlikely that the plots will kill anyone in actual life.

Later, when nearly all the lights are out in the bookstore I ask Piper Fields, "Why did so many of your fans give me boxes of chocolate?"

"Oh, you really never have read the books, have you? Just a tip. Don't eat any of those chocolates." To my surprise and almost slathering delight, she slips me two one hundred dollar bills. "Believe me," she says, "I should pay you triple."

Later—it must be almost 2 a.m.—my phone rings. I pick up, breathless with hope.

It's Piper, even though we just left each other hours earlier. "Is it too late to be calling?"

"No, never," I lie, deflated.

"I always find it comforting to make fudge when I can't sleep. Anyway, I had a thought. You like to write and you're broke. Obviously."

"Does it preoccupy you—my finances?" I ask.

"I used to be broke too. I sympathize, and I know all the signs. Pretty obvious, those signs. The thing is, I hope you got a good sense tonight of what my life is like by signing those books, and I hope you understand how hard it is for me to pretend to be somebody I'm not. I hope you're now a little more sympathetic about what I go through."

"I can't imagine why you'd ever want to give it up. If you're not the author of those books, why don't you become an author? You could write both children's books and novels so that you could stop pretending that you're not an author. You could become what you say you're lying about."

She sighs into the phone. "You try writing children's books. Just try it. I mean, that's the idea I had. Why don't you write for children?"

When I'm silent, she says, "I really mean it. You probably could write a children's book. You're not going to make any money now that you've given up writing about me. You need money. Real money. Maybe you could whip off a children's book?"

"Oh no. I'm not violent. Plus, I bet it's really difficult. No one can 'whip' one off."

"Children enjoy mayhem. I know you don't believe me, but I think you'd be good at it. I can't write the stuff. I don't even want to. You probably could. Why not? Write a children's book. Really! You could flatten everyone's arse—no one expects anything from you. It would be—impressive. Don't you want to be impressive?"

"Arse?"

"I know. It sounds so much worse than 'ass.' "

She must be stirring her fudge. A spoon rattles against the side of a pan. "I know it sounds like a strange idea," she says, "but I do feel bad that you're so obviously out of luck in so many ways. Maybe you could try writing something new. Or you could collaborate with me on making people believe Maryann writes what everybody thinks I write."

"You're all gangsters. Whatever I would write about you, you would still be stuck in a web of lies. I'm certain you're not telling me the truth."

She keeps me on the phone until she finishes making fudge. It strikes me that she's lonelier than I imagined.

I Attempt to Write a Book for Children, Not Out of One Single Noble Impulse

It's an interesting idea, isn't it—my writing a book for children? I haven't had what anyone would call extraordinary luck writing for adults. What if I've been peddling to the wrong crowd?

Must try to convince myself, despite all internal evidence, that I can write a book for children out of goodness of heart and interest in bringing light to the world.

But how?

Source of inspiration? Try to remember own childhood? What I do know: children should feel love, not guilt.

Sins of childhood: putting rubber snake in mailbox to annoy mail carrier. Confessing to adultery as seven-year-old because lacked enough imagination to name a proper sin during First Confession. Buried a doll.

Children: what sorry lives they lead. Must write to give comfort!

Animals: children love animals because animals don't neglect or judge them.

Will not name nonhuman animal in possible children's book after famous human animal. No duck named Dostoevsky. For one thing, have hard time spelling Dostoevsky repeatedly. Keep trying and keep missing. Will not create cartoon-like dog named Dog-stoy-ev-sky. Besides, probably has been done.

Maybe I could write about a giraffe. Why not? Neglected in children's literature (how would I know for sure though?). Such beautiful animals, such long necks, like stepladders. How do they ever lie down? Strivers. Ambitious. Must have evolved by attempting to reach beyond all other creatures and their own innate capacities (at first).

I suspect this much: you have to keep things moving for children. A minute in time is experienced by a child in the same way that three days of ironing shirt collars is experienced by adults. Poor helpless kids. The way adults almost never leave them alone. And the way adults force children to sing in staged performances! And then adults applaud, no matter how poorly the children did. It's hard to believe how often children have to be fooled!

A name for the giraffe?

Gloria! The slow, long "O." The flirty "ee-uh." The name practically arrives with an invisible exclamation point! Yes, the giraffe's name is Gloria and her long neck grazes high leafy branches, and she loves to complain!

"Me neck. She's more trouble than she's worth. It's like operating a crane, me poor neck. I've got a backache from holding up me neck. Me poor poor neck."

Gloria's companion could be a fly? A fly lands on Gloria's long sooty black eyelashes, and the fly can talk too!

"You think you've got it bad! Half the day I'm washing me legs with me own nose."

"But me neck, me poor poor neck!"

Or Gloria's friend could be a Raindrop. A raindrop sullied by industrial run off.

Maybe there could be a series? In the next book Gloria could have a brother. And Gloria's brother could have a brother. Except it's a porpoise. They're half-brothers.

No, time to give up already. Cannot write for children, especially because children don't like me, and I have no governing inspiration. Will leave that up to professionals. Plus, fear doing psychological damage to most vulnerable among us. And I don't mean only children. The power of those authors of children's books is immense—the power to imprint stories upon us all. They might as well be making woodcuts out of brain tissue.

TEXT FROM BRENT VINTNER

Sorry I can't stop over tonight Reshoots

Response from me:

Shoot away

Text from Brent Vintner:

Tomorrow night? 6:45—for dinner?

Text from me:

Ok what do you want me to fix?

Text from Brent Vintner.

I'm taking you out It's on me Hope that's clear

SUSHI

We're at a place partially devoted to sushi, unfortunately. I don't want to be insensitive, but I can't understand. Evolution meant we appropriated fire. Sushi—an unhealed wound.

I have to hold myself back from telling Brent Vintner, "Please don't eat anything almost alive in front of me," and then of course I tell him.

He laughs, throwing his head back and almost hitting the skull of the man in the booth behind us. "Oh, Tabitha, this sushi roll is looking less appetizing by the second."

I'm trying very hard, again, not to be insensitive. Toni and Arturo learned everything they could online about sushi and give credit in the menu to their sources. And their sushi displays look fabulous—like bouquets of shining flowers, sushi in pinwheels, sushi in what look like windmills. And radishes whittled into sharp little tulips. I am always impressed by shaped food—bread twisted into braids or sculpted into a moon with moon rays or cakes that look like actual antique books with clasps and a red ribbon place marker. And yet the more beautiful the food the less edible—so often. My mother has always told me she and I have nothing in common, and yet we both cannot pipe frosting roses on a cake in any way that doesn't look like frog eyes.

Brent Vintner keeps smiling at me in a way that suggests he has a secret. Little filaments of hilarity beam off his perfect teeth. "What is it?" I ask.

"I was reading one of your biographies on the set today. It was impressive."

"Then why are you laughing?"

"It was—refreshing."

"What do you mean?" I ask. "Be careful. I was at a book signing the other day and I'm still recovering. I hope you're not going to hurt my feelings because my feelings are raw. I can't help it. Plus, yesterday I tried to do something I have no capacity for—writing a book about a giraffe—and, predictably, I failed. Still, it never feels comfortable to fail, no matter how much you're used to it. And then, too, my terrible intern keeps coming over to my apartment and asking why this person—Piper Fields—remember her?—won't talk to her. And I have nothing to say that can help my intern. Except for a few celebrity profiles—and working on a biography of you and for a while working on something about Piper Fields—I've only dealt with the dead. It's easier to write biographies about the dead, especially if they have no living relatives. You can intuit what their lives were like."

Brent Vintner taps my hand then pulls back. "You wrote one biography about a dog."

"Well, the dog was dead."

"You really got into the dog's mind."

"It was an experiment, admittedly. All sorts of remarkable writers have written about dogs, and so I'm not alone. Virginia Woolf, she wrote a book about a dog. No one reads it. It was the best thing she ever did. I don't mean the book itself, I mean writing about a dog. I myself found it so rewarding writing about that beautiful dog."

"You acknowledged that it was a compound portrait, right?"

"I was upfront about that, though it probably sounded like cheating. One dog's life isn't always very interesting. I had to play around with the possibilities. It will be easier to write about your life than about a dog's."

Brent Vintner taps my hand again. "Are you sure?"

I admit I'm not sure.

"Tell me about your regrets," I say, and then—jokingly I add, "and don't include this dinner."

"I'm not going to regret this dinner."

"I don't know. I just don't know."

"Regrets? I regret about two thirds of my movies. I shouldn't—they were opportunities. I should be grateful. Still, I'm gut punched when I see or hear anything about some of those movies. Not that I sold out, it's just that I said lines that weren't right for the character. I'm not going to tell you the titles—I'm loyal to the people I worked with. What else? I regret that I can't ride a horse no matter how hard I try. Horses don't want anything to do with me. Is that enough regrets?"

"Oh my gosh, you have so few regrets. What's wrong with you? Really, I'm disappointed. And that regret about not being able to ride a horse. Obviously you just haven't tried enough. I rode a horse once and we had a wonderful relationship. I let the horse do whatever he wanted, that's the secret. He just munched around and I sat on him and it seemed like a perfect relationship. That's the secret: don't interfere with the horse."

We eat in silence, and Brent Vintner does that strange thing: occasionally tapping my hand, grinning, eating his sushi while I try not to look at either him or his sushi.

"Tell me about your parents," I say.

He clears his throat. "Wonderful people, so caring and imaginative and kind and I'll always be grateful. Church every Sunday. They're retired. My mother was a nurse, my father was a high school teacher."

"Oh high school teachers—he must get so much hate mail. That always happens. You can be the nicest person in the world and some repulsive teenager wants to blame you for everything ten years after they graduated."

Brent Vintner taps my hand again. "That's about right. My parents would adore you. They would understand you."

"Why?"

"I don't know. You remind me of a cousin of mine."

"Is she dead?"

"No, thank god, but she has your sense of humor. I used to want to marry her when I was a little kid."

"Incest is interesting, don't you think? The family, you know? Can I ask you a few other questions? They'll seem very simple, maybe obviously stupid, like the questions middle schoolers ask when they interview the principal for a puff feature in the yearbook. But, you know, stupid questions can be revealing."

"Certainly. Ask away."

"If you were an alcoholic drink what would you be?"

"Easy. One of those bellinis your nephew makes. You told me you like them so much. I'll have to try one."

"Yeah, overpowering. Seemingly sweet, but the next thing you know you're milking a cow or something?"

". . . ?"

"I don't know where that came from. I've never milked a cow. Okay, if you were an illegal drug what would you be?"

"I don't know. What about you?"

"I've thought a lot about this. I don't think I could be an actual illegal drug already known to humans. Instead, I might be an undiscovered illegal drug. A really compelling fungus—one that's orange and looks slippery. With maybe these crystals all along the edges like salt on the rim of a shot of tequila. Let's get down to the really inane questions. What's your favorite color? No need to answer that actually. I know—from the internet—that your favorite color is green."

Brent Vintner asks, "What's your favorite color?"

"Green and purple."

"You don't have a preference for one over the other?"

"No. I hate to make choices. I always feel like I'm offending someone. Not that colors can be offended, although who knows? You know that Robert Frost poem about two paths in the woods and you have to choose the one less traveled by? I hate that poem. Okay. Here's another question. If you were an animal what would you be?"

"I really—I've never thought about it."

"You couldn't be a horse because you'd fall off yourself."

"That narrows the possibilities. What about you? If you were an animal?"

"You know, my name—Tabitha—it means either gazelle or ocelot. Isn't that odd? Whoever made up the name couldn't choose. In Greek, the name Tabitha is Dorcas—which makes no sense whatsoever. My mother told me she chose my name because it means elk. That's absolutely incorrect. Actually my name has biblical roots. There's a person in the Bible named Tabitha. She shows up first as a dead woman. The apostle Peter is brought to her poor dead body by her friends and he looks at her corpse and says 'Tabitha, get up.' And her eyes open and she sits right up. Then you never hear about her in the Bible again. Okay. Another question. If you were a tree what kind of tree would you be? You know what? I'm not going to ask these questions. I'm feeling embarrassed. I must be lowering myself in your estimation."

"Impossible," Brent Vintner says.

"I'd be a shrub, not a tree—in case you're interested. Do you have any hobbies? I'm sorry—I need to know everything about you."

"I used to fish with my dad. Painting. Painting fish."

"You paint fish or you paint paintings of fish?"

"The latter," Brent Vintner says. "Do you have any hobbies?"

"You know, I don't. I don't understand how anyone has the time. Getting out of bed in the morning—that takes a long time. You have to kind of force yourself out from under the blankets and trick yourself into thinking that the day will be different from every other day. But hobbies. I know these people who lord it over everybody with their bee hives. Like the rest of us don't deserve to live because we have no hives. I don't want to be like that—arrogant about a hobby. Do you know what the etymology of the word *hobby* is? It means a tiny rambunctious horse. That's what a hobby should be: not a hive. But painting portraits of fish, that sounds like such a nice hobby."

"The fish never complain," Brent Vintner says, smiling. So many lovely teeth.

"Okay. Last question. Do you have a favorite memory, a memory that's like a tattoo, it will be with you forever?"

He's quiet for a while. I wait patiently.

"I do have a memory I can mention," he says. "A really early one. I couldn't have been more than five. For some reason I'm outside my parents' house on the driveway and I run and fall. I look down and my knee is cracked open. Blood spurting. I remember thinking, 'I can take care of this. I'm not going to tell anyone about this.' I remember feeling proud and not telling anyone about my knee. My parents would have done anything for me then, and they're still that way now. But I think in that moment I developed a sense of self, of responsibility toward myself. I had the first sense of being separate from other people, not that I was different. We're all different."

We look at each other.

"So you went right into the house and pretended you weren't hurt and that's when you learned you could act?"

"I've never thought of it that way."

"You learned you could act like you're not hurt."

"You must have learned that too," he says.

"I bet you needed stitches. Maybe I should write all about any scars you have. Next time. Remind me. Just say the word 'scars' in case I forget. Oh, one last final question. Because you're an actor you have to act like another person. How do you snap back into being who you used to be?"

"I don't think I do. Every role can change you. You integrate it into your life."

"Like how after you lose someone you're never the same although maybe you look the same? It's like you lost an arm and everyone sees both of your arms and everyone thinks those are the only arms you have. You don't snap back into place because you've changed. And you like that?"

"I like that. I feel pretty fortunate. Don't you feel—fortunate?"

Interlude: Thinking About It

I know I'm fortunate. Of course I'm fortunate. I'm becoming more and more fortunate. I know how to live alone in ways that sustain me. Like, for instance, as I noted earlier, a little trick: I order a discount box of chocolates, and I never know when they'll come in the mail and so when they do come it's a surprise—like someone sent the chocolates. Little things like that can make you feel good and spoiled. Maybe frivolous too but you need attention sometimes.

But then, why do I feel like I'm having a slow heart attack? I have nothing to complain about. I have purpose: a biography to write. And there are people who'd chew off their own fingers to be sitting across the table from Brent Vintner, although my heart feels like tied-together bedsheets are being pulled out from the blood vessels, like prisoners are trying to escape and the bedsheets are tearing. How will I live once Brent Vintner leaves town?

The same as always, that's how I'll live. I will calm myself. I'll grow a crust over all my internal organs.

Returning to the Subject

"Yes, I feel wildly fortunate. I'm very lucky. You can probably tell that by looking at me. All this luck." I brush at the front of my shirt where the pad thai has made a map of some country I'll never visit. Brent Vintner is pretending he doesn't notice what's happened to my shirt by grinning at his raw fish.

How will I write about this man? How to do him justice? The only one I've ever got down almost right in words was Annie.

"Do you have recurring dreams?" I ask Brent Vintner.

He pushes his plate aside. "Regularly. I'm on stage in front of everyone I know—or that's the sensation anyway, that everyone I've ever met is watching—and I can't remember my lines. A pretty standard dream. I have it too often. What about you, Tabitha?"

I am thinking that Brent Vintner is one of the nicest people I've ever met. It's my job to ask him questions. He doesn't have to ask me any, especially about my dreams. Dreams are always boring. Nevertheless, I can't help myself and tell him about the bear at the top of the bridge. He's already paid the check—he insists on it—before I can finish telling him.

"And then what?" he says.

"And then the bear escorts me over the bridge. And there's someone there—it's God except there are curlers in his hair and a man is giving him a manicure."

He looks at me, his eyes shining.

I say, "You know, if pregnant women aren't supposed to eat sushi I don't know why the rest of us should."

Afterwards

I had only told Brent Vintner part of my dream. Yes, a bear escorts me over a bridge, and yes, God is on the other side in hair rollers and he's getting his nails done. But that wasn't all that happened. In the dream, the bear escorts me over the bridge and then unzips his fur and out of the fur walks Brent Vintner. The detail about how we then find God in curlers and getting his nails done—that's accurate. It's like God sees Brent Vintner and God realizes he isn't all we've cracked him up to be and has failed at grooming.

Transformations

How to write about Brent Vintner when he's so obsessively NORMAL and POLITE and KIND? I told Rosamund that I had an intuition that he'd do something ABNORMAL and thus warrant attention. He keeps on being hopelessly UNTHREATENING. As a consequence, I'll have to gussy up the context that surrounds him, but how? Must find something new and of some interest in Brent Vintner's background to make biography readable. Do not imagine will find murder or larceny. Incest?

Trial Sentences for Biography of Brent Vintner

Brent Vintner finds himself daily among indie actors with strong proclivities for illegal substances and the most dilatory of occupations: knitting. Knitting keeps his co-stars from doing what they otherwise might do: manslaughter.

Or: Brent Vintner sits in a sad little bar not far from the sad little piano and drinks draft beer from a chipped mug. An actor and a man of the people and for the people, if he weren't such an introvert.

Or: Just try watching one of his films and speed past his face if you can—it's a face full of light. Every morning he not only shaves off a nascent beard but a layer of cells until his skin resembles a well processed cheese, it's that smooth, that formidable.

Or: Brent Vintner is unusually empathetic about dogs. Reads about them, shows uncommon respect for any breed. He laughs often, a sound like change being spilled on a sidewalk and falling into an open drain.

Or: Brent Vintner finds himself dreaming the same dream repeatedly. He's on stage and has forgotten his lines. Even while dreaming he has high standards, and yet it's likely that he forgives himself for forgetting lines. Because he is refreshingly healthy and capable of almost obscene levels of courtesy, even toward himself.

How can I suggest to Brent Vintner that he needs more drama in his life without sounding patronizing? Given that he doesn't seem to need more drama in his life.

He needs, apparently, nothing more in his life.

Whereas, I am always asking: What am I supposed to do with myself, even when I'm doing with myself what I thought—yesterday—that I was supposed to be doing with myself? Why do I need so much and want so much? Know thyself: Socrates. Very sad advice given human limitations and what Athens did to him. Save thyself: that's what I would have suggested to Socrates.

Text Exchange—Afternoon After Sushi Night

Text from Brent Vintner:

When can I see you?

Response from me:

You can't I'm too busy writing about your life

From Brent Vintner:

What do you really know about my life?

Response from me:

You've given me some raw material that's almost enough.

From Brent Vintner:

I'd like to give you some really raw material

Response from me:

Is that a sushi joke? I'm too busy for really raw material I have plenty of my own

WHILE I'M WORKING AT HOME TRYING TO ACCOMPLISH SOMETHING, ANYTHING AT ALL, A PACKAGE ARRIVES

I open the package, wondering what it could be. Raw material from Brent Vintner?

The package is loaded with styrofoam peanuts. Those things should be outlawed. Good god. Slivers float into the air, possibly others attach to my lungs. No return address.

Inside, under all the layers: a teapot.

Immediately I send a text to Piper Fields:

I'm not returning your stolen goods for you Even though we're friends now

Response from Piper Fields:

Please keep it That teapot should be yours. All I ask is that you reconsider why not free me from a life of lying now that you know the truth?

Text from me to Piper Fields:

Take your teapot elsewhere holy man That's a paraphrase of a quote from Kirk Douglas in The Vikings You should watch that movie It must be about your thieving ancestors.

Text from Piper Fields:

My identity has been stolen from me What's a teapot in comparison to my identity?

Response from me:

I am not responsible for your teapot or your identity

The Royal Dispensation

I have enough "facts," don't I? And Brent Vintner deserves the benefit of my intuition, doesn't he? The authoring days, these days of composing his biography, I call these the days of royal dispensation, as if I don't have to be responsible, I don't have to pay attention to the normal world. My mind becomes like an enormous fold-out couch on these days. I just have to bed down some ideas!

Perhaps, upon its completion, Brent Vintner will be very very very pleased with the biography, built as it is from the foundation of my daily note-taking. He will see I have so much to offer: insight, loyalty, professionalism, self-discipline. Perhaps lack of self-interest on my part will be impressive? My highly developed sense of duty?

I feel like I'm writing my own eulogy.

Self-respect: where are you?

Pert and Pretty are no help as I grapple to get my bearings. Monstrous cries for attention, wrestling with one another. I play with them for an hour and they only want more.

My mother calls, without leaving a voice mail first: "What ho! Tabitha, how's the biography coming? Has Tinker helped you out?"

"Never."

"Are you sure? I thought she was working on both of them—the one about the actor and the one about the pornographer. Two for one. She wants to get them together too. A cute couple! How are the cats?"

We spend a half hour analyzing Pert and Pretty. They like to sleep with their feet hanging off the edges of chairs. It's charming.

After my mother stops talking, the question that her call provokes needles me: is Tinker Flatts taking over both biographies? Not just the biography of Piper Fields?

Is Tinker Flatts free-lancing? I want her to write about Piper Fields only. Or to try to do so. That's her right and Piper Fields's right to lie to her. But Brent Vintner? I've already interviewed him about his humiliations. She can't have him. She can't walk away in her big boots with his pretty face.

Awful thought: What if Rosamund's plan is for me to do the initial research on Brent Vintner and uncover eccentric, prurient details, and then she'll have Tinker steal my material, slap together twenty full-page photos of Brent Vintner, and turn my research into a coffee table book with minimal text?

Text to Brent Vintner:

Has a girl with big boots been following you?

Response from Brent Vintner:

Where are you Are you in big boots

Response from me:

Her name is Tinker Flatts?

From Brent Vintner:

Never heard of her

Response from me:

Be on the lookout

From Brent Vintner:

Where are you

From me:

Home

From Brent Vintner:

I can come over at 7 tonight

From me:

Great I will have questions for you

From Brent Vintner:

Do you need me to bring anything

From me:

Your body

From Brent Vintner:

You got it

From me:

I don't have it because you're not here

From Brent Vintner:

See you soon

From me:

Not if I see you first joke!

THE BROCHURE

A booklet addressed to me has been dropped off in the foyer of my apartment building—an advertisement for my ex-brother-in-law's macabre jewelry business: Keep Your Beloved Next to Your Heart Forever.

Why isn't there a term for former in-laws? Thomas calls himself "your outlaw" but that hardly covers the criminality.

COCKTAILS & TIME TRAVEL

"You brought limes!"

I am delighted that Brent Vintner brought limes. I can't look at them enough. Perfect green bumpy balls. Perfectly perfect. Like citrus representations of Brent Vintner.

He says, "And vodka—peach vodka. And more."

If I didn't know better I'd think he was guilty about something—the way I catch glimpses of his face quaking. Frankly, though, I'm so happy about the limes.

I ask, "How did you know I would love limes and peach vodka?"

"Something told me."

"Whoops—my phone! Oh, it's nothing. A mortgage payment is overdue. I don't even have a mortgage."

I look at him and wonder why he's here. And then I remember. "Oh—I need to interview you a bit more. We probably should go through some of your experiences on set."

"No one will be interested."

"Yes they will. Earlier today I went through descriptions of all your movies." I pull out a list. "Let's start with the one about time traveling."

"If we drink first, the interview will go more smoothly."

"You're right."

He makes the drinks, tooling around my kitchen. "You're like an absolute lawn boy!" I say. "Or do I mean pool boy? I can't imagine having a pool boy, can you?"

"You have a pool here?"

"No, and I still can't imagine it. Oh, you brought orange juice too—and squeezed peach juice. You could run your own smoothie business!"

"That I could. Tabitha, let's sit down. Let's go through those movies as quickly as we can and then I have something I want to—"

"You want to leave right away? Is that it?"

"Tabitha, no. I want to stay. But I don't want to talk about myself."

"Been there, done that—for you. I don't know hardly anything about you and I have to write the blasted biography. I'm thinking that it may have to be a kid's edition at the rate I'm going, or some little paragraph for *Entertainment Yearly*. I want to hear your perspectives. Your first big studio film—the one where everyone travels through time."

"I'm traveling through time now, Tabitha. Listen, I won't be in town forever. We're wrapping up in about two weeks. Money's running out. The film's a disaster. I'm a disaster. I don't think a biography will work, Tabitha. I don't think I'm going to get much work in the future either."

"Are you going to do something incredible to get in the limelight? I told Rosamund that you might assassinate a political figure, but I was joking, trying to sound like a solid forecaster of trends."

"I don't want the limelight. I'd be happy with regional theater. I'd be happy with heavy construction work."

"But you dated top models!"

"I know and look where it got me."

"I know—it's sad, you're in my living room drinking peach vodka with me. It's very sad. You deserve more."

"I'm glad that I'm here. You know what? I'll act again. It will work out. That was self-pity talking."

"Your self-pity even sounds better than my self-pity! You should hear my self-pity. I start feeling so sorry for myself, so sorry that I'm so lonely I could eat my own arm! I could peel off my skin and hang it off the balcony—that balcony, right past the sliding glass doors?" He glances over. "Sometimes, my skin is strange, like it's percolating. You know, for the sake of your life story, I really hope at some point you lived out of a car."

"I did."

"Me too. It was awful. I may be living out of a car again very soon. I don't know how I'll pay my rent—yet. Let's not talk about that. Please. What do you think of our quaint village?"

"I like Midlothian. It's peaceful. People get along. When locations were scouted they wanted a quiet place. Actually, they thought, for atmosphere, that it should be grittier."

"We have a cement factory."

"They didn't scout in spring. They didn't expect things to be so—blossoming. The director, Alberto, he wants to wrap up before things get even more spring-like. He's aiming for the whole atmosphere to be pretty sinister. Tragic."

"Do you get to die?"

"I do. Toward the end."

"It hurts to think about that. I hope you get a happy ending, even so."

"Alberto thinks happy endings are cheap. At most he goes for ambivalent endings. Maybe an absurdist twist. It's about status and punching the audience, leaving them reeling. That's why he's taken seriously."

"Well, I think comedies are deeply serious. And true to life in a certain way. Comedies hurt just as much as anything. It's just a different kind of hurt. Have you ever laughed at a funeral?"

"Sadly, yes."

"Me too," I admit. "I didn't want to either. I had to turn the laugh into a coughing fit. Like projectile coughing."

"Why'd you laugh?"

"A woman fell."

"And that was funny?"

"I know. I know. She was wearing these very high heels with elaborate straps. Like gladiator sandals except with five-inch heels. And she slid and fell right in front of the casket. I was so ashamed of myself for laughing. But she wasn't related to the man. Just nosy. She goes to all the funerals. And then she got up, not even embarrassed. And she bowed."

"She bowed?"

"She bowed. Like the funeral was all about her. Her funeral and she's still alive."

I don't know how Tinker Flatts got in, but she's standing in front of us, and good manners force me to introduce her to Brent Vintner. "I didn't hear your boots," I say. She looks enormous because Brent Vintner and I are sitting down and also because she carries herself with such authority, like she's climbed every mountain.

She makes a brushing away gesture. "What are you two drinking?" she asks, looking directly at Brent Vintner.

"Oh it's fabulous," I say. "I can make you one?"

"I'd like that," she says. "I'd like that very much." She's still gawping at Brent Vintner in the way she gawps at lobster bisque. I know because I watched her once at a restaurant when she didn't know she was being observed. She didn't even eat the bisque, she just watched it. Something about her tilts the entire living room of my apartment. The way she stands over us, like a scene in a movie. Strange how nearly everything seems like a scene in a movie before we recognize we're inhabiting reality. All those layers—a memory or a dream or a movie—to swim through. No wonder everything seems to be happening simultaneously. It's difficult to touch your life, to pat it, to make sure it's real.

I hustle out to the kitchen, assemble ingredients. Voices are floating in from the living room—mostly Tinker's. I catch snatches. Nothing she says is unexpected: words and phrases like "incompetent," "really not capable," "sorry you have to deal with . . .," variations on a theme.

The drink sloshes a little on the counter. I wonder where the cats are. They knew Tinker Flatts was coming before I did.

When I reenter the living room with the drink I decide to be forthright and ask Tinker, "Aren't you busy with Piper Fields?"

Tinker exhales heavily. "That's why I'm here. She's furious. She says you've been impersonating her."

"What?"

"She says people think you are her. You pretended to be her at her own book launch. People took photos. Now they think she's actually you. It's your face they're recognizing. She says your face is too bare—no makeup. This big face that people think is her face. She's enraged."

I'm almost speechless. "How ironic on so many levels! She asked me to sign books for her. She pretty much demanded it. I didn't even sign any name that was legible."

"You always make things work out in your favor—no matter what."

"Nothing has ever worked out in my favor."

Brent Vintner is looking between the two of us. "Should I leave?" he asks.

"God no," I say. "One sane person in the room would be helpful."

Tinker doesn't finish her drink. "My work is done here," she says, setting her glass too hard on my coffee table "Now you know what trouble you've caused."

When the door closes I put my head in my hands.

"It's going to be fine," Brent Vintner says, patting my back.

I look up. "Oh I know. I didn't expect Tinker to be such fun. She's really risen in my estimation."

"She doesn't understand you at all, but you understand her. That must be infuriating to her."

"Thank you."

Brent Vintner nods, touches my hand, withdraws his own hand. "As I was saying before that woman showed up, my life isn't worth a biography, but if you want to do a short profile—something you'd get paid for, I could help you. We can continue with the interview for that at least."

"Oh—this drink—I'm not quite myself," I confess. "I think we've blown our wad on this interview."

"Good. I have a question though: how will you earn a living if you're not writing biographies?"

The thought of what I might do swims before me. "I can always go back to working at the credit agency. Or maybe I can't. I can also wait on tables. People never tip me though. I suspect I'm too arrogant. I kept getting fired. No restaurant in town will have me."

"How could you, of all people, be too arrogant?"

"Advising people on their dinner choices, their wine choices. I couldn't bear to see people eat anything that had already fallen on the floor in the kitchen. I'm not cut out for waiting on anybody."

We are both silent for too long. "I have an idea," Brent Vintner says at last. "Come to the set. Meet the director. He might be able to use you. He's acting like an idiot lately, but he might be able to use you."

"Why is he an idiot?"

"He wants to remake Alfred Hitchcock's *Vertigo*."

"Oh my god. How is he allowed to live? That's not possible. *Vertigo* cannot be redone. Has he even seen the movie? A man falls in love with a woman who resembles another woman and then finds out the woman he loves was impersonating the actual dead woman whose husband had planned the actual dead woman's death. And then the woman impersonating the dead woman dies because she's spooked by a nun. And who could play the Jimmy Stewart character? And his best friend, his Miss Moneypenny type of friend who designs bras? I've always thought she was the movie's true hero, designing those bras. Or maybe she was drawing bras? I can't remember. You can't help but wonder—"

"It's been a long time since I've seen the movie." Brent Vintner sets his glass down. "Tabitha, there's something I'm finding hard to tell you. I should confess. I'm here under false pretenses. If you want to, you can still write a short profile about me, as I said, but it's not the right time—if ever—for a biography. You won't want to write a biography about me now."

"You really think it's not the right time for a biography about you?"

"There's something I've found out."

He's not looking at me—a bad sign. I don't look at him, but that's natural—he's too hard to look at.

Brent says, "My ex-wife—"

"I didn't know you were ever married! I researched online and there was nothing about marriage. Nothing even about a divorce. That's impossible!"

He sighs and taps my hand. "We worked pretty hard to keep it a secret. Tabitha, she's written a book. A memoir about her life. I'm in it. It's not a good time for a biography about my life, Tabitha, if there ever was a good time. I'm sorry. I know how much you wanted to write one."

I try to look at him and bleat.

He goes on. "Tabitha, I had to okay the book—because of lawyers. I got the PDF this afternoon, right after I invited myself over. It's a short read. Once you read it you won't want to write about me, I can assure you. And the fact is, I really don't think I could take reading what you'll write. I'll send you the PDF—you deserve to see it. You've put a lot of time into thinking about my life. But, Tabitha, there won't be a biography. If there were one, I'd want you to write it. I'd trust you. But trust me, there's nothing about my life that merits a biography. And my ex-wife's book will be released soon. I don't think it's a good idea for there to be another book out in the world that's in any way about me. I should have told you that as soon as I came over. Pretty selfish of me not to tell you as soon as I got through the door. Please know how—"

The Ex-Wife's Story

I am an ex-wife, and thus I am inclined to agree with other ex-wives, and so I can hardly breathe when I open the PDF. What has Brent Vintner done? How has he ruined this woman's life?

Can I Bear to Read the Manuscript?

Just because you download something doesn't mean you have to read it.

Her name is Joyce Pernell. Oh crap, she begins with her family history. I really wish memoirists wouldn't do that. If I have one piece of advice for memoirists: avoid discussing your parents. WE DON'T CARE. Your family, they're dull and they're your problem.

She includes, upfront, photographs of her parents and two sisters and one brother. These people don't look alike. It's when siblings look alike that it gets eerie. It's like you're examining a flock, not individuals. You have to keep turning the knobs of your attention to get a fix on any one of them.

I am skimming away, allowing myself little bursts of egotism and outrage. The way she keeps using the word "robust." I suppose that's to hint at the future moment when she will discover Brent Vintner, whose body is nothing less than robust. This woman is using the word "robust" when referring to a sand castle at Cape Cod.

As a child she performs in dance recitals. Thank god she soon becomes an adult after which she undergoes months of auditions. At last she gets roles on television, usually playing a murdered woman. Too many scenes spread out on a morgue table. I'm feeling sad for her. A difficult life, playing a dead woman.

I skim faster. Oh no. Brent Vintner comes into her life. The intimacies. The obscene moments of candor. The various locations for their unnatural natural acts: once at a funeral parlor! No! Her great uncle dies and this is how she honors the man. Then the wedding ceremony on a beach. Like one of those destination weddings that earn your relatives' hostility as you snort up their vacation time and retirement savings. Except this woman and Brent—they don't invite anyone and neither Brent Vintner nor his bride are as famous as they will become and she has a different name before she has any genuine luck acting and he has a first name: George. Brent is his middle name. I didn't know that. Gradual diminishment of affection on her part. She complains that he reads too much! Good god, she's a monster.

As if a man could read too much. Thank god Brent Vintner reads too much. In fact, it would be impossible for him to read too much. Poor Brent Vintner, formerly married to a woman who has no appreciation for reading even though she's expecting us to read her book.

Does this woman never get rejected—for anything? At least I don't have to wallow around in page after page about rejection—that's a plus. It's not like I'm reading a printed-up version of a reality show. It's always painful when anyone asks why they have been rejected in those shows, isn't it? Asking why you're rejected: it's like pushing a tack into your eye and attached to the tack is a note that says "Not you." There's never a reason. Although once when I was subbing for Leon behind the bar a woman told me she had a reason for rejecting a man on the first date. She showed him a few of her drawings she had on her phone and all he said was, "I don't really like art." So all she said was, "I really have to go, it's an emergency" and then moved one barstool over. That same woman, she's the one who told me about bears. She read somewhere that bears give birth while hibernating. The cubs get born and suckle while the mother bear hibernates, totally unaware, and later the mother bear wakes up to find cubs frolicking beside her in the cave. The bear hadn't even known she was a mother. Those mother bears lead lives that even Kafka couldn't dream up.

At the bar this same woman—I wish she hadn't only been passing through Midlothian—told me she had a unique ability: whenever she saw a movie starring Matthew McConaughey she could smell him. "That's right," she said. "I see him—on television or in a movie, it doesn't matter—and I'm sure I can smell him." I asked her what he smelled like. She said it depended on the movie. I asked if she could smell anyone else, but it didn't work with anyone else. She said, "It's like there's some oil that collects on Matthew McConaughey and it transmits fragrance through the airwaves." Why am I remembering this? I guess it's because of Brent Vintner's ex-wife's memoir—as I read her memoir I could smell perfume inserts.

Two more chapters. Why did Brent Vintner think this is a quick read? Much cleverness involved in buying a floor lamp. Perhaps this person's book is a vanity project meant to burnish her reputation as not only beautiful and wealthy but literate. Oh, here we go: she's buying a horse sired by British royalty. No, something squirrely with the syntax. The horse was only mounted, possibly, by a member of British royalty, a dim cousin. So much good luck otherwise—this woman is drowning in it.

You have to appreciate someone with good luck, don't you? Sometimes when I'm especially sad and disheartened and wondering how I can be a more purposeful person I try to think about a friend from ages ago and her good luck: her career as a pioneering engineer, her successful marriage, her twin children who are often seen on Facebook wrapping their arms around her neck (lovingly) . . . It seems like her good luck might rub off on anyone who contemplates her. Maybe this book is meant to create good luck for the reader by showing how there are a lot of dead spots in our own luck but it's still, basically, luck?

Why can't I jump into the practice of wicked optimism! Optimism so far-reaching that it is a force unknown in nature. Then again, how did Brent Vintner ever survive this woman?

And yet, he's lucky. His ex-wife doesn't report many truly ugly things about him at all. He was only nineteen when they were married and she's gone on to other alliances. What can she hold against him? He snores? So do I. Leon told me the truth when I stayed over in his guest room. Apparently there are high pitched moments when I sound exactly like a weasel. Her other complaints? Brent Vintner is boring? She doesn't know him, obviously. It doesn't sound like they ever had an actual conversation. He has trouble advancing himself and saying exactly what he wants? Oh no, flog him! Or don't! She put him through such a sexual obstacle course. But outside of all that exercise she found him too Midwestern for her taste, like he was her own little flyover country.

Nevertheless, I can see why he doesn't want another book about himself or even a pamphlet floating around in the world right now. The book will be available in early August—still in time for beach reading. And it will sell because his ex-wife is highly descriptive about not only Brent Vintner's body but the body of men and women with far longer careers in movies than Brent Vintner has enjoyed.

I study every photo of her in the PDF. Reader, he married her. He married the long dark glossy hair and the heart-shaped face and the wide, luminous eyes. How could he have helped himself? She looks so crushingly small . . . which makes me feel tenderness toward her. How could Brent Vintner not have felt the same?

The book is called *My Life's Journey Through the Stars.*

I really hate that journey metaphor and yet—here I am at a waystation. It appears to be an old stage coach that I'm stepping out of so that the horses can be watered and unsaddled. I'll stay for the night in a small hostelry (in my mind).

I will say this: Brent Vintner's ex-wife can really handle a frothy sex scene with various women and men, including Brent Vintner. I never knew condiments could or should be involved. Now I am suspicious about Tinker Flatts's tattoos.

The thing is, Brent Vintner's ex-wife isn't what most people would call "nice." Is that what attracted him to her?

The Problem With Niceness

What if niceness is a form of capitulation and spineless conformity? Not at all! Or evidently! I want people to be nice to me. But do I have to be nice to them? And yet I am—possibly. At any rate, I want to be.

Or am I just jealous of some not-nice people because their bodies look so nice it would upend the balance of nature if their behavior turned out to be nice? Cleopatra experimented with poisons on people and watched them drop dead. Not nice. But she was the memorable one. She got the perfumed barge.

Calling Brent Vintner Late at Night Against My Better Judgment & Not Mentioning the Unnerving Memoir Written by his Unnerving Ex-Wife

Me: It's just me. I'm sorry it's so late to be calling. [Remind myself yet again: do not mention his ex-wife's memoir to him—ever.]

Brent Vintner (voice groggy): It's okay. Are you all right?

Me: No—I mean yes. It's just. I have questions.

[Note to self: must not allow own voice to suggest how good it is to hear another human voice at this time of night]

Brent Vintner (voice even more groggy—near snore): What? What? Okay. Okay.

Me: For my project, even though you're requesting that I write only a short celebrity profile because you don't want another book floating around that's in any way about you, I need to hear about something you did that you're ashamed of.

Brent Vintner (sound of starched sheets, blankets being pulled—probably he's sitting up. Snapping sound: bedside lamp is being turned on): Tabitha, really?

Me: I could use your help.

Brent Vintner: I set myself on fire once.

Me: Oh, that's great. That's definitely helpful! Why'd you do it?

Brent Vintner: It wasn't a political statement. I was a stupid kid. Sixteen. I forgot that when I gassed up the car I got some gasoline on my pants and then later I lit a cigarette. I dropped and rolled and a friend threw a coat over me and I only got singed. Lucky. I was lucky. What about you? It's your turn. What are you ashamed of?

Me: I don't have to answer that.

Brent Vintner: It's only fair that you answer that. You woke me up.

Me: This is very embarrassing.

Brent Vintner: Good.

Me: It happened a long time ago. Remember that.

Brent Vintner: Remembered. I'm awake now.

Me: Okay. It was at a music festival and I was wearing a suede vest with fringes.

Brent Vintner: That must have been really long ago.

Me: It was, you weren't even born yet. Or no, you would have been very young but born.

Brent Vintner: I'm sorry I wasn't older.

Me: Oh don't say that. You would regret being born to witness what I'm going to tell you about.

Brent Vintner: You're delaying telling me. You're trying to come up with another, less embarrassing story. Not fair, Tabitha.

Me: All right. I guess I can trust you. I'm going to tell you this very quickly to get it over with. You know that suede vest with fringes? I was proud of it. I felt—in that vest I felt free and easy and beautiful. A music festival: local bands so you can imagine how bad it was. Anyway, people kept staring at me. I thought they were admiring my vest. An old man called out to me, "Hey, Davy Crockett!" Anyway, I felt special and admired. Then I saw myself in a mirror and realized that my right breast must have been poking out all night like a dog nose.

Brent Vintner: Oh, Tabitha.

Me: I know. Okay. That's all right, I guess. One more question: Who was your first love?

[Realization: oh no, am I bringing up the subject of his ex-wife—without meaning to do so?]

Brent Vintner: This is going to sound like Charlie Brown.

Me: That's cool. I love Snoopy.

Brent Vintner: My first love was a little dark-haired girl in second grade. She had the roundest face—like her face was traced with a paper plate. She wore these glasses with clear plastic frames. I liked her so much I could hardly face her. I used to squint when she was around. I squinted so much my eyes hurt.

Me: Thanks. That's all for tonight.

Brent Vintner: You're having trouble sleeping, Tabitha?

Me: I'm going to hang up now. Good night!

Note to Self

You should never have told that story about the vest/breast. Now your guts are hanging out.

Note to Self

A mystery that haunts: hard even to imagine that Brent Vintner and his ex-wife were legally wed. Painful to think of how easily and quickly she disposed of him and now uses his fame and the fame of other celebrities to catapult herself forward. How disorienting that secret marriage must have been for him.

Must stop rereading that PDF and erase from my consciousness Brent Vintner's ex-wife's prurient descriptions of his body. Why does this woman focus so much in her memoir on that intimate aspect of her life with Brent Vintner and with so many others? How was she raised? If I had a daughter I'd never refer to anything even vaguely related to the act of copulation in any form. I'd just throw a pamphlet on her bunk bed and be done with it.

Reading that PDF = torture. Again, must stop. Feel a bit filthy afterwards. Must not take more notes regarding PDF.

Message to Publisher

Dear Rosamund,

I'm afraid I have to return both advances, eventually. Nothing is quite working out as planned, despite my due diligence. Perhaps this is for the best. Brent Vintner has acquiesced, as a kind of personal favor, to my writing a short profile about him and has explicitly requested that I not write anything longer. In other words, I won't be writing a full-fledged biography about him. Not to be repetitive but just to be clear: at most, I'll compose a lean little profile about Brent Vintner fit only for online distribution. I seem to have backed myself into a corner now that I won't be writing biographies of either Piper Fields or Brent Vintner.

Thank you for all the support you've given me. I should mention, however, that it may be some time before I'm able to return the advance monies. I hope you understand. I should never have adopted those two cats. They're wildly expensive and generally ungrateful.

Who Needs Biographies Anyway?

Biographers? They need biographies? Selfish of them?

Now what do I do? Of course I had wanted to focus solely on Brent Vintner, interviewing him, talking easily with him, learning about him, smelling him, feeling his finger tap my arm and wrist. And now, given that I'll only be writing something short and possibly not publishable or postable, there's no reason in the world for Brent Vintner to spend time with me.

I am like a woman on a ship drawing away from port, away from a country she had only begun to discover. I must sail away—and where am I sailing to? No, this analogy doesn't work. And yet—I keep seeing a woman on a ship and the ship is going nowhere. It's like the ship is stuck. Like the sea has turned to taffy.

Those people who talk all the time about the dignity of failure, how you have to keep going, how anything of worth includes hundreds of thousands of hours of failures (do not remember the exact research), those people who talk about taking the wrong path until it becomes the right path, that's easy for them to say. And to say again. Well, they're failing to be comforting, they ought at least to admit that.

Not good thoughts.

An Expected Voice Mail

"Tabitha! I saw you on the sidewalk today and you looked so strange. Like a wolf. Your nose was crinkled in a very unattractive way. You're letting yourself go, Tabitha. You don't want your rear end to intimidate the moon. Remember that! The best way to tell if you're expanding is if you get the gripes because your waistband digs. Is it the beer at The End of the World? I used to know a tall man with a beer gut—he looked like a drinking straw that sucked up a possum. I'm referring to his pouch. Or what do you call it? Paunch? Anyway, must skedaddle. Things to do, places to go."

The Lives of Twins I Have Known

I don't think my mother has ever been lonely. I don't know how she manages it. It's like she's her own twin. Whereas I think I've been lonely since I was born. Even when I'm with Leon.

I went to high school with two sets of twins. The most attractive people in class, they also had the best grades. They were also the most confident. They were so popular they acted like they didn't need us; they had each other. I mean, each twin had a person from the other set of twins. I know all twins differ. Those twins—they were like beings descended from the gods and goddesses. And so beautiful that the lords of creation made two of each. Maybe for some twins it's a gift on the order of upwardly mobile reincarnation.

Never to be lonely—what could that possibly be like?

Insomnia, Again

The worst thing: the gate is lowered and memories attack and you see by enemy-light. As a counter-offensive, I labor to remember lovely things: first birthday cake. Five years old. I'm sitting on the next door neighbor's garden fence and the neighbor runs to me holding a cake: white frosting, pink, yellow, and blue roses. My first birthday cake. The neighbor is crowing: "I just had to see your face. Before your mother comes!"

I don't remember eating the cake, only how surprised I was. A memory like that might sustain a person. Cake.

Bits of flotsam spin around, and more memories swirl: my mother and her work as an upholsterer. Much stuffing pulled out. Elementary school: back then I cannot understand why the word "what" contains "h." Someone—who?—cutting an apple for me with a shiny knife and handing me a slice. Mattie saying, "I love you more every year. I didn't think I could love you any more than I do, that that wouldn't be possible. But I do." Getting a $20 tip from a kind woman when I had to wait tables and my glasses broke. Buying my first laptop and writing, writing, writing notes to myself. Lilacs.

Bad thoughts slide in. What is the name for a group of flying bats? A cloud. A cloud of bats. Bats not flying inside my head. No, bats hanging upside down on wall inside my head. No need to make notes about those thoughts. Will remember. Disgust at self for bleating when talking to Brent Vintner.

The heart-cracking sensation. I've made a mistake and don't know what the next mistake will be.

Self Report

Sometimes, you know, you just need to check in on yourself because otherwise . . . otherwise what? I've had this lingering sensation before and have been able to wait it out, you know? I just typed "you know" as if anyone is listening.

And maybe that's the problem. Who would listen? I don't even know what's wrong except that there's a kind of loneliness I'm overly familiar with and it threatens to become a howling meteor that's miniaturized enough for me to swallow it, and now it's inside my throat and growing and growing and soon there won't be an inside inside of me. No, the meteor will come rushing out because I'll be a bubbling ball of space gas. Does that make sense? I don't know how to explain it any better, the sensation that I don't quite have skin. Years ago that feeling manifested in a whole other way. Back then I always felt I was behind an enormous glass panel. I tried to explain it to myself: it's because you're wearing eye glasses, Tabitha. And then I felt better. Using my own name made me feel better, as if I wasn't alone.

What Is It That Has Pulled Me Under So Many Times Before?

Why should I believe that sadness, which afflicts so many, can pull me under again? Sadness has no independent existence. Sadness is not swamp monster patrolling. And yet—sadness must poke from inside me to be recognized by me. Like old movie, *Alien*. Sadness eggs were implanted long ago and I have been warming them for appropriate moment. Self-fertilized eggs. Why does sadness pull *under*? Because weighty. Like rock. No, boulder. No, rock. Rock because I am glass house.

The End of the World

"Tabitha, why are you here?"

"I'm not allowed? It's not a public bar?"

"It's late. You're never here this late."

I don't see Blowman tooling around cleaning up tables. "It looks like you need help. I really want to help. I want to help you, Leon."

Predictable, what people leave behind. Sticky quarters and dimes. Crumpled napkins. Beer mugs festooned with industrial strength lipstick. It won't be easy getting those mugs clean even in Leon's steaming dishwasher.

Someone abandoned a bag of corn chips on the mini baby grand. I attempt to hustle over to the piano, protectively. My legs sink in invisible sludge. Partway there—everything seems to take so long, even walking across the barroom—that's when I notice how soft the piano looks, and I imagine that if I ever put my weight there the piano would sink like a scorched marshmallow.

"You didn't walk here, did you?" Leon calls over to me from behind the bar where he's cleaning out the cash register. "You did, didn't you." Normally at night I'd drive "to confuse the perverts," Leon likes to say whenever I pull up in my car.

He insists on walking me home but first says "Wait." He comes out of the kitchen with a carton of eggs. "You can use these," he says. And this: he hands over $10 in a wad of one dollar bills.

"Why?" I ask.

"You bring in customers—that pissy Piper person came in the other day and your buddy Brent Vintner stops by too. You clear away glasses. You swept up last week when Gilbert blew off coming in. It's not The End of the World without you."

Normally I'd refuse the money. I feel a little desperate, admittedly. Funny how Leon's kindness makes me feel worse.

As we walk toward my apartment the trees along the sidewalk are melting, the dark shadows as soft looking as the piano at The End of the World.

"What's wrong?" Leon asks. "You never walk this slow. Did someone hurt your feelings? Every day if someone doesn't hurt my feelings that means I haven't been awake."

The shrub at the corner shrugs. It must be so tired.

Leon comes into my apartment with me. Pert and Pretty run to him. He sits in the biggest armchair and they swarm him.

"You brought bacon bits, didn't you?" I say. My voice sounds far away and slurry. I know he brought bacon bits. Pert and Pretty are inhaling him.

"I love these monsters," Leon says. "They love me and my bacon bits." He addresses the cats. "Do you love me for me or for my bits? Huh? Huh?"

Pert and Pretty dance on his chest, rising to his shoulders in slow, tail dripping motion. Their meows sound like they're coming from under the city's sewer system. Everything is so far away.

Self Report

Have turned off phone.

Have enough food for cats. Set out three extra bowls of wet food and three of dry food and four bowls of water.

Must pause.

Notes unnecessary.

Resurrection

The difficult thing is that you have to die first.

A Scene of Panic (Condensed)

Is it comical when men burst into your apartment and one of them says "Get her a glass of water" and one of them brings in a pail of water and the other man says "Not boiled water—she's not having a baby"? That is a scene from many movies—never a scene from my life.

It is not easy for me to retrace how I came to be lying on the floor with two men standing above me and looking down uneasily. I want those men to believe it's a bout of the flu or that I hit my head on a drain pipe. Anything. But as I lie on the floor and Leon lifts my head to enable me to drink a glass of water it's apparent that he and Brent Vintner are considering if they should call an ambulance.

I must convince them that I would be mortified, that this sort of thing isn't unusual, that perhaps they've simply never noticed how common it is for a person to find themselves going down for many hours, almost imperceptibly, until the most natural thing is to end up on the floor.

While Leon puts a glass to my lips I review plausible excuses. I sit up partway, attempting to stretch my arms over my head. It hurts to do that. My arms have taken time off from their usual job of being arms and now are stiff.

"Careful, careful," Brent Vintner says.

"I'm fine," I wheeze.

How long had I been lying there? Longer than they could have guessed. I will say I was impressed that Pert and Pretty hadn't taken advantage of me.

As I warm to the job of convincing Leon and Brent Vintner I'm all right I begin to feel that way, that this period of hibernation, of a loss of all meaning, has served a purpose, resetting my mind.

I'm still only half sitting when Brent Vintner folds himself down beside me and puts his arm around my shoulders. It is a brotherly gesture, a gesture of solidarity brimming with such kindness that my eyes water. It is evident to me that he too has experienced a sinking down, that he too has found himself stretched out on the floor and viewing the dust debris under his couch and an ancient empty bag of Fritos and a busted ink cartridge. That when he looked up the room spun and a spider on the ceiling became a facial mole in search of a face.

Leon says, "You're covered in cat hair, Tabitha."

"I'm so glad," I say.

"You're dehydrated, Tabitha," Leon says. "That's all it is—dehydration."

"Thank god." Brent Vintner jiggles his legs. "I'm really sorry. Do you need anything? Can I do something?"

After Leon assures him more than once, Brent Vintner apologizes again. "I'm really sorry that I have to get back. I should have been back hours ago. Will you be okay?" He waits until Leon gives me another glass of water. I forget to thank Brent Vintner before he leaves.

Leon sits with me at my kitchen table. "That's not going to happen again or at least not for a while?" he says.

"I didn't know it would happen. I thought I was doing okay overall. And then it was like I kept getting shorter and shorter and then the floor was so close and cool against my face. Was it awful? Were you embarrassed? I'm sorry."

"Do you ever think about seeing someone?"

"I just needed to fall down the rabbit hole, Leon. Lewis Carroll was brilliant. That book describes the stages I go through. Maybe I'm the only one who goes through them. Although maybe—do you?"

"Yeah. But I come out quicker. You linger, Tabitha."

"Kind of lazy of me. I'm okay now. If I just let myself feel things all the way to the bottom after a while I wake up."

"What's it like when you're all the way on the bottom?"

"I won't remember—not for hours. And then it's kind of a secret."

"Tabitha, you need to see someone."

A Feat of Memory

It doesn't take a few hours to remember. It takes twenty-seven hours and then I see the place where I had been sunken—so deep but not quiet. The roar in my ears. The sand turtles and rocks and the low sky, storm clouds boiling, and the grayness of the water, a long slick covering the sand, and I couldn't look anymore because my eyes wouldn't open again.

To not travel there—how busy I'll have to be. How necessary that I undertake a meaningful project that will not sink under me, that I find a way to keep my life afloat despite the coming waves.

A Very Kind Phone Call

Brent Vintner calls me the next day, apologizes again and again for having to leave the day before, says something about how things are going to be very busy for him—something about rewrites, reshoots, everything going wrong with the movie, being needed on set, and then he apologizes again for having to leave and not being able to see me today or tomorrow or the next day or . . . and then he says he really hopes I'm feeling better, much better. And as he speaks it is a wonder that I don't fall through the floor with shame. How it all must have looked to him when he and Leon found me laid out like a ragged old pelt from some extinct animal. How sorry he is that he must protect himself by not seeing me again—that is what he's telling me. That is what every sorry, sorry, sorry means.

Assembling Oneself

Must not burden others. Must be own burden. Must change my life.

Each day: make bed. (I read on three websites that this simple act allows self to assume control over circumstances.)

Each day: Gratitude. Remember how lucky you are.

Each day: Consider options fully even if options mean reversing earlier options? Take every opportunity to fulfill need to write about another person's life (reconsider Piper Fields biography?) thus crafting a way to understand how a life might be shaped, even if subject of biography lives by lying? Must have faith in ability to ferret out truth? Must continue—somehow—to tell the story of someone or some thing's life?

Each day: Help others.

Helping others in action: Take action by texting Leon. Remember less fortunate.

Text to Leon:

Me: Do you need any help today?

Leon: No.

Me: None?

Phone rings ten minutes later.

Leon: You're broke? Is that it? You want to charge people for tarot readings again?

Me: No, never. It was probably illegal. People got upset. Even Blowman.

Leon: Especially Blowman.

Me: I couldn't help that someone put all Death cards in my deck. Anyway, the Death card is supposed to mean transformation. Not actual physical death. Some people are idiots. Can I help that? I only texted to see if you need anything.

Leon: I'll think about it and get back to you.

Me: Thank you.

An Attempt to Renew Health

Recommit to exercise. Don't just sit around all day and self-mummify even though enjoy being seated. Must reconnect fully with body. Don't want to be like head pickled in jar in old science-fiction movie. Must become useful to others and to culture at large. Volunteer at The End of the World more often? See if old group Clean Water! wants to reconvene?

Trying yoga again but keep forgetting to breathe, and yoga program online makes me sleep in corpse pose. Plus, the session leader keeps nattering on about peace. Decide that fresh air is best. Will not forget to breathe while outside.

Fear I am having palpitations—from yoga. And from profound sense of loss. What did I lose? I had nothing to begin with? Self-pity. Am not enjoying it as much as usual.

I Engage in Movement

Walking around the block is not only good exercise but connects me to the neighborhood. Let's me notice little things—particularly neighborhood dogs. I prefer those on leashes. The wisteria at the apartment building three doors down are coming along nicely—with long tendrils. I pretend to myself that I am having a close encounter with neighboring shrubs.

Remember that the roots beneath the earth are living. It might be helpful to hear the soft cheep of a sparrow.

I breathe in the warming air and feel myself coming more alive with little gusts of resentment.

I cross over the street and head into Jesmun Park.

So many memories of walks in this park. Talking about the word "dapple" with Brent Vintner. Other memories—not all of them good: last fall's community scarecrow competition. Each scarecrow numbered. A scarecrow woman with a scarecrow dog. A scarecrow doctor with a stethoscope next to a scarecrow patient on a table, the scarecrow patient's stuffing spilling out. A musical scarecrow holding a guitar, like the guy you avoid at a party. A scarecrow at a desk bent over a laptop. (I identified: how did I manage when I didn't take notes? Mistaken conviction: that not taking notes would allow me to "live in the moment." Forgot too many moments. Denied myself pleasure of self-gossip.) A scarecrow woman in a flowered dress, her face a burlap bag, her eyes blue painted circles. So sweet. She was holding a bouquet of pink and red paper roses. Simplicity. "You're not scaring anyone," I told her. That's when a couple stopped. I stepped aside to get out of the way and the woman startled. "We thought you were part of the display!" Her husband cried out, "Don't move!" and took photos. I laughed to regain my dignity and said, "Oh, it must be my hat!" And my dungarees.

I'm so glad I'm not wearing a hat and dungarees. No one's going to confuse my identity today.

Ahead of me, two women are speaking loudly as they stroll. So loudly that I don't have to pretend not to be listening. Obviously they intend to be heard.

Woman 1: I want to go to Stone Harbor. She always wants to go to the mountains, any mountains, even dipshit mountains like the Poconos.

Woman 2: Well, Rod never wants to go anywhere. It's funny. He's really really passive—like Jabba the Hut lately.

Woman 1: I don't know if I can stand going to the mountains. She wants to go to the mountains because she wants to frustrate me.

Woman 2: Can't you do both? I wish Rod wanted to go anywhere. We go out to dinner and he orders the same thing. Crab cakes. Nothing changes. I don't know how I can go on much longer.

[Note to self: I LOVE these women. Why can't I have a friendship like theirs?]

Woman 1: I know I'll wind up going to the mountains just to make her happy. She always gets what she wants.

Woman 2: What's her secret? I'd like to get what I want the way she gets what she wants.

Woman 1: Endurance. She enjoys arguing. Which she doesn't call fighting. She calls it "exchanging points of view." And then she does all the talking.

Woman 2: Have you heard a lot of screaming lately?

Woman 1: From that house behind your house again? The acoustics aren't so good where we're at.

Woman 2: I hear everything. The guy who lives there keeps yelling "I'll kill you all."

Woman 1: Have you called the police?

Woman 2: No, I know him. He doesn't mean it. He says what I think.

The women leave the park and turn east on Liberty. I keep walking west, feeling almost refreshed, as if I've run a block and built up a healthy sweat from holding back on joining those women's conversation.

In the Dark Woods of Life

You know what I love in novels? When a woman runs through woods. Unless she's about to be murdered. I love when she drives through a wooded countryside too. Or somehow, in any way, passes through an area lined with trees. It's like all her old ways of being and all her old habits fade away behind the woman. The woods become her or she becomes the woods and not in any way that suggests she's captured. No, it's like she's moving into her own—for lack of a better word—soul.

When she emerges into the daylit, necessary, agreed-upon world, she's not quite the same. Although no words will suffice to explain herself to herself or to anyone else.

When I used to pick elderberries, I came upon a bush that was so lush, the lushest ever, lit up with bright purple bead-like berries. Then I realized my mistake. I was looking at the shining eyes of birds clustering. The birds lifted at once and sent the bush shaking. I don't know why I'm remembering this except that afterwards I ran through the woods with my heart thumping and aching and I felt so much wonder.

I would like to feel that sense of wonder again, but my mind is skittery. I even fight back flashbacks of my own wedding day, in the deep misty past. I can't help but recall my mother insisting on giving me away. A year later I found out that, after she let my arm go, she executed a comical, vaudeville-style kick to the back of my gown for the benefit of onlookers. She wore a long white dress at my wedding (at least she skipped the veil) and invited her most boisterous female friends to tell jokes so filthy they unsettled the father of the groom. If only there had been a nearby woodland to run through.

Seeing Someone

I think I'm all right by now, but Leon keeps saying I need to "see someone." That's what Leon calls it: "seeing someone."

I suppose I do have to see someone because forks are sticking out all over my body. To go through a doorway I have to pass sideways. Of course I know that actual forks are not sticking out from every inch of my body, but the sensation persists.

I make an appointment with a therapist. Her office is only five minutes from The End of the World, she has a four and a half star rating online, she will accept my pitiful insurance, and her name is Irene. A good sign: my beloved grandmother Mattie loved that song "Goodnight, Irene."

The photo on Irene's website shows a muscular young woman lying on her back and stretching to touch her toes, thereby executing what's called "Happy Baby Yoga Pose." Evidently she has no inhibitions, and I am full of admiration. I tell myself: you are taking control of your own well-being. You are being responsible. You are going to "see someone." You are going to do what fortunate people do: pay someone to listen to you.

Good Afternoon, Irene

The office is small. A beige couch, a laptop on a desk, a black leather armchair where Irene sits. No windows. Much lavender scent. A white noise machine at my feet which, presumably, will keep our conversations private and not channeled to the dance studio across the hall. A box of tissues at my elbow as an inducement to tears.

We're in an encased chrysalis from which I hope to emerge, winged. This association is not arbitrary. On each wall hang framed prints of butterflies emerging from their twiggy wads.

Irene immediately wants to know about my past.

Irene: Your family—are all members alive?

Me: My mother, very much so. My father was no longer alive by the time I was two years old. But I don't want to talk about my family.

Irene: Are you married?

Me: I don't want to talk about that.

[Summary of what I immediately tell Irene: My husband was a choir director for two high schools and occasionally taught voice lessons. Eventually I learned that he was involved, each of those seven years of our marriage, with a recently-graduated high school senior. There must have been, in the end, three of those tragic young women. Because of him I learned to detest every number from *The Sound of Music*.]

Irene: My my my.

Me: Can we not talk about my past? It's over.

Irene: I need to know the basics at least.

Me: Can we do this quickly?

Irene: Please go on.

Me: Okay. Quickly. We lived in Maine during my marriage. I never fit in. Everyone was so self-reliant. They made their own soap.

Irene: How awful.

Me: It was, it really was.

Irene: And after your divorce?

Me: I came back to Midlothian and took classes at the college in Hiram, working my way through by waitressing and clerking—not a lot of job opportunities. It was difficult in my classes—I was older than the other students. But I loved my English courses at first. And a course in mythology.

Irene: You didn't finish?

Me: My grandmother—Mattie—was ill. She couldn't live alone any more.

Irene: How did you feel about not finishing college?

Me: Some of my professors weren't very encouraging. They didn't love what they taught. I knew I could love what I read on my own. And while I was helping out Mattie I was educating myself. And I wrote—I starting thinking about how to write about people's lives. Which led me to begin to write biographies and profiles. But that's not—

Irene: I see. Time flew by too quickly, so much time, and here you are, trying to find meaning and purpose and to be alert to—

Me: That's not why I'm here. I'm here because of this physical sensation I have that isn't really ultimately a medical issue.

[I explain the problem about having to walk sideways.]

Irene: You feel like you're covered with forks?

Me: I do—on every part of my body—a fork is sticking out.

Irene: That's your unconscious trying to tell you something. You realize that many physical manifestations of pain are actually rooted, like dreams, in a literalization of the language that we use to describe our realities?

Me: No.

Irene: Okay. You say you feel like you're walking around with forks protruding from your body? You know what that means? Your plan—whatever it is you're planning to do or whatever relationship you're pursuing—it's not going to work out. In other words: stick a fork in it, it's done. Now do you understand?

Me: . . . . . . Oh. Oh.

Irene: You're grieving the past, Tabitha. You're grieving for all your mistakes, all that lost time. Human life is a series of crises, I always say, and time for healing after any crisis, no matter how long ago it happened, cannot be rushed.

[What I do not say: Then why am I paying you and on time too, otherwise you charge a late fee?]

Irene: So resistant, so resistant, Tabitha. It's time for you to tell me much more. Otherwise, what are you paying me for?

Reflection

Difficult to write these notes with forks stuck on forearms and finger tips. Must not pity self. Must move forward. Must pull out of muck. Must act.

A Reconsideration

That popular idea about how making your bed each morning causes you to gain a sense of strength, order, and purpose?

That idea doesn't work.

At least not anymore. I must have been deluding myself. Have difficulty attaching meaning to concepts and objects. The words all seem wrong. What is a bed? Why are we told to "make the bed"? How did such an expression emerge? It could have been "clothe the bed"? Or "squeeze the bed into its ghastly wardrobe."

Remind self: you have a large life. A large, large life. At any rate, it's going to get large. About that, I am determined!

Then again: smallness, underestimated, frankly.

Message to Piper Fields

Dear Piper Fields,

I'm reconsidering the substance of the earlier email I sent to you. Perhaps I can, after all, write a biography about the so-called author "Piper Fields." I will entertain the charade that another woman wrote the books published under your name if I can indeed interview both you and that woman (Maryann) at length and if you will herewith withdraw your complaint against me in which you claim that I usurped your identity because I followed your own directions at that book signing and your cult followers thought I was you because they're sincerely confused people. Please call very soon. We can arrange a meeting at your earliest possible convenience.

Message to Publisher Written Immediately After Message to Piper Fields

Dear Rosamund,

Please ignore my earlier email about my being unwilling to write Piper Fields's biography. I was out of my mind. Temporarily I lost my sense of indignation and my mature ability to confront two challenging situations. My mind has now recomposed itself after profound sleep-hibernation. I missed more than fifty text messages from Leon and Brent Vintner, and I don't know how many emails, and at last woke to find the actor Brent Vintner standing above me as well as my nephew Leon who has the keys to my apartment and let himself in. I was blessed—they hadn't called an ambulance.

I confess that I succumb to freakish incidents of torpor at times of greatest challenge. Perhaps it is related to the survival instinct: the tendency to lose all hope for a meaningful life, and while facing the void to lose conscious connection to other living beings. And then slowly to be drawn downward to the floor.

At this point I'm writing to make it clear that I will focus on writing about Piper Fields and have no intention of returning in any capacity to the credit agency or to any restaurant that will have me as a waitress despite my ability to speak honestly in any situation.

I insist that Tinker Flatts assume the position of intern—and intern only, not as a subversive substitute for me—and agree to learn the ropes instead of roping herself into a project that I initially was contracted to fulfill. Is that too much to ask?

Another advance would be nice. For Brent Vintner I will continue with the more modest project I mentioned earlier: a celebrity profile for online distribution, most likely, and thus I will at some convenient point be returning the portion of the advance that involved my earlier agreement to write a full-length biography about him. Anyway, I really don't have the heart to interview his family members or the razor-thin models he dated, etcetera, or any other love interest past or present. No reason—I simply don't have the heart. I prefer to concentrate my attention on writing a full-length biography of Piper Fields.

Thank you for your understanding.

Why Am I Losing My Voice Even Though I Took Action and "Saw Someone" and Have Just Now Re-Committed Myself to Biographical Project?

I sound like I'm climbing out of a well, and then I don't sound like anything at all.

The voice isn't separate from the rest of the body and requires the entire body's assistance.

One's voice reveals our health and our emotional state.

The voice is an alarm, and each voice is individual—that's why there's such a thing as a voice print.

I am relatively sure that this speechlessness is being enjoyed by those who know me. Very much afraid to tell therapist, Irene. She'll think it "means" something.

Responses to the Loss of My Voice

Leon: Have you ever heard of a moth that makes a high pitched squeal? Your voice has that quality? Maybe keep on being silent, so you don't strain it.

My mother: No unnecessary blabbing—it may be for the best.

Piper Fields: Why aren't you answering my calls? Why are you only texting? That's not like you. We need to meet.

Brent Vintner: Nothing from him. By that I mean: silence. And more silence. Silence upon silence upon silence.

Irene, thank god, is out of her office for a week, and so I can't report this strange new symptom even if I wanted to (and I don't). Anyway, I know what she'll say: that I've lost my voice because I'm afraid of what I might say to someone. Or she might say that I'm angry about something I won't admit. Or she'll think of a common saying: "Silence is loud." Or . . .

I'm not evolving anymore. I could happily live like a jellyfish except at an earlier point I developed a brain stem.

The lilacs from Brent Vintner—I keep changing the water, but they are beyond dying. They've been very dead for a while now. Maybe I can dry them and press them in a book if that doesn't sound pathetic, like a jilted teenager does with a never-worn prom corsage. My voice—I still find it hard to talk, as if forks migrated onto tongue.

TOUR OF MY APARTMENT

Ever since Brent Vintner was in my apartment—twice in fact, no, three times because of the time when I couldn't get up off the floor—I've come to see my apartment—differently. Maybe I never really saw it before, and as a consequence my apartment went unseen and neglected.

The fact that I don't put up pictures? Is that wrong? Aren't I, in a sense, freeing the wall to be itself, undisguised? And the fact that there are still unopened cartons from my last move, doesn't that suggest a certain casual, ready-to-take-action personality trait which in turn reflects on the apartment itself, making it seem the perfect place for undisclosed adventures? Or is the apartment a reflection of something in my personality that remains opaque? Or maybe the apartment isn't about me at all. My apartment is itself the narcissist, waiting for the right inhabitant.

Couldn't it be much worse? You don't come into this apartment and think: this is where someone is going to be killed. Nor is there, as I've mentioned previously in another context, diphtheria. It's clean and serviceable. The kitchen is a little too narrow, but the linoleum is attractively cracked: yellow and pink patterning, the colors merging so that it's like walking on broken clouds. I suspect that linoleum was laid upon generations of earlier linoleum which gives the kitchen floor a nice rubbery bounce. My apartment may have its secrets, like what's behind the refrigerator, but otherwise it's a tranquil place. True, sometimes the guy on the first floor experiments with putting his mouth on various implements not usually considered musical—a garden hose, etcetera—but otherwise it's often relatively quiet here.

And then I look around at the room I'm in, the so-called living room, as if the other rooms are deceased, and I'm trying to be kind to the apartment, and it seems to me that there are beautiful things here, maybe not on the walls but on the shelves in the alcove. All the books, especially that red and gold set of Trollope, the sea shells given to me by a little girl who suddenly ran to me and placed them in my palms, and the golden pony—that perfect little plaster statue, gilded gold, that I've loved very much because it reminds me of Mattie. And there's also the tin cat statue that Pert and Pretty knock off the shelf every week and, of course, the dried up lilacs. My apartment—there's nothing to be ashamed of. I'll defend this apartment. It's been loyal to me, after all. No echoes. Being silent means nothing echoes.

A Sad Discovery

Found on the counter in the vestibule of my building: an envelope with my name on it. I immediately regret tearing open the envelope when I recognize my ex-brother-in-law's handwriting. Inside: a spoonful of what must be my ex-husband's ashes. Panicked, I don't know what to do. Then, the seldom-seen Emmie Gootz, who pays for part of her rent by cleaning around the building, hustles up, pushes the ashes into her hands, and runs out the exit and tosses them into the street. "This place is such a mess," she says. "They should pay us for living here."

I try to thank her and my voice comes out in a croak, but that croak is progress.

Unexpected Visit

Am I experiencing an apparition?

"Tabitha, please don't think you're a pain in the ass to me. You have been and sometimes are, but I think I know what you need and I'm not here to ask you for a favor."

My mother hands me a cup of coffee—very hot, encased in a steel cylinder.

"Don't expect this treatment ever again, Tabitha. Mother's intuition. Sometimes we all need a little help. You may have lost your religion, but I know you still think of coffee on the order of a gift from the outstretched hand of Jesus Christ on the cross. Tabitha, you have to wipe that dead look off your face. Look. I brought you an entire bag of coffee beans. Unground. It says here on the bag that this coffee has afternotes that taste like cherries and chocolate and caramel and citrus. Too bad. I know you're like me on one count: you just want to taste coffee in your coffee."

"I'm so glad you're here. I'm really really glad."

"Speak up. You sound like you're stuck in a tin can."

My mother won't sit down when I point to the couch.

"Tabitha, I remember like it was yesterday the day you were born. Before I could even see your face the nurse whisked you away to clean you up because you got yourself all gunky. Then they brought you to me and you were wrapped in a blanket, this teeny tiny newborn, and I looked into your face and my first thought was: 'Who is this little old woman?' I knew from the start that it was unlikely we'd have much in common, but remember: I'm your mother. I've never once forgotten that. Even though you came twenty years after your brother, who made me a mother by being born. You are not at all like your brother, I'll say that."

"When's the last time you heard from him?"

"Not long ago. Not really. His wife—what's her name—"

"Gaia."

"They both care so much about you. Gaia sends you those self-help books and you need self-help books."

"I want to choose my own books. Those books—"

"What was that one that bothered you so much?"

"*Aging Gracefully.*"

"I don't know why your brother married such a dolt. Aging gracefully! Tabitha, grace has nothing to do with it. You should listen to me, not read some antiquated book. Someday you'll learn something from me."

"That's what Mattie always said."

"Oh she was a piece of work. She was right about one thing. Listen to me and learn."

I'm so grateful to see my mother—someone who's always known me and even has a gift for me—coffee—that I'm weeping. Leon will laugh when I tell him about my mother's visit and say: why? why? Why should it matter so much that my own mother does something unexpected, appearing in person when she knows I'm in distress and bringing me coffee? Even at my age, I need her. I'll need her even after I'm dead.

I miss her while she's standing right in front of me.

It makes perfect sense that my mother is adept at upholstering. She takes shapeless things, worn down by years, flattened and slumping, and builds them back up by aggressively stuffing them and then sitting on them and applying all her weight. This is not a small talent, I'm beginning to realize.

"Don't expect this again," she warns as she moves to the door. "You're stronger than you look. Remember: there's a good likelihood we're related to members of the Donner Party. Which tells you a lot about the survival instincts you inherited from my side of the family."

Already I can feel it—my throat coming unstuck.

A Special Offer

A warning directed to myself: because I don't have the excuse of writing a full-scale biography of Brent Vintner or ever seeing Brent Vintner again, I may be tempted to lean too hard on Leon for companionship. I have to avoid that—Leon has his own life—and I have to remind myself repeatedly that Brent Vintner has no reason in the world to want to see me again now that I won't be writing his biography—per his request. He's a busy man, an actor. He can see anyone he wants. For all I know, in future years he might be knighted by a king or queen. And I'll be able to say: I interviewed him. He introduced me to Captain Morgan's rum. I will not say that one afternoon he found me stretched out flat in my living room. I'll make myself forget that, won't I?

"Take this," Leon insists. He's in my apartment, propped against the refrigerator.

I flip open the booklet. "These are massage coupons," I say in a firm, nearly clear voice—my almost fully restored voice, "and they're all seven years old."

"I called and they're still honoring them."

The coupons are inscribed "Happy Fingers." Under four hands are two slogans: "Unwind from the Grind" and "Glow & Go." The coupons have to be from a friend of Leon's—someone he is no longer talking to. Someone who paints ceramics.

I ask, "Does this mean you think I need to relax more?"

"You do need to relax more. At least take one."

"Okay. One."

"That coupon covers full price and includes a tip," Leon says. "Don't let them squeeze you dry. When are you going?"

"This isn't one of those places that exploits women and requires them to do more than massage anyone?"

"They're certified massage therapists, Tabitha. It's entirely therapeutic. I've never even gone."

"How do you know then?"

"Word gets around. Ask for Gwyneth."

HAPPY FINGERS

I don't usually do things immediately, believing as I do in the ultimate value of procrastination, but I am trying to change my life so that I can be more helpful to others and more stable, and less prone to making Leon worry. Last night I felt a strong attraction to the floorboards in my living room and had to fight to stay upright. I must take action.

Therefore I immediately arrange an appointment and drive to the outlet mall on the south side of Midlothian. A massage must be valuable. It's possible to imagine one's body rebalanced and restored. A stranger's hands palpitating my body—something about that makes me queasy, admittedly, but massage is an ancient and highly developed practice, even spiritual?

"Do you have anyone to drive you home afterwards?" the woman at the reception desk asks. She is wearing a long white coat, like a physician. Her lower teeth resemble the opera singer Pavarotti's—like those of certain small dogs.

"I came alone."

"Well, then, you'll have to wait at least a half hour after your massage before you're capable of driving. Not to sound like we're giving you a colonoscopy or anything!" Crisply, she hands me a pen and a paper form to fill out.

I experience the dulling of all my mental faculties—the same dulling that occurs whenever my body is about to be examined, which only happens in a doctor's office.

No one else is in the waiting room. Ferns, armchairs, a tank of fish swimming from one end to the other of the glass. The tank looks well-tended but the fish look depressed.

I leave blank any question that would violate my privacy and shuttle the form to the desk.

Minutes later my name is called by a short, officious looking woman who appears incredibly clean, even polished. She escorts me to a dimly lit room, hands me a robe, instructs me to undress. Before I can undress, the woman—she is, by all evidence, the masseuse and has a sorrowful face—looks me up and down in almost a proprietary way.

"You know, you have this cute little tummy." She bats at my stomach. "That could come off. We could freeze it next door. They have the equipment. You'd look so much better."

"I don't want to look better. I only came for the massage. I just want to relax."

"If you don't care about how you look you must already be relaxed."

"Maybe I'm relaxed and don't know it because I'm so anxious."

"Please be sure to take off your glasses. I don't want to get them all smudgy-mudgy. I'm going to be using our special lavender and violet lotion, okay? You'll notice a slightly warm, tingling sensation."

She leaves while I undress. When she returns her timing is uncanny, like she's been peeking through a hole in the wall.

"Oh, like this, sweetie," she says, "you have to lie down on your stomach." She adjusts my head until it fits in the opening on the table. A funny thing—without my glasses I lose not only most of my sight but my sense of smell. She could rub me down with Crisco straight out of the can and I wouldn't know it.

I feel pelt-like stretched on the table and horribly shy. She pushes my head back into the hole. This is all done with the authority of an executioner before the guillotine blade drops.

She thrusts an elbow into my back. "I can tell you're all knotted up. Toxicity. Fear." She presses her other elbow deep into my left shoulder blade.

I visualize chicken bones dropped into a dumpster after a barbecue.

"Keep your head in place," she says. "What are you afraid of? Nothing can harm you here. Your fears are being pushed out, out through your ribcage, out through the massage table, out to the floor, and from the floor down, down, down into the big old belly of the earth. Your fears are being pushed right down and out. Your fear that your love will never be returned, that you'll die in tremendous pain, that you'll only be able to communicate by moving your eyelids. Your fear that you'll be strapped to a goat's carcass and sent to wander in the desert. Those fears have to go. Go, now. You have a right to be here, to be in the universe. You are stardust."

I want to turn over to see her face. It would be a relief to tell her that I fear being driven off a cliff. I fear that when trying to help someone I'll accidentally cause their death. I fear that I'll vanish from the face of the earth and there won't be even one trace of me. My books will be burned, and not because they're dangerous.

"You have many, many, many knotted places. Has anyone died in your family this week?"

"No."

"I can't hear you, your voice is muffled. That's okay. Whether someone died or not, there's so much dead meat on you. We'll loosen you up right quick. Here's your spine, like a long line of beads or like a long train track, and where's the train? Oh, the train skipped the tracks!"

Late that afternoon Leon calls. "How was it? Great, I hope!"

I answer him.

"I can't make out a word you're saying. You haven't lost your voice again? You haven't had a stroke?"

I am able to say "No," and "Call . . . back . . . in . . . hour."

He calls back, almost on the dot. "Tabitha! What the hell!"

"Sorry. I could hardly get words out. I'm still blubbery. That massage—I never want another one as long as I live. That one can last for the rest of my life. Leon, you didn't warn me."

"Tabitha, I'll sue them if they hurt you."

"I'm not hurt. I'm just—it's like the person working on me liquidated my muscles."

"That's a good thing, right?"

"I couldn't stand up for nearly an hour. When I finally managed to walk out to my car I couldn't feel my hands on the steering wheel. I was treated like a piece of raw beef that had to be tenderized with a hammer. And the hammer was that woman's hands. And then I was treated like I was something that had to be poured into a loaf pan and the last bits of dough were sticking to the side of the mixing bowl. Then she did this weird dusting thing with a feather, a purifying ritual and I felt so dirty."

"Did you ask for Gwyneth?" Leon asks.

"I didn't think you were serious."

"You should listen to me. Maybe you got someone who was transferred from the other place—the one that was closed down. All Hands on Your Deck. You can imagine the fun people had playing around with the name of that place."

"I don't want to imagine that."

"You feel better now though, right?"

"I feel less human. Not that I'm without hope. It will just take time. I can't wait too long, though, for my skeleton to re-calcify."

"I'm sorry, Aunt Tabitha."

"Don't be. At least she didn't hit me with a stick and treat me like a witch and feel me up for an extra nipple."

TEXTING

From Brent Vintner:

Your intern invited me to party U going?

Response from me:

What party?

From Brent Vintner:

Your mother's house?
Friday night? 9? Meet you there?

From me:

Oh that party See you there

Note to Self

Poor Brent Vintner. I never thought I'd hear from him again, but of course he doesn't want to be left alone with Tinker Flatts! So good to think I can serve a purpose! Perhaps I do not have to fear he no longer has use for me now that I cannot write a full-scale biography, because of his (somewhat infuriating) modesty and fear of drawing too much attention to himself while his ex-wife peddles her own version of their wild nights? Obviously he is too kind to reject Tinker Flatts's invitation and now wants to be defended from her.

Why is Tinker Flatts holding a party and why am I not invited to said party? Is it a party for two? If so, dear naive Brent Vintner didn't get the message. What to wear? What to wear? Must go to mall. Must not allow Brent Vintner's last impression of me to linger.

The anticipation that surrounds another party. Socializing = exhausting. Exciting in terms of anticipation, debilitating in terms of execution. Must not spend time afterwards reviewing awkward encounters in minute-by-minute analysis. Will NOT list and annotate said encounters.

Midlothian Mall: I could be blindfolded and know where I am: fragrance of jasmine and molasses and burnt rubber, probably coming from the tire outlet on the other side of the parking lot. Should have opened another credit card—hope springing in spring.

I engage in Mystical Shopping. If I concentrate the right clothing will appear and be affordable and compliment my body. The right clothing will say: Yes! This is who you are—someone not to be trifled with or if trifled with then trifled with by the right person. Someone you won't find lying on her own living room floor forever.

Must appreciate own health and good fortune and not compare myself, once I'm at party, with beautiful friends of Tinker Flatts in case any are in attendance. For instance, you do not know if their intestines are full of worms.

Friday cannot come soon enough. But need time to prepare.

GETTING GROCERIES AS ADDITIONAL STEP TOWARD RE-ESTABLISHING HEALTHY PATTERN OF LIVING

Have squeezed all life out of extra limes Brent Vintner left at my apartment. Must grocery shop to maintain life. Am in the market for orange juice and other citrus. Plus cat supplies, milk, cheese, strawberries . . .

Unfortunately, I'm being followed by Bubboy, the market robot who resembles a giant malevolent pez dispenser with attached googly eyes. Ostensibly protects shoppers by alerting us to hazards: rolling avocado in aisle three. Bubboy is the genuine hazard. Children are lining up ketchup bottles in aisle nine so that Bubboy will declare a hazard in creepy hazard voice.

Bubboy insists on following behind me like a stalker so self-confident he beeps to make sure his presence is known.

I wish I could save money on Pert and Pretty's needs. They only take premium cat food and only step upon premium litter. A true hazard if I don't fulfill their wishes.

Checking prices and feeling creeping despair. I settle on low level boxed cereal in faded container. Price is right though may be more crumbs than flakes.

A woman in an immense Eagles sports fan jacket passes me, her cart loaded with fancy noodles—at least eight boxes. I endure a wave of jealousy.

A man in very high thigh-rubbing shorts squeaks by with a cart almost entirely filled to the brim with frozen meat products. It's like Survivalist Wednesday.

I linger by the aisle with greeting cards because that's where the boxes of Whitman's chocolate samplers hang out. I snag one—for the chocolates and for the vintage cover that makes me feel that somewhere a little sampler is being stitched unendingly by a hardy frontier woman. A silver-haired man bumps me with his cart. Annoying. I apologize. He does not.

A box of chocolate-covered cherries hovers on a rack nearby, like a perfect mirage. Resist.

Isn't grocery shopping nearly spiritual—fulfilling needs that aren't usually met, considering possibilities arrayed like gorgeous temptations to sin. That covetous way you can't avoid reacting when staring into other people's carts. And then, too, how you have to swing your cart away from other glances or, when putting your comestibles on the conveyer belt, you know the person behind you is making more judgments about your lifestyle than the Holy Ghost.

You think no transaction is simple, and it isn't. Nevertheless, I am feeling accomplished.

It looks like no one I know is in the store—a plus. An additional plus: at the checkout counter the clerk doesn't call out the names of what I'm purchasing although she does have a question about the hair dye.

I bag everything, making sure the Whitman's sampler is on top of the last bag for easy access on the drive back to my apartment.

And then—just as I'm about to experience victory—my credit card won't go through.

It must be because I shopped at the mall and that was the final straw that maxed me out.

The clerk looks at me. I look at her. My eyes sting, maddeningly.

I have no money in my wallet. Stupidly, I left my checkbook at home.

The people behind me in line look away at first and then gawp. I have no rights, apparently. In the eyes of everyone here, I am less than vermin. Where's Bubboy when you need him? He should mow me down.

The clerk tells the other customers to go into the next slot while "this one here figures things out." I'm searching for other credit cards. I know I'll be denied again. I know my own credit history.

Thank god I didn't forget my cell phone. I call Leon and apprize him.

"Never fear," he says. "Just give me a minute."

I am sweating through the stares of strangers.

And then—quicker than I could have hoped for—Blowman stalks up. He nods to me and pulls out his wallet. He passes a platinum credit card to the clerk. It's approved instantaneously.

The people in the next lane, the ones who had been judging me, are trying to catch surreptitious glances of Blowman, who terrifies them, I'm happy to say!

It's his big fists and enormous hammered-looking Hellboy face. As they consider my possible relationship to Blowman their thoughts are pornographic. At last I am real to them again and even occupy a position of respect. If they don't mime respect they might find themselves injured—that's what they must suppose because Blowman is looking around with glinting nail-gun eyes. I wish Blowman and I could stay here for a long, long time.

Blowman, silent as usual, takes hold of my cart and wheels it into the parking lot while I trot along behind him.

I thank him at length as he shoves groceries into my car's trunk. I promise to pay him back, and he says something incomprehensible before hurtling away.

Once I get back to my apartment the obvious occurs to me. Maybe I can be helpful to someone after all! Maybe I have a genuine reason to contact Brent Vintner even before the party that Tinker Flatts has arranged!

I email Brent Vintner. Because he hasn't encountered Blowman at The End of the World, I send a photo from last year's New Year's Eve party.

Brent Vintner calls me. "Great idea, Tabitha. I'm sending this to a casting director I know—for future reference."

"That's good to hear," I say. "I don't know if Blowman would ever consent to being in a film, but he should have the opportunity. He's a true gentleman. He makes you think he skins people and eats them alive and then throws what's left of them down a well."

"Right. That's what Hollywood is always looking for."

"I don't know, though, if he could ever leave Midlothian, even for an audition. I don't know if I ever could either."

"Why, Tabitha?"

"It's the one place I know. Every peaceful inch of it."

Brent Vintner groans. "In my hotel every night I hear screams."

"Well, that's true about the entire township. Leon named his bar based on what someone was screaming. But there are peaceful aspects. And the cement factory—it doesn't spew granules every day. One year my car got pock marked. Not too much trouble since then. I know what to expect here in Midlothian—that's important, that's serenity-inducing."

"Don't you want to experience the unknown?"

"You sound like Rod Serling," I say.

"That was the idea?"

"Oh."

"Midlothian can't have everything you need."

"True," I admit. The town is indeed seeming smaller to me lately, and yet stickier, a haunted town. "The conditions aren't always conducive to—much of anything."

"Anyway," he says, "you're more than those conditions."

"Am I?" Realization: I must never allow him to meet my mother.

Breakfast the Day After Grocery Shopping

I am almost looking forward to Tinker Flatts's party, and I never thought I'd feel that way about any sentence that includes the words Tinker Flatts.

The luxury! The cats are delighted by their premium cat food, and I am delighted by the following: orange juice and toast. And butter! I am slathering butter on my toast. Never even thought about the word "slather" before. A perfectly wonderful word. I'm glad nobody I know has to churn. I'm dressed, practically slathered, in a fluffy violet housecoat—very Duchess-like in the frills and with the butter. I totally forgot I owned this housecoat, which happens when you have hidden laundry.

And just to extend the sense of wanton self-indulgence, I fall into a trance watching Netflix and it's not even 10 o'clock in the morning. It's 9:50. I watch a wonderfully witless series with a forgettable name—maybe it's called *Love Ain't It*? and I can't yet be sure I haven't seen this episode before. Apparently some family secret is involved.

Why is a family secret always involved in anything entertaining—like, always? I can't even consider a novel recommended for me on Amazon without reading a hopped-up description about a family secret. In the Netflix movies I've been watching recently the secrets are anticlimactic. I'm sorry, they are. So deflating. Like Grandma loved a purveyor of skin cream more than Grandpa. Or Eustace is actually the son of the mad industrialist. Or your wife isn't really dead she's hiding in the barn.

Every plot would be destroyed if people were honest and candid.

At the same time, it's difficult to be honest and candid, even in small things. Like pretending to understand what Blowman is saying, for instance. Or telling Leon that his mustache makes him look like he has a neck. And of course I want to be lied to too. Sometimes I've had enough reality.

I butter my toast yet again for a layered wedding cake effect and consider that secrets can never be entirely explained.

Later I stop over at The End of the World. In the kitchen Blowman is bent over a broom, sweeping. I want to thank him again for rescuing me at the grocery story. At first, he doesn't notice me, so fierce is his attention on the floor. I reach over and take the broom out of his hands, rest the handle against the wall, and hug him. It's not like hugging a bear, it's more like entering a bear cave. A smell like cedar chips and cut grass, a lovely smell. As usual, he says nothing. It hardly seems necessary. Always, Blowman has been on my side.

More Prepping for Tinker Flatts's Friday Night Party

Golden light, the sky endlessly blue, so blue from my balcony that the blueness seems like an incredible heaven-made dye. Tiny gusts of wind, almost like the wind has decided to relax and exhale. I must screw my nerves on tight. As if that ever solved anything, the nihilist in me complains. The wicked optimist in me says, Oh please, remember, you can be happy. Everything is possible!

As I get ready for the party Pert and Pretty balance on the rim of the tub, interested as always. Raise water level so Pretty can pat bathwater with her paw. Foaming body wash combined with bath oil creates wonderful cat diversion. Baths—so useful for thinking. *Bubble*—such a remarkable word. It sounds like what it is. Bubble.

Large afternoon meal is required for strength: scrambled eggs with cheesy spread. Much coffee. Then too much coffee. Feeling peaceful yet giddy: like Dalai Lama if drunk. I step into the lilac dress. Fitted, a little tight. Breasts are not in denial. Very much foregrounded. I do not feel they are objects of pity. Only a soupcon of polka dots along ridge of scooped neck. Subtle. I suppose the dress could serve as a particularly elegant graduation gown at a clown college—I'd tell myself that if I wanted to tease myself. Frankly, I have never looked better. I'm sure eating so many eggs has helped.

Tinker Flatts, forehead wrinkling and nose twitching, looks confused when I walk into my mother's house. Of course she wants to ask, Why are you here?

She relaxes when she sees a use for me. It's obvious she's itching to gossip about herself. As if I know any part of the story, she whispers that she has a new girlfriend. She points to the new girlfriend over by the kitchen island. The new girlfriend is very young—everyone in the house—there must be a dozen people—is very young and in dark clothes and intriguingly pierced—and the new girlfriend is not from New Zealand, after all, but from the Netherlands. Her skin is so pale it's blue and her freckles resemble blood spatter.

Tinker leads me into the living room where young people cluster. "I don't know why your mother isn't back," she shouts above the whiny vocalizing from a mini-speaker on the coffee table.

"Oh—it's Clinique Sales Day," I inform Tinker. "She and her friends always go right before closing time to get the free makeup bag and extra mini tubes of makeup that you get if you buy outrageously overpriced toner. Then they go for what they call a smash and grab. They get smashed and grabby at The Ranchalot. It's a bar. Mostly octogenarians go there. It's too wild for anyone younger. They'll be gone for hours."

Tinker pinches the fabric of my dress at the waist. "You look like a farm," she says. "I mean—a garden. What is that print?"

"It's lilac," I say, proudly. "From the mall." It's the nicest thing I've ever owned. Form fitting. I still have a form I'd like Tinker to know, and the lilacs are gorgeously fulsome on a white background, big heaping lilacs, lilac colored lilacs.

"One of my professors used to always pick on girls who wore flowered outfits," Tinker Flatts says. "He used to say to them, I'm not kidding, he said, 'You are not the soil from which flowers grow.' "

"How awful to be taught by such a hideous man. I'm so sorry, Tinker!"

By then I'm looking around. Where's the hanging spider that shed black fibers into my soup? Or the lighted skulls on the buffet? Where's the dangling hag whose bat wings rock? It's as if my mother's house has been robbed by a Satanist.

I climb the stairs. Where is the skeleton with the always-open mouth and the long dangling arms? Where is the Chucky doll with the sparkling angel wings? I peek into my mother's room. The Edgar Allan Poe life-size cutout should hover near her bed, but no. Who has performed this terrible exorcism?

Where's the caldron? Where's the cauldron?

Where's the witch hat my mother kept on her bedpost?

It's not like my mother to pack away Halloween decorations. For decades she has paid homage all year long to the Day of the Dead—except on Halloween. When I was a child and trick or treaters were set to arrive, she shut up the house and turned off the lights. That was the signal for Mattie to stop by and pick me up. Together we walked the neighborhood, which meant I couldn't be terrorized by the other kids. My grandmother borrowed my mother's witch hat and deployed her fierce glare, rich cackle, and kitchen broom against my detractors. I always had such a hard time with the other kids. Probably because I didn't talk until I was four (at first it seemed unnecessary) and then, for a year and a half, I couldn't stop talking until I learned what "unnecessary blabbing" meant, and then I didn't talk again for a while. It must have been hard for anyone to take. Mattie took it—first the silence, then all the talking, then the silence, then the new way of talking, when I learned to write and could talk part of the time in my head and no one could hear me, and so no blabbing had to be unnecessary.

It's true that thc basis of the word *nostalgia* is pain. It's possible to be nostalgic about anything at all—even a sudden homesickness that strikes at the memory of a witch's hat that used to dangle, first, from a hook in the hall and later from a bedpost. Sometimes you can't help but gasp with a memory of loss so sharp, loss that is all sensation, unattached to any one memory, loss that makes you double over. Then undouble. You remind yourself where you are.

On a long table in my old bedroom: needle-nose pliers, a tack hammer, a claw tool, a webbing stretcher. You'd think you stumbled into a torture chamber if you didn't know my mother still upholstered furniture on the side. A piece of good advice she gave me: always pat down your own couch. Always, always, always, you'll find something in a couch.

No cauldron anywhere, not even in the upstairs closets.

If I didn't know where she is, I'd think my mother is buried somewhere on the property.

I retreat down the stairs. One of Tinker's agile friends lies full-out on the couch with another friend and they're kissing frantically, performatively.

And then the air thickens, a current of energy whirls, and I know he's here: Brent Vintner. All the young people turn like one many-headed squirrel. Tinker Flatts rushes to him, and Brent Vintner in his creaking leather jacket nods over her head toward me. He's carrying a six-pack of beer because somehow he knows that Tinker Flatts would want a six-pack, and then he's surrounded by her friends. It's like a little picket fence of her friends encircles him. And there he is, being polite, mumbling niceties. I think of the Lady and the Unicorn tapestries, and how the unicorn in at least one of those tapestries is held behind a small white fence. Brent Vintner, the closest I will ever come to being in the presence of a unicorn. The joy at seeing him is that immense. He only nodded, but I can tell he's not embarrassed by me, that he's not remembering the last time he saw me in the flesh, on the floor in my apartment, with Leon helping me drink from a glass of water.

He's looking toward me again. "Beer?" he mouths. I nod and he heads toward the kitchen. When he comes out—it takes a long time—he stops to talk to someone. Surprise! It's Piper Fields. She angles her hips toward him by the buffet. I move closer until I see I shouldn't, that something important is being spoken about between them.

They're waylaid by a goateed person who looks no older than fifteen and who soon carts Brent Vintner off to a corner of the living room.

Maybe Piper Fields doesn't recognize me although she's usually the one hard to recognize? I tap her shoulder. "Not now," she says. "We can talk at another time. Not here."

The desire to be back in my own apartment is fierce.

I'm at the door when Brent Vintner catches my elbow. "Let's leave," he says. "Your intern doesn't need us here."

We step out into the night air. The cool spring air.

My plans, I tell him as we stand on the porch, are clear to me. If he'll still cooperate, I'll write what amounts to an extended profile about him—not a full biography, but I would still like to write something of at least some length about him, if only for online distribution. I'll be sure not to violate his wishes. I won't write anything that will see much distribution. I don't tell him about my pride, how leaving anything unfinished makes me angry at myself. It would embarrass me to recount my weaknesses. As he listens he's looking out across my mother's yard where I used to wander lonely as a cloud and it seems clear to me, and not entirely uncomfortably so, that he probably already has a pretty good idea of my weaknesses. Actors are trained observers. He pats my hand, looks down at me.

"That's a really nice dress," Brent Vintner says.

I smooth the skirt of my dress and cannot help but say, "You have saved the entire night for me."

Brief Phone Call From Piper Fields Late That Night

"I apologize for treating you like that. I can explain. Pick you up tomorrow at 11:30? We can visit Maryann. Advise your intern not to contact me ever again."

"You know what? No need to apologize. I totally forgot about you!"

Phone Call From Brent Vintner in Early Morning After the Party

"Tabitha, Blowman IS an actor."

"No."

"Under the name Scott Farrell. You can see him on Netflix in a film from the eighties, *To Russia From Russia*. He's a hired killer known for ingenuity. He kills with everyday objects. Wet wipes. Maybe don't tell him you know that he does some acting—or did some acting."

"Does his character in that movie kill with a credit card?"

"No. With a stamp collection. Just joking. Tabitha, pretend you didn't hear this from me."

"For your own safety?"

"He might be sensitive."

Oh, Blowman. Dear kind Blowman.

Blowman must have been a bearlike little boy who as early as nine years old had the physique of a healthy sixteen year old athlete. Because of that, no doubt people treated him oddly, like he should behave more maturely. And that must have confused him: he wonders what's wrong with him. And no one tells him what he needs to know. When he reaches adulthood he tries entering a monastery and of course that doesn't work out because it's not his true calling, and soon he's spotted by a talent scout who is actually legitimate, not like one of those people you meet at the mall. And the next thing you know he's got a role as a violent criminal in a low-budget movie and what happens? Another role and another? And then presumably he found Hollywood unsatisfying, deadening. Producers probably treated him like a two-eyed Cyclops, and so he fled and created a spiritual harbor at The End of the World.

I bet that's exactly what happened. Exactly.

So good of Brent Vintner to let me know that Blowman had a movie career. All I ever knew about Blowman was that he used to be a monk and that the monks in his monastery made mustard and coffins. That's really all I knew.

A quick brisk rainfall. After talking with Brent Vintner on the phone I lay in bed listening to the whisk broom of the rain. A rain that comforts because of its efficiency, a tendency to tidy up. A late spring shower, clearing the air, not so much falling as intentionally releasing itself.

RESEARCH NOTEBOOK/VISIT TO THE COUNTRYSIDE

It's pleasant to take a country drive, the breeze rushing through the car's open windows.

Piper Fields and I are heading toward Maryann's and I am making plans. What I'm going to do, how I'm going to make the best use of the interview—it seems evident to me now. Except suddenly I fear that perhaps Piper Fields will pull off onto a lonely dirt road and stuff me in the trunk. Does she regret denying that she's the author of the novels published under her name? If so, does she think that a country drive would allow her to murder me more easily? Does the fact that murders and orgies occur in her novels suggest that she is the true author and is inspired by the actual murders she commits?

I tell myself to breathe. Focus on the moment. Clasp purse more tightly. A purse can be used as a weapon in case of attack.

The side of Piper Fields's face is benign looking, yet the right eyebrow is puckering, and now pinched. In general, Piper Fields appears pinched today. Psychologically run over. Would be tempted to help her if I did not fear she wants to kill me.

"That Brent Vintner," Piper Fields says as she steers around a truck, "I like him, now that I'm getting to know him a little bit. He's shy for an actor. Or maybe more actors are shyer than we know. When they don't have a script they don't know what to do with themselves. They have to inhabit another personality to have a personality."

I say nothing. I hate to correct anyone.

"I've visited him on set," she says. "I promised Maryann I'd promote her novels—for the movies. It's like another world on set."

"Do they knit a lot?" I ask.

"I never noticed. The director is very—ugly. It's interesting to see all these beautiful actors and then an ugly director."

Genuinely curious, I ask, "Is it like he's compensating for his face by directing?"

"I wouldn't repeat that if I were you—if you ever meet him."

"I don't intend to meet him."

Piper Fields hasn't even shut her car's door before Maryann bolts out of the house. It's like a parody of those videos where the dog gallops toward the returning soldier. She hugs Piper Fields in an effusive show of affection that Piper Fields doesn't return.

The house looks different today, perhaps because now I know I'll be referring to the house in the biography in a way that suggests a haunting. Even if Piper Fields is lying and she actually is the author of the books that bear her name, I'll recount this odd episode. I'll depict the interior of the house, accurately, as homey, quaint, all floral curtains. Yet sinister. You can feel it in the house, something coy and well-protected and yet portentous. That something being Maryann herself.

As soon as Piper Fields and I sit down Maryann glides out of the room and comes back with a plate of sliced date nut bread. "Beer or milk?" she asks.

Piper Fields says, "You don't happen to have coffee brewing or tea?"

I'm asked my preference and opt for coffee. I'm sure I need a stimulant. Preferably rough coffee—caffeine at an extreme. Coffee that turns stomachs into saddle leather. It would be such a lovely thing to curl up on the couch with that rose patterned cushion under my head.

I sit up straighter and whisper to Piper Fields. "Are you tired, or is it just me?"

When Maryann reappears I waste no time, in case I fall asleep and in case she has put something in my coffee, for how can I trust this peculiar woman?

"This is my plan," I tell both women. "It's going to be a dual biography. I don't know if either of you are telling me the truth, but even if you're lying, it's intriguing to think about why you'd lie. Piper Fields, it does seem clear to me that you don't want to be known publicly as the author of those children's stories and those incredibly filthy novels. That's obvious. You could be paying Maryann to take on your identity in the future. Or, conversely,

Maryann, you may have been paying Piper Fields for years to take on the burden of representing you in public."

Maryann interrupts. "You'll have to do interviews with a lot of people—right?"

I feel the stirrings of pride. "Oh yes. I'll interview all your relatives, your former teachers, your neighbors. I'll ask to review your correspondence, possibly your tax returns, and I'll want to know all I can about your relationship"—I nod at both women—"with each other—whether this is a love story, a friendship story, a tale of bitter rivals. Or I could do something more ambitious, more fluid, less commercially successful. My publisher—Rosamund—would hate that, but I have my ethics."

Piper Fields gawps. "You're doing all that with Brent Vintner too? You're going to interview everyone he's ever known?"

"I'm not writing a biography anymore about him. Just a profile."

"That means you're almost finished with him, right? And so you can spend more time on Maryann and me, without getting sidetracked? I like that. I don't want this to take forever, the interviews with us and all. The biography can be completed swiftly, I hope."

My mouth is full of date bread. The coffee is too scalding to help me swallow. Maryann's date bread—date bread, date bread, date bread. There was something in an excerpt from one of those erotic novels she or Piper Fields wrote. Something done to date bread. Hard to swallow after that.

"Why," I ask Piper Fields, "why do you want me to hurry?"

"Because I don't want any more people to be deceived. I don't want any more 'followers.' I don't want cultish readers who think I actually know anything about the bizarre sexual practices that those books champion—"

Maryann interrupts. "Don't accuse me of championing—"

"All right. Okay. Anyway, I want a life that's calmer. I want to be able to eat at a restaurant in peace."

I study both women and then turn to Piper Fields. "Do you realize how rare your life is? That there's hardly an author in the world who shares your fate—the fate of being popular?"

"It's only because half the books under my name are for children and the other half are for—never mind, I don't want to characterize adult readers. It's because the youngest cultists probably had those children's books read to them when they were toddlers and then they grew up and read the novels and it's like they're imprinted. Maryann, you did this to me. You did it."

I push the plate of date bread away and decide against the coffee. Nothing in this house can be trusted. Maryann sits demurely in her armchair, one of those armchairs that seems to demand you wear a smoking jacket, and appears to be sleeping. Her eyes pop open.

"See," she says. "Tabitha, can you hear the misery in Piper's voice? That's why we need you to write for us. To take time to contextualize our choices. When Piper told me about how you went after that guy bothering her—that's when I thought: she's the one. And the fact that you're somewhat naive and literal minded, that made me think you'd be the right person to convince our usual adult readers. You don't like the date bread? It's a little dry, isn't it?"

I ask, "Why—if I assume you're the real author of books sold under Piper's name, why'd you do it—really? The truth."

"Obviously we all want the truth," Maryann says. "Have you ever heard of the Church of the Holy Mother of God?"

I stare at the date bread, hoping it will evoke a memory. "Is that a Catholic organization?"

"God no," Piper Fields says.

Maryann shakes her head. "No, not even Christian. I mean, it borrows some iconography, that's true, but it's more like a new religion that's based on reverence for the moon and its sacred power."

"That sounds like an old religion," I offer. The date bread looks like it's crawling.

"Did you put something in this date bread?"

Piper Fields shoots out of her chair, "Maryann, you didn't!"

"Sit down, you maverick," Maryann says. "Of course not. Tabitha, you have a vivid imagination. What on earth do you think you're seeing?"

"I thought the date bread moved."

The women look at one another and Maryann swoops up our three plates.

She hustles back from the kitchen, "All right," she says. "Back to the Holy Mother of God. My husband, bless his heart, was an officer. His whole life revolved around the church. I suppose that's hard to understand."

I attempt to understand. "At least they weren't entirely patriarchal if the church is named after the holy mother of God?"

"You have no idea," Maryann says. "Needless to say, I was not a holy mother. A mother yes, but not a holy one. Who is? Anyway, I loved my husband and tolerated his beliefs. I started writing partly as a means to keep sane. The children's books—those came naturally. Really, I was using words in those books to get my husband to sleep after a late-night ceremony, you know, after the chanting and mooning and moon ogling. He'd come home all hopped up. I learned that a certain sequence of sounds calms the nervous system."

"And what about the adult novels?"

"Oh, those are pure revenge. Once my husband joined the church he took on chastity as a cause. Three children and he thinks he's done his work. Holy Mother of God—those officers of the church asked too much of him. Three of those officers hit me up. I told him and he wouldn't believe me. My husband thought I was jealous of the whole Holy Mother of God congregation."

"How many worshippers are there?"

"Oh god, I think there might be twelve or maybe a few more of them left. They're not a threatening force anymore. That's another reason why I feel that I should free Piper from the burden of pretending to be who she isn't. The ones who are left—they're weak fellows. They've done their damage. They've had their nights howling at the moon. Don't get me wrong. I had some fun too, and I don't want the congregation, small as it is, to dissolve. But now—I want all the falseness regarding Piper to end."

Piper Fields shifts in her armchair. "Maryann, tell her why you chose me." I try to gauge Piper Fields's expression. Is she furious with Maryann? Shouldn't she be?

"I was her babysitter years ago," Maryann says. Both Piper Fields and Maryann laugh. "Before I married Oswald. I told her stories. I've always thought the world of this here person." She reaches over and tugs at Piper Fields's ear. "I knew she could use some money, too, like any of us, and I could give her a percentage. Plus, she has the best name, doesn't she? A great name for both a children's book author and a quasi-pornographer."

"But what about Bunny Swift, your pseudonym for the novels?" I ask. "You used a fake name for the novels for years."

"I couldn't toss Piper into that maelstrom—in the beginning. The publisher for my children's books wanted a physical presence to promote the books. A face and a body for the launches and interviews and all that. Piper, with prepping, worked perfectly. When it came to the novels I thought I could get away with not being seen. No promotions. I never imagined they'd gain a following. Maybe that's why the books gained a following—because the author was invisible. I had used Piper, though, for the contracts and for communicating with my agent. And so when Bunny Swift was outed, it was Piper who got outed."

I ask, "Maryann, what's your full name?"

"Let me spell my last name for you. D-A-M-M-I-T. I put the accent on the last syllable. No one else does. You know, my husband always claimed that Edgar Allan Poe had a character with the same last name. I bet he didn't have a character with my maiden name too. My full name is Maryann Bougher Dammit. I pronounce it in a certain way and it sounds French. Very sophisticated. But, you know, I mean it: no one pronounces it correctly. So there was Piper with her perfect name. We both thought it was a great idea, right Piper?"

"Initially."

"You could have used a pen name for anything you wrote," I say. "Wouldn't that have been easier?"

"No. My husband would have suspected. It was easier to have mail go to Piper and for Piper to sign contracts and checks and for Piper to make appearances. As I said, my publisher for the children's books wanted an actual body behind the books."

"And they got me," Piper Fields says. "It was such fun until it wasn't. And now I'm afraid no one will forgive us unless our story is told carefully by someone very compassionate who has lots of time on her hands because she has no ties to anyone else."

Maryann Dammit says, "Like me, I guess—although I can't tell my own story. I mean of course I have ties to my children. They're adults. They know the truth. With my husband out of the picture, basically, there's no one I can hurt anymore. It's Piper who's being hurt. We need someone to tell our story who can pretend to be objective."

"Excuse me." I head out through a screen door that leads to a small yard and the bright sunshine. I vomit into the grass. It's a bad habit—vomiting. But it's kept me clean, clean of lies.

Interlude

It is my belief that possibly we are each part of a giant puzzle and, if held to the light, our edges examined, we might reveal something of importance to other members of the human race. Perhaps some basic particle only useful in a rare instance. I hope that before all traces of who I am vanish from this earth that I will hold up some piece of needful truth.

As for needful truth: so much was occurring to me as I listened to those two women. Holy Mother of God—I mean, if I were younger I'd join a moon-worshipping congregation in a flash. Maybe not if there was a drum circle. Otherwise it sounds exhilarating. Even just saying those words: I'm a member of the Church of the Holy Mother of God! That's a prayer in and of itself. Get me into that nunnery.

Then I was thinking that everything fit too nicely and that Maryann Dammit didn't seem like she'd be too careful with any husband. For one thing, Dammit must be her married name. It's an improvement on Bougher but not much. Still, if you agree to marry Mr. Dammit you have enough power over the man that he can't ask too much of you. Just the fact that you don't continually call out his last name during domestic tiffs would be another line of credit. Say, if you resist the urge to shout, "Pick up your own damn socks, Dammit!" Or "My mother-in-law, Dammit, is on the lawn." Just by not using your husband's name in vain you're already filling pot holes in your marriage.

The age gap between the women: that seemed about right. Yes, Maryann could have been the babysitter. But why would Piper Fields agree to become what basically amounts to a stunt woman?

As I stand under Maryann Dammit's walnut tree I text Brent Vintner: "Why would someone lie about their identity?" At first he thinks I'm accusing him of lying about his own identity (which of course makes me suspicious) but then he supplies an answer: "Because they have something to hide." He texts again: "I've said that line five times in three different films."

Searching for Truth

When I come back into the living room both women are looking up at me from their chairs, expectant as baby birds.

"What are you lying about to me now?" I ask. When they don't respond I say, "What are you hiding?"

From somewhere in the house a deep vault is opening. Giant barrels are being rolled. The air stops moving. I hear what sounds like the hard clump of a large dresser being shoved across floorboards. A chill scurries up my spine.

Around the corner, from somewhere in some distant room, comes more thumping and creaking.

The woman who at last appears must be about my mother's age.

"Hello, Mrs. Bougher," I say. "I really didn't appreciate what you did to that date bread."

"Please," she says. "You're free to call me Modesta." She pulls herself up to her full height. She steps closer in that heavy-booted way of hers that is surprisingly attractive, like she's stamping her sense of self into the earth, never to be eroded. It's like she has roots she needs to pry up with each step, and that's what accounts for the grating noise. She reminds me so much of my mother—that same remarkable ability to dominate an occasion.

"I hope you don't think you're Agatha Christie," she sniffs at me, not without admiration.

"I do feel like Agatha Christie," I say. "Because of my advanced abilities of detection. Although I can't help you. I do have someone who can be of use to you possibly. My intern. She'll believe anything. No one will ever discover the truth."

She smiles benignly. "Tabitha, how I do like your name. I've often thought of naming a character Tabitha. Possibly in my next children's book—perhaps a hippo. A very good name for a hippo."

This woman really can fire the imagination. Immediately I imagine a plum-colored, plum-shaped hippo with a giant mouth that's wide open. The hippo's teeth look pounded into its jaw with a mallet.

Maryann's mother continues. "I also very much like the name for a character in one of my novels, possibly someone with a fetish involving sudoku at the entry level. Can I get you something more to drink?"

"Oh—nothing for me," I say. "I do like sudoku."

"Piper, how about you?"

"I know nothing about sudoku."

"No, I mean anything to drink."

"Nothing for me."

Modesta Bougher smiles above my head while addressing me. "So, Tabitha, I understand now, fully and entirely, that you believe you're not going to help us. Nevertheless, I hope you'll reconsider. You might think of your spiritual life. You might consider joining the little group I assemble regularly. We're conscious of our place in the universe. So few are. You would feel released, sinless, absolved."

I ask if she includes sins of omissions in the absolution. There's so much I haven't done.

She chuckles, disarmingly. "Oh, everything in our temporal world is probably meaningless anyway," she admits. "But it's such a pleasure. Such good fun to be among like-minded souls. And to keep at least some mysteries intact. One must never let one's talents go to waste. I have always inspired love."

I don't risk my life by staying for supper, although Piper Fields stays.

I manage to get an Uber out of there.

Poor Piper Fields.

Such a complicated life.

I myself prefer an uncomplicated life with all its inherent mysteries that arrive complicated in simple ways.

A Plea or: Will Piper Fields Ever Leave Me Alone?

Piper Fields calls me late that night. It is very hard to get her to stop talking.

"It's not a lie," she says. "Admittedly, Mrs. Bougher does write the books, not Maryann. That's the truth. Maryann memorized a script to try to convince you—everything she said was exactly what her mother told her to say. That's why Maryann sounded like a very old lady. She did pretty well, I thought. But please, Tabitha, you should know that I haven't always been lying. When you and I first met and I told you about the bunnies that were run over by my father's lawnmower? Maryann was babysitting when we found traces of what was left of the bunnies. And then when her mother came to pick Maryann up I was crying so hard Mrs. Bougher drew happy pictures of the bunnies for me—that was the start for her, for her bunnies. It took her years before she tried to get her work published, and by then I was twenty-four and heading off a cliff in my own life—"

"You stole things and got caught?"

"How did you know?"

"That teapot."

"Okay. Sometimes I like to keep in practice. Anyway, Mrs. Bougher imagined I'd be perfect as her 'stand-in'—my name, my being only in my twenties by the time she submitted anything to an agent, my excitement about the prospect of acting like I wrote those kiddie books.

"She had me sign all the paper work, meet her agent and publisher. Be the face—although I always made sure my face wasn't easily recognizable in photos, you know? I had to keep something of my own. By the way, some of that's true, what Maryann said about her husband being an officer in the congregation. He really followed his mother-in-law's teachings. You don't often see that kind of loyalty from a son-in-law. They're an unusual family."

"It's so funny," I say. "Almost everyone I know is pretending to be someone they're not. The strangeness of life and the lengths people go to . . . they'll go to the moon. It makes so much sense. So Modesta Bougher's church—she believes in what she's—"

"People really need something to believe in and she wants to be believed in."

"I can understand that."

"But can you understand how it started for me? I really was flattered about pretending to be her and I didn't have a job and I've always been attracted to transgressions and I was broke—like you."

"You always remind me I'm broke."

"Anyway, I do like the money. I'm just tired of the same old pretense. How to get out—without harming Mrs. Bougher or the books or both our reputations? She thinks people will reject erotica if they find out it's written by a woman in her eighties."

"That's absurd. I bet it takes at least eighty years to even get a handle on—"

"Anyway, she loves her congregation and doesn't want the publicity, but she thinks Maryann can handle it and can take over for me—the age difference won't be so alarming if people think Maryann wrote the novels. Maryann will do anything for her."

"I feel that way about my own mother. Oddly enough. It must be biological."

"Tabitha, do you know how many places I've lived in the last three years—to escape attention? That man in flannel who showed up—"

"Paul Bunyan?"

"Although lately I've noticed that this is the funny thing—other than Paul Bunyan, locally, no one else besides him bothers me. Even after that signing. I really think only out-of-towners attended the signing. Obviously no one in Midlothian reads. It's becoming almost a relief to live here."

"That is not entirely true—that no one reads. You know, Piper, you really don't look the same way twice. I'm getting good at recognizing you because I have practice, but you really are good at going incognito."

"Can you even begin to understand how much energy that takes?" She breathes so heavily that the phone echoes. "Tabitha, you just have to tell part of the truth—delicately. We want you to write that Maryann wrote the books. We think you'd be perfect for presenting that story. If people get outraged there's ultimate deniability—with you. We might even look victimized—by you. Well, we'd pay you for that, even though we'd have to pretend to sue. But I don't think anything will go wrong. You'll slide the truth in front of people and make it, maybe, acceptable. Maryann already dreamed up a story for you—and if it all works I'll then be free of the playacting and Mrs. Bougher's identity will remain intact and secret and she can parade around with her followers and no one will know that a woman in her eighties can—"

"teach us so much about our bodies. I'm so sorry, Piper. It's just—I can't lie for you. I wanted to write the biography, really, but I can't lie and so I can't do it. It's that simple. I'll let Tinker Flatts know. She can take over. She can do your lying for you."

There's silence between us for nearly a minute.

"You are missing so much fun, Tabitha."

Thinking About the Meaning of "Battle-Ax"

Something is haunting me about Maryann's mother. I forgot to put this in my notes, but before I caught my Uber, Modesta Bougher said, referring to herself: "I may be the leader of a congregation, but I'm especially proud to be just a regulation style battle-ax."

How interesting! I go on Wikipedia for more information. *Battle-ax*: insult against vigorous, opinionated women. Should be compliment. Carrie Nation, temperance leader: presented as exemplar. Used hatchets on bars, destroying endless bottles of liquor. (Misguided.) That woman could out-hatchet Lizzy Borden. Must recuperate term outside of temperance movement.

Perhaps I am from a long line of battle-axes? My mother—so far into her ninth decade and still wearing metallic undergarments. Considers red lipstick crucial in the defensive arts. Has had both knees "done"/joints replaced and talks about it the way botoxed people talk, like it's a "cosmetic." The wonderful thing about having a mother like mine—you never have to feel desperately guilty because you know she'll always take care of herself and prevail in any situation!

Pert and Pretty are becoming more affectionate. At night they crawl under the covers with me, Pert on my left, Pretty on my right. It's comforting. Like sleeping with animated Russian muffs. And yet they also are possessive, hissing if I change position. If they had the right sort of agility and thumbs they would tie me to the bed, like Gulliver, except asexual in terms of species.

TEXTING

From Brent Vintner:

I can't stop reading Annie Her Life Story

Love it

Me to Brent Vintner:

I'm glad So you're the one

Text from Brent Vintner:

Plenty of copies on your publisher's website and online Can't stop reading

NOTE TO SELF

Very much tempted to tell Brent Vintner that I adore him for reading *Annie: Her Life Story*. So kind of him. Delusionary, some would say, admittedly, but kind. And generous.

How could anyone deserve him?

MESSAGE FROM PUBLISHER

Tabitha—

I've heard from Tinker about your once AGAIN formally handing on Piper Fields's biography to her. I am assuming you've now made up your mind for good. I assume you will not be waffling once more in such a mysterious and counterproductive way as previously. Tinker's delighted and ready for the opportunity—again. It is my understanding at this point—to be entirely clear and to guarantee that you don't reverse your decision yet again—that you have reneged on our agreement, and that you are now no longer writing a biography of either Piper Fields or of Brent Vintner, although you are intent on peddling a short profile of that actor to some online outfit that won't pay you a cent.

I realize you're in a financial bind. Call my office and talk to Rene, but please know that I can't allow you to drag your feet on paying back all that you owe from the generous advances you received. Perhaps there's a silver lining. You could let the problems you've encountered teach you about what opportunities might be more profitable for you. Many of us have to recalibrate our compasses, Tabitha. Failure is part of life. Recently I came across, on a coffee cup, a quote about failure. It goes like this (paraphrase): Fail, fail, fail. Fail like you mean it. Tabitha, I know you enough to know you mean it.

Confession: your book on Killdeer—his grand niece bought it out so she could destroy it. I did reasonably well on that one, thanks to that indignant woman. Obviously, withdrawing the book did not translate into royalties.

I Do Not, At This Moment, Deign to Write Back to My Publisher. Instead, I Text Piper Fields With Admirable Restraint

Me to Piper Fields:

I'm sorry I can't help out with the lies you want me to tell but I have mailed that teapot back to the restaurant

I'll send you a bill for postage

Piper Fields to me: Did you look inside the teapot

Me to Piper Fields: Too late Already mailed

Piper Fields to me: Too bad

Me to Piper Fields: What was in the teapot

Piper Fields to me: You'll never know now will you

What really was inside the teapot? Funny that in the same day that Rosamund mentions Killdeer in an email Piper Fields tells me there was something inside the teapot that she stole and subsequently mailed to me. Was Piper Fields compelled to steal the teapot and then give it to me because she was receiving directions from the afterlife? Did Killdeer want me to have that teapot because he believed the interior of teapots held spirits?

If it was a gift from Killdeer from the afterworld, the pot is gone now. It's the thought that counts.

Anyway, it took me forever to get to the post office but at last that tea pot is off my hands. Yes, at last I've accomplished something.

The Bar at the End of the World

I am, apparently, considered a reliable friend by Brent Vintner. Someone to kill time with when his unreliable actor friends aren't available. What terribly unreliable friends he must have.

Remind myself daily: this will not last, Brent Vintner needing my company. Must prepare self for day he leaves. Which must be soon. Do not wish to ask when. Time can be manipulated in one's own mind.

We meet at The End of the World and sit in a booth far from the door. Now that he knows I'm not writing about him at any length he seems oddly happy and more relaxed. It must be lonely for him, making the movie. He has nothing in common with those knitters. So far he has not brought up anything about my fringed vest or the spectacle of my being laid out on my own apartment floor. My gratitude makes my eyes hurt and my throat close. Must think silly thoughts to control myself. Can only think of a man I once met who said he wanted to eat chili so hot it would burn a hole in his neck.

Then too, Brent Vintner must be glad that I have remained silent on my opinions about his ex-wife's memoir and her intimate descriptions of their time together and her intimate insults about him—insults which, to my mind, are so minor that I almost question if she and Brent Vintner actually met let alone performed acts that defy gravity.

Leon comes over and I ask for a bellini and he laughs. "Like I'm going to have peach juice today! You'll have a Michelob and like it!" I know he doesn't mean it.

I tread carefully by saying to Brent Vintner, "I heard that Piper Fields visited you on the set?"

"She's flogging one of her books—seeing if it could be made into a movie."

"One of the children's books or one of the others?"

"One of the others."

Leon comes back with bellinis for both Brent Vintner and me. It wasn't what Brent Vintner ordered. Leon can't compartmentalize.

"I've been thinking about your book, the one called *Annie: Her Life Story*," Brent Vintner says. "I laughed a lot."

"It's a sad story," I say.

"Is it?" he says. "It's just—Annie is really quite—something."

"She was everything to me, even though it turned out that she wasn't who I thought she was."

"That happens," he says. "God almighty, this is what's called a bellini?" He turns the glass to the light, swallows more.

"Yeah. Leon specializes in them. He once worked in a peach orchard. He knows what really good peaches taste like. He's awful to go grocery shopping with. You can't get him out of the produce section."

A commotion at the door. Brent Vintner waves over four people. I recognize the woman from the time she was pasting herself on the piano. Once again I experience a strange jigsaw-like sensation, her face reassembling and then detaching from a double exposure. She is very beautiful, and maybe that's what's disconcerting and initially made her look unattractive. Her husband accompanies her and two other friends—young guys who can't take their eyes off her. It's very calming. No one looks at me and nothing is expected of me.

The conversation is lovely—truly—all talk about the movie that's being made here in Midlothian and then about other movies. The voices swirl around until I feel very peach-like and quiet, and the husband of the actress kisses my cheek in a fatherly way. And then—very soon—everyone leaves except for Brent Vintner and me. I ask Brent to tell me again those people's names. The second bellini has interfered with my memory. He tells me their names, and moments later I can only remember one name, and it's the name of someone who wasn't even in the bar but someone they kept talking about: the director: Diverto. Which seems like such a perfect name that I keep saying the name to Brent Vintner, who is laughing.

"Is he the one who wants to remake *Vertigo*?" I ask.

Brent Vintner affirms that he is.

"But it sounds like he's nice, and sane. Not like a madman at all."

And then—it is so strange—the actress and the actor who is her husband and their two friends are back in the bar again because the actress wants to sit on the piano and sing. This time, maybe because of the bellini or because I know that no one is laughing at her, I feel an outpouring of love for her. How she gives herself away. It may look like she's smushing ants with her bottom but she's entirely unselfconscious about it, and that's something I could learn from her, surely.

Leon offers her a bellini—he's gone out and got more peaches apparently—and in minutes he puts down an entire pitcher of bellinis on the table and everything around us turns golden.

"Have you ever gotten up on a piano to sing?" the actress asks me.

The entire table except for Brent Vintner laughs. It is such a ridiculous idea that as I'm walking toward the piano I watch myself—I'm in slow motion—and I hop up after a few tries and sit atop the piano and sing "Happy Birthday"—in the way Marilyn Monroe sang it to John F. Kennedy. In other words, I sing softly as if breathing is difficult, and everyone at the table laughs so hard they cry. And then Brent Vintner leads me back to the table and says, "Time I got you home," and I realize that I've humiliated myself. I also realize that I don't care, that I am beyond humiliation.

"Was I that awful?" I ask Brent Vintner as he unlocks the door of my apartment. "Did I embarrass the world?"

"I loved it," he said. "Absolutely. I didn't think your rendition was funny. I felt like bawling. I felt you were singing Happy Birthday to every dead president and dead actor in the world. You're going to vomit, aren't you?"

An Expected Voice Mail

"Let me be straight forward, Tabitha. I always want to be the person in your life who tells you the truth, not like the usual cowards I suspect you run with. This is the truth, Tabitha: you used to be a pretty woman when you had short hair. Whatever you do, get your hair cut off and shaped. By shaped I don't mean like that haircut you had three years ago. More overhangs than a Swiss chalet. These days you look like you're coming out of the water in a horror movie. A woman's hair is her crowning glory. Getting yours cut short will be a choice you won't regret! Just say to the hair dresser, 'Chop it off, chop it all off,' and they'll try to convince you otherwise and you'll argue and you'll wind up with a decent compromise. Take my word for it, Tabitha. Tinker says Hi!"

Looking Farther Into the Mirror

Why, in novels, do people look in mirrors? So that the first-person narrator can tell us what they look like. But that's so unrealistic, doesn't everyone know what they look like? Actually, I don't. So I'm not the best person to ask.

I know perfectly well that when I look in the mirror I'm not seeing my face. For one thing, it's reversed. For another, to deflect the psychic blow mandated by my culture and every other culture, I rearrange my face before I can see it. That is, I am relatively sure that I change the size of my lips.

Advice I saw in a magazine: look into the mirror and say nice things to yourself.

I try "You can really layer those spice jars like a spice pro and sell dozens of them for the firefighters' charity." Or: "You want happiness for all sentient beings except if their happiness depends on the destruction of others and then it's so tough!" Or: "You're ready to tackle anything if 'anything' is small and in bad shape." Then I try kinder possibilities . . .

It's so disturbing—that Sylvia Plath poem about looking into a mirror, the one where a woman sees a fish coming right at her? At the end of the poem an old woman (the young woman's older self, like the young woman knows what she's going to look like years later, and it's not promising) is rising toward the young woman, and the old woman looks like an awful fish. Depressing. Keep hearing theme song from *Jaws*. Plus, why a fish? Why couldn't the young woman's elderly self jump right at her like a spectacular kangaroo because life moves so fast?

PHOTOGRAPHY

I'm embarrassed even as I take a bunch of selfies. I'm doing this not because I intend to post a single one of them. Of course not. I'm doing this because I am interested in what Brent Vintner sees when he looks at me.

Fifty selfies. I move through the camera roll. Not one of those selfies looks the same, yet they're all of my face. Maybe no one looks like themselves. Brent Vintner frequently pauses when he sees me, pauses and then, slowly, a smile spreads across his face. Is it possible that initially he doesn't recognize me?

DOGGED QUESTIONS

Have I, for weeks, taken many notes and written many observations as a way, from the start, to avoid writing any biography of any sort, let alone what is now my only option: a short profile of Brent Vintner?

If a life is unconsciously guided by the sentimental fantasies projected in movies is that life doomed to failure and lingering grief?

If a life is unconsciously guided by outrageously cruel fantasies projected in movies is that life better adapted to limitations of human life?

Does the avoidance of pain limit a life when avoiding pain means things hurt less? Is that a tautology?

Why do people say "You're not thinking straight" when thinking cannot be straight in a curvy world?

Now that enough time has elapsed so that remembering it doesn't stir absolute agony, why did I get atop that piano at The End of the World and sing? Was I possessed? By what sort of demon? Before I crawled back to the table I imagined I saw a sudden flash of sequins. Then—regret?

GOODNIGHT, IRENE

Irene is careful to spacc hcr client's appointments at intervals so that we avoid seeing each other. It doesn't matter. I can tell who's been here before me. The person, every time, might as well be a tomcat spraying. The scent of chlorine pervades the air and the couch is wet. Obviously, it's a member of the senior aquatics team from across the street—someone who hardly bothers to towel off before skipping on over.

Today the framed prints of butterfly wings struggling to free themselves from their chrysalises are crooked. Perhaps a dissatisfied client scrambled up from the couch and swatted them. I'm wondering if, when one of her clients finally graduates from therapy, Irene hangs up prints of butterflies fluttering their stained glass wings, freed of their creepy former environs and fully accepting of the larva they used to be.

Irene says, "Something you've never told me—"

"There's a lot I haven't told you."

"My my my. I know. Tell me. What was it really like when you were married all those years ago? You haven't given me a sense of the atmosphere in the marriage."

"At first it was wonderful and then it was like being in the waiting room of a dentist's office. And then Conrad changed and I didn't—not much, not entirely. And then there were all those eighteen-year-olds who needed private voice lessons."

"That must have been a blow to your self-confidence. As I always say, human life is a series of crises. Are there ever any moments when you still feel like forks are sticking out all over your body?"

"No, those went inward. And now I just feel a strange heaviness. Like there's cutlery in there melted into a hard lump."

My life really has to change. But how? I want to be a fierce warrior for my own life and those of others instead of small simpering rat in brain hole. Must stop. Must stop punishing self for being self. Must, as Irene at this very moment is insisting, allow thoughts to float by, without judgment. If so, isn't that a judgment: thoughts as flimsy clouds drifting? Unacknowledged legislators of my inner world. Know thyself? Not if you don't examine own thoughts? So many contradictions.

I would consult well known works of philosophy except so many seem hateful . . . Don't mean to be hateful myself, close-minded and cruel to philosophers, many of whom suffered. Syphilis.

"I'm glad we're making progress," Irene says. She settles deeper into her chair, pops a gold-colored lozenge into her mouth. "You have to realize, Tabitha, that the end of any relationship is like a death, even if the relationship happened a long time ago and the person is actually dead. Do you understand, Tabitha?"

"I do. If the end of a relationship is a death, then it makes sense never to begin a relationship so no one has to die."

My therapist is excellent—so excellent that I may never need to return!

TURNING MY HEAD OVER

At least the woman moving my head around isn't someone I knew in high school, nor do we have relatives in common.

She studies my reflection in the immense mirror. "Can you take off your glasses?" she asks.

Without my glasses I can see nothing but blurry bunches. Gradually my eyes adjust and I make out the outline of the dark cape around my shoulders, and I assume that explains why my head is floating. I don't know why there are mirrors in this place. I can't think of a place anyone would less enjoy seeing their own face.

I read somewhere that the angle of your neck when you're leaning back into the basin for a shampoo can cause nerve damage. I manage to keep calm.

Afterwards, I find my way back to the chair where the hair dresser—her name is promising: Divinity—will begin clipping. She wags my head around, and the scissors make soft snips. From the waiting area comes the sad crackling sound of old magazines that someone previously took with them into the tub, and I hope that no one I know comes in and sees how vulnerable I am with my head wet and Divinity working me over. Her stomach is pressing against my back and I wriggle to get free of so much physical contact.

"There," she says. "Do you want to get a good look?" She hands me my glasses.

I can't help myself and cry out, "I'm turning into my mother!"

Divinity, behind me in the mirror, scowls.

"You don't understand," I exclaim. "I'm happy! I look like I could break a cow over my knee!"

My eyes are so much wider than ever before and my mouth takes up more of my jaw. Divinity has spread my features out.

I can't stop looking at myself in the mirror. My hair—it's an amazement. So short. I never knew I had so much face in there.

I tip Divinity extravagantly—more than I can afford. She has earned her fortune.

Hair in a Baggie

Hair. Hair does tell a story. And so when a person has their hair cut it's like they're telling a new story. Or an old story. Or a story they don't want to hear anymore. No matter how trivial it may seem to anyone self-important, I *am* changing my life.

The smell of the historical society: mothballs, dry newspapers, and pine cone sap. The society was very good to me when I researched Killdeer for my first biography and read through his diaries, thanks to the caretaker, Lauralie Thompson. She even gave me a baggie of Killdeer's hair as a souvenir after I begged for it.

An impulse—coveting Killdeer's hair. I took the lock of hair in a baggie home with me—until suddenly I wished I wasn't alone in my apartment with the hair and made up my mind to return the baggie of hair to the historical society the next day. In the meantime, I hung the baggie on a nail on the balcony. The next morning the baggie was on my kitchen table. I picked up the baggie to look at the hair in the light from the window. The hair had GROWN! I couldn't get it back to the historical society soon enough.

What that experience taught me: maybe you shouldn't take what you think you want. Maybe what you think you want will look very different in the morning.

Maybe you should think harder about what you want because what if what you want keeps expanding.

I wish I hadn't remembered that hair.

The End of the World

The End of the World is almost empty by ten p.m. Three customers—the usual widowers, retired—and they're not even drinking. When Leon comes out of the kitchen I look closely at him. The warning light of intuition is going off. "Is everything okay?" I ask. "I hope you're doing okay? Leon, you—I don't know—you seem unhappy lately."

"You're asking this question of a man in the middle of a divorce?"

"Are you trying to evade the question? You have practice at getting divorced. It's not divorce that's bothering you, is it?"

He turns to the cash register and pops the drawer open. "Oh, Tabby, I'm fine. Never better, buttercup. Wait a minute. Have a seat. I'll be with you in a sec."

A minute later Leon dances over to me, toting the new nonalcoholic drink he's experimenting with: peach-aide. It's wonderful and just needs vodka.

"Are you really okay, Leon? I want to help in any way I can. You're doing okay financially?"

I stare hard at him until he says, "Knock knock."

"Who's there?"

"Donna."

"Donna who?"

"Donna ask questions if you donna want answers."

"Leon, I do want answers. I've been thinking about ways to raise money for you—for The End of the World."

"No reason to worry. You got your hair cut? Nice."

"Does it make me look—different?"

"You looked different, like Eleanor Roosevelt, as soon as you hit puberty. Bam! National icon."

Warmth rises to the top of my head. Mattie loved Eleanor Roosevelt. To think that I look like the woman she most admired—that warms me.

"You don't look so much like Eleanor Roosevelt anymore," Leon says "You'll always look only like yourself. Like Tabitha."

"I thought I look like—your grandmother?"

"God no."

"Okay . . . This is what I really want to talk about. You paid my car insurance, didn't you? You can't afford to do that. I wondered why I didn't get a bill and then I talked to Denise Ogabe at State Farm. She told me you paid. Leon, I'm going to pick up extra work.

I just need a little more time to figure things out. I don't want you to pay my bills for me—ever. You could use extra money, right? I was thinking—what if we had a benefit in support of The End of the World? We could name it after you—the Leon Acrete Benefit."

"People will think I'm dead."

"That's the idea."

"No, Tabby. No. Not in this lifetime or any other."

I keep thinking: what if everything I love is lost? What if The End of the World ended? All the luscious darkness, beautiful and haunting, and the tangible aura of kindness. The End of the World welcomes everyone, shyly but surely.

In the corner I press down one key on the piano and the sound rings, true and resonating. The widowers at the bar turn and smile. I wave and they wave back and only briefly do their eyes ding against my chest. Where would any of us go when we're miserable? What other place would take us inside so fully, so comfortingly?

I do have bar experience, and so it's not as if I don't know what other bars have to offer. My ex-husband Conrad and I used to go to bars years ago. I never found any bar to be as—I don't know—enthralling?—as The End of the World. For example, Conrad and I went to a bar named Winterfell. It was very much what you'd expect: white couches, iced drinks, blue light—a cold and sterile environment. Another bar: I don't remember what it was called but it had a Western, gunslinger theme, high balconies, with tiny doors behind them, like where Miss Kitty in those old *Gunsmoke* re-runs stashed her mole. The smell of saddle oil. The enormous stone fireplace, so enormous two full-grown men could be shoveled into it. A bartender in a sweaty-brimmed cowboy hat.

And then there was this other place. Animal heads all over the walls. Very small heads. The owner had to be a game hunter, but not a big game hunter. More like a little game hunter. I was sad for the animals and couldn't identify them. Mouse or hamster or guinea pig? Conrad insisted the heads weren't real, but he was lying. I petted several of those heads and those were real skulls, with real hair.

None of those bars could compete with The End of the World. People don't even drink all that much at The End of the World because, as I always say, being at The End of the World is already like swilling around inside a shot of whiskey.

And then—my skin grows quills of alertness. All my senses crispen. Everything is louder. The ice cubes in my glass chuckle. I'm fully aware I'm being watched.

A flash of silver. A silver-haired man who must have just arrived is sitting at a round table and smiling toward me. I've seen him before. In the grocery store? His cart nearly jolted mine right by the Whitman samplers. A full moon is beaming through the high windows and lighting up his hair.

Later, when I'm back in my apartment, Leon calls and tells me that the man with silver hair asked about me.

"Is he from the IRS?"

"Possibly," Leon admits.

No Texts

No more texts from Brent Vintner. Why should there be any? Why would I expect any? No reason for him to contact me.

Beautiful Discoveries: Part 3

A beautiful man is a stunning man. You are stunned—like you've been frozen by how beautiful he is. Parts of you are not working. Does that make sense? I don't know if I'm making sense. I got so stunned whenever I saw Brent Vintner. Why should I ever have let myself be stunned? It wasn't his fault. I have no one to blame.

Seeing a beautiful man—it's like a bruise inside your mind. No one can see it, but you're tender inside your mind. You have to learn to toughen up. Armor yourself.

Beautiful people are like mirages. In books and movies a beautiful young man must always disappear and the older woman who loves him must die alone or be shown exhibiting helpless spitting fury as the man goes off with her daughter—the rightful love interest. I'm feeling more justified than usual about not having children.

Worrying Is the Practice of Imagination

Leon's sitting outside the kitchen entrance on the steps. Behind him, through the window, Gregory is shaking his head to something on the radio. The bar won't be open for another hour. The maple sapling by the dumpsters looks waifish in the early afternoon light. I imagine the sapling being bulldozed, the entire building that houses the bar hollowed out and collapsing, the lot sold for new construction—for an ugly, squat office building, mystery-less.

I ask Leon, "Do you have any idea about how long your finances will hold out?"

He smiles, winks. "Don't worry, Tabs. Even if things don't work out they'll still work out."

This statement is worrying, coming as it does from a nearly twice-divorced man. Supposedly, optimistic people live longer, but that's all they've got going for them.

"You worry too much," Leon continues. "I'm making ends meet. Last month I even made a profit. So don't sneak into my room at night and stare at me while I'm sleeping or anything."

If Leon were drowning he'd believe a dolphin would float along and give him a ride. Trapped in a burning barn, he'd assume a horse would kneel, insist he saddle up, and leap with him over the flames. He could be freezing in a block of ice in Michigan's upper peninsula and he'd put his faith in a flash thaw.

Worrying is a form of imagination, isn't it? No need to be ashamed for being imaginative. But if The End of the World ever were to close, what would Leon do? And what about Gregory? The End of the World is his life. Half the time he's not even working. Gregory would be lost without the stool he sits on, the kitchen window he looks out of, the *First Magazine* he borrows from the chiropractor's office where his niece works. His joy: to camp out in the kitchen and read while Leon runs in regularly to dunk fries in the fryer.

And Blowman? He has money socked away somewhere, and investments, I'm betting, and I have the feeling that anything Leon pays him winds up back in the cash register through some magic stealth Blowman learned from his time in movies. But something keeps Blowman at The End of the World too, keeps him revolving in place. Perhaps penance for failing as a monk?

And myself? Right now, the way my mind has been in recent weeks, I'd fare the worst if The End of the World closed. Where else could I pop in and feel at home when my loneliness hardened all around me? What other place eases out at least some of the sharpness digging into my sides? And the piano—I love how it changes shape depending on the viewer's mood, like a mystical piano. What if the piano were auctioned off or carted away to be junked? The end of The End of the World would not just be the end of the era. For some of us it would be the end of time itself.

I may have been embarrassed a number of times at The End of the World, that's true, but I never felt the place wanted to push me out through the exit and past the dumpsters.

SPICE JARS—GOING FAST

Leon buys five more spice jars that night. The firefighters will appreciate it, I tell him.

"Are you sure?" he asks.

"Tell people not to rub spices on their skin. I've been layering so many spices I've got a rash."

I refuse a beer (trying to keep clear-minded) and sit in a back booth with iced tea. I startle when the silver-haired man, the same one I first saw by the Whitman samplers, slides into the booth to sit opposite me. "I hope you don't mind," he says.

I don't have the energy to tell this stranger the truth: I mind! I mind deeply!

He says, "It's—it's like I'm compelled to talk to you. I apologize if I seem rude."

I'm not attracted to him. Nevertheless I keep touching my hair. "You don't only seem rude," I say. "You seem like a very clumsy stalker, with no subtlety whatsoever. You feel compelled? Compelled?" His hair is streaming with light.

"I do," he confesses. "I don't think I could avoid coming over here and sitting down across from you. You're—enchanting."

A small part of me already hates this man. I ask, "Do you feel like someone put a spell on you?"

He whispers, "How strange that you'd say that." He slides both of his hands across the table, perilously close to my iced tea.

I study his gray eyes and know that my intuition should be obtrusted. I am pretty much positive that the silver-haired man is obviously enchanted, and not by me.

I tell him, "You're a member of the Holy Mother of God congregation."

Obviously Modesta Bougher has sent this man to tempt me to do her bidding and convince me to claim that her own daughter is the author of her salacious books. This man is an overly shiny, fussy fishing lure.

He lifts his hands off the tabletop and speaks through gritted teeth. "Lower your voice. I didn't know you were a member."

"I'm not."

"Yet you know about us."

"Don't worry. I won't tell anyone anything about the congregation. I've sworn myself to secrecy. I don't want to sacrifice my own self-respect."

Where is Leon when you need him? He's behind the bar, shaking a spice jar.

The silver-haired man sits back. "Did you know that the moon is a satellite?" he says, "and that what we see from Earth happens to be not only craters but great bodies of hard lava?"

I am Wikipediaing away on my phone and answer. "Did you know that the moon is about 400 times smaller than the sun and is always moving away from the Earth?"

An Interlude With Balcony Light

From my balcony this morning the sunlight brushes against the railing and settles on the patio below. No matter how miserable I complain about being in these notes, that is, afflicted with the sort of loneliness that being with most people doesn't solve, I still have this balcony and the view down toward the patio and the courtyard. True, some trash gets trapped there—lids of coffee cups and cigarette packs and candy wrappers flashing in the light, along with the occasional hypodermic needle—but it's easy to clean things up and I can contemplate the fresh shoots of grass and the peony bush. Soon that bush will release its wild glory of blossoms with their scent and Leon will stop over with a friend or two.

Last spring we spent evenings down in the patio with Leon's buddy Clover softly singing and calling me Auntie even though he's only a year younger than I am. I felt a certain gravity and authority that night and Clover, always curious, asked me why I wrote about other lives. I told him about how each book I wrote gave me an extra life.

"But doesn't it feel like maybe you have less of a life—that their lives dominate your life?" Clover asked.

And Leon reached over and said, "Clover, man, let's talk about your marriage and how it's going."

Of course that got Clover to change the subject. He loves to talk about the secret of a good marriage. I could never find out the secret—it never made sense to me. All I remember is that his wife makes wigs.

It's wonderful to have a balcony. I feel a little selfish. It's the only balcony on this side of the building. The apartment below me is empty, which is good. A woman who worked nights used to live in that apartment and shouted up through the floorboards, "Take off your god damn boots!" I never even wear boots.

Once a crow or some other immense black bird landed on the railing of the balcony. In its mouth was an actual stick. Not a twig. The stick was bigger than the bird. The bird looked at me, tilted its head, flapped its wings twice, and made a low, gentle squeak as if trying to tell me something. It flew off with that stick like it was the easiest thing in the world to speak softly and carry a big stick.

I can't continue languishing in this self-defeating way. I have to accept what life offers, don't I?

Lunch With the Man of Silver

I won't accept a dinner invitation from the silver-haired man who has stalked me at The End of the World. I do accept a lunch invitation. Just to be kind and not squeamish and somewhat more open to the accidents of life. We agree to meet at Scandals—his choice. The restaurant's name strikes me as especially presumptuous.

In order to continue to be more tolerant, I accept the silver-haired man's recommendation of the wine—some rare red variety—and my head swims instantly after the third sip. I do, however, manage to listen to him.

"If you ever come to my farm," he intones, "you'll see how bright the moon can be there—and the stars. Living in the countryside, the sound of the leaves in the trees, that sound, greets me each night. I like to keep my windows open so I can hear the old oak."

[I picture a barn where someone's killed.]

He asks, "Do you ride horses?"

"Never more than one at a time," I say.

"Is that a joke?" he asks, good naturedly.

"It was—just a way of—speaking. I once did ride a horse and let it have its way with me."

The man in silver nods. "They're sensitive animals. They feel your feelings. They want to please, as in a healthy relationship."

[My vow: I will never see the inside of this man's barn.]

"I have cats," I say. "Basically, they model what an unhealthy relationship should look like—it works for me."

[My macaroni and cheese can't come soon enough.]

Like a vision, the waiter appears and places our loaded plates before us.

"Oh," I say, after my first bite, "this is the fanciest macaroni and cheese I've ever tasted. Gourmet style. With seven cheeses. I didn't even know there were seven cheeses."

The silver-haired man waves a fork at me. "Camembert, feta, gouda, brie, roquefort, colby, mackengo, cheddar, gorgonzola, asiago."

"Do you think that impresses me?" I ask. "Because it really does!"

[I will never, never, never see the inside of this man's barn.]

Happily, gelatin is on the dessert menu. Anything that pops out of a mold—I'm all for it. And anything that quivers. Gelatin—the most alive of the dead! My mind is full of gelatins—pistachio-colored gelatins fluted and embossed like family crests. Rose-colored gelatins in the shape of clustered rose petals, em-pinked and glorious. Moon gelatins—silvery and quaking and stenciled with astronomical signs on quivery skin.

The gelatin is undecorated—and turns out to be a dollop of vanilla ghost pudding in a bowl, but I like the modesty. And it pairs well with the macaroni and cheese.

"You have an incredible speaking voice," the silver-haired man says. "Do you sing?"

I tell him I don't sing and have never sung, even as a child. Especially as a child.

"How sad," he says.

This comment freezes the conversation.

"If you can talk, you can sing," he says.

Silence.

He shows me a photograph of his deceased wife and my heart brims with sympathy. Feeling numb, I am tempted but don't dare bring up my deceased ex-husband. Would sound callous and competitive. I tell him that I bet he has a nice singing voice.

This uncorks him. Soon he's singing softly at the table. We're now the only customers and I still want to die.

The silver-haired man (perhaps his name is George?) stops singing to attend to his pudding. When he looks up his pupils enlarge. It occurs to me that if he didn't seem to be thoroughly enjoying himself he should be deprogrammed by an expert. Then, what would his life look like without the Holy Mother of God congregation? He'd be just another silver-haired man with a horse and a barn.

"You're really very beautiful," he says. "Do you know that?" He winks, pleased with himself, and licks his fingers.

That does it. There are two human acts that are beyond my power to defend myself against: people who lick their fingers and Bob Dylan singing "Lay Lady Lay." I'm sorry. I recognize that Bob Dylan is purported to be a genius. Nevertheless, every time I hear him sing "Lay Lady Lay" with that invitation to "lay across my big brass bed" like a collie named Lady is being instructed, it becomes very hard not to run through streets screaming.

"I'll be back in a minute," I say.

I hurry outside, bend over on the sidewalk, do not vomit. Make myself breathe. Tell myself: you never have to see that man again.

When I unfold, I picture the silver-haired man on his farm, a hobbyist's paradise. He ties his horse to an old oak tree. On a hillside one small sheep bleats. If it were a much earlier century the silver-haired man would be on the waiting list for a mail order bride. If the mail order bride had any sense she'd leap off the packet boat before ever catching sight of his woodland thicket. Then I picture the silver-haired man untying his horse and galloping around his barn while oak leaves thrash, and I force myself to go back inside.

As I walk toward him he's looking at me with beaming adoration. It's useless, I want to tell him out loud. But it would be awful to say so: like branding a chicken: delicate, and unnecessary, and cruel.

Love, I think, is this man's crisis. His loneliness, deeper than some cavern in Kentucky. It's like a phantom has been waiting—and I recognize it in him. Seeing it in him makes a recognition rise up in me.

All that yearning in his face—that's how I must look, although not with him. And it's like something has cracked open, something brittle that had encased me.

I hope this man with his shining silver hair finds someone wonderful to love, it just can't be me.

No use denying it any more: I don't want to be the sort of person who needs to be loved and touched—but I am that sort of person once again, after years, and more than ever.

Dance Sequence

The next morning I wake up irritable and coffee does nothing to help. I turn my sculptures of Dutch heads to the wall and play Radio Roulette. That is: I dance to whatever is on the radio. Including local news. I hate that old saying about how you're supposed to dance like nobody's watching. Mix a little bit of hate with my dancing. Almost feel better! That lunch with that sad, strange man. Other people—they are our best mirrors?

An Expected Voice Mail

"Tabitha, be a doll and pick me up some wax—for the candles for the firefighters' charity. It's counter-intuitive, I know. Firefighters put out fires and candles start fires. Well, that'll keep the firefighters in business. It all works out in the end. I hope you're getting busy on those spice jars. I've signed you up for twenty-five more. I know you're not busy these days. You have all the time in the world and then some. Don't waste it!"

I CALL BACK

It's foolhardy to call back after receiving a voice mail, but I call back anyway.

"I can pick up the wax on Wednesday—is that soon enough?"

"No. I need it for tonight. I want to sell some at my reading group."

"You have a reading group?"

"We don't call it a book club anymore. A reading group—I know, I know, we sound like a bunch of socialists! Anyway, we're reading poetry to please goddamn Polly-Allison. It was her turn to choose and she always does the unpopular thing. She's one of those people who believes in self-improvement. For herself, fine. She's such a masochist she wants all of us to suffer. So we're reading Keats! Of all people. It's hard for me to concentrate. What I could have done to that man! La Belle Dame Sans Merci? We're all working hard to pronounce that correctly. Those translation and pronunciation apps—they're worthless. For one thing, his French would have a British accent. I'd ask to borrow one of your books full of Keats's poetry but there's already a lot of his crap online. I know you love poetry but it's a slog for me, especially because Juana insists on reading stuff aloud. It takes every effort not to strangle her. I have to be nice, though. She left me some frozen shad for my freezer. Such a bony fish. And she's going to be our designated driver tonight, thank god, because Polly-Allison always gets out of hand. Anyway, we've been allowing a man into the group, just for fun. The things he says—so sentimental. He uses words like: refreshing, comforting, absorbing. We can't decide if he's mocking Keats or writing copy for Kotex. We really should record the sessions."

"I can get the wax for you the day after tomorrow."

"That's the earliest?"

"That's the earliest. Or you could pick some up yourself maybe?"

"Oh, Tabitha, that's not like you. Think of the firefighters!"

Finding Meaning in Life by Serving Others

Picked up and dropped off wax. Then made fifteen spice jars. Will double that number. Is that not a goal?

Good news. Leon says the spice jars are going fast at The End of the World—once he got the clientele to figure out they weren't for smothering cigarettes. Smoldering, they smelled terrific though.

"What kind is selling most?" I ask.

"There are different varieties?"

"Oh yes! One is for beef, one is for fish, and one is a general deodorizer."

"Are they labeled?"

"Of course they're labeled." [Question to self: did I label them?]

"Well, anyway, they're going."

"Tell me the truth. Did Blowman buy most of them?"

"You know he did. He's your biggest fan. Like Kathy Bates in *Misery* with James Caan. Just don't drive into a snow filled ditch and make him lug you up an embankment like a frozen heifer."

The mention of snow makes me think of Brent Vintner. He joked once about Michigan's upper peninsula—where he grew up, where his parents still live. Deer flies the size of hummingbirds. The peninsula is known for pasties: dough-filled survivalist pies. People lose their minds and go snow-blind.

I decide to experiment with a cider mix—cinnamon, cloves, nutmeg, allspice, dried lemon peel . . . or should I just stay the steady route with garlic and herb rubs? Unhappy thought: handling the ground spices reminds me of my ex-brother-in-law and how he still thinks that eventually, if pressed, I'm going to buy one of his memory lockets filled with cremains. How many years do I have to say no?

Emmie Gootz is lumbering around in my apartment changing the filter on the air conditioning unit—her task each spring, before the summer heat arrives and turns the entire building into swampland.

"Have you seen that guy—Brad Victuals—that movie star guy?"

"Brent Vintner?"

"Right. I'll have more of that please." She rolls her eyes before she says, "Tabitha, don't pretend you don't know what I mean. They're filming out by Costco today in the parking lot. I'm going to head out there as soon as I get all the filters replaced. I hear that that guy—Brent Vinkler—is down to earth and courteous. A nice guy. That pretty much ruins the charisma, but I'm going out to Costco to catch a look. This filter doesn't even fit. Forget it."

After she leaves I drive out to Costco. The lot is half full of cars. Nothing suggests that filming has taken place or will take place. At the service desk one of my old classmates from high school spots me and calls me over.

"Ancient times," Connie Schutz says. "Great to see you."

I ask if there was a film crew in the parking lot.

"That was at like 4 a.m., pumpkin. Sorry you missed it, pumpkin."

I hate how, even though it's been over thirty years since we were in high school together, Connie Schutz still calls me pumpkin. It's not like the shape of her face is any better than mine. She has one of those very white faces that blushes purple around the chin and I don't call her Turnip.

Her face rearranges into an expression of pity. She has a reputation for kindness and thoughtfulness, for hugging and expressing concern, for regularly reading the obituaries and keeping an entire box of sympathy cards at her elbow. She can fool a lot of people, but I know she's one of those kind people who's secretly cruel. The opportunity to express thoughtfulness—that's too tempting. If you lost your gall bladder she'd be the first to jump on it, send a card, tell the entire town, and make your gall bladder more diseased than it ever had a right to be. Vicious.

Porter Plus lunges from a back room and stops in front of me.

"Are you avoiding me?" he asks. He's a friend of Leon's and this is his joke. He asks that question every time he sees me. Unfortunate name: Porter Plus. He likes to say his name is Porter Plus Size. Everyone has an acquaintance just like this guy, so I can't even accept Connie Schutz's sympathy.

Next Porter Plus says, "You hate me, don't you?"

If you fall for the bait and say, "I'm not avoiding you" or "I don't hate you" you're caught. He'll make up scenarios: how you never accepted his invitation to duck under the flaps of the beer tent. How he once offered you the maraschino cherry from his high ball and you turned away. How he laundered your gym uniform decades ago and you never thanked him.

Such bad luck to see both Connie Schutz and Porter Plus on the same day.

An Expected Voice Mail

I'm heading back to my car when I get the voice mail.

"I just heard you were seen making moves on a man with white hair. No grass growing under your feet. Tabitha, you may look pickled but you're not puckered. Take my word for it. Like kids used to say years ago: 'You go, girl.' This too shall pass unless you snatch opportunity out of the jaws of death."

I am so confused. Are these koans?

Finishing

"This too shall pass": one of those hateful sayings. If you're having a good time why tell yourself "This too shall pass"? It's all right if you're being tortured.

Finishing. I used to want to finish whatever I started. I hurried and hurried to finish. Ending was a way to feel competent. Look at what I made: a cake. I made a cake and it's OVER. You did something and you basked in the done-ness.

But then—to finish what I would like not to end. How to suspend oneself within those moments, turning and turning and not being tossed away? Shouldn't I have finished writing about Brent Vintner by now? He'll be leaving Midlothian soon. He too will pass and I'll remember everything.

Nobody gives Freud credit for anything anymore. In fact, he's treated like a positive embarrassment. Granted, some of his theories are embarrassing, and deny people who identify as my gender, for instance, pretty much of a full human soul, but he was really right about the importance of love and work, which makes it so hard when you have neither.

STANDING IN FOR LEON

And then as if summoning Freud for once amounts to good luck: an opportunity to be of use arrives! I can be so busy I won't think about anything but the present moment. I can "be here now" by working!

Leon calls and asks me to bartend for him. He's feeling sick, he says, although I don't believe him. He's met someone. The thing about my relationship with my nephew: he can lie to me but never about me.

I haven't been behind the bar for three years. "What if I forgot how to make drinks?" I ask.

"It's like riding a bike."

"Actually it's not."

"It's like riding a bike without wheels. Half the time you just stand there. No one will come in anyway."

I am nervous, of course, but I tell myself I'm excited. Being a bartender means that inevitably you exert magnetism. People must come to you to express their wishes. The shining mahogany bar is between you and the customer. It's like you're an executive behind a stand up desk and people have to earn your attention. And you're so busy you can pretend not to hear them over the jazz squeaking from the speakers. You guard the liquid sustenance and people make their nervous requests. It's like you're a cow and they can't get the milk for free.

I couldn't tend bar regularly even if I was good at it. It's too hard for me to make change and often when people hand over money it's wet.

An hour in, and I'm doing okay and have managed to resist hearing the next episode in the story called "the meaning of each of my tattoos" narrated by a tattoo artist who calls himself Avery Blotch.

"I'll give you a discount," he says. "Anything you want. You get one, you'll want a dozen."

I think about Tinker Flatts and her tattoos and wonder how she's doing. She hasn't contacted me ever since I handed her another chance to write about Piper Fields.

Avery Blotch puts his arm on the bar like he's throwing down a ham. He points to his wrist. "See this squirrel?" he says.

I don't—the portion he's pointing to looks like a rhododendron.

"This squirrel is in memoriam. A squirrel got stuck in my tool shed and tried to chew its way out. But where it chewed there was a metal plate by the roof and one day I saw that the squirrel was stuck."

"Squirrels are slim and appear pliable," I say. "I didn't know they could get stuck. Aren't their bones flattenable? Or maybe this one's hips were large?"

"I don't know. Anyway, I get my bush trimmer and peel back enough of the metal for the squirrel to escape. Do you think it escaped?"

"No. This is going to be a tear-jerker. You said it was a memorial."

"Right. But it did escape, though it took a long time like it was afraid of the sharp edges where I'd peeled the metal back. It didn't even try to get out for a long time. And that's why I put the little guy right here on my arm. The great escape artist. Houdini."

"A slow escape artist."

"What does it matter? The little fucker must have escaped. No one ever saw it again."

So many questions I have for this guy: what is it like to wear one of those electronic ankle bracelets? Why do some women crawl all over themselves to marry serial killers?

Hunched on the farthest bar stool is a face that looks familiar. Then I realize: it's my first floor neighbor.

"You play the garden hose!" I say. "You live on the first floor! I live on the third floor!"

"I don't play the garden hose."

Such a mystery.

"I used to know a man who played a carrot." This comes from the woman on the next stool. His sister, my neighbor says, introducing us.

"Tell me more," I say. My neighbor's sister has bright orange hair and I can't help but wonder if what she says is a double entendre.

"You have to carve the carrot," she says, "and cut holes in it. Not easy to do without slicing open your own hand."

"Does it sound like a flute?"

"It still sort of sounds like a carrot," she says.

I jump, startled, when Leon hurls himself over the bar. How agile he is. Leon: fifty-one years old and still wiry as a rat, bless him. "You're free," he says.

I turn my back on my neighbor and his sister and whisper to Leon, "What happened?"

"Nothing much."

"I'm so sorry."

"Don't be. You're free now. Unless you'd like to stay."

I do stay, acting like I'm helping Leon out. Watching him, I can tell he got his feelings hurt earlier in the night. He's cheering up, though, because my first floor neighbor's sister is telling him how to make a flute out of a carrot in so much intricate detail it's obvious she finds Leon attractive.

When things get quieter I go into the kitchen. Gregory nods at me and doesn't appear to want any help. He's too busy reading *First Magazine* in the armchair he keeps by the stove. Only minimal bar food is available at The End of the World: French fries and fried cauliflower, boiled eggs, mini gherkins, and unshelled peanuts with their dusty good smell, like sunlight and dried dirt on a country road. Gregory takes care of orders and deals with all the extras: the cut up lemons, limes—and maraschino cherries, neon red, like they popped up from a pile of nuclear waste.

I open what has to be a new refrigeration unit. Those craft beers—Leon is extending his range. That's a very good sign in favor of his financial stability. I endure a wave of tenderness toward him. The bar must be doing better than I imagined? Maybe Leon can survive without me? I'm less useful than I imagined?

That night I have trouble sleeping. Insomnia. Such a pretty name for such an empty experience. I didn't have coffee late in the afternoon, and so there's no reason for me to be lying awake. Maybe it was seeing Leon looking unhappy when he came into the bar and then seeing the way he got excited about the carrot flute after he returned. His resilience. Within a half hour he was bouncing. I'd like to bounce and maybe that's what's keeping me awake. And then it occurs to me: I'm awake because I'm excited. I'm sure—somehow—that Brent Vintner needs something from me.

A premonition is hovering. Something is going to happen. Something is going to happen to me. I'm like one of those animals that goes to higher ground before the tidal waves strike. I try to calm myself. I'm often wrong but the premonition is so strong—an energy all around me, butting its head, like goat energy.

The next morning the apartment doesn't feel the same. The latch on the door leading to the balcony is broken. The rain-scented air washes into my apartment. I make my way to the balcony and under my feet the wetness from where the rain dashed feels good.

ANNIE: HER LIFE STORY—TRANSFORMED

I see Brent Vintner's name on my phone and pick up immediately. I'm desperately hoping that my intuition is correct and he needs some sort of assistance.

"Listen, Tabitha," he begins. "Don't reject this idea out of hand."

"Too late! Rejected! I'm kidding. I reject nothing!"

"Seriously, it's from Alberto, the director? We talked a lot about him at the bar a while back?"

"Diverto?"

"His name is Alberto. That's his last name too."

"Fuck me with a spoon. That's such a great name."

". . .?"

"Are you still there?"

"Okay. Tabitha, he wants to use your book *Annie: Her Life Story*."

". . .?"

"Tabitha?"

"Really? This is a joke, right?"

"He wants to use it, overlaying it on the plot of *Vertigo*."

"That's not possible."

"Now—try this experiment. It's a mind experiment. Just—okay. Tell me the plot of *Annie: Her Life Story*."

"You read the book. You said you read it. You tell me the plot."

"I want you to be open-minded. What's the book about? Pretend I'm a stranger who hasn't read the book and you're explaining it."

"Like for Wikipedia?'

"Right."

I start slowly, concentrating. "Okay. It's the true story of a dog. My cats know 200 words of the English vocabulary and they're listening. I may pay for this later. But okay. The plot. It's the story of Annie. How I took my dog Annie to the vet and got her trimmed and bathed and looking beautiful. She was a mutt—I have no idea about her ancestry. Generations of mismatched animals had to be bred accidentally to create her. Anyway I adored her. The vet really worked on her, bathing her, giving her a haircut, the works, and then I brought her home. For at least six months I didn't realize I had the wrong dog. It wasn't even Annie. It was a total mix up. The thing was, I felt that this other dog I had mistakenly taken home knew that she wasn't my dog. She was deceiving me. Pretending to be Annie. It was ridiculous. She answered to Annie. She wagged her tail like Annie. She ate like Annie. She had a way of taking her food into her mouth, walking with it into the living room, dumping her food on the floor, and eating it in front of the television. Then one day I noticed that under all the hair around her neck there was a little collar. It was such a tipoff."

"You see? Keep on."

"Well, it was a tipoff. But I thought—wow, the vet must have really liked her and gave her a little collar because of her incredible cuteness. I started thinking more about it. Something didn't seem right. I experienced this uncomfortable sensation almost daily back then—like those people who endure an ailment that makes them think their own family members aren't who they say they are, although maybe those people are just being realists. Annie kept looking away from me like she was guilty, and then I started to feel really dizzy, and Leon came over and before the screen door could slap shut Annie was out of the apartment and running down the stairs and she ran right into the road and nearly got whacked by a Buick with a trailer hitch. I caught Annie and called the vet and they checked their records. The fake Annie had a chip. The real Annie had no chip. There was a dog exchange—and my Annie, the real Annie—ran to me and knocked me down. I was unconscious for about ten minutes, otherwise perfectly fine. We had a good life together for fifteen years after that and then Annie fell off a rock pile while we were hiking."

"That's partly the plot of *Vertigo*—right?"

"But in *Vertigo* the woman who pretends to be the other woman dies. Both women die."

"Alberto was thinking of doing things differently. No dog will die."

"It's okay to have a woman murdered but not dogs. I understand."

"He thinks your book could be the basis for a comic treatment of *Vertigo*—with dogs. And he could option the book. And he would pay you. Or your publisher?"

"I have the rights to the book. Rosamund, my publisher, demanded it."

"That makes it easier. I loved the book. I laughed a lot, Tabitha."

"Because it didn't happen to you."

NOTE TO SELF

It is hard to imagine my deceased dog in the role that Kim Novak made famous. Maybe this is a weakness on my part?

Possibility: I'm dreaming anyway. Ideas for films are batted around, yes. Always problems arise, don't they? And then the film doesn't get made. Yes, some films get made, but a film about Annie? I loved that dog. And when she was returned to me she showed so much love. She'd never forgotten. And the other dog—also named Annie—she loved me too, in a less overt way. I never heard from her owner again. Resentment must have built up. Apparently my Annie was not demonstrative enough in the other person's home, which makes sense given that she was accidentally kidnapped and a changeling was put in her place!

Brent Vintner says films are built out of the remains of other films all the time—they're all towering corpses, he says. How much Annie would have loved knowing that her life story might be made—despite all obstacles—into a movie. She was one of those dogs you could watch late night television with. She'd sit up on the couch with her long head on my shoulder. Very relaxing. Pretty and Pert can't compete, sad to say. Annie used to look at me like she was trying to get me to understand something. Like a teacher with a pupil she pities. She used to hide her toys and try to get me to find them. Annie . . .

I Take a Walk & Think About Life's Meaning and Get Interrupted

Mid-spring is the time for changing your life, the time when the earth is making such an effort. The lily of the valley—poisonous to cats, otherwise I'd love to pick some—are dangling their tiny pelvis bone flowers, and the bleeding hearts have already bled, and the earliest lilacs make a last stand, already browning at the edges after being lightly toasted by the sun. I hate how I feel in spring, but then I hate how I feel in autumn too—those seasons when everything is turning over and it's like something in me is turning over too. Like having allergies inside your heart which is sneezing and watering. Does everyone feel this way?

Walking in the park, like I am, among all the lushness, only exacerbates the problem.

Why should I feel as if I'm ready to shed my own skin? Am I one of those people who is never satisfied with life on earth? It would be nice to have a dog again. I could run with the dog. The dog would make my way of running look natural, like I was running at that pace for the dog. But no dog could ever replace Annie. I am a one-dog woman although I am perversely polymorphous enough to be a two-cat woman. But having cats if you're a woman alone—it's about survival.

A tarnished silver color between the trees. I duck and scurry to avoid the silver-haired man charging up the northern path, no doubt on his way toward some meeting where Modesta Bougher will tilt the axis of the earth for her suggestible hell hounds. A brilliant flash of light breaks through the scalloped edge of a cloud. The silver-haired man's head disappears. I blink and he's there again, striding, head and all.

A woman fast-walking past me says into her phone, "He wasn't a sociopath he just loved to party" and I feel better already. She's helped me and will never know it. I love when people defend other people. It's clear, as I follow behind her and eavesdrop, that the person she's talking about is very much dead and she can't help him, so she might as well help me.

My phone vibrates. I'm so lonely that I don't even look before answering.

"I left you some of Conrad's ashes. What did you do with them?"

"Why? Do you want them back?"

"Do you have anywhere to put them? Because I've started a new line. Chokers."

"If I invest forty dollars in your business will you finally stop trying to sell me jewelry?"

"Okay. Listen. That wasn't even Conrad so don't worry about it."

"Who was it?"

"I don't know. I always have leftovers. Some people don't want to put the ashes in the pendants themselves. They want me to do it for them."

The woman chatting about the person who wasn't a sociopath has turned around. She flashes past, still talking into her phone. She says, "He had the best parties."

To get my ex-brother-in-law off the phone, I say, "I never realized how hard your job is. I'll mail you a check. Must go now."

"Why such a hurry?"

"A party," I say, inspired by the woman who is now far ahead of me on the pathway. "I'm going to a party."

Life Is Strange

The funny thing is—within an hour I am invited to an actual party. At the director's house. Brent Vintner—such a wonderful, kind man, what will my life be like when he's no longer part of it?—calls and extends the invitation.

"Alberto Alberto wants to meet you."

"Was his name always Alberto Alberto?"

"No," Brent Vintner says. "Remember—I mentioned it? His wife's last name is Alberto and he took her name. He likes the sound of it."

"So easy to remember. Except that I still keep thinking of him as Diverto."

"He very much wants to meet you—the author of *Annie: Her Life Story*. Tabitha, it's going to be fun. He's fun, Alberto is, and his wife—I should warn you. She's about thirty years younger than he is and acts like his daughter. It's a very loving relationship but I know you, Tabitha, and I know you'll ask if she's in high school."

"Why do you think you know me? Are you studying me?"

Brent Vintner snorts into the phone. Even his snort is attractive.

"Oh my god," he says. "By the way, Alberto's wife is named Collette. She's French and Italian."

"I don't speak either of those languages."

"Don't worry. I'll translate."

When I return to my apartment the golden pony is gone. I notice its absence immediately. I call my mother.

"Think of it as safekeeping for now," she says. "I know you'll want me to have it someday."

If I hadn't been contemplating the meaning of life earlier in the day I would be more selfish. "It's yours," I say. "You need it more than I do."

My mother has always had a nose for resentment, although it's almost impossible for her to detect irony. "You say that almost resentfully, Tabitha. But I know you're not a resentful person, unlike Tinker Flatts."

"Things aren't working out?" I ask, my voice vibrant with hope.

"I reorganized the whole house for her and now she wants guest towels. Honestly, girls these days are very conventional. At her age I would have shot myself in the head before wiping my hands on a guest towel. Next she'll be wanting monogrammed sheets. If she was like people in your generation she would have had to take a Home Economics class and might have been sensible and managed to get out of it by claiming she had her period. Those classes were like inoculations. You never wanted to make a home again. Tinker—such a throwback, like the fish you catch but toss because it's too bony to fry. She actually made dinner last night for her Dutch girlfriend or was it the New Zealand girlfriend and tried to pass off tuna noodle casserole as edible. She's been talking about how interesting it will be to can tomatoes in the fall. Canning tomatoes? I'd rather boil my own head. And she wants to bake with yeast. Next she'll be wanting to wash her panties by hand."

"I'm glad you have the gold pony—at least you have that."

"You're a doll, Tabitha. I've always said that. Like a big doll. Like a big cabbage patch doll! Bless his soul, these days you look just like your daddy."

COFFEE

After my conversation with my mother, as usual, I want to hold a cup of scalding hot coffee.

I'm at Dieter Bros Coffee Emporium, third in line at the cashier stand. Someone is demanding too many specifications. It would take less time for a full medical exam. Nevertheless, I can't leave because I want coffee. Really heavy coffee. Coffee like newly erupted lava. Coffee that leaves your tongue rough for hours and hours and hours.

My skin prickles and I whip around. Behind me is the same man who accosted Piper Fields while she was contemplating her waffle.

I head out the exit. When I hear the slap of feet on concrete I turn and shout "Go away!"

The man stops, crouching. "I didn't mean to scare you. I know who you are."

I'm walking again, and all at once he's ahead of me, half-kneeling. "I'm sorry," he says. "I wanted to tell that woman at the breakfast place thank you. That was all. I could never get up my nerve. And now I'm glad I didn't thank her."

"I bet she's glad too."

"I should have thanked you."

"For pushing you into the street. I can do it again." I am brave on my own behalf. This man cannot be anywhere as difficult to deal with as my mother. I am steeled.

"I want to thank you for writing those books. I saw it was you. You signed your book for my wife—at that signing. I knew then that you had been using that other woman as a decoy."

I look at him with awe. There are people in this world who always, always, always, always, get things wrong. He is my brethren.

"Your books," he says, "saved my marriage. We got the kids to sleep with the books written for kids and then my wife and I read through all your novels. Before then we didn't have a lot of—intimacy."

"Oh too much information!" I find myself squealing. He's not one of my brethren, after all.

It does no good with some people to try to convince them of whatever is the truth. They have another truth in their minds and their truth is wound around with the thickening lard of belief. To make them change their minds would slap the lard, and I cannot do it. I haven't even had my coffee.

I am running, his breath no longer upon me. Only the fair tentacles of spring weave through my hair.

Partying With the Albertos

A party is an opportunity for laughter or disaster, or both, although who is doing the laughing? Alberto Alberto—just thinking about the name fills me with admiration. Was he attracted to the woman who would become his wife as soon as he discovered her last name is his first name? Should I pity her?

The Albertos' palatial temporary home is located less than twenty miles from Midlothian so that they're close to "location." A funny thing to say: "palatial home." I had no idea places like this existed except in actual movies.

The mansion appeared to float like a steam boat on the outrageously Martian green lawn. We had arrived in Brent Vintner's rental, fumed up by new car smell from two hanging air fresheners.

Before we step into the Albertos' place, Brent Vintner says "Tabitha, your dress is—what—three-dimensional? Patterned?"

I look down: my black dress is dusted with granules from the cement factory. I shouldn't have stood outside on the sidewalk too early, which meant spending a lot of time in the wind while waiting for Brent Vintner to pull up. Leon and I protested last spring against the factory's lax environmental standards. It looks like we're going to have to attend city council meetings again and pound away about the obvious. I explain this to Brent Vintner who says, "Alberto is all for community action. He'll think you're wearing your dress as protest."

"Oh no," I cry out, suddenly remembering. "I bought a decorative frog as a hostess gift and forgot it."

Brent Vintner takes my arm and tucks it under his own.

Once inside, we confront two walls of giant windows, marble flooring the color of an orange creamsicle, the soft swishing of expensive fabrics, and the low voice of a person circulating with a tray of what appear to be sprouts on crackers. It's evident that there are many dim recesses in the mansion, almost like at The End of the World, except here there are corridors. I endure a wooly sensation that lets me know more bodies are clustered throughout the property. Passing close in front of me: a tall, outrageously good-looking man, wearing a faded greyish yellow t-shirt that looks like he stole it from a corpse. The shirt only adds to his perfection. It's easy to look at his face, though, because it's one of those faces that appear digitally-generated, everything as slotted into proportion as a jaw in a shaving commercial.

Someone is stepping on my shoes. Brent Vintner introduces us.

"I luff dogs," says Collette Alberto, a woman so beautiful she looks like one of those sweet little infants you see advertised in diaper aisles.

"You love dogs!" Brent Vintner says, translating.

"Oh, you luff dogs," I say.

"They luff me too," she says.

"They love you too!" Brent Vintner echoes, too loudly.

"She says they luff her too!" I translate for Brent Vintner.

Collette Alberto is laughing, throwing her head back. "You are the funny one who wrote about your Annie. Funny little dog."

I am humbled by her. "I wish I could speak your languages," I say. "I can hardly speak English in a way that can be understood."

She touches the collar of my dress and shakes her head. "What a little drab dress," she says.

I look at Brent Vintner for a translation. He bites his lip.

"You mean vintage?" I say. "Vintage? A vintage dress? It's been to more funerals than I can count. It's my go-to dress, and I've been to too many funerals, let me tell you. Not like there's a preferred number. Other than less than zero. What are you drinking?" A whole orchard grows in her glass. Floating at the rim: a bird's nest.

"It's called Mutual Intercourse."

"It's a mule," Brent Vintner says. "A drink called a mule."

"But what about the intercourse?" I ask, vaguely astonished.

Collette slaps Brent Vintner's shoulder. "It's Mutual Intercourse, ghoul flea!"

"It's Mutual Intercourse, goofy!" I inform Brent Vintner. "I really wish I was good at naming things. I would love to name drinks.

Cocktails have such great names. It's like drunk people invented them. I don't know how they do it."

"But you are a writer!' Collette Alberto says. "Your business is names." It is apparent at last that English is her first language.

"I'm a biographer, not really a writer, not really. It hardly feels like that story about Annie was anything I wrote. It's like the story was summoned through me. It would be a good thing if everybody kept a dog diary—to commemorate their dogs. She was such a good dog. I'll never get over losing her."

"But you did lose her," Collette Alberto says. "You were not able to identify your own dog at the dog—how you say—dog beauty parlor. Such a delightful idiot to be like that! We will find a new name for your doggie. Not Annie, no. Alberto, come meet the author of the doggie book. The distinguished idiot, you know!"

I turn to Brent Vintner, hoping he'll translate. He's studying floor-length curtains that shimmer with eye-catching gold threads. On a side table I spy an orchid—a gorgeous purple like some of Rosamund's—and next to the orchid is what might be an Oscar. Or else it's meant to look like an Oscar, although the little gold plated man is shorter than the Oscar statuette, thicker too. Like Pizza Oscar. I want to ask if it's a joke Oscar but Brent Vintner, reading my mind, shakes his head.

I am clasped in a hug. The lapels of Alberto Alberto's jacket stretch over my ears. His chest is redolent of sandalwood and lavender, of many showers in a stall handsomely equipped with arrays of dials and spigotty shower heads. He is a man who carries a weather system with him.

I draw back, breathing heavily because I don't want to forget what it's like under that man's jacket. If I could breathe his scent every day I'd never have to worry about drawing up my self-confidence.

"So you're the woman who wrote the book," he says, and once again I want him to enclose me in his jacket, for I feel my face is growing hot. Behind my eyes thick tears are forming. I realize what my self-consciousness has been trying to tell me: I'm allergic to this man. Luckily, after thumping Brent on the shoulder and kissing his wife on the mouth, Alberto Alberto leaves, circulating among the other party goers, patting backs, sniffing cheeks, very handsy.

Brent is soon surrounded by other actors. He reaches out to draw me toward the group, but I shake my head.

Two small beige colored dogs I assumed to be stuffed turn their eyes toward me. I go to them, sit with them in an enormous armchair, and pet them until they fall asleep, their little nervous systems calming at last.

From my perch I observe the party. Brent Vintner is moving from group to group. A well-liked man. Maybe that could be the title of the post I write about him? *Brent Vintner: A Well-Liked Man.* Not too intriguing, except it's unusual to be well-liked.

I startle when I notice that a young woman is sitting on the floor at my feet. She looks up, smiling.

What it is with breasts at parties? The woman at my feet is wearing a see-through loin cloth that stretches to her shoulders. It makes me feel better about my fringed vest from all those many years ago. Still, why aren't men baring themselves at this party? I remember when men did bare themselves—those horrible five years when gold chains tangled in their chest hair. Disturbing. I want to tell the girl sitting on the floor that it's not a requirement for her to dress uncomfortably and with more see-through netting than a sack of onions.

She leans back, resting against my knees. We must look like a painting called *The Two Weary Milk-Maids*. I don't move because this young woman—this girl really—has a small head and I'm afraid it will slip between my knees.

"You remind me of my mother," she says, looking up from my knees. "I miss her so much."

"That's sweet," I say.

I'm glad I'm not her mother. I'd be tempted to tell her to put on a sweater. No, I wouldn't be that kind of mother. I'd educate with stories. Passive-aggressively. I'd say things like, "I knew a girl who wore a dress so low-slung that she got the croup and the doctors had to cut out one of her lungs." Or: "I knew a girl, and the slit in the front of her dress got caught on a door knob and she twisted her neck and had to wear a brace for six months." Or: "I knew a girl who dressed like that and a bobcat rushed up and scratched the girl's chest and her entire body, feet to scalp, had to be dipped in stinging iodine."

The girl leans her head back and says, "You look so much like my mother I feel like you are my mother."

"Is your mother all right?" I ask, fearing that the girl's mother is dead.

"Oh, she's right over there," the girl says. She picks herself off the floor and wanders away to be hugged by a woman who doesn't even remotely look like me. In fact, the woman has a very large head and a very small body, like a cartoon character. Betty Boop.

If I were that girl's mother I'd tell her: "I knew a girl who told women they looked like her mother, and this made women feel peculiar and more like a cartoon character than usual, but you don't care, do you? And so someday some girl will sit at your feet and say you look like that woman over there by the window and that woman over there by the window will be Donald Duck."

I stare toward Brent Vintner's direction long enough for him to understand I'm ready to go home.

He grins and the entire room lights up. I don't know how people can bear to stand too close to him too often. Do they feel stewed by his beauty or lightly roasted?

Later: After having been at that party, such a sophisticated party, a purportedly famous director's party, I feel like a traveler returned from a far distant vista who must bring back to the village some kind of meat. Not actual meat, because I don't eat meat. Perhaps I can bring back the living bison of my experience. However, am not shaggy like bison and do not have sordid tales to tell around camp fire. In fact, when in strange land did not conform to local customs nor intended to. For instance, will never dress own breasts in netting from sack of onions. Nor capture own breasts behind transparent sheeting like fancy take-out bag. At parties with celebrities or near-celebrities, will not sit on any laps, like small duffel-shaped dog.

Reconsidering *Vertigo*

Could Brent Vintner be any kinder by trying to get my Annie book made into a movie and introducing me to the Albertos? I want to be grateful, given his efforts to help me.

So many questions. Because I am part of Annie's life story, will Alberto Alberto turn me into the Jimmy Stewart character, deceived, afraid of heights, bumbling? Also, grouchy and controlling? Demanding. Obsessed. Sputtering.

It might be much worse. They could have planned to overlay *Annie: Her Life Story* on *Old Yeller.*

Rosy-Fingered Arrivals

The rainstorms we get around here start off like an insult. First, a giant "splat" against one window. The "rainball." The warning shot before the deluge. And then the sky opens and there are no raindrops, only rain sheets. The storm shakes the windows that lead out to the balcony. Pert and Pretty are, weirdly, in the bathtub as if a tornado is on the horizon and they expect me to throw a mattress over them both. It's okay, I tell them again and again.

The morning dawns golden with the fresh-washed calm that only a good storm can make possible, shaking out the atmosphere.

It had been a cleansing ritual, giving Midlothian a much-needed bath.

Contessa, the newest apartment manager, lets me know a basket has arrived for me. She hauls it up from behind her desk. So beautiful! Lily of the valley and ranunculus and colorful leaves and a balloon heart tucked in among branches of sweet grass. My hand trembling, I open the card:

> Do you think this basket needs artificial baby breath? I hope you can pop over to the craft store and pick some

up and tuck it in? This has to go to Polly-Allison's house and it's on the other side of town (44 S. Dodge). Tell her she can mail me the check if she doesn't want to hand it over to you to bring to me. I hope you can take this basket to her by early this afternoon. She's trying to win the heart of a retired horticulturist. It ain't gonna work!

What We Shouldn't Do During a Series of Crises

Do not mention the baby's breath when phoning Polly-Allison to let her know you are bringing over her g-- d--- basket. The basket does not REQUIRE the floral addition of baby's breath.

Do not continually whisper "Très diabolique!" (Impossible not to be haunted by that French movie.)

Do not self-deprecate to anyone by announcing, "Don't mind an old bag like me"—even though vast portions of our culture are determined that such words should be said by any woman over the age of thirty-five.

Good Morning, Irene

I have been avoiding a session but Irene is charging me anyway and so . . .

Irene has reorganized her "consulting room" and as I enter she's sitting on the couch where I normally sit. She gestures toward the office chair, her usual spot. I sit, uneasily, and then realize: her chair confers such a sense of power that it's a miracle Irene ever listens to a word I say.

"Go ahead," she says. "Tell me what's bothering you this week."

It occurs to me: that is a very good line to use when meeting new people. Whoosh—you're right at the heart of matters.

We sit in silence. I encourage Irene to lie down on the couch if she'd like to but, no, she sits clutching a tissue, her legs curled under her.

Finally I tell her about a waking dream I'm having. A funny thing: lately while relaxing, my mind floods with images. "It's probably nothing, but in this waking dream or fantasy or whatever you call it—"

"No need to call it anything, Tabitha."

"Well, okay. This is what happens. I see a strange woman and she opens her mouth and all this dirt flies out and circulates around my head."

"Eat my dust. My, my, my, that's what the message is. That's what someone wants to tell you—the hostile part of you is communicating with you."

"Oh . . . oh. And then the scene changes and I'm working as a butcher with this huge carving knife. It's more like an ax really, and in my fantasy, or whatever you want to call it, I cut off my own arm!"

Irene sighs. "Think about it. A part of you is defending the rest of you. That part of you, that courageous part of you, is asking you to consider the question: 'What am I, chopped liver?' "

"And then I'm resting on a bench and beside me are all these birds. The birds are quacking. That means I'm a sitting duck, right? I made that one up. Because if I told you I was beside some birds I know you'd say I'm a sitting duck."

She brings the tissue to her eyes. "The fact that you thought you knew what'd I say and that out of all possible cliches you chose the sitting duck reference—that fact suggests that you are indeed a sitting duck. The mind is a wonderful thing. Why do you think I made sure we changed seats today?"

"Because your back is bothering you and you thought the couch would be more comfortable."

"No. Try again."

"Because my back is bothering me and you thought I'd be more comfortable in your office chair. Or because you wanted to show me that you normally occupy a position of power. Or because you want to get a sense of what this chair looks like with a person in it. Or because you want a change of view. Or—"

"Please stop. I did want you to have a change of view and a realization as well. A realization that I wanted you to arrive at independent of my prodding."

"That takes too long."

"True, Tabitha. Unfortunately true. I changed our seating positions because I want to make the point that *where* we are positioned in relation to another person is a matter of perception. In our personal relationships we may allow others additional power even though our own power should not be diminished in relation to theirs. For instance, consider any of the queens of England."

"I'd rather not," I admit. "They had such a bad time of it."

"Consider perhaps a contemporary queen from a small European nation—any nation with a monarchy. As a queen attired in her bright-colored dress-suits she is a recognizable figure, admired and loved by many. But put her on the sidewalk pushing a shopping cart and wearing a funky old pantsuit and what happens?"

"We identify with her?"

"No. Or possibly. What I mean is that we participate in giving people power. I'm not referring to institutional power at the moment, although there's so much to be said about that sphere and various abuses. I'm simply speaking interpersonally."

"So you're saying that I'm treating some people like royalty when actually they're just bargain shoppers like myself?"

"Exactly! Tabitha, I don't know how you ever got the idea that there's anything that's terribly, terribly much wrong with you."

"From therapy. I got the idea from therapy?"

"The idea predates therapy, I'm afraid. I always tell my clients, 'Walk into the light.' You're a creature of light. Tabitha, you should be raging against the dying of the light . . . That sounds so familiar. Who said that?"

"Dylan Thomas."

"Right. Dylan Thomas. Welsh and couldn't keep his pants on. That's all I remember about him and that's enough for our purposes."

Anticipating the Midlothian Month of May Parade—A Phone Call

"She's insisting on a wheelchair this year," Leon informs me.

I endure a wave of anxiety. "Something's happened? She hasn't told me—"

"Tabitha, when does she ever tell us anything?"

"But why—"

"This is what I think. Several of the other women are using motorized wheelchairs, whether they need to or not. Most of them need to. She wants a regular wheelchair and she wants me to push it."

"I could push it," I say. "You don't have to." And then I realize: my mother wants to show off her grandson. If I ask to push her, I can predict she'll say what she's said on many occasions: "Tabitha, honey, you don't have the figure for it."

And then I picture the parade. Every year the oldest mothers head the parade, before the garlic float, the shad float, the bacon float—each float signifying a Midlothian festival—and before the high school band and before the John Deere tractors and the Boys & Girls Club with their annual tolerance and solidarity banners and the Midlothian Propane Gas Exhibit with empty, purportedly safe tanks, and the Smoky Garden Store Display on the back of the biggest truck, exhibiting artificial grass and an electric fountain and wilting carnations. The parade used to be held earlier in the month until the anti-communist league from Clinton got pushy. Now it's an event that honors the oldest mothers in town among other facets of local culture.

Always in front, the mothers. Only the most ancient. It's that much of an honor. Usually the mothers are in three rows, with new candidates replacing others each year as the limitations of life on earth require. At her age my mother deserves to sit down as she parades, but the real reason she doesn't want to walk or to ride a motorized wheelchair is so she can be pushed in a conventional non-motorized wheelchair by Leon and thus show off her fifty-one-year-old grandson who looks twenty years younger and acts even younger, she would say, with mock disapproval.

My mother—she needs to make an impression. She'll make sure balloons are tied to her wheelchair. She's not going to get out there on the street without making the parade not only a moving spectacle but an occasion. Throwing candy is no longer allowed, ever since a little girl nearly ended up under the wheels of a tractor, but of course my mother will toss candy, will argue that her grandson Leon is incapable of harming a child, and she'll get away with it.

My ferocious mother. It is impossible not to love her. Not if you're her child—at any age.

"I'll tell her I'm sick and can't push her," Leon says. "So you can push her."

"Oh god," I say, laughing. "Don't tempt me. I could push her into a tractor. Not meaning to, you know. But I can be impulsive."

"Oh if only, Aunt Tabitha."

I remember how frustrated with me my mother was when I invested in Leon's bar. Something I've never told Leon. "It'd be better to put your money into the funeral parlor business," she said. "They're always coming up with new incentives. You can't go wrong."

"Sometimes I wonder if she's disappointed that I never had children," I tell Leon. And then I reconsider. "No, she wouldn't want the competition."

That night Pert and Pretty sleep with me again, one on each side. "We've changed, in a good way, haven't we?" I whisper to the cats. They don't yawn, at least. Their quest goes on—for premium treats, for attention. Am I such a different sort of animal?

Lust That Travels

There are things that do not belong in these notes because even if I dropped dead I'd still be embarrassed if my thoughts were discovered. Especially thoughts about lust.

I do not understand how human beings could ever think they have sinned because of what was once called "lust in their hearts."

The lust in my heart stays in my heart. It is not like the lust of Brent Vintner's tattle-tale of an ex-wife. Her lust went places.

I Break It to Brent Vintner by Phone

And now I have to be true to myself. Again. Will tests of character never end?

"It won't work," I tell Brent Vintner as soon as he answers his phone. "*Vertigo*—no. I don't luff those people. You are wonderful for wanting to help me, but no."

"They really want your book," he says. "I'm sure of it."

"They don't luff me or the book. I'm tired of not being luffed." And then I'm laughing. I tell Brent Vintner, "I would rather go back to working in the credit agency or at one of the restaurants than give them control over Annie's story."

"Is it because Collette referred to you as a stupendous idiot?"

"Those weren't her exact words, Brent, but close. Very close."

"She has trouble with the language. She meant genius. You've never called me Brent before, do you realize that? You always use my full name."

"Speaking of names, I looked up the name Annie after that woman—Collette—said they were going to change Annie's name. You know there are an awful lot of Ann's in art—Anne of Green Gables, Anna Karenina, Anne Elliot of *Persuasion*, Princess Ann in *Roman Holiday*, Little Orphan Annie? And then there's my Annie. I don't think I could bear seeing what they'd do to her. They wouldn't know how to respect her memory. They'd make her a stupendous idiot too. And they'd ruin *Vertigo* for me. I have principles, Brent."

"I know," he says, sorrowfully.

The phone echoes and it sounds like he's ended the call. Then I hear his breathing.

He asks, "What are you going to do next, Tabitha?"

"What about you?" I ask. "What are you going to do next?"

"Something's in the works. It looks like I'll be in Nova Scotia. Another independent film that won't make money but that's okay—it's art."

We're silent until I say, "That's really great, Brent. I'm sorry you tried to make something work out for me."

"Tabitha, they'll take the idea anyway, and they won't give you credit. That's how it works. They'll change the plot a little. Change the genders. If it was already going to become *Vertigo* they could do anything."

"They can do it without my participation then. Nova Scotia? Have you ever been there?"

"No."

"I heard it's beautiful. From my mother—and she finds next to nothing beautiful. The light there—all the colors look very bright, I was told. Like in an ad for a laundry detergent."

We're silent again. I imagine he wants to end the call and doesn't know how to do it without being abrupt. He's breathing heavily, as if he has a cold.

"Come with me," he says.

"When I mentioned laundry detergent—did that make you think of me there, in Nova Scotia?"

"Tabitha, there is nothing about you that reminds me of laundry detergent. Think about it, Tabitha. Come with me."

"What would I do to make a living?"

"You could be—"

"You can't think of anything."

He hardly pauses before he says, "My publicist."

"I can't even write about you now. It's like you're my secret, and I don't want anybody to know anything about you."

"Those are the perfect qualifications for being my publicist. Think about it, Tabitha."

Thinking & Not Thinking About It

Piper Fields doesn't phone before she shows up and convinces someone to let her into my building. She looks ready to weep.

"Is that Holy Mother of God woman dead?" I ask.

"Oh, God, no. It's just that—that Tinker person is useless. She isn't going to help in any way. She sits around with Maryann's mother and talks about yeast and composting. I've never met someone so irritating and ingratiating in my life. She wants to learn to sew. Next she's going to be wearing one of Mrs. Bougher's vestments and leading services on top of a rock."

Speaking with my new shining confidence now that I've turned down a movie director, I say, "I'm sorry I can't help you. Although, come to think of it, I've already helped you. Your stalker thinks I wrote the books. He won't follow you again. He's terrified of me. He won't follow me either."

"Nobody's terrified of me," Piper says.

"I'm sorry. But you can change that."

It occurs to me that Piper Fields has pretended to be the author of those books Modesta Bougher wrote, pretended for so long and with such authority, that maybe, unbeknownst to herself, she really has become the author. If you pretend long enough I suppose you start trusting yourself even if you're lying.

I'm relieved when—without dragging me into more of her problems—Piper Fields leaves my apartment. I think of her as a friend and I know how precious it is to have a friend, even one who wants me to ruin my self-respect, but it's impossible to think with her in front of me. It's not easy to think anyway, not about Nova Scotia. It would only be a short assignment in Nova Scotia—it wouldn't be forever, would it?

A sense of self-respect. I want it for everyone! And not just a creeping sense of it! Admittedly some people don't need any more of it, but I know only a few of those people.

I wish I could say that I felt self-respect earlier in my life, and of course I did, although sometimes in feeble squirts and at other times in big gushers that depleted me. But being appreciated, having the prospect of eventually being paid as a publicist—how can I not be wildly grateful? And yet?

If I have to be honest I should at least be honest with myself.

And of course I love Brent Vintner, who wouldn't? Who doesn't? Maybe I loved him the moment I was born—that's how much I love him. Which would mean I loved him way before he was born, given that he's fifteen years younger than I am. And now, knowing he's leaving Midlothian so soon, I fear that the next time I see Brent Vintner my feelings will come bubbling up and I'll have to hold them like a soft boiled egg in my mouth. One of the difficult things about being alive is predicting one's own behavior. I have to admit that I'm harmable. Living = Harmable. And won't it hurt me if I go to Nova Scotia and see him with other women, those hairdressers and models and social activists who are liable to come for him in his profession? And there I will be, my heart bobbing in my mouth.

For someone else, someone different than I am, the choice would be simple. What do I have to lose? But I know myself. I know that I would be a cannibal to myself and each month would be worse and worse, and one day I would tell him how I feel about him—it would blurt out, words of astonishing clarity—and they would fly past him and he would blink and try to be kind. And I would not survive it.

And then again I imagine the clear skies of Nova Scotia, the wind with a chill through the deep summer, and the pretty white houses against the brilliant blue of the ocean on days when the sun is both bright and yet gentle, and I think that Brent Vintner's invitation will be remembered always, like a precious dark cameo I could keep in a drawer, and if I went with him I could see him every day and perhaps I could come to feel part of something and even babysit his future children.

No!

Getting Back the Golden Pony—I Make a Phone Call

"Are you going to be home at three today?"

"Why? Tabitha, I'd love to talk more but I've got laundry."

"I'm coming over and getting the golden pony. You really shouldn't have taken it from my apartment. You can have it after I'm dead."

"Is that a promise?"

"Certainly. You can have it in writing."

"Thank you, Tabitha. I don't want Tinker to haul off with it, so you might as well keep it safe while she's still here with her sad New Zealand girlfriend."

Message to Publisher

Dear Rosamund,

Enclosed please find my first partial payback on the advances. It may be only a check for $25 but if you consider how much my bank could charge me for an overdraft that's a healthy sum.

Please know, too, that I appreciate that for a very long time you had faith in me. I continue to have faith in myself. In fact, recently others have felt the same. The wife of a famous movie director has called me (I understand that the words had to be translated from English into English): a distinguished genius. Based on *Annie: Her Life Story.*

Message From Publisher

Dear Tabitha,

I'll never entirely regret publishing *Annie: Her Life Story*. Oddly, we're out of copies. All copies. Amazon has the e-book.

They're out of all other copies, including used copies. Which is unexpected because they have everything. The absolute junk they sell. Bottles of hand lotion filled with motor oil. Buyer beware. And now all the physical copies of *Annie* are gone. Not that I'm suggesting a second printing. Still, it's a puzzle.

I do wish you well, Tabitha. You've always got a friend in my office. My assistant Rene speaks about you often. The print run for *Annie* was never large, and so don't expect anything in the way of royalties. Possibly, we may come out even.

Why Should I Let Brent Vintner Ruin My Life and Every Chance I Have of Happiness?

Dear Mr. Vintner,

This is not a text because I find my fingers are far too large for texting at any length. This is an email statement of intent. As your publicist, should I accept such a position, I would expect at some point to be paid. Also, I would hope never to have to run around to any studio parties or to any awards ceremonies where I would be photographed. I would hope not to have to create press releases that simply praise you and your capacities. I would want to strike a more philosophical note in that department. In addition, I would hope to decide about whether or not you should accept certain interview requests. Generally, I'll authorize anything because I know how painful it was to have my own requests rejected.

If you marry again I will not be the third wheel in your relationship—the pitiable companion who tags along so that the possible bitterness that attends your marriage will be blunted by my presence as a witness or inflamed by my presence as a witness. If you have children I will not be referred to as "Auntie Tabitha" and I will not babysit ever, knowing that I will love them and will not be able to lead a life truly separate from any beautiful child you might have. I will not be present at any of your children's school concerts of any type because I cannot bear to hear children sing.

I am able to promise that I will be your faithful publicist and will labor to keep your secrets ever more secret, for a true publicist, like an itinerant magician, hides more than she reveals.

If you agree to these terms I will go with you to Nova Scotia, as long as your offer was not extended out of any emotion resembling pity.

Most sincerely,
Tabitha Acrete

Brent Vintner Makes a Proposal by Email

Dear Ms. Tabitha Acrete,

I accept all your terms. I would like to discuss in person some additional terms of my own once the dust dies down over here on set. Pity has nothing to do with my terms. Unless it's your pity.

Most sincerely,
Brent Vintner

An Unexpected Visitor

How strange. Collette Alberto is inside my apartment. She announces that "the bartender at that place Brent talks about" told her where to find me. Her voice no longer sounds at all like someone pretending to be French or Italian. I don't judge. When I was a teenager I used to bounce around in my bedroom pretending to be British and saying to my own reflection "Top o' the mohrnin' to ye, guvnah!"

I would ask her why she's visiting except that would be impolite. And then I know: she hopes to convince me to give over the movie rights to *Annie: Her Life Story*. Or maybe she wants me to write her biography. I'm struck once again by how soft her skin looks, almost velvety, and how large her eyes are.

"For you!" she says, handing over a bottle of wine with a big blue bow on it.

"Would you like me to open it?" I ask.

"No. I'm just here to talk. We can talk?"

"Oh yes. It's been done before! Talking."

"We can be friends?" she says, stepping closer. I am engulfed in a cloud of musky perfume—very expensive, surely extracted from the glans of a defenseless animal.

"Certainly!" I say, although it's hard to imagine being her friend. How could I even afford to go to lunch with her? I once knew a wealthy woman who offered to take me to lunch. When we finished she said, "If you'll just take care of the tip." Two weeks of earnings went to that tip. Of course those were from my very poor days. I can afford even less now. Yet how good of Collette Alberto to come to my apartment, like we know each other so well we can drop in on each other at any time.

"I confess," she says, "that I've been thinking about leaving Alberto. Don't look like that. Alberto is insane. He's a director. They're all like Mussolini."

Mussolini—I think of my mother. Whenever his name comes up I think of my mother. Terrible habit.

"Alberto is so busy making movies he neglects me, horribly."

I begin to rally. "You have many interests, don't you—so you don't have to feel neglected by anyone? Why feel neglected when you have interests, right?"

She turns away and then swings back, her dark hair whipping my face, rather horse tail like. "What are my interests?" she asks. "What do you know about my interests?"

"I don't know about your interests. You look like you have interests. Don't you?"

"Alberto won't even give me a cameo in any of his films. He says my face detracts from the scene. He says no one will stop looking at my face or body."

She paces toward the kitchen and then back to me. "You don't know what it's like to be beautiful," she says.

"You look like a baby."

"My face is a magnet," she says. "Alberto claims my face is a big glowing sun."

"You could act for other directors? Or even onstage? Or community theater?"

"Any director will say the same thing. No one will let me act."

I am almost at a loss for words before I say, "But, really, don't you have other interests? What do you do well that you'd like to share with the world?"

I gesture to the couch. When she sits down, the couch makes a soft mewling noise.

She tosses her purse next to her and out spill three tubes of lipstick, tissues, pill bottles, a magic marker, a notepad, a miniscule lint roller . . . stuff keeps coming. She gathers everything up and stuffs it back into her bag. "I know what you're thinking," she says. "You're thinking why don't I conduct tutorials on how to fill a purse or how to pack clothes in a rolling suitcase."

"Honestly," I say, sitting beside her now that she's cleaned up her things, "that never occurred to me. I was wondering if your purse holds an inflatable life raft. Pretty incredible—all your purse holds. It's a magical purse. Like there's a stepladder in your purse and you can climb to Mars."

"Not really," she says. "I'm an interesting person. I just don't know how to communicate that."

It's hard to concentrate on what she's saying. "Everyone has something interesting about them," I say.

"Obviously that's not true."

"Well, yes. Sometimes people just don't know it. Did you read about that woman whose body is a brewery and she never knew it? It's called gut fermentation syndrome. Yeast and carbohydrates in her body turn into alcohol. She didn't know this for ages until she took a breathalyzer. Bizarre things happen all the time. For years my mother made a living as an upholsterer and she still does some upholstering on the side. This is a story she heard and apparently it's not a rare occurrence. A sofa was brought in and when the upholsterer ripped out the underside he found a man. Alive. And it's not uncommon. Burglars hide inside sofas. Maybe everybody's heard of that, but I still find it interesting. The fact that you live on or near movie locations, that you mingle with actors . . . you must know gobs of gossip. You have an incredible bird's eye view of some very peculiar people. Charities. You could do charitable acts and help many people. With money."

She adjusts her thin red shoulder strap. The entirety of the top of her dress is a mess of strings.

"Brent said that you write biographies and profiles. How's that going?"

"Beautifully," I say. I wonder if it's possible not to lie to this woman. All the saints in heaven would lie to this woman. Saint Agatha would deny that those were her own breasts on the platter.

She says, "Weren't you—"

"I still am." (I have no idea what she's referring to.)

One of her eyebrows rises. "What is that weird smell?"

"Oh. Spice jars. Three dollars apiece. A donation for the Midlothian Fire Department. If you're interested."

"I'm on the board of five charities. I've already budgeted for all my charitable contributions for this year."

"Spice jars—make an impact. Everyone loves them. Really, only three dollars apiece. I lose money on them."

She straightens her shoulders. "Are you writing another biography about a sick pet?"

"Annie wasn't sick. Mistaken identity at the groomers. I came home with the wrong dog, but Annie wasn't sick."

"A problem for you—mistakes like that. So I take it, you're not really writing."

My throat is starting to close. "Oh—I'm writing about fascinating people always. Very spicy. I have notes."

"I suspect you'll recount meeting me."

"God no."

"You must not be very busy writing."

"Oh I'm so busy. Always writing about fascinating people."

I look down to hide my lying eyes. Collette is wearing golden sandals with thin straps, very high heels. Her sandals ought to look cheap, like something on a Barbie knock-off in a dollar store, but they're exquisite. Like sandals worn by a goddess who expects goats to be slaughtered to appease her. I dress for comfort and camouflage. I still wear Mary Janes because I broke my foot a few years ago and nothing else keeps me as stable. To compensate, I often tell myself my shoes look adorably French. It may seem superficial and petty to care at all about what either of us wears. But let me tell you, if clothes make the man they are my g--- d--- downfall.

Collette blinks rapidly and pulls out a small atomizer from her purse and spritzes the air. "Lavender. Very calming. So a little bird told me you're tagging along to Nova Scotia with Brent? What's up with that? You know the next film he's in? He must be researching the part. It's about a man who spends time with a very ordinary woman. A woman no one would look twice at."

I say, "There are no ordinary women. I know that sounds sentimental. My grandmother used to tell me, 'All people are precious in God's sight.' That idea doesn't go over in many places. She was a revolutionary."

Collette Alberto stares hard at me. "You seem—asexual, are you?"

"God no. I was married to a choir director."

"What is Brent doing with you? It doesn't make sense that he's always with you. That's what I keep hearing—that he has to see you. I don't get it. I've known him for a long time. We have a history."

I realize that I'm smiling because my jaw aches.

"Is there something you want to ask me?" she says. "You can ask me anything."

Of course there is, but I won't ask it. Instead, I say, "How do you keep your lipstick from getting on your teeth or disappearing altogether? When I wear lipstick it always disappears right away. I might as well just apply it inside my mouth."

She clears her throat before she says, "You seem like a very undemanding sort of person. Brent must like that." She rests her head against the back of the couch and gazes at the ceiling—like someone smoking in a movie. "Brent's devoted to his craft. He's never the same in any role. That will insure he has a long shelf life."

I think about cheese, about eggs. I silently remind myself: check expiration dates.

"You really don't care what anyone thinks about you," Collette Alberto says.

I don't tell her that I hear that a lot. Instead I say, "I'm so lucky. It's a family trait."

She frowns. "It doesn't make sense. You don't make sense. Brent's good at disappearing. That's what I've heard."

"He always knows where I am," I say. "He doesn't let me disappear."

She shifts on the couch and pulls her purse strap over her shoulder. "I never even read that book about your dog. Alberto read it. But Alberto's insane, what can I say?"

"He must be," I agree. If I had to, I would compose this woman's life story by pressing dried flowers between waxed paper and above each flower would be a speech bubble. And the speech bubble would be empty.

"I'm off," she says. "You're smart not to listen to Alberto about the dog movie. It would never get developed. That's how things go."

I thank her again for the wine, walk her to the door, and listen to her rattle down the steps. I peer over the balcony railing to see her when she emerges on the sidewalk, expecting her to stumble or put her hands over her face. All her suffering must be under her velvety skin. But no, she looks happy, radiant. Do you remember the Teletubby sun? She looks like that sun. Alberto is right about her. I don't think she'll ever leave him. He must really love her if he can't bear to look at her.

I do a rush order online for the book *Five Types of People Who Can Ruin Your Life.*

Something occurs to me: she had to ask Leon where I live, even though Brent knows. Either Brent wouldn't tell her where I live, or she didn't want him to know she intended to show up at my apartment.

The Genuine Prospect of Friendship

Piper Fields understands practically everything about inauthenticity and rampant hypocrisy, and so I contact her by phone. She picks up on the second ring.

"Piper, I love how you fool everyone and people still think you write the books that Modesta Bougher writes so that her leadership of her freaky little congregation isn't threatened. I love how direct and straightforward you are otherwise."

Piper whispers, "Hello, traitor."

"I'm not a traitor."

"I know. It just felt good to say that. What's up, usurper?"

"What are you talking about?"

"You. Because of that signing and all the photos of it on Instagram people still expect me to outfit myself like you did—in an obscene pink dress. Piggy pink. In the pink. Readers adore that disgusting dress. The imagination floods with the awful prospect of matching accessories."

I can't wait any longer and reprise my conversation with Collette Alberto.

"Did she bring you an apple?" Piper Fields asks.

"No. Wine."

"She's a very angry woman."

"Oh—you mean an apple—I get it. Like the witch in *Snow White.*"

"You were being poisoned."

"She went to all that trouble—for me. Her purse spilled all over my couch and her life flashed before my eyes. Maybe she didn't mean to make me feel miserable? Maybe she couldn't help herself?"

"She could help herself. I bet she practiced in a mirror before going over to your apartment."

"Oh, Piper, you are so right. It's like she wanted me to think I'm Jane Eyre. She practically called me 'poor, obscure, plain and little.' How loathsome."

"We've all been Jane Eyre. Listen, call anytime. Especially when you're insulted. I'll cheer you up. I could run classes on how to cheer people up. It's a gift."

I feel myself growing lighter, unburdening. Who would think that Piper Fields had such a gift? So unlikely. Like getting instructions about gymnastics from a mortician. Makeup, yes.

And then I can't help myself. "I'm so wildly glad you're my friend!" I say. "So grateful!"

"You're gushing like a goddamn firehouse, Tabitha."

"You're so lucky to get the blast from my hose!"

"Oh no, Tabitha. Promise me you'll never say that again."

"Done! But it's true. You're a great friend."

Before she hangs up I hear a soft, "Sure."

POSSIBLY MY LAST SESSION WITH IRENE?

Irene greets me in the parking lot. She's arriving late for everything today, she says, apologizing. We hustle into her office together. She throws off her coat, settles into her desk chair, pops a lozenge into her mouth.

Me: I want to thank you for all you've done for me. I feel so shallow and superficial—and that's a wonderful way to avoid pain. My wounds have crusted over.

Irene: Those are only scabs, Tabitha.

Me: Oh, no, please.

Irene: My my my. Nothing is wrong with the word *scabs*.

Me: Irene, there's something I've been wanting to say. Maybe it's not my place to make a suggestion?

Irene: It's not your place. Don't worry. What is it?

Me: Well, you know all these prints of butterflies on every wall here and how they're all coming out of a chrysalis? Yesterday morning I had to take my left shoe off because it felt spongy. One of my cats had deposited a hairball the size and consistency of a tiny cigar inside the toe. And that's okay that those drawings on the walls make each chrysalis look like that hairball. But I want you to know that I don't think these images are inspiring. Our lives are not hairballs that we are trying to cough up and leave behind.

Irene: I'll admit that, Tabitha. After all, if I've said it once I've said it a hundred times, human life is a series of crises.

The office smells like butterscotch.

Irene makes an incredibly annoying clicking sound, her front teeth meeting up with the lozenge. At last she says. "Pay attention to your own heart, Tabitha."

My face heats instantly. "Are you serious? That's the most banal advice, Irene! I hoped for more from you. That's like advice a deluded person has stenciled on the wall of the family room. Enough to make everyone in that family run away from home."

Irene crosses her arms. "Maybe you ought to run away from home."

When I say nothing she continues. "Listen, it's sophisticated advice, what I'm giving you. A true cliché: the human heart is the size of a closed fist. Think of that: a closed fist. The most dangerous organ. Every day we have a choice—to wake up and be alert to the world. Truly alert. And that takes strength. A person like you can be very brave because she is very afraid. Think of your heart—not to cold cock anyone but to remember your strength. Without resorting to violence."

"I never was contemplating violence."

"Well, I have been, Tabitha. But I'm not you."

The Midlothian May Parade

Parades always make me uneasy. The town celebrates itself, grasping its past and rubbing it in our faces. The town puts bodies on the line, closes traffic, and demands to be noticed. At any rate, there are four tractors, the most mammoth ever, though the farmland in the county is being suffocated by warehouses.

I count about seventy mothers. The parade is slower this year because of all those mothers upfront. There are more than usual—and the pot holes cause delays for two of the motorized wheelchairs in particular.

There's been scuttlebutt that Claudine Rochet horned in and lied about her age, adding two years so that she was eligible. At the start of the parade she was pressed by the other mothers into the third row, among the walking mothers, and given one less balloon—quickly supplemented by someone on the sidewalk where we all line up to clap and hoot.

I don't think any queen of England—and I count all of them—could wave with more dignity than my mother. And Leon, bless him, nudges her wheelchair forward, with the most stately decorum, until he spots me in the crowd and shoves the wheelchair toward me despite my mother's shrieks and the fluttering of her heels against the foot rests. He pushes her right up to me so I can lean down and kiss her cheek. I accomplish this act quickly. He wheels her back into formation, a little rudely, given that he bumps another wheelchair and it's frail Mrs. Gaither's.

My mother's eyes are wet, I see, when I scramble ahead to get a good look at her face. Impossible to tell: tenderness or annoyance, those emotions being close to the surface for many of us. Or it could be the wind—it's come up and blowing into her dear eyes.

Moonlight

I watch the full moon that night from my balcony. Of course there's a face in the moon and an entire race track. It's amazing what you can see in the moon.

I imagine the members of the Church of the Holy Mother of God worshipping this moon, baying at it. No doubt Maryann's mother stands on an immense moon-like boulder while her acolytes squat on stumps, and she accepts their caterwauls as her due. Strange thought: what if my mother and Modesta Bougher ever met? Enough power to light a cement factory. A country of cement factories.

The moon tonight looks like that disturbing man on the box of Quaker Oats. And also, more than ever, like Modesta Bougher, the Holy Mother of God. No higher perch than that. If she's God's mother, she can tell him flat out how much he disappoints her.

It occurs to me that a woman like Modesta Bougher is inspiring, really. She inspires worshippers because she's steel plated, casting her own cold moonlight. Like my mother she must be part of that Margaret Mead generation who told one another how fabulous it is to be postmenopausal.

I don't think I could ever tell her secret to anyone who would believe me.

Saying Goodbye

From my mother: "Then I can have the golden pony back—eventually? You won't need a horse in Nova Scotia! Don't just shake your head. Think about it!"

From Tinker Flatts: "I really think you never should have called yourself a biographer. If you're going to be a publicist you're a hired gun. I stopped calling myself your intern ages ago."

From Piper Fields: "I haven't seen that awful man in flannel again. Thanks, Tabitha. I know you didn't intend to help, but you actually did. Maryann's mother says she'll pray for you. Watch yourself in crowds."

From Blowman: No words. He presses his forehead against mine and pushes a wad of cash into my hand with a note: "Emergency plane fare. Just in case."

I haven't yet had the heart to talk directly with Leon.

Message to Publisher

Dear Rosamund,

Not long ago I sent you an email accidentally (no, I was not drunk—one of my cats climbed atop my laptop. I won't peach on which cat sent the email). In that email, as you may recall, I implied that you don't care anything about books. I care desperately about books, but it was a projection on my part to say that you are dedicating your life's work as a publisher only in order to meet new people and hold insane levels of power over authors, and not because you have any feeling, whatsoever, for the contents of books. That was brutal of me to say, I realize, although maybe what I accused you of is partly true about me. Maybe I tried to create biographies about two living people because of a need to meet people and to be listened to as much as to listen to them, a need I couldn't accomplish otherwise. Even when I wrote *Annie: Her Life Story* I was hoping desperately for readers, and for a response from those readers. You were my reader, and I will always be grateful for that.

No doubt in the future I'll be sending you a manuscript from Nova Scotia where, most likely, I will soon be peeling off. I'm accepting a position as a publicist and, knowing myself, I imagine that I'll still be writing biographies or profiles. It's a habit, imagining my way into another life. It is, admittedly, like being a parasitic worm. (I looked up parasitic worms yesterday and believe me I had to shut my laptop, the news about those worms was that bad.) But that doesn't mean I can't face the more negative aspects of my vocation. I use the term "vocation" because it is indeed a calling: wondering about other lives makes it easier to avoid wondering about my own. But isn't that salutary at some points in one's life? Doubling one's own life or halving it—who's to say which it is?

No longer will I require an advance. Even the word "advance" strikes me as perilous. It sounds militaristic and also confusing. Given that an advance necessitates from you a withdrawal from one of your many bulging bank accounts.

I must say that the one time I was in your apartment I admired not only your orchids but your fish tank and all your many fish. You said you were a scrupulous vegan with one exception: you ate fish "because they eat each other." You must have a whole crew taking care of that tank, all those fish undulating their brilliant gold or purple or blue feathery fins. I confess that I felt almost intolerable sadness watching those fish. What is their life but a series of movements, back and forth, back and forth, bumping up against the invisible? So human of them. If it's at all possible to do so with their safety and the city's ecology in mind, I hope you'll set those fish free.

Thank you again for supporting me and also for letting me know that *Annie: Her Life Story* has been selling at last. I have an idea who the reader is. And now I have to get ready to travel.

All About Travel

The pleasure of it: telling Rosamund I'm going to travel to Nova Scotia. I've always thought of travel as something other people do. The sort of travel I imagined when I was a kid: by boat. One of those big ocean liners where harrowing things happen—bodies thrown overboard, buckets of vomit in the hallways, endless raw seafood platters. The better side of it all: I love how in old movies everyone on shore waves hankies at the departing ship and how once a woman enters her stateroom a giant cellophane-wrapped tub of fruit awaits her. The giant bouquet of flowers too, wrapped in cellophane. That should be what travel's like, I used to think. You would hardly need to leave your cabin. I could enjoy that.

Biting The Bullet

It is past time, in fact way way past time, for me to watch an entire movie with Brent Vintner in it. Past time for me to look squarely at my future employer's face. I choose *Bachelors on the Pick-Up Bus.*

The premise is simple. The wheels fall off the bus when the occupants—men seeking love of any sort—with women, with other men, etcetera—discover that touring by bus to find mates isn't an efficient or successful means of fulfilling their desires. Brent Vintner plays the best friend of the bus operator who started the business and drives the bus. To make Brent Vintner a best friend and not the lead, that is, to turn down his attractiveness, he's given a mustache, a beard, and bangs, thereby his beauty—his infernal and yet heavenly beauty—is partially obscured. They also give him a teacup pig, though, which makes him possibly even more attractive. Every time he answers the door when his buddy comes over Brent Vintner is cuddling that teacup pig he rescued from a dealer who stunted the pig's growth.

The movie wasn't a hit. Probably it did much better than it would have otherwise because of Brent Vintner cradling that teacup pig. The pig's name is Poison Dart—a misnomer that renders the pig even more adorable for the high contrast with its obliging nature. It's possible, I learn, to feel insane amounts of jealousy toward a pig.

Brent Vintner's face behind that extraneous hair—I see it and manage not to look away. It's like aversion therapy except the reverse. I'm not repelled by Brent Vintner's face. I endure the opposite, equally uncomfortable sensation. I watch, finding that I can move my eyes around his face in tight circles. Or I turn my attention to his perfect ears, which are less communicative than his eyes and mouth.

Then I turn my attention to the pig and replay a scene. The pig is trying to look up, which is hard for a pig because they have virtually no neck. The pig is raising its snout to look into Brent

Vintner's eyes and Brent Vintner is looking down at that pig with such tenderness. I know that look.

Brent Vintner has to believe he's a normal man who would have a hard time finding love in order to be convincing in this movie?

I have, very often, wished to be perceived as a more normal woman. That might strike some people as sad and inauthentic, but that's because lucky people don't know what it's like not to be viewed as normal.

I make myself watch the movie without having to tie my arms to a chair.

I laugh often and, generally, enjoy myself.

I'm glad Brent Vintner plays a pig rescuer.

Is it possible that Brent Vintner thinks he's rescuing me? Or could I myself ever rescue Brent Vintner from a future life of emptiness, triviality, and superficiality? I can supply all three!

It occurs to me that any other person watching this romantic comedy would call it a guilty pleasure. People call guilty pleasures such things as reading a romance novel or watching a detective movie or eating corn chips off somebody's stomach. Much more interesting: shameful pleasures. The kind you'd never admit to yourself. Like, say, a person visits your apartment and this person obviously wishes you harm, wishes you would destroy yourself but, first of all, that person spills the entire contents of her purse on your sofa and days later when you're sweeping you pull back the sofa and discover she's left a packet of false eyelashes and Pert and Pretty have chewed them until they look like balled-up spider corpses, and as a consequence you don't have to return the eyelashes to their owner, and for this small blessing you go to the refrigerator and eat a couple of pats of butter for the absolute joy of it.

About that bachelor bus movie—I never felt a moment's guilt watching it, although I did feel like a voyeur because I actually know Brent Vintner and there I was watching him without his knowledge. Watching and judging. And he could do nothing about it. If I hadn't been alone, I could have talked to someone about him behind his back.

It's still mysterious to me, how actors do it. They give over their bodies to the roles they play. Maybe it's like dreaming, how you can walk through a palace in your dream, yet the next morning you're not any richer. Maybe your body's commitment to the role fades like a dream. Still, I don't know how Brent Vintner snapped back into his own personality after playing a man bonded with that teacup pig. The whole movie should have been about that pig and the relationship between that poor little pig and the character Brent Vintner played. More romantic that way, more of a love story. I'd ask Brent Vintner about the pig but don't want to cause more sadness.

Still, it looked like a very happy pig during the time it had, given the shortness of any pig's life span. Maybe the teacup pig kept growing. Maybe it became violent with the crew and other actors, all except for Brent Vintner who really has so much love to give.

Strange Package

The large envelope is in the apartment manager's office waiting for me.

"I hope you're not dealing drugs," says Anastasia, the assistant apartment manager.

"I hope not!" I say, taking the package, surprisingly light.

"You best not have weed in your apartment," Anastasia says, "or else you better let me in on that stuff!"

I open the package on the kitchen table because something tells me a mess is going to be left behind. Maybe glitter and little paper stars. It's one of those diabolical, resistant packages. I have to use a knife and operate.

At last a flap opens and a dusty crumbling substance explodes onto the table.

I dig out a note from among the crumbles: *This is a special herb for traveling although it's best not to bring ON your travels (Customs officers) but BEFORE you travel to Nova Scotia. Do not ingest. Place in warm bath and allow the fragrant steam to open your sinuses and relax every inch of you.*

A sudden fear: are these herbs, or is this a trick and these are the ashes of my former husband? Would my ex-brother-in-law do this to me?

My heart is choking. I think I see a bone chip among the dusty crumbles. I turn the note over. In gold calligraphy: The Church of the Holy Mother of God.

Just the same, that doesn't mean this grey ash-like substance isn't human remains.

What to do? I don't want to pour anything down the drain in case these are human remains and thus should be attended with respect. My fingers are oily from touching whatever these crumbs are. A smell is rising—vaguely like mint and paprika. I feel somewhat like Rosemary from *Rosemary's Baby* sniffing that awful tannis root Ruth Montgomery foists on her. Next I'll catch my reflection in a toaster gobbling raw meat. No, this stuff won't enter my bathtub. I use a knife to decrumb my table and sift the exploded crumbs back into the envelope. I go to the balcony and shake the envelope. The last of whatever was in the envelope floats, catching light.

Oddly, I do feel that every inch of me is relaxed. But I'm not going to write a thank you note.

TEXTING PIPER FIELDS

Text from me to Piper Fields: Can you tell me now what was in the teapot you sent? Herbs?

Text from Piper Fields to me: No herbs a $100 bill I thought I could buy your cooperation That was before I really knew you

NOTE TO SELF

I'm glad about the teapot, and wonder if the teapot, unopened, was put back immediately onto the shelf at the restaurant.

Old saying: Money talks. True, but I'm just not listening, right? Tempted to visit restaurant.

No, just no.

Will not refrain from looking inside teapots again. Will look gift horse in mouth, etcetera.

More Squirrels

"Tabitha, it's me. I need five blocks of wax—orange this time. Tabitha, I want to tell you a story. Funny how I almost forgot this story. Are you ready?"

"I'm ready," I tell my mother.

"It's a long one."

"That's okay," I say, as if I have a choice and could still remain my mother's daughter.

"Maybe put me on speaker so your hand doesn't start aching. This is the story. I knew this woman and a squirrel got into her house."

"How bizarre, this is the second time in days that I've heard about squirrels."

"As I was saying, the squirrel was apparently coming down through the chimney regularly, that's what this woman thought. Anyway, the squirrel starts running all over, even up and down the walls! Knocking off framed photographs! The squirrel gets on the fireplace mantle and knocks off all the gewgaws, including this handblown glass figurine of a swan made by the woman's dead husband, an accomplished glassblower. The horrible thing: that swan contained her dead husband's breath! And now the breath is lost! All because of a squirrel. Now what does that woman do? She's furious. She calls an exterminator who manages to get the squirrel out of the house by—get this—dropping a trail of bread slices and leaving a window open on the second floor to get that squirrel to climb out on the roof. Voila, the squirrel's out of the house.

"Well, that wasn't enough for the woman because that squirrel dissipated her husband's breath. What does she do? She tells the exterminator to put up squirrel traps. Every day she comes home from work and sees four squirrel traps on her roof and each of the traps has a squirrel in it, because the cages are baited, and irresistible to squirrels. She has to pay twenty-five dollars a pop for each squirrel the exterminator catches. After two weeks she's out of a lot of money and there are more and more squirrels in the yard and on the roof and in her garage. It's like the squirrels are coming out of the woodwork to get that bait. She fires the exterminator. By then it's too late. The squirrels get to digging a hole in her roof and set up camp in her attic and have their babies there. It's like a maternity ward.

"And then right where the squirrels made a hole in the roof all the rain gets in and when water gets in mold gets in. Are you still listening? Anyway, she had to move out of her own home and then couldn't sell the house because of the black mold and the squirrels too. Horrible. The thing about squirrels. They're deliberate animals. They remember every nut they hide. They run around chittering and also using sign language, if you've ever watched them you'd know."

"Do you have a squirrel infestation?" I ask, trying to sound sympathetic.

"I do. That's not the point."

"How bad is it?"

"It's awful. I hear them in the walls. Busy as Caligula in there."

"I can call the exterminator for you. There have to be some that don't hurt the squirrels. Just transport them. Although the title exterminator suggests . . . maybe I'll try going for an animal rights group."

"They'll come back, those squirrels will. I don't have any hope. But, again, that's not the point. I didn't raise you to be obtuse. Think. There's a moral to my story. You know what it is? Don't make a little problem into a big problem. Don't be like that first squirrel either and get trapped in a place where you don't belong."

LIGHTWEIGHT RED FLANNEL

Because he's not alone and he's with his family in the park—a wife and two little boys in lightweight red flannel—I don't recognize him. It's only when he calls over and waves his arms that I realize who he is. He doesn't say my name—only "Hey, Hey, Hey." He drags his boys, each by the hand, his wife holding up the rear.

He points at me. "Boys, this is the lady who writes the books you love. The bunny books!"

I could correct him, except it's an awful thing to correct a parent in front of their children. It's hard enough for a parent to get a child to respect them, and at some point all that respect goes down the drain. Why accelerate the process?

The two boys look enough alike that I wonder if they're twins. They're at that stage in life where they're both missing teeth. I don't know why that's supposed to look so cute in kids when it doesn't look so great in adults. Anyway, they're staring up at me with confused expressions, probably not only because they think I'm Piper Fields but because they always fall asleep before they get to so much as the middle of one of those books.

What square-shaped faces these little boys have. Like someone created their heads out of alphabet blocks.

The mother looks away from me. It's evident: she believes I know her worst secrets. I want to tell her that I haven't even read an entire book written ostensibly by Piper Fields. How could I know how her marriage has been rescued on the physical or spiritual plane?

I stoop to the boys. "Hi, guys! So nice to meet you! I bet those bunnies enjoy knowing you guys! Those bunnies are thinking about you! You're not just thinking about the bunnies! They have eyes. When you're reading they're watching you!"

The boys shy away from me. I like them more already.

The man in flannel looks so proud to have shown me to his children that it's endearing. His wife is tugging at his arm. She's dying. Dying to leave before her husband says something she'll never forgive him for.

"Well, I have to be off!" I say. "Can't keep the bunnies waiting! They're watching me too!"

The wife gives me such a look of solidarity that I know I'll feast on that look as much as I can—for days. Although it is a not entirely unfamiliar sensation: to feel you've done someone a favor by leaving their presence.

What Is That Line From Milton?

I can't quite remember that line from Milton but I think it's: "They also serve who only stand and wait"? It could be: "They also serve who also get up and leave."

I hope I didn't go too far with those little boys, telling them the bunnies are watching them. I meant to suggest a level of cuteness. Hoping not to scar anyone.

It occurs to me: even though I stopped writing about Piper Fields it's almost as if I became her anyway. It was a pleasure to bounce out of myself for a bit. Being a biographer is such an attractive pursuit. You have access to another life but don't have to live it forever.

Still, you snap back into place, but who you are—you're not in the same place, are you?

Some part of you has to relocate?

Warnings

TEXT FROM LEON:

He's here With a woman

RESPONSE FROM ME:

I'm not his nanny

TEXT FROM LEON:

What's wrong with you

RESPONSE FROM ME:
I'm sorry

THE TERRIBLE WAIT

TEXT TO LEON, one hour later:
Has he gone yet?
RESPONSE FROM LEON:
They're both gone Sorry Tabitha

THE END OF THE WORLD

It's still early in the evening when I walk to the bar. Just Leon and a pack of regulars are there—three retired men slumped on stools. Widowers.

Eduardo says, "Hello, Tabitha, come sit with us old goats. You never sit with us."

I take a seat at the bar with them.

"Bellini?" Leon asks.

"Just—whatever you want to get rid of on draft."

"So, Tabby, how's it shaking?" Bruce says, his eyes flicking at my blouse.

My phone vibrates in my pocket.

I slide off the stool and take the call in a booth.

Brent Vintner sounds jubilant. "Where are you?" he asks. "I'm outside your place with someone I want you to meet."

"Your girlfriend?" I ask.

"A screenwriter. She wants to work with your book *Annie: Her Life Story*. She'll keep *Vertigo* out of it."

I tell him where I am and in instants he arrives at The End of the World with a very young woman. She has a gorgeous buzz cut and her dark lipstick is smeared, as if she's been eating chocolate all day like a mule. I want to like her instantly and I do, although the polka dots on her blouse are distracting, like portals into another world.

I once fainted in church and the air filled with gray polka dots, and I once had a polka dotted dress and realized when I passed a mirror that the polka dots galloped. It's so interesting that polka dots on fabric used to stand for leprosy, pock marks, and diseases until in the natural progression they evolved to represent clowns.

"What a story," the woman says after she's had her second drink. It takes me a moment to realize she's talking about *Annie: Her Life Story*. "Mistaken identity. Not quite *Prince and the Pauper* or *Parent Trap*. More experimental and searching. Like: how well do we really know our dogs? I think of it as an animated feature, an adventure classic. For kids. With enough subversive humor for adults. Would you consider partnering with me?"

I have to look away because polka dots are covering her hair. Annie would like her. Annie would lay her long head on this woman's shoulder. She might, if overexcited, snap playfully at the polka dots like floating bubbles and quickly realize her mistake. How Annie would appreciate knowing she wasn't forgotten. I shake my head until the woman comes back into focus.

"I'm going to Nova Scotia," I say.

The woman answers me: "There's such a thing as the internet, Tabitha."

I wonder if Modesta Bougher would be the better person to write something for children. Then I realize that movies are probably meant to keep children awake. I assure the woman—her perfect name is Patsy—that I'll think about it.

Brent Vintner asks to drop me off back home. I tell him I'm going to stay a little longer and talk to Leon.

After the door closes behind Patsy and Brent Vintner, polka dots hang in the air everywhere I look.

Leon comes over to the booth and slides in opposite me. "I hear you're going to Nova Scotia," he says. "I hear everyone knows but me, even my grandmother."

"I wanted to tell you myself. That's why I'm lingering."

"No more End of the World for you for a while, huh? And you're going to be Brent's publicist, that's it? He's a good guy, Tabitha. You should pay more attention to what he's saying."

"I don't know what you're talking about. I do pay attention."

"Not really. He's probably not used to that, the way your head is always swinging around. Maybe he likes that. Maybe that's why he's always with you or else looking for you."

"Because my head keeps swinging around?"

"I'll miss you, Tabitha. I can take Pert and Pretty off your hands for a while, if that makes it easier. Are you sure about Nova Scotia?"

"I shouldn't have told anyone. He hasn't finalized it yet. He's going to impose conditions."

Leon looks at me. "Oh god, Tabitha, accept whatever they are."

Upon the Concept of Accepting Conditions

What is self-respect?

What is self-confidence?

Don't those both seem awfully limited? All that selfing.

And what if Brent Vintner's conditions are too narrow?

Piper Fields Tells the Truth

I call Piper Fields, intending to tell her it's likely that I'm going to Nova Scotia to work as Brent Vintner's publicist. Before I can tell her my plans she says she's coming over.

She drives us to Palmenong Lake. The lake is calm, a long stretch dazzling with light. The wind comes up and brings a touch of menthol with it. We sit on a bench and watch five geese circling in the water. I know how nosy I used to be about Piper Fields's life. I don't want her to think she can take the same liberties with me.

"I owe you a good deal, you know that?" Piper Fields says. "I suspect that if I hadn't met you I wouldn't eventually have fully accepted my identity as a certified liar."

"No one ever guesses?"

"Only you guessed I was lying when I was telling part of the truth. I stopped reading the books, by the way. When her fans question me I don't even bother to sound like I know what they're talking about."

A lone goose patrols toward us, lifting each webbed foot as if there's tacky glue on the ground.

I ask, "Are you going to stay here—in Midlothian—past the summer?"

She shades her eyes, looks out across the lake. "Who can resist the cement factory? You probably don't know that I just got put on the board at the Sputter Museum because they think I actually write books and might have at least rudimentary aesthetic values that I can communicate to the whole county. Believe it or not, I might be able to make a difference, bringing art to the area. Someday I'll be appreciated. Does that sound overly idealistic?"

"No. It sounds perfect. You have your own identity at last."

"Well, I'm still pretending to be writing those books so I guess I have multiple identities. But I get such great kick-backs from Mrs. Bougher. Money money money. The money remains pretty irresistible. And I'm afraid of Mrs. Bougher. There's not a lot of choice involved."

"How is she—and Maryann?"

"Maryann is the same as ever, carrying the psychic load of being that woman's daughter. And Mrs. Bougher—I think she's building her congregation. She was always meant to reign over an empire."

The goose turns its back on us, waddles into the lake.

"Please tell Mrs. Bougher I think about her often," I say. I don't believe I'll ever again look at the moon without her face appearing there, along with that of the Quaker Oats man.

"You really want me to let her know you think about her? Do you know what you're asking for? She'll try to convert you and you'll be howling at the moon within a week."

I tell Piper Fields about Nova Scotia and my fear that everything will go wrong. She laughs so hard she puts her head on her knees. When she straightens up she says, "Oh this is wonderful. This is exactly perfect. You'll love being a publicist. You just need to trust yourself. I've been pretending to be someone I'm not for years and getting paid good money for it on behalf of a cult leader. And I still can trust myself, so why can't you?"

"You're like one of those women with Charles Manson."

"No," she says. "No, I'm not."

"I apologize. I don't know what I'm saying. My mind is—"

"Your mind is in excellent shape. Good god. You'll be freed when you go to Nova Scotia. You're going to have to fight to keep away from all the people who will want to get to know you. You've been in Midlothian for so long you don't realize how easy it would be for you to find the right person anywhere else. It's like this place has put you to sleep. You're like someone cast under a spell."

"I met a man cast under a spell—one of the Church of the Holy Mother of God congregants. He was always talking about his horse and his barn—I'm not at all like him."

Piper laughs again. "Remember that night when you had me meet Brent Vintner at your nephew's pathetic bar—what were you thinking?—and every time Brent Vintner looked at you his eyes did this weird thing—they shot out rays. At first I thought he hated you and I couldn't figure it out. Then I realized that you made him happy and he felt more alive because of you. I bet he's been in relationships with women where he felt dead."

"His ex-wife often played the part of a dead woman."

"See?"

"She really did. More than once she played a corpse."

"I understood you the first time, Tabitha."

"You know, I've never had many friends."

"You always say that and I never doubt you."

"What I mean is that—I think you're a remarkable person and a good, true, genuine friend. And it's all right that I'll never understand why you stole that teapot. Maybe you're just attracted to acts of wrong-doing because you've been doing something wrong for a long time—although, really, why do people have to know the identity of anyone who writes those books? I swear I will never turn you in. You paid me for helping you out at that signing—when I was at a low point and needed quick cash for rent. You also meant to help me by suggesting that I try writing a children's book. I couldn't do it, by the way. I lack the criminal gene—in fact, I still think you should be the one to write those books. Why not become what you're pretending to be? Maybe you could write about a teapot—a teapot that gets lost and has to find its way home in a heavy rainfall. And it gets cracked. But everything turns out okay because a dog brings the teacup in its mouth to a ceramics class. What I mean to say—"

"How could anyone not love you?"

"I know how."

"Oh, Tabitha."

"When I'm gone, we'll still talk on the phone?" I ask. "We'll text? You could visit me? But I'll still miss you. Whoever you are."

"Oh stop. You know who I am. It's you I'm not so sure about."

Conditions

Brent Vintner shows up at my apartment the next morning. Nine thirty a.m. I haven't had my coffee yet.

"This is a condition I'm imposing," I tell him. "Don't show up at my apartment before I've had my coffee."

"But I brought you coffee."

"Oh," I say. "Oh, that's different. If I'm your publicist I'm not going to be bringing you coffee, though. I have my self-respect."

"I know. You've earned it."

"And how would you know?"

He pauses. Puts the coffee in my hand. "Drink this," he says. "Completely. And then we can talk."

After a minute Brent Vintner asks, "How do you like the coffee?"

"I don't just like it, I never want to leave this coffee. I want to marry this coffee and bear its children. Actually, I'm too old to bear children, but I would try to bear children just for this coffee. You wanted to talk about conditions for Nova Scotia? I can't just accept any conditions. I'm turning my life over to be your publicist—not that I have a job here or a life, but I could be made very happy here, and it's not like me to take a risk, in a foreign country, and there are other issues too."

He sits beside me on the couch. "What issues? I don't want this to be a terrible decision for you, Tabitha."

"I know myself and how much I need my privacy."

"You'll have your privacy."

"My privacy is very extreme."

"Like how extreme?"

"I just—there are whole days when I can't be available. When I have to visit florists and parks, you know. When I have to mope around to get my balance."

"That's not a problem. I understand your need for that. It's funny—I'm very much the same way. We're more alike than you realize."

"We both probably need to relax more," I say, tentatively.

"Definitely," he says. "Are you through with that coffee?"

"Yes. I asked it to marry me, but before it could answer it disappeared."

"I love you, Tabitha, I really do."

"That's so sweet," I say.

"No," he says, his face changing color, darkening more. "I mean, I love you."

"You love me like you love an auntie. That's very nice that you can think of me as a relative."

He sits forward on the couch. "I don't think of you like you're a relative."

"I guess not. We look nothing alike."

"Tabitha," he says, taking my hand. "Do I have to write you poetry? I love you. I *love* you."

"I really hope you don't write me poetry. That would disturb me. Don't play around like that, Brent."

"Do you notice that you're using my first name again? You've started doing that lately. I like it. I've pointed that out to you. I don't know if you even hear me."

"That's so funny. That's what Leon said—that I can't hear you. I think it's because you're so beautiful. It's like listening to bird song, your voice."

"Listen," Brent Vintner says. "I have loved you almost since the first time I saw you at The End of the World. I love you passionately. I don't love you like I'd love an aunt. I don't even have an aunt—"

"Then you probably don't know what aunt-love is like."

"So I take it that you don't love me. That all this time I've been deluded."

"Of course I love you, Brent. I love you so much I'm sick."

And that was that. That really was that.

"We'll never get married, will we?" I say.

"Not if you don't want to," Brent says, shaking his head before tilting it at me.

"I've been married before. He divorced me and married other women after me and then he died. I always thought I was bad luck for him."

"It sounds more like he was bad luck for you."

"No, it was just one of those awful things. I was too young to know what I was getting into. Are you too young to know what you're getting into?"

"Tabitha, I'll be thirty-six in a month."

"When I was thirty-six I would have been too young for you."

"Exactly, that's why it all works out now."

"You know," I say, "I could talk to you forever."

"That's how I feel," he says. "We could go on like this and I'll never exactly predict what you'll say. I'll never understand everything you mean. But I think I understand you more than I ever have anyone else."

"You really have been lonely."

WALKING AND CONSIDERING

To be a publicist means discretion is required. So different from being a biographer, where the less discrete you are the better you are. I do not know exactly what I'm supposed to be in this life, except that there's no rule against being incompetent. I know plenty of incompetent people and they're cherished, frankly.

If you love someone you must lose them and then find them again—that's what a philosopher said. I can't remember who. Or was it a novelist? I want to tell Brent Vintner that he has to lose me and then find me again and then I don't have to.

He loses me. I lose him.

I am living inside a movie of my own, and it's called *Vertigo* just like the actual Hitchcock movie called *Vertigo*.

I am myself and look like myself and walk like myself but don't know myself. Who am I impersonating? Who is the better actor, Brent Vintner or me?

Because as I'm with him, doing little things—he likes to help out while I engage in occupationally boring things (fold laundry, scrape dishes, scrub sink)—he laughs often. He is delighted. As if it's natural to be delighted.

Meanwhile, thoughts rummage through my head like starving rats:

Is he doing research for a role about a man involved with a woman who does common everyday things to summon laughter because of absurdity of inherent dullness of everyday actions?

Why does he want to dance with me in my living room and does not feel embarrassment?

Is he doing research for another role? He has not told me in any detail about the new movie he's going to be in. Can only anticipate it's like famous movie *Dirty Dancing* except it's called *Grubby Stumbling*?

Brent Vintner says, "Tabitha, happiness is just an unfamiliar feeling. It's not uncomfortable." That word—*uncomfortable*: what women in childbirth are told they experience while in searing pain.

Have spoken on phone with his confused and wonderfully kind and welcoming cousin. I had to lock myself in bathroom afterwards because emotions threatened to do a tidal wave thing. Had visions of *The Shining* with blood pouring through door.

But the movie I'm living in is not *The Shining*. As I mentioned, the movie is *Vertigo*. When will Brent Vintner discover who I am, and then will I accidentally fall off my balcony? More ironies than can be counted.

I Receive a Check

The check is my own check. A message is tucked inside the envelope:

Dear Tabitha,

I'm returning your check for $40. A good investment. Nevertheless, I realize—hearing a bit of scuttlebutt—that you are in need. Conrad always regretted divorcing you. It was no fault of yours, though he liked to say he picked a daisy and discovered thorns. A man for metaphor.

You Know Who

NOTE TO SELF

What sane adult signs a note You Know Who? Of course I know who it is. The question is: what honeypot has my ex-brother-in-law found? I am very much hoping it's not Rosamund after all. Will not pursue the issue.

So glad to have the check back. It would have bounced.

I have a disturbing dream. I'm walking in giant drifts of snow. Then I realize it's not snow, it's white ashes. I'm walking through my ex-husband. A black spot appears in the distance. A giant bull. I get up on the bull's back like in that myth about Zeus and Europa (took Mythology 101 in college and cannot forget gruesome torture scenes—those myths = rugged stuff) and then the bull turns out to be a piano and I slide off the piano into more ashes. And coming toward me is a snowman. Except made of horrible ashes. And the snowman says, "Wasn't Conrad buried?" And I wake up and wonder if my former husband was actually buried and not cremated. It would be like his brother to play tricks. Bad form.

Then I fall back to sleep and the dream continues! Even while I'm dreaming I'm thinking, What is this, a sequel? But the beautiful thing: all around me white flower petals are falling, like apple blossoms. I wake up, feeling grateful to myself for that dream. It's like something in me said: you've had enough horror for now. Really enough.

I crack two of the eggs that Leon gave me a while back and then check the expiration date. Oh no—old eggs. It's such a shame. I have to throw them out. Very old eggs. I hate the symbolism.

And then I go out on the balcony and look down and watch a squirrel eating the very last tulip—a lingering hold-over. I keep watching, hoping to see something more hopeful. And then I see that the squirrel has one red petal stuck to its little foot. It looks marvelous—like the squirrel is wearing a tiny velvet slipper fit for a prince.

Walking and Considering Again

I only have to walk five blocks and I'm in doctors' row, a section of Midlothian that used to be inhabited by well-to-do physicians, and thus the trees are enormous and old—sycamores and ginkgoes and maples and horse chestnuts. Beautiful trees, all leafed out, a fresh new green, amid the ancient mansions. The properties are starting to look sunken. It costs too much, apparently, to keep the mansions entirely erect. People with enough money to tend places like these choose newer properties and another part of town. And so they are missing out on the giant horse chestnuts holding up their candelabras of ivory blossoms and the three robins that are cocking their heads right now and listening for worm song. It's sad to think that some women during the Victorian era wore those robin breasts on their hats—imagine those soft red feathers skimmed off those robins.

So much blossoming—peonies and azaleas splurging themselves on the air. Still, the real stars now are the leaves—that greenness on the new span of leaves, greenness unfurled. There should be calendars featuring portraits of green leaves. There should be statues celebrating leaves. The leaves are not whispering anymore. They're heavier in the wind and don't expect to be admired but should be.

I mistake the sign for a realtor's. When I get closer I see that the placard reads "Filming in progress. Artificial Gunfire." A perfect time to murder someone with a handgun. I walk two more blocks before I come upon the cameras and the vans and the cords snaking across the street. Somewhere Brent Vintner is here, of course. Maybe he will be shot soon in the movie. Maybe this is when he dies . . .

A cluster of my fellow Midlothians are jostling to get a better view, bending the taped area where they're kept back.

At first I think I'll join the others to watch, and then I can't catch my breath. I'm gasping. I hang back, pray no one hears my choking and runs to me and tries to help.

I wait until I can breathe again, until my heart stops punching.

The relief of not being rescued, of not being, mistakenly, given the Heimlich maneuver. The relief, too, of not seeing Brent Vintner getting shot, even in a way that's entirely fake.

When I return home I check the clock. I'd only been gone about twenty five minutes. It felt like hours, like time expanded and shrank continually—like the accordion that one of Leon's old friends used to play. He'd dress up in plaid and play until you had to beg him to stop. Time, breathing in and out and almost panting.

How It Happens

The woman isn't beautiful and is about my age, although maybe a few years younger, and the way Brent Vintner reacts to her lets me know. We're in the mall, strolling, holding hands. Why we're in the mall I don't know. Something about how he needs to pick up a few things, how he wants to lead an ordinary life, as if I'm the ticket to all that's ordinary for Brent Vintner.

The woman stops him, rests her hand on his arm. "Brent," she says. "Dear dear Brent." Much air kissing, then hugging. They were in community theater years ago. She teaches acting now—a college class.

He is blooming in front of me, and it is a terrible sight. He has everything in common with this woman, and she delights him. She mentions her travels—a castle in Spain. She's telling the truth apparently. She mentions bathroom fixtures. More air kissing. Delight. Brent Vintner's shining face. The woman bobs her head at me as if she will never place me. Brent Vintner introduced us immediately, but my name doesn't stick. She only has eyes for Brent, as she should. I can hardly look at him, but she has looked at him often, without a problem, and with joy.

And I am writing this and living this because otherwise in every report, book or movie, the older woman loses everything, but if her dignity is already lost what does it matter to her, and why should she be punished and why shouldn't the beautiful man choose her and be happier because of his choice? Why shouldn't my story be that story?

And yet my life isn't a story, finally. No one will write my story for me. And this story is already written many times over—the older woman dies or the man only wants her money. When a woman only wants a man's money it's a comedy. When a man wants a woman's money that means she'll die soon and alone. I'm so glad I don't have any money. And yet—I can't ignore what I can only call pain, this doubling-over pain.

The pain of being with Brent Vintner—how to describe the pain. I'll never be at peace. I'll be self-conscious and not self-aware. To be jealous—such an ugly, ugly thing, and I see my jealousy whipping in front of me. I'm like the woman in the fairy tale whose mouth is stuffed with snakes that come drizzling out. Jealous men are terrifying, aren't they? But more acceptable. Jealous women—they get shot in the bathtub where it's easier to clean up afterwards.

What if I'm cruel to Brent Vintner?

What if I punish him, even if I don't mean to punish him?

I have been trained all my life by life itself to expect so little, and I have no one to blame anymore. I finished all the lessons myself.

But why do I have to suffer? Brent Vintner's old friend must have wondered why his hand is in mine. I endure this fear that she thinks he's doing something charitable, like there's a charity called Big Brothers for Old Broads. And then I want to lambast myself for my own biases against age, against my gender, my submission to cultural constraints that have led me to judge myself harshly by standards that have been erected to disqualify me from meeting my own desires let alone needs.

The horrible thought intrudes: my mother is more advanced in her thinking than I am. Never in her life has she questioned her own worthiness. Not once.

Brent is pulling me into the chocolate shop and pattering on about the woman we just met. "Great singer," he says. "*Guy and Dolls*. They threw me in at the last minute when one of the dancers bailed." Much of his life is unknown to me. If I'd written his biography perhaps I'd know more. I'd understand why someone with such a lively, glamorous past . . .

"Your past is glamorous," I say as he's paying for two pounds of toffee.

"Oh no," he says. "Lots of ugliness. You should have seen some of the reviews I got. Some of the reviews I still get . . ."

"Do you read them all? Or does your agent cull them and send you a selection?"

"I used to read them," he says. "Then I decided life's too short to suffer when you don't have to."

I can't stop thinking about his words. *Life's too short to suffer when you don't have to*. Brent Vintner—I suffer because of him. It's not his fault. It's my fault. It's the way I'm made. There's a boundary and I stepped through it, not realizing the boundary was an electric fence. Is that the only way I can understand what's happening to me? Shocks. I feel shocks traveling up my arms. It must be an invisible fence, like the kind people use to keep dogs in the yard.

That night I tell Brent Vintner I want it all to end, that being with him is too much for my nervous system. That my jealousy is a giant weight on my soul, that I am plunging down into the ocean of my own ugliness, that I lack the self-forgetfulness to be with him, that he's making me sick, making me miserable, that I never stopped being sick and so I might as well be sick alone.

He leaves for Nova Scotia. My mother's response shocks me. She returns the golden pony.

The End of the World

I go to Leon's bar early, before the arrivals start. "I'm making you a bellini," he announces.

"There was a woman—" I begin.

"There's always a woman," he says. "Sorry, Tabitha. So she's with him now."

"No."

"She's not with him? Was she ever with him?"

"I don't think so."

"Then she doesn't count."

"I'm not meant for being with another person."

"No one is. It's like we all live in a tragic fairytale. Some of us find a way to make it work. Not me. You know what? You're the loneliest person I've ever met, Tabitha. I'm alone and I mostly like it lately. You're alone and you're—not well. You look like you have a fever. Also diarrhea. You just look—limp."

"I'm fine."

"Call him. Has he called you?"

"Yes. I know he'd be better off with anyone else."

"He will be, if you don't hurry up and become sane."

Leon takes a long time making the bellini. Several regulars enter, already looking like they've visited Tappity Doo Dah. They sit at the bar, watching Leon's back. I wish they'd leave. I wish I'd leave too.

After Leon hands me the bellini he looks away, like my drinking anything is too intimate, embarrassing. And it is. My hand shakes. And I think of Brent Vintner and what I've lost—and the loss is so sharp I'm choking. Leon brings me a wad of napkins and I thank him.

"See?" he says. "Can you begin at least for once to understand?"

"Leon, he's an actor. He could only be pretending to care about me."

"Have you seen his films? He's not that good of an actor."

THE RAIN STORM

At first it's just a matter of something striking the window—a thump, maybe middle schoolers tossing a pine cone from across the street. And then, without more than that warning—a singular hard splat—the rain pours and pours, a curtain growing heavier until nothing can be seen but grayness. The cocooning of that rain, the way the outside world vanishes. It reminds me of movies where someone in love is caught in the rain and the one she loves appears, or she runs after the person and that person turns and they embrace. Or possibly they dash to a cottage that's conveniently open or, less romantically, a gazebo. Time suspends. The rain is their inner world, I always think, a beautiful gray realm where they can hide from the outer world.

Gradually the rain lessens, and I step out onto the balcony and let my face and hair and shoulders get nicely wet. I feel better then, as if something in me has been released. I pat my own arm.

Leon calls. "Did you lose your electricity?" he asks. The bar hadn't lost electricity. A few times the lights flickered, that was all.

I tell him I haven't lost anything, then thank him, and he goes back to work.

Late that night on cable an old movie comes on. Bing Crosby wakes up in King Arthur's court. When I was twelve I first saw that movie on television after midnight. I had tiptoed downstairs and watched with so much yearning. To wake up in another time and place. To think that time could be changed fully. It was one of those movies that, for me at least, can't replicate itself when seen again. It had become an entirely different film.

I never asked Brent Vintner what his secret sorrow was. Because I could not bear to hear it.

To care for someone—how often that means that their suffering is unbearable to us. And would his secret sorrow explain what I was to him, what I was to heal—if that's a possibility? I don't want to know already how I might have failed.

Staying in Bed

The remedy is simple: sleep. Bad dreams wake me—some inner imp that functions as an alarm clock keeps shouting in my ear: You have to get up! They'll find you if you hide!

I check the clock and calculate: I've slept for twelve hours.

I tell myself: go to the park.

You can admire the glossy leaves of the rhododendrons lining the pathway.

You can think your own thoughts, undisturbed.

Better yet, you can stop thinking.

What are the chances I'll meet anyone I'd rather not see? Excellent, I'll say.

I don't go to the park.

The Irises Far Below My Balcony

My apartment might be small, admittedly, but the balcony opens out to the wider world. If you have a view, if you can look out beyond your own kitchen, you are blessed.

Blessed is what I've always wanted to be. Not knowing that of course I was and am.

I thought they didn't bloom, the irises, that the blooms were eaten away or that those stalk-like leaves were too self-interested to flower. And now I think it must have been the person on the second floor—the person who moved out—who always cut the irises as soon as they bloomed during other springs. Because the irises are now in full spectacle mode. These are the bloomiest. So much so that I head down to them. I want to kneel before these irises, their purple and white veiny bodies, to protect them.

Why would I ever give up the irises now that they've blossomed and I live in such a peaceful apartment building? Why, when my life has a prescribed order and there's always Leon and The End of the World where I'll be able to drink relatively unaccosted unless some man is widowed long enough, say thirty years, to lose all inhibitions, not that there's anything wrong with that. That's twice the age difference between Brent Vintner and myself. Not that age is anything but a means for calculating the number of years before you're likely to die.

Oh the irises, the tallest of them. No one has ever been able to duplicate their scent. Brent Vintner used to say that my neck smells like crumb cake—somewhat of a disgusting thing to say. Although memorable. And sweet. And affectionate. That is the problem—I may have a very good memory for the rest of my life.

A plastic bag blows into the patio. The image comes to me as if I'm in the midst of a dream—the bag blowing over the face of the iris, over that stunning face. I catch the bag—it's sticky—and toss it into the dumpster on the other side of the patio.

The street is full of parked cars because a little girl is having a birthday party on the lawn of the apartment building across from mine. A cake loads down the picnic table and a mother ferries bowls in and out of the house. Balloons flicker and bob on a post. Children run shrieking across the lawn, chasing one another. And then the mother gathers all the children and they squirm in place, seated at the picnic table. I cannot help but stiffen when all the little girl's friends begin to sing.

Sunlight and Houses

It is true about Nova Scotia, true about its beauty—a scrubbed beauty that heightens colors. From the window of the airplane, the houses far below seem to refract light. I don't even text Brent Vintner to let him know I'm arriving. That way if I catch him with anyone else I'll know all the truth and I'll settle into that truth, freed. It is not kind to him but it is kind to myself, this decision.

I did not reckon on my mother's greed. For there Brent Vintner is, at the airport, holding a giant bouquet of many colored roses in cellophane, and he doesn't look at all lost but like he has known, always, that I would arrive, that I would rather be sick with him than sick without him.

It is, as I've indicated, my dear mother's doing, for she has always wanted to keep the golden pony for herself. And it is, I suppose, my own doing too, for it is a very odd thing to be loved. It is wildly unexpected, except that is has been wildly craved.

The role of a publicist: I cannot help but see my future, traveling with Brent Vintner from location to location, even doing a little voice work for the movie *Annie: Her Life Story*, and writing a few profiles (some long and possibly some full-scale biographies) but mostly being in the world and moving across the world's surface and knowing that things will end and will not end, and that the ending doesn't have to be anticipated because it will always be a surprise, for isn't Brent Vintner the great surprise of my life, as I am, he says, of his? It is an unfamiliar feeling, this feeling of not being lonely.

Even so, there are little pinpricks in that feeling, places where even love can't reach, and in those places I want to find my way toward the other beauties of the world—the ocean, for instance, or the houses on the shore, their clean clarifying colors, white and gray and orange and blue. How much we have to see around the edges of things, and how, even if we don't know what those things mean, they give us so much, and how our gratitude, even our gratitude, can't be quite enough. I keep using the first person plural—"we"—

in this really aggravating way. It's just because I'm happy, and why should I be alone in my happiness, why should we?

And if Brent Vintner years from now or even weeks from now or even days from now (or hours) realizes I'm the wrong woman—that in some vertiginous state he chose poorly—who am I to correct him when I cannot be sure either of us hasn't made a mistake?

And now, in the beautiful now, I can see him in the distance from the high balcony in this little place we're renting. I can see that long stride of his, and I know it's his particular walk, his hurrying toward what we both want to be happiness, are determined to be happiness, and I know it's him, even though I can't, not quite entirely, see his face.

ACKNOWLEDGMENTS

With immense gratitude to Sagging Meniscus Press and Jacob Smullyan. For insight about this novel, for seeing what I was attempting—Jacob, thank you. And thank you for bringing Tabitha outside of my house.

Thank you to my supportive friends, especially Jennifer Gilmore and Steven Belletto, who took me to dinner after this book was accepted. Champagne! My gratitude also goes to BJ Robbins, who read an early draft of the novel and offered encouragement. Thank you as well to Joseph (Jody) Bates for listening to me with such care and warmth. There should be a medal for that.

For my inspiring, high-spirited daughters—Theodora and CeCe, loved beyond all measure. What sheer luck to have such daughters.

For Eric, always—whose absolute love, incredible heroism, and faith in the future sustain me.

This book is dedicated to Alice Faye Upton (our Faye), whose unexpected death in 2023 devastated us. How wildly fortunate I was to have had such a loving, large-hearted sister. How we miss her in this life!

Lee Upton's poetry has appeared in *The New Yorker*, *The New Republic*, *Poetry*, and in many other journals as well as three editions of *Best American Poetry*. She is the author of books of poetry, fiction, and literary criticism.

Printed in the USA
CPSIA information can be obtained
at www.ICGtesting.com
CBHW030353020424
6232CB00002B/3

9 781952 386893